"Hilarity, intrigue, the magnificent landscape of Sicily and food! Mario Giordano has created a world that spins in Technicolor like a Sicilian *carretto* and, like the traditional donkey carts painted in an explosion of color, this novel is a celebration of the palette of Italian life and the Sicilian experience in its specificity, warmth and drama. *Delizioso!*"

—Adriana Trigiani,
best-selling author of *Kiss Carlo*

"A masterly treat." —*Times Literary Supplement*

"Giordano keeps the tension in check with an anonymous narrator whose affection for his eccentric relation can't be disguised."
—*Washington Post*, "6 Beach Reads That
Will Bring You More Pleasure Than Guilt"

"As types of amateur sleuths go, the category of lusty Bavarian widow has been woefully underrepresented—until now . . . Fans of international mysteries or just those who fantasize about good wine and languorous meals on the Italian coast will devour this mystery debut."

—*Booklist*

"There's a new star in the mystery firmament, and her name is Auntie Poldi. Mario Giordano has created a character who will be the envy of every novelist, mystery and otherwise."

—Alan Bradley, author of
The Sweetness at the Bottom of the Pie

"This book is absolutely delightful. Reading it felt like a mini-vacation to Sicily, full of colorful characters and all the twists and turns I crave in a mystery . . . If you're looking for a book to read on the beach, this one is perfect!"

—*BookRiot*

"The most enchanting novel I've read in ages! . . . A lush, sexy, and slightly madcap romp, much like Auntie Poldi herself. Mario Giordano has a gift for eccentric storytelling, snappy dialogue, and sly wit, making this a tart and delectable treat that you'll press on all your friends. I can't wait for the next installment!"

—Amy Stewart, author of
Girl Waits with Gun

"A lively, humorous portrait of Sicilian society and gastronomy."

—*Times* (London)

"The whole book is alive with a tang of lemons to set the senses zinging. Refreshing."

—*Spectator*

"Poldi is flamboyant, earthy, and always forthright . . . The mystery is well plotted and red herrings abound, [but] the true draw of the book is the Sicilian setting and the eccentric Auntie Poldi. Fans of quirky stories such as Alan Bradley's Flavia de Luce series may enjoy this amusing romp."

—*Library Journal*

Auntie Poldi and the Lost Madonna

Auntie Poldi
and the Lost Madonna

MARIO GIORDANO

Translated by John Brownjohn

MARINER BOOKS

HOUGHTON MIFFLIN HARCOURT

BOSTON   NEW YORK

2021

First U.S. edition

Copyright © 2019 by Mario Giordano
English translation copyright © 2020 by John Brownjohn

First published in Germany in 2019 as *Tante Poldi und die Schwarze Madonna*
by Bastei Lübbe AG, Köln

hmhbooks.com

Library of Congress Cataloging-in-Publication Data
Names: Giordano, Mario, 1963– author. | Brownjohn, John, translator.
Title: Auntie Poldi and the lost Madonna / Mario Giordano ; translated by
    John Brownjohn.
Other titles: Tante Poldi und die Schwarze Madonna. English
Description: First US edition. | Boston : Mariner Books/Houghton Mifflin
    Harcourt, 2021. | Series: An Auntie Poldi adventure | "First published in Germany
    in 2019 as Tante Poldi und die Schwarze Madonna by Bastei Lübbe AG, Köln"
Identifiers: LCCN 2020034218 (print) | LCCN 2020034219 (ebook) | ISBN 9780358446279
    (trade paperback) | ISBN 9780358251392 (hardback) | ISBN 9780358251415 (ebook)
Subjects: GSAFD: Mystery fiction.
Classification: LCC PT2667.I5617 T35813 2021 (print) | LCC PT2667.I5617
    (ebook) | DDC 833/.92 — dc23
LC record available at https://lccn.loc.gov/2020034218
LC ebook record available at https://lccn.loc.gov/2020034219

1 2021
4500822803

A Brief Prelude

The woman on the ancient massage couch writhed as if she'd been hit by a power surge, grunting, growling, and snarling like an animal. She foamed at the mouth and rolled her eyes, gnashed her teeth and uttered blasphemous oaths. Every time the priest sprinkled her with holy water, the three nuns had their work cut out to force her back onto the couch by her legs and shoulders without getting bitten.

The middle-aged woman was barefoot and wearing a cheap patterned tracksuit. She seemed highly dissatisfied with the whole situation.

The wobbly phone camera zoomed discreetly back and panned once more across the treatment room. It revealed a sink, three old wooden chairs around a kitchen table covered with floral oilcloth, two espresso cups, a small altar, and a Madonna. Hanging on the pastel green walls was a crucifix flanked by several pictures of Padre Pio, a team photograph of Juventus F.C. 1986, and a framed portrait photograph of the pope. The two windows, which overlooked some kind of garden or park, bathed the room in sunlight. However, the room's monstrous couch and the old flagstone floor made it look about as snug as a Gestapo interrogation chamber.

Nothing could be heard but the woman's snarls and the exorcist's sonorous voice.

Panning further, the phone camera lingered for a moment on the youngest of the nuns, who smiled coquettishly.

Then came a dramatic close-up of the priest, a plump, jovial-looking sixty-year-old with a healthy Mediterranean complexion and laugh lines around his eyes. But for his cowled soutane, one might have taken him for the proprietor of a slow-food restaurant.

He inscribed the sign of the cross on the woman's forehead. "Renounce your satanism, Rosaria! Renounce your witchcraft, your drink and fornication!"

The exorcist sprinkled her again with holy water, and Rosaria instantly snarled at him like a cornered cat. This didn't seem to faze him in the least.

"What is your name, demon?"

No answer, just more snarls, grunts, and growls.

"I ask you again, demon! Tell me your name!"

He repeated this procedure several times: holy water, cross on forehead, demand for a name. Rosaria yowled and twitched like the lead singer in a heavy metal band. The nuns had to pin her down.

"Tell me your name!"

"*Nigra sum sed formosa!*" Rosaria yelled in Latin. And again: "*Nigra sum sed formosa!*"

She rolled her eyes, then went quite rigid and opened her mouth wide.

"Die!" she growled in Italian, her voice a sudden, unnatural basso profundo. "She must die! Die in agony!"

"Who are you, demon? Tell me your name!"

And this time Rosaria did answer. In pure Bavarian German, what is more.

"Kiss my arse, you *creepy gobshite!*" she yelled at the exorcist. "I'm Poldi. One more time, just for the record, you cowled cunt: I'm Isolde Oberreiter from Torre Archirafi. Got that?"

Auntie Poldi and the Lost Madonna

1

Tells of graffiti, start-ups, chakras, pirates, learning the sitar, uniforms, envy, and death. Sicilian summers bring out the abs and pecs, Poldi embarks on a spiritual journey, and her nephew is once more devoid of a plan. On the plus side, Poldi has taken in a new in-home helper with a cock-and-bull backstory. When Montana gets serious, she first develops cold feet and then receives some nocturnal visitors.

K RAZZZ AB! This misspelled German injunction to kick the bucket had been sprayed on the front of No. 29 Via Baronessa, right beside my Auntie Poldi's pretentious brass plate. Glistening in the midday sun, the black paint did, one had to admit, contrast most dramatically with the sunny yellow of the façade. Black and yellow is, after all, Mother Nature's favorite color combination for venomous reptiles, killer wasps, and no-entry areas of all kinds. Visible from afar, it is an unmistakable warning that the fun stops here. Even the dimmest birdbrains get the message at once; either that or they're hoodwinked. The drips oozing down from the spidery capital letters, which had clearly been applied in a hurry, may have been meant to lend them a certain emphasis. They looked more like the product of a Halloween stencil from a hobby shop, but the message itself was disturbing nonetheless.

"What the hell!" I said, taking off my rucksack, which was sticking to my back.

"Quite," Poldi said happily. "My sentiments entirely."

I was just going to ask what it all meant when Totti, my Aunt Teresa's dog, came hurtling out of the house. Beside himself with delight, he leapt up at me, almost knocking me over, and licked me from head to foot. He also gave one of his habitual farts, needless to say, but my weary heart melted and I reciprocated my smelly friend's welcome by patting him and ruffling his fur.

"What's Totti doing here?"

"Well, Teresa thought it'd be better if I wasn't all alone in the house for a while."

Mind you, no animal could be less suited to the role of watchdog than Totti. A typical Sicilian mongrel, he's yellow with a black muzzle, huge, batlike ears, and a thoroughly ill-designed body that looks as if it's been put together out of components from every breed imaginable. I strongly doubt that his appalling farts would suffice to keep a potential murderer at bay.

"Is this the only threat you've received?"

"There were similar messages sprayed on walls in Via Filandieri—in English and Italian, presumably to demonstrate the troll's language skills. I made a record of them all, of course."

She got out her mobile phone and proudly showed me photos of various menacing messages. All it said on one wall was POLDI GO HOME!, which I found quite mild.

"That's how it started," Poldi explained. "The wording

was rather ambiguous, though, because 'home' is a relative concept to a citizen of the world like me. Besides, my 'home' is here in Torre Archirafi, and because that probably occurred to the troll, he resorted to threats of murder—"

"He?" I broke in on impulse.

Poldi stared at me in surprise. "Well, I never! Bravo, *cento punti*! This time you didn't fall into the primary hypothesis trap. Could be a she."

She stepped back with her head on one side and contemplated the threat on her façade like an art expert.

That gave me a brief opportunity to inspect my Auntie Poldi, because we hadn't seen or spoken to each other for a few weeks—not until the previous day, when she had unequivocally summoned me back to Sicily right away.

Although rivulets of sweat were trickling down her cheeks from under her black wig, I thought she was looking well. She had acquired a bit of a tan and was wearing hot pants made out of truncated jeans from which her bare thighs bulged in a rather unflattering way. With these she wore a skintight orange top with a plunging neckline that emphasized her Bavarian baroque appearance, and peeping saucily out of her décolleté was the tattooed phoenix on her left breast. Completing her outfit were a pair of strappy gold sandals and a whole collection of cowrie-shell necklaces that clicked and clattered softly whenever she moved. Only a woman as self-assured as my Auntie Poldi could have ventured such a hippie look at the age of nearly sixty-one.

What really took my breath away, however, was the screen-printed image on her top: a kind of silhouette of herself with the words DONNA POLDINA below it in bold capitals.

"Did *you* get that made?" I blurted out.

"No, your cousin Marco designed it. It's a logo. The thing is, I thought I'd open a discreet little detective agency — a sort of start-up, you know." Poldi tweaked the top straight and stretched to give me a good view of everything. "Like it? I've got one in your size too."

I sighed. "Yes, don't tell me. *Moderation* is a sign of weakness."

"You can stick your sarcasm where the sun don't shine. It's what they call image-building. Marco says you've got to pull out all the stops from the word go: home page, blogs, logo, merchandising — the whole shebang."

She turned back to the graffito.

Wafting toward me through the open front door came a gust of air-conditioned air mingled with the scent of patchouli and the soft, plaintive strains of a sitar. So Poldi was on a spiritual journey, and also champing at the bit with her new business idea. This could only mean that her plan to drink herself to death within sight of the sea had been temporarily shelved. On balance, this was a welcome development — or would have been but for the KRAZZZ AB! on her wall.

Poldi concluded her art expert's analysis and shook her head. "No, that was a guy all right. Three *Z*'s . . . It's suggestive of all the insecurity of a pubescent prick without a girlfriend, don't you think? The sort that's lost his grip on life — spends all day watching movies on the internet and gets a hard-on if he can spook someone. Want a beer?"

"Finally," I grunted. I picked up my rucksack and went inside.

Totti trailed after me, farting.

I was naturally itching to hear about the background to

4

these threats and all that had happened to Poldi while I'd been gone—all that she had done, botched, and straightened out again. I had to admit that I had missed her, even her eternal bullying. And I was positively bursting with curiosity about her adventures and escapades in the past few weeks, and could tell that she herself was finding it hard not to come out with it all. I knew better than to ask—in the first place, you must never badger Poldi if you want something from her; second, the Italian *bella figura* principle precludes undue curiosity; and third, it was really hot and I could have used a beer after my journey and all the chaos in France. I felt like I could use much more than one beer, in fact, but I'm not too fond of losing control of myself, and besides, I always get a headache after the third.

The first thing that struck me inside the house was the heavy, sweetish scent of joss sticks, fighting a losing battle with Totti's farts. In other respects, No. 29 Via Baronessa made a neat and tidy impression. Specifically, there were no empty booze bottles to be seen.

But then there was the sitar music, which was live.

I was just going upstairs when I glanced down at Poldi's shady inner courtyard and saw a guy of about twenty sitting there, dreamily playing the sitar in a white salwar kameez, the combination of long shirt and baggy trousers traditionally worn in India and Pakistan. He gave me a friendly nod. Rather puzzled by this apparition, I nodded back. From below me, Poldi called, "No need to look so surprised. That's Ravi. He's giving me lessons."

Shaking my head, I trudged on up the stairs to Poldi's attic guest room, which I regarded as *my* room at this point. The freshly made bed, which seemed to have been waiting for me, was coated with a thin layer of Totti's fur. I flung my rucksack into the corner and sat down at the wobbly little desk beside the window, where I figured I would finally, after a longish break, resume work on my novel, a great Sicilian family epic spanning an entire century. I checked my mobile for messages (there weren't any), or rather checked to see if Valérie was online (yes, she was), gazed at the phone with mounting despair, then turned it off and promptly on again. I could hear Poldi clapping to the sitar downstairs, and I strove vainly to feel at home. Somehow, I was completely out of gear.

"What's keeping you, for God's sake?"

"Just coming!" I called back, lying.

Thirty-four years old, I was devoid of any qualifications, job, or plan. All I had was a fragment of a botched novel and —this was a novelty—a broken heart. I was a living, breathing zero, and nothing and no one seemed capable of remedying this situation.

I went out onto the roof terrace to smoke a cigarette and collect my thoughts. The midday sun was dazzling. The heat, which felt like a punch to the face, was burning off the remains of spring. It was still springtime, but there wasn't a breath of wind. Across the rooftops I could see the sea stretching away to the horizon, glittering and motionless. Behind me, Etna jutted into the midday haze, its peak already free from snow and a sluggish, irresolute plume of smoke issuing from the main crater. Air conditioners were humming the length of the Via Baronessa. The air smelled of tomato sauce and coffee. Sounds of hammering were coming from the esplanade, where workmen were busy putting up snack bars and sunbathing decks on the seafront's jagged volcanic rocks.

The Sicilian summer was bringing out the abs and pecs again. It would once more reduce all movement to the consistency of molasses while enervating people with the sirocco, plague the countryside with tiger mosquitoes and forest fires, and make people closet themselves behind their shutters even more suspiciously than usual. But summer belongs to Sicily like mountains to Switzerland. It's only during the long, hot months from May to October that the island is entirely at ease with itself, rediscovering its rhythm like a cat that has strayed and found its way home again. Summer would also bring mulberry *granita*, silken nights filled with promise and the scent of jasmine, and days bathed in the sand-colored light of which you can never get enough. The coffee would again taste as it does nowhere else—in fact everything would again taste like the very first time, for that is the Sicilian summer's hypnotic trick: everything feels pristine, over and over again.

I was surprised to see that Poldi had embellished the roof terrace with several flowerpots containing a variety of succulents, a palm tree, and a little lemon tree—there was now even a bistro table with two basket chairs and a sun umbrella. It all looked really nice. Noticing an ashtray on the little table, I was touched to realize that she'd done it all for me.

Poldi was waiting for me in the inner courtyard. There was a bottle of Birra Moretti on the table, but she herself was drinking something that looked like a mixture of duckweed and mud from the pond in a horror film. Ravi, sitting cross-legged on an embroidered cushion, was still playing the sitar. I briefly introduced myself.

"My pleasure!" he said in English. He played on, using a species of wire plectrum on his right forefinger to evoke gently quivering overtones from the instrument's twenty strings.

My overwrought nerves quivered along with them.

Totti, lying in the shade beneath the table, blinked at me cursorily.

"You look kind of tired, my friend," said Ravi. "I shall play something cheerful for you."

Not good, I thought in alarm, *not good at all.*

But Ravi had already adopted a different rhythm and the sitar was buzzing out a florid, coquettish medley of fifths and thirds.

Totti emitted a sigh.

"Could you take a break, please?" I interjected.

I sounded a bit brusque, perhaps, not that Ravi seemed resentful. He stopped playing but beamed like the sun.

"No problem, my friend."

"Hey," said Poldi, "what's the matter? Aren't you feeling well?"

"No, I'm fine," I muttered, lighting a cigarette. "What on earth are you drinking?"

"It's a laxative ayurvedic smoothie. Totally organic."

"Looks that way. What's in it?"

"Don't ask."

"How does it taste?"

"Awful, but it's good for the anahata."

"What's that?"

"Why, the heart chakra, the seat of unconditional love

and so on. Like to try some? You're looking a bit constipated, heartwise."

I ignored the offer.

"Is he living here?" I asked without looking at Ravi.

"Oy, oy!" Poldi exclaimed in amusement. "Could someone possibly be jealous?"

"What does Montana say about it?"

I should have known better. Red line. Poldi glared at me for a moment, then tore several strips off me. "You impudent young twat!" she thundered like a summer storm in the Alps. "You can get stuffed! Who do you think you are, taking that tone with me? This is still my house and my life, and I'm not accountable either to you or to Vito. It's nobody's business but my own if I screw every available male from Taormina to Siracusa. If you don't like that, you tobacco addict, you can pack up your things again and piss off. Is that clear?"

Silence reigned for a moment. Poldi continued to glare at me.

"I like the sound of the German language," Ravi exclaimed. "It's very lovely."

"I apologize," I mumbled meekly. I gave an embarrassed cough and stubbed out my cigarette. "I'm sorry, Poldi, especially now. I'm, er . . . I'm going through a rough patch."

"Yes, I thought as much from the way you're looking, back in your nerdy old jeans and navy-blue polo neck. You make an emotionally dehydrated impression. Having trouble with Valérie? Or is it your *pesciolino*? Can't you get it up?"

I took a white paper napkin from the table and waved it in the air. "Poldi, please!" I sighed. "I already apologized." I turned to Ravi and said, "Sorry."

"You're welcome." Ravi folded his hands on his chest and bowed. "*Namaste.*"

Totti farted.

There it is again, I thought, *Poldi's parallel universe.* As I did so, some of the previous weeks' heartache dissipated. Drawing a deep breath, I felt something akin to a cool sea breeze blow through me—I felt *there* again at last. In a nutshell, at home.

A trifle more reconciled with the world, I changed the subject. "Tell me something, Poldi. Why did you call me back from France? And no hedging, please. Just be straight with me, okay?"

She stared at me in surprise. "I didn't call you. I thought you missed me, that's all."

"Er . . . Just a moment! You called me. You told me to shift myself and get my arse back to Torre in double-quick time. I know your voice, after all."

Poldi suddenly looked kind of tense.

"Fake news," she said, studiously casual. "It wasn't me, I don't talk like that."

"You don't? Since when?! Who else was it, then?" A thought struck me. "You haven't had another of your mental blackouts, have you?"

Poldi angrily dismissed this. "Get on with you!"

"What's your explanation, then?"

She drew a deep breath. "There are things for which there's no so-called rational explanation. Want another beer?"

That's her usual way of evading an unwelcome subject. There was nothing to be done, I knew. She exchanged a glance with Ravi, who seemed suddenly in a hurry and took his leave. Poldi escorted him to the door and returned with another beer for me.

"Ravi is my new helper," she explained before I could say anything.

"Aha."

"Yes, not what you were thinking, okay? Housekeeper, not toyboy. Besides, it turns out that sitar music has a favorable effect on Totti. It stops him farting."

As though in confirmation of this, Totti let rip from under the table and I instinctively held my breath. Poldi put on a playlist of classical sitar music, and sure enough, his vile flatulence ceased.

"These death threats, Poldi—when did you say they started?"

"Soon after you dashed off to France like the biggest love-sick idiot in history."

I let that pass.

"And since when has Ravi been here?"

"Don't go down that road!" Poldi made a dismissive gesture. "Ravi's a kindhearted soul. He's an absolute pearl."

"Maybe someone in the town has a thing about Indians. Or foreigners in general."

"You reckon so?" she said.

I shrugged.

"Ravi comes from a highly respectable family," she said. "Three weeks ago he was going from door to door, offering his services as a cleaner, and I could have used a bit of help in the house after you and Valérie . . . Well, never mind. Anyway, Ravi told me he had majored in economics at Harvard and gone to Europe on a voyage of self-discovery. He was completely broke because—get a load of this—his father is a Mumbai multimillionaire who wants him to take over his entire hotel chain someday. But Ravi, who's got a lot of talent, would sooner play the sitar. That's why his father has brutally disinherited him and blocked all his credit cards. Sad, isn't it?"

I was dumbfounded. "And you bought that cock-and-bull story?"

"Good God, how dumb d'you think I am? Still, it's a good story, and a good story bends the truth a little, here and there, until a truth of its own emerges. Bear that in mind for your novel. No need to roll your eyes like that, just tell me what happened in France. Did you break up?"

Instead of replying, I pointed to her ayurvedic pond potion. "Heart chakra, did you say?" Before she could say anything, I swapped my cool Moretti for her slimy anahata smoothie. "I think they'd be more appropriate that way around—for both of us."

Poldi sighed. "It never ends, does it, the old heart palaver?" She clinked her bottle against my glass.

The smoothie was lukewarm and tasted like what I'd imagine a turtle's stomach contents might.

"Any alcohol in it?" I asked.

"Sure there is, I enhanced the flavor with a wee shot of grappa. It's all vegan."

"Bottoms up!" I downed the enhanced turtle cocktail in one, shook myself like a wet dog, and slammed the glass down on the table.

The "wee shot" of grappa was already going to my head.

"And now," I exclaimed, "I want to hear what's really been going on here. The whole story, mind you, so don't leave anything out. Oh yes, and I also want to know what sort of birthday party you'd like."

Because—who would have thought it after all that had happened?—Poldi would be celebrating her sixty-first birthday in a few weeks' time.

It was almost a year ago, on her sixtieth birthday, that my Auntie Poldi had moved from Munich to sleepy little Torre Archirafi in Sicily, where she planned to drink herself to death in comfort with a view of the sea. However, a few things had supervened since then. Specifically, three murder cases that Poldi, sporting dramatic outfits and seldom entirely sober but fully committed, had solved. What had also supervened was a handsome *commissario* of police (to quote Poldi, a sexual force of nature) to whose pulsating, unflagging *sicilianità* she regularly succumbed. She had also acquired several new friends, for instance sad Signora Cocuzza from the café bar in the piazza. Or Padre Paolo, Torre Archirafi's chain-smoking priest. Or Valérie, the owner of Femminamorta, but I'd prefer to pass over her here for emotional reasons. Or Poldi's peculiar, cheesy-smelling, clipboard-carrying, imaginary friend in a hoodie—the one whose surprise visits she likes to describe but whose existence none of us is wholly convinced of.

By "us" I mean my family in Catania, notably my Aunts Teresa, Caterina, and Luisa and my Uncle Martino. They were the ones who had periodically flown their nephew—the dropout with the lousy command of Italian—from Germany to Sicily to look after Poldi and keep destroying her stocks of booze. A thoroughly Sisyphean task, I can tell you.

With a small inheritance and the remains of her savings, Poldi had purchased the little Via Baronessa house with the roof terrace that affords a view of Etna and the sea. I usually sit up there by myself because of Poldi's bad knee.

I enjoy being on my own, but Poldi needs people around her. She needs to make a big entrance, needs a stage on which to argue, flirt, grumble, blaspheme, be helpful, forge plans, and flaunt her leopardskin look. And, after solving three murders, she had found the perfect stage in peaceful little Torre Archirafi, with its esplanade and mineral-water spring.

She had soared to the heights of local celebrity like a comet. "Donna Poldina" was now well known throughout the Catania-Taormina area. For all her natural modesty, this went down well with Poldi and may possibly have gone to her head a little. Seldom did a day go by but someone rang her doorbell to ask her advice, request an autograph or a selfie, nail an unfaithful husband or the author of a poison pen letter, christen a fishing boat, mediate in a family feud, or find a pubescent Angelica who had run off with some acne-ridden Enzo. But these, of course, were all small fry to a sleuth of my Auntie Poldi's caliber. She was made to solve really major crimes, so she needed harder nuts to crack. It would have been like using a high-performance laser cutter for fretsaw work, except that a high-performance laser cutter doesn't drink itself to death when it's disconnected from time to time.

The other aunts were afraid that too much inactivity would sooner or later get Poldi down and drive her to drink, which was why they had set my cousin Marco on her during my absence. Hence the idea of the detective agency, the business plan, the logo, the T-shirts, and so on—all intended to keep Poldi on the go and off the booze. Perhaps the aunts and Marco had rather overdone it, though, because success, initiative, and self-assurance inevitably attract envious trolls who spit in your soup, key your car, leave dead cats on your doorstep, or—just for fun—threaten to murder you. For, sad to say, envy is as much a part of Sicily as Etna, the Cyclopses, Cosa Nostra, *pasta alla Norma,* suspicion, melancholy, and fatalism. It doesn't matter whether you start a business or build a house, open a bar or stand for election —as soon as you venture out of the safe haven of universal indifference, envy strikes, blighting your mood, testing your endurance, and setting traps that eventually spell disaster. Sicilian envy is a legacy from centuries of foreign occupation. It has saturated the Sicilians like *omertà,* the law of silence, preserving the status quo and ensuring that the ruling structure of money, power, and misery isn't displaced. Like *bella figura,* the look-good principle, it forms part of the glue that holds Sicilian society together. Envy tends to mean that you've made it to the next rung on the social ladder and want to stay there, thanks very much.

"Why so indignant?" Poldi demanded. We were still sitting in the courtyard. "Have I put your nose out of joint again?"

"No, it's all good."

"Oh, I get it. It was just that I thought you were too busy with Valérie and *voulez-vous coucher avec moi ce soir.*"

After Poldi had cleared up the Owenya case in such a spectacular fashion and John Owenya had returned to Tanzania, Poldi went off to Rome with Montana for a week of canoodling. Me, I flew back to France to join Valérie and heard nothing more from Poldi. Nix, *niente,* zilch.

I sighed. "Have you forgotten already, Poldi? I thought we were a team now."

"You didn't get in touch either."

"Eh? I sent you at least three texts a day."

"Poof! You know I hardly ever check my mailbox because of the negative vibes those electronic gizmos give off. I'd have answered if you'd sent me a letter."

"I *did* write you a letter."

"A proper letter. Fancy!"

"Yes, six pages of my best handwriting, plus an amusing little sketch. What more did you want?"

"I was very busy too, for God's sake!"

"With sitar-playing and 'it,' eh?"

Poldi shook her head reprovingly and drank some beer.

"No, with a new murder case," she said casually. "What did you think?"

I stared at her. "Are you being serious?"

"Yes. You don't think these graffiti write themselves, do you?" She leaned forward and whispered, "I'll just say this: Black Madonna!" After a brief, dramatic pause, she went on. "Somehow or other, I've got mixed up in another fine mess. Want to hear about it, or would you rather go on sulking?"

"*Forza*, Poldi!" I said with a sigh, and went to fetch myself another beer.

The fridge was full of little bottles of Moretti, no hard stuff. Since Poldi had been activating her ayurvedic chakras, I concluded that she'd always expected me back, and I inferred from the number of bottles that she intended to tell me everything in minute detail. I found this both galvanizing and flattering, I must admit, because my Auntie Poldi knows a thing or two about murder and thirst.

But first things first, perhaps.

After John Owenya returned to Tanzania, Vito Montana, Poldi's bearded, mustachioed police inspector with the crumpled suits, frown lines between the eyes, dense thicket of chest hair, compact little tummy, and Cyclopean virility, had invited her on a surprise jaunt to Rome, where he had served in the special Antimafia Commission during the eighties and where his daughter, Marta, was studying medicine.

To Poldi, this was an unmistakable sign that the man was getting serious. And as usual when a man was getting serious—when she'd achieved her aim of being introduced to his family and included in medium-term plans for vacations and Christmas—she developed cold feet. It was no use, the lights went red and she panicked a bit. It had been the same even with my Uncle Peppe, the love of her life. Poldi simply couldn't resist the impulse to flee. My Uncle Peppe had managed to capture and even marry her, however, for—don't get me wrong—Poldi was a staunch believer in love, loyalty, and devotion. Although she could be flighty and had a thing for stalwart, uniformed traffic cops, she preferred a safe harbor to the open sea—but only if she could head for the harbor mouth whenever she thought fit. In her heart of hearts Poldi was a pirate, and pirates must sometimes go marauding so as to expand their horizons and make the world a bigger place for us all. I know of no one better equipped to do that than my Auntie Poldi.

Now that I know her somewhat better than I used to, I often wonder how Poldi and Peppe stayed together for so many years, because Peppe was a hothead, a bit of a rogue with an erratic lifestyle characterized by too little sleep and an excessive zest for life. Poldi always prevaricates when I broach the subject, and I can't ask my Uncle Peppe because he's dead. I sometimes think it must really have been a grand passion. Or sex, maybe. Or a shared love of booze. Or fate. Or my Uncle Peppe simply knew he had to give Poldi room to breathe.

Whether Montana would realize that remained to be seen.

"On one condition only, *tesoro*," Poldi said gently when Montana suggested the trip three weeks ago.

"I'm listening."

"Once we get to Rome, don't go fishing out a ring or proposing or anything of that kind, is that understood?"

"No worries," purred Montana. This not only relieved Poldi but almost immediately rankled a little.

She's like that, though, because she also knows a thing or two about the zest for life and the fragility of the human heart.

The trouble with the little trip to Rome was getting there, because Montana insisted on flying them himself in a friend's single-engine plane, and Poldi was terrified of flying. Montana dug his heels in, however. He needed another couple of hours' flying in order to extend his pilot's license in any case, and besides, I think he wanted to make a statement.

"Forget it, *tesoro*!" Poldi told him emphatically. "I don't need a vacation, let alone a lesson in humility."

"It's not about that," Montana replied gravely.

"So what is it about?"

"Trust."

"Are you being serious? After all we've been through?"

Montana just shrugged.

Poldi bombarded him with imprecations in Italian and Bavarian. She told him to go to the devil, she blocked his texts for three days and cursed, swore, and haggled like an Uzbek carpet seller. She pulled out all the stops, but in vain.

The evening before the planned trip to Rome, someone rang Poldi's front doorbell. Assuming that Montana had been worn down at last and was prepared to travel there in comfort by car and ferry, Poldi breezed to the door, ready to graciously forgive and engage in uninhibited, conciliatory sex.

But instead of a contrite *commissario,* she found two strange men standing there in the light of the streetlamp: a young priest in a soutane and a forty-something policeman in a blue uniform and a peaked cap which Poldi, for all her expertise in this field, could not immediately identify. The priest looked pale and exhausted. A thin film of sweat glistened on his forehead, and the bluish stubble on his chin intensified his thoroughly unhealthy appearance. He was incessantly kneading his very hirsute hands as though rubbing something off. Dust, perhaps, or—given that he was a Catholic—original sin. Anyway, Poldi thought he made a sickly impression. Not so the policeman, who looked great —just her type: muscular but not too tall, with a chiseled, clean-shaven, Hollywood-cop type of face.

"A face like a bronze sculpture," she enthused to me. "Pure testosterone, believe me—in fact the sight of him took my breath away for a moment. He remained absolutely impassive, of course. If policemen smile at all, you know, it's only off-duty or after sex."

"Poldi, please!" I sighed.

Now, even Poldi knew that strange men who ring your doorbell at night aren't to be invited in just like that, even if they are wearing a police uniform or a cassock. Criminals come in many guises, after all. On the other hand, she was used to receiving strange visits at unusual times of the day or night. Besides, where knowledge of human nature and intuition were concerned, Poldi had one gear more than us normal individuals. The Oberreiterish superbrain took only nanoseconds to absorb the whole appearance of the pallid priest with his film of sweat, his fluttering eyelashes, his kneading fingers. It scanned his figure for lethal weapons, registered the high quality of his cassock and luxury footwear, and came to the conclusion that this young man genuinely was a priest.

"Moreover," Poldi told me, "a priest who could afford to have his clerical garb made for him by Gammarelli of the Via di Santa Chiara in Rome. They are *the* clerical tailors in Rome. Only popes and cardinals shop there—remember that in case you ever change track."

"How would you know something like that?"

"Why, because I used to be a costume designer and had to deal with such people. Anyway, he didn't look the sort who would hit an old lady over the head and steal her cheap jewelry. Only killers do that, and he just wasn't cool enough."

And Poldi had registered all this within moments, as I said.

Where the policeman was concerned she had no misgivings at all, because she simply had a nose for cops of all kinds. It was only his insignia that gave her pause for thought. She conducted a seconds-long mental review of her five photo albums containing all the policemen she had photographed (and sometimes screwed) in the previous thirty years. It wasn't until she noticed the badge on his left sleeve — a triple crown and crossed keys — that the penny dropped.

"Well, I'll be buggered!"

"Signora Oberreiter?" rasped the policeman.

"Please forgive us for disturbing you at this hour," the priest said in a low voice. "I am Padre Stefano. This is Commissario Morello of the Vatican gendarmerie. We've come here straight from Rome."

"Really?"

"May we come inside?" growled the *commissario*.

Poldi then had a rather X-rated impulse, because detective inspectors are, as everyone knows, supreme manifestations of humanity, above all sexually, but she just managed to control herself.

"What's it about?"

"We'd like to ask you a few questions, that's all," said the Vatican *commissario*.

And, as ever when a policeman spoke of "a few questions" in that tone of voice, Poldi knew she was in trouble again.

2

*Tells of respect, sexy glances, the Song of Solomon,
improvisation, and pinups. Poldi gets drunk with her
nephew, comes under suspicion, and offers a dirty
deal. She turns a no into a yes, drinks tomato juice,
and buys a calendar. Then she has to shake off two
individuals, visit a cemetery, and traverse a museum.
That was the plan, but like so many plans, this one
ends in front of a doorway it would be wiser not to
enter.*

As usual at such junctures, Poldi paused for a moment
and eyed me contentedly.

"I'm going to make myself another root-chakra smoothie.
Want one?"

I knew the move. It was a little battle to see who would
crack first. I strove to extinguish every last spark of curiosity
inside me and became a Zen master of absolute vacuity.

"No thanks. You carry on, I'll wait."

"Aren't you curious?"

"There's no rush."

Poldi stared at me appraisingly. "You used to be more impatient."

"That was in the old days."

"Perhaps it's just that the fire of curiosity has died inside you," she said, glaring at me. "Permanently."

I held her gaze. "Maybe you simply need a break, so you can dream up something else."

"You think I'm inventing it all?"

I shrugged. "You said it yourself: a good story bends the—"

I got no further. Poldi grabbed me by the ear and yanked me to my feet.

"Ouch! That really hurts!"

"I'm still your aunt. That means I deserve some respect, get it?"

Still gripping my ear, she towed me into the kitchen.

"D'you think I daubed those death threats on the walls myself, just for fun?"

"Listen, Poldi, I—"

"Not another word!" she snapped. "While you were making *amore* in France, I became innocently embroiled in a conspiracy. Dreamed it up be damned!"

Grumbling and vituperating, she chopped up some celery, beetroot, and spinach, slung them into the mixer together with a handful of mulberries, plenty of cumin, some hot water, and a generous slug of grappa, and pressed the button. The brown gloop smelled of male perspiration. Poldi filled two glasses and handed me one.

"No thanks," I groaned. "I'm feeling a bit woozy already, to be honest."

"Drink it or I won't tell you any more."

My Auntie Poldi is an expert at subtle persuasion, and I always know when I'm beaten. With the stoicism of Socrates draining his cup of hemlock, I downed the contents of the

24

glass. As before, the grappa unerringly found the shortest route into my circulation.

"Hang on a minute," I said. "Got to fetch something from upstairs."

"Like what?"

"You'll see."

On the stairs I had to cling to the banisters for a moment. There was something wrong with my legs.

It was a relief to flop down on the plastic chair when I got back to the courtyard soon afterward. I opened the big black notebook I'd bought in Paris.

"Well, I'll be damned," Poldi exclaimed. "So Mr. Author has been making notes."

"My memory's not improving with age," I muttered, "that's all."

"Show me!" She snatched the notebook out of my hand and examined it closely. "You mean you write down everything I tell you?"

She sounded rather touched.

"Just bullet points," I said with a shrug. "More of an aide-mémoire."

She nodded, gave the notebook an affectionate stroke, and handed it back.

"And then you'll make a book out of them? About an aging nympho who's trying to drink herself to death but never succeeds? About the cases investigated by a useless old dear?"

"Poldi! I'm just making a few notes, okay? Relax."

She took a crumpled handkerchief from her trouser pocket and loudly blew her nose. "I'm an emotional person, that's all," she said. Having trumpeted into her handkerchief once more, she sniffed and finally went on.

. . .

My Auntie Poldi isn't easily disconcerted, not even by a prize specimen of a detective inspector standing on her doorstep at night with a dog-collared priest beside him. "Perhaps you'd like to be a bit more specific?" she said boldly.

Commissario Morello took a photo from his breast pocket and held it out. "Do you know this woman?"

The photo was of a forty-something woman in a cheap patterned tracksuit. Her chin-length brown hair was unkempt. She looked as if she'd been caught doing something reprehensible.

"Her name is Rosaria Ferrari," Morello went on.

"And? What about her?"

"She's disappeared."

Poldi was a trifle disappointed. "No one's been murdered, then?"

"Yes!" the priest blurted out. "That's to say, we don't know for sure if —"

"Father!" Morello hissed angrily.

"I'm sorry."

Poldi beamed at the two men. "Call me Poldi. Maybe that's too personal, though. Better call me Donna Poldina."

She showed the priest and the policeman into her living room and went to the kitchen to put some coffee on. When she returned the priest was sitting meekly on the sofa with his hands folded on his lap. Commissario Morello was pacing up and down. He had removed his cap and was scanning the room with a look familiar to Poldi from her experience of detectives.

. . .

"It's a very special look that goes right through me," she told me. "It's like being felt all over by big, exploratory hands—inside and out, of course. It makes me go all horny. You can make a note of that."

"Poldi!" I sighed.

"My, how uptight we are today! Anyway, he was looking sexy with his buzz cut and his muscular neck. I couldn't help picturing what the rest of him must look like—without his uniform, I mean. I'm not stupid, though. I grasped at once that he suspected me."

So Poldi kept her cool. Patiently, she sat down in an armchair and poured some coffee.

"Do sit down, *Commissario*."

Morello pointed to the antique muskets on the wall, which Poldi had inherited from her father.

"Have they been deactivated?"

Poldi had been expecting that question.

"No," she trilled innocently. "If you want to defend yourself, *Commissario,* you'll have to use your service automatic or wrestle me to the ground."

My Auntie Poldi knew a thing or two about flirting with detective inspectors.

Morello's face remained expressionless. He went over to the sofa and cleared his throat because the priest was seated in the middle.

"I'm sorry," muttered Padre Stefano, hastily making room for him.

"There was an incident," Morello began. "Two days ago. During an exorcism."

He paused for a moment and looked at Poldi, but she coolly held his gaze. They might have been playing who'll-blink-first.

"Can you give me a bit of context, *Commissario?*"

Morello turned to Padre Stefano.

"Of course, I'm sorry," the priest mumbled, realizing that it was his turn to speak. "I am the assistant of Monsignore Amato, the Vatican's chief exorcist."

"Congratulations."

He ignored Poldi's sarcastic tone of voice.

"Monsignore Amato has conducted more than fifty thousand exorcisms in his life. No one knows the Devil better than he."

"You'll pardon my skepticism."

"There are innumerable demons in this world," Padre Stefano went on eagerly. "Satan is everywhere."

"Really, Father! I'm sure people would do better if you sent them to see a good psychologist."

"If you'd seen what Monsignore Amato has seen, you wouldn't talk like that, Signora Oberreiter."

"Donna Poldina."

"I'm sorry. The *monsignore* has seen people hover in the air in front of him or spit nails!" Stefano drew a deep breath. "Besides, we do send most people to see doctors. Sometimes, though, if the doctors make no progress, they send them to us."

Poldi sighed. "What about this incident the *commissario* mentioned?"

"I'm sorry. I took a video. May I show it to you?"

She sighed again. "Go ahead."

Padre Stefano fished a big smartphone out of his trouser

pocket, tapped the display with a hairy finger, and handed the phone to Poldi.

"Just tap Play."

Poldi took the phone in both hands and bent over it in order to see better. She struggled with the controls at first.

"Hang on, almost there!"

She watched Rosaria's transformation on the massage couch. She saw the woman arch her body, grunting and snarling, saw her sprinkled with holy water. And then she heard her swearing in Bavarian. In *her*, Poldi's, voice.

The video ended abruptly. Poldi stared at the display for a moment, trying to compose herself and think of something nice. Then she drew a deep breath and slid the phone across the coffee table. Morello had apparently been watching her the whole time.

"I realize this must come as a shock to you, Donna Poldina," the priest said in a low voice. "I was just as shocked just now, outside the house, when I heard you swear in German. *Madonna*, I thought, the same voice!"

Poldi interrupted him with a gesture. "What was that she said in Latin?"

"*Nigra sum sed formosa*," the priest repeated. "'I am black but beautiful.' In the original Hebrew the conjunction is simply *ve*, which can also—"

Morello frowned at him disapprovingly.

"Sorry," he mumbled.

"But she isn't black," Poldi exclaimed.

"Nor did she speak either Latin or German at other times," growled the policeman.

"The Song of Solomon, one, five," said Padre Stefano. "The song of the Queen of Sheba: 'I am black, but comely,

29

O ye daughters of Jerusalem, black as the tents of Kedar, as the curtains of Solomon.'" He glanced at the *commissario*. "Sorry."

"I see," said Poldi, who had always liked the Song of Solomon for its erotic allusions. "But the video must go on, surely. What happens after that? Did she say anything else?"

Morello and Stefano exchanged a quick glance.

"Monsignore Amato ended the session immediately after that outburst," said the priest. "Rosaria couldn't remember a thing afterward."

"You really don't know the woman?" the Vatican detective interposed. "Never seen her before?"

Poldi shook her head.

"Think carefully."

"Good God, you can tell I'm thinking! I've never seen that woman in my life!"

"That's rather hard to believe, you must admit."

"Heavens alive, what's so hard to believe? You breeze in here in the middle of the night and show me a video whose authenticity I can't check, then make a bunch of assumptions and suspect me of something. Is *that* believable?"

"Nobody's suspecting you of anything, Signora Oberreiter," murmured the priest.

"Donna Poldina."

"I'm sorry."

"So who's dead?" Poldi demanded.

Morello showed her a photograph of an angelic-looking young nun in a white habit.

"That's Sister Rita."

"Of the Society of the Merciful Sisters of the Most Blessed

Virgin and Dolorous Mother Mary," Padre Stefano amplified.

"A Clement sister," said Morello.

"Sorry."

Poldi studied the photo more closely. The way the young nun was pursing her lips struck her as a trifle vulgar—as though Sister Rita had been posing for a selfie. Despite her austere habit and wimple, however, her beauty was unmistakable.

"I think I may have seen her somewhere after all."

"Sister Rita assisted at the exorcism," said Morello.

"How did she die?"

"She fell off the roof," Stefano whispered in horror. "More precisely, the roof terrace of the Apostolic Palace. That's four stories up."

Commissario Morello grunted impatiently. It seemed they'd agreed on a different strategic line of questioning.

"Sorry," mumbled the priest.

"The terrace forms part of the papal *appartamento*," said Morello. "Which is still unoccupied because the Holy Father prefers to live in—"

"I know," Poldi broke in. "What does 'fell' mean? Did she just fall, or was she helped on her way?"

"Everything points to suicide," said the policeman.

"Did it happen immediately after the exorcism?"

"No, a good four hours later. We're still reconstructing what went on in the interim. For instance, how long Rosaria spent in the Vatican precincts and whom she may have met."

"But your first job, surely, is to discover how Sister Rita found her way onto the roof terrace of the papal apartment."

Morello shook his head. "That's not so hard. Ever since F1 moved into the Santa Marta guesthouse, Curial officials have enjoyed using it."

"F1?"

The policeman cleared his throat, sounding slightly embarrassed. "Pope Francis. The Holy Father."

"I'm sorry," said Padre Stefano.

"So, if I understand you correctly," Poldi summarized, "a nun fell from the roof terrace and you assume her death is somehow connected with Rosaria, whose exorcism the nun attended. And because Rosaria spoke in my voice during that hoary old Catholic hocus-pocus, you think I'm also involved. A bit far-fetched, isn't it?"

"We simply want to know what happened."

Poldi burst out laughing.

"It's quite simple: I employed satanic methods to manipulate this Rosaria at long range, maneuvered Sister Rita onto the pope's roof terrace, and persuaded her to jump off. But not before leaving behind a subtle clue to my identity, tadaaa!"

She shook with mirth, but neither of the men joined in. They simply stared at her.

"You can't be serious, guys!"

"I'm sorry."

"What do forensics say?"

Morello coughed. "I can't comment on that for the moment."

"And the State Police?"

He harrumphed again. "The incident took place on Vatican State territory, which means the Vatican gendarmerie are responsible for the case, not the Italian police. I may request the latter's assistance in due course, but for the moment we're treating it as an internal matter."

"I see. And what does the press say?"

Morello didn't reply. Padre Stefano started to speak, but a curt gesture from the *commissario* instantly silenced him.

"Sorry," he mumbled.

Poldi shook her head. "The way I see it," she said, homing in on Morello, "you've got a huge problem. A nun falls off the roof of the Apostolic Palace and gets killed after an exorcism, and the only possible witness or perp has vanished without trace. That in itself would be meaty enough for a scandal, and the Vatican hates scandal even more than free love."

Padre Stefano started to object, but Poldi shut him up in Bavarian.

"Zip the lip, *Burschi*!"

"Sorry."

"And then," Poldi continued serenely, reverting to Italian, "your instinct tells you that Sister Rita did not leave this life of her own volition, otherwise you wouldn't be here. Murder in the Vatican? *Madonna,* an earthquake pales in comparison! So what do you do? You try to keep the affair under the radar for as long as possible and sort it out by yourself. Bravo! Except.. . . . How long will it be before someone in the Vatican leaks the whole story to the press? And so, because it's a time bomb and you're out of ideas, you jet over to Sicily and, in the middle of the night, corner a lone pensioner in her prime" — she pointed down at herself — "in the hope that if you bully her enough, something will come of it. But what if nothing does? You'll have to hand the case over to the Italian State Police or sweep it under the carpet. You're experts at that in the Vatican, aren't you?"

"I beg your pardon!" the priest said angrily.

Poldi sat back in her chair.

"A beer, anyone?"

Morello had listened to Poldi with his jaw muscles tightening spasmodically.

"Where were you between six-thirty and ten o'clock the day before yesterday?" he demanded.

That did it. Poldi got out her mobile phone and tapped the display meaningfully. "Know what, you comedians? I'm now going to call Commissario Montana at police headquarters in Acireale and ask him to look in, because the way I see it, you've absolutely no business here."

"No!" Morello barked. He drew a deep breath. "Donna Poldina . . ."

"Yes, Commissario Morello?"

"I, er" — more harrumphing — "wouldn't mind a beer."

"A sensible remark at last!" Poldi smiled at him and went off to fetch three bottles.

This, as may be imagined, was because something had long ago awakened inside her, namely, the hunting instinct. And Poldi knew a thing or two about the hunting instinct and making the most of one's opportunities.

"Cheers, gentlemen!" She clinked bottles with her two nocturnal visitors. "I don't believe in Satan," she said firmly. "There must be some rational explanation for Rosaria's behavior and Sister Rita's death. If you really want to find it, you're out of luck, because for that you need me. But you're also in luck, because you've now got me on board."

Morello almost choked. "Eh?"

"Unofficially, of course. I'm not only a hundred percent professional, I'm inconspicuous. A shadow. A ghost. So here's the deal: You don't interfere with me. I'll operate in the background, completely independently. If problems arise —though why should they?—you can simply deny you've had anything to do with me."

Morello and the priest stared at my aunt with their mouths open.

"I know," she said brightly, before either of them could speak, "this wasn't the way you'd imagined your little jaunt to Sicily, but get this: happiness equals reality minus expectation. And from now on—*ecco là!*—I'm your reality and your luck."

"No!" said Morello.

"Yes," Poldi blithely said. "Because without me you'll get nowhere. Not even to the airport, because the State Police will arrest you both first, and tomorrow the whole shemozzle will be splashed all over the newspapers." She spread her arms with an innocent air.

"Not on your life!" Morello growled. "It's out of the question. Over my dead body."

"That was the moment," Poldi told me later, "when the *signor commissario* should have stood up and walked out, because I was only bluffing. But he didn't."

I was flabbergasted. "And he actually agreed to this deal?"

I may have been slurring my words already. I was also feeling a bit dizzy and had the beginnings of a headache, and I made up my mind not to drink any more.

Poldi bridled. "Well, not in so many words. The man's no

35

fool. In his sternest official tone of voice, he told me bluntly that he'd lock me up in the Vatican jail if I interfered with his investigations in any way or went nosing around the Vatican on my own account."

She inserted a brief pause and waited for me to finish making notes. I was having trouble wielding the pencil and doubted I'd be able to decipher my scrawls the next day.

"Er, what happened then?"

"Why, he and the hairy priest took their leave. I realized by then that he'd unofficially given me carte blanche."

"Hang on," I said. "So he said no, no, three times no, and you interpreted that as a yes?"

"I'm a woman with a lot of antennae," Poldi told me without turning a hair, "and a woman always knows what a man really means when he says no. Want to see the video? It's a bit creepy."

"You mean they left it with you?"

"Of course not." She grinned. "I forwarded it to my own phone while I was watching it. Very practical, what you can do with a single click these days. When I bent over, those two thought I was simply being butterfingered."

I've said it before: my Auntie Poldi possesses an extra gear. She's an ice-cold pro with a heart of Turkish delight and nerves of steel.

She pressed Play, and I heard for myself how the woman mimicked Poldi's Bavarian cursing. I felt a bit queasy at the thought that it had been Rosaria who had actually called me in France in my aunt's voice and summoned me back to Sicily.

"What do you think this Rosaria woman is after?" I asked hoarsely. "Where I'm concerned, for instance?"

"Absolutely nothing." Poldi made a dismissive gesture. "Why should she be interested in you?"

I stared at her.

"I'm joking, for God's sake!" She stroked my cheek and eyed me with concern. "You're really out of kilter, my lad. Relax, pin your ears back, keep taking notes, and prepare to be amazed."

"Is there another beer?"

After her strange visitors had gone, Poldi conferred with herself and then with the internet, railing against the irony of fate. For a week she had cried blue murder and moved heaven and earth *not* to have to fly to Rome with Montana, and now she would have to fly there after all, but without him.

"Yes, very funny, universe!" she grumbled aloud as she defied death and booked a seat on the first available flight to Rome, which was scheduled to take off shortly after seven the next morning. "Thanks for the lesson, *grazie mille*! You must be splitting your sides, I know, but if you think I'm going to chicken out, you've got another think coming. You got me into this, so give me a bit of a hand, you hear?"

Because no, she didn't want to fly. She hated flying more than thirst, boredom, or her native Augsburg. She would far rather have embarked on a leisurely drive to Rome with her hand on Montana's thigh. In default of that, she would at least have got blind drunk before takeoff, but neither of those was an option, for once my Auntie Poldi has tasted blood she becomes a terrier. This was now a personal matter, so to speak. She had to get to Rome as quickly as possible. Sober, what was more.

. . .

"Just a minute," I asked, puzzled. "You mean you left Montana in the dark?"

"Stop interrupting. Are you crazy? How was I to let him in on it? I was operating undercover, sort of. If I'd told him about it, he'd never have let me go sleuthing again. Besides, it was better for him not to know anything just in case I came unstuck, know what I mean? I was protecting him, that's all."

"Come off it, Poldi! You simply wanted to handle the whole thing solo again. Besides, if I know you, a certain Vatican detective was ever so slightly involved as well."

She glared at me. "May I go on now, Signor Goody-Two-Shoes?"

I drained my latest bottle of beer. "*Forza,* Poldi!"

Early the next morning Poldi climbed into her leopardskin trousers and bomber jacket and, weak at the knees, boarded the first flight to Rome. No Montana to hold her hand and distract her with a bit of mansplaining. No Montana to lecture her at exhausting length on meteorology and the physics of flight or explain that "air pockets" didn't exist.

Instead she had an aisle seat beside two buzz-cut, heavily aftershaved young men in brightly colored sneakers, who made themselves comfortable without a word, as though they owned the whole plane. They were twins distinguishable only by the color of their footwear. The one next to her, who was wearing fluorescent red sneakers, showed his companion, who was wearing fluorescent green, some photos of young women on his smartphone. These the latter either dismissed with a shake of the head or approved by clicking his tongue. The hand holding the phone was callused and covered with little scars like that of a craftsman or agricultural laborer.

Increasingly stressed and apprehensive before takeoff, Poldi mopped her brow and panted audibly, but the twins simply ignored her.

My Auntie Poldi has undergone many experiences in the course of her tumultuous life, but being ignored by men is certainly not one of them. From this, and their hands, her razor-sharp brain inferred that the two sprawling twins could only be plainclothes policemen let loose on her by Morello. She resolved to keep her nerve.

Nonetheless, when the flight attendant secured the forward cabin door, Poldi rather lost it. With one swift movement she grabbed the man's phone—which, she was amused to note, had a Madonna sticker on the back.

"Right, let's put that away for the moment. You can have it back when we land."

"Signora!" the young man protested.

Poldi gave him no chance to speak. Swiftly stuffing the phone down her cleavage, she let fly: "Okay, so you've now got two choices. Either you shut up like a good boy and let me have the goddamn armrest to myself, or you can try to retrieve your phone. If you do that, though, I'll kick up such a fuss they'll throw you both off the plane. All clear?"

It was an uneventful flight. The two brothers merely ground their teeth the whole time and stared straight ahead. Poldi sweated and panted and clutched the armrests at the slightest turbulence, but her professional instincts helped her to preserve her composure. She even drank a tomato juice.

• • •

"Now you're exaggerating," I protested when she told me.

"Not at all," she said firmly. "I engaged in self-therapy. That surprises you, doesn't it? Fear's the thing—write that down! If you stand up to it instead of running away, it shrinks like a limp . . . well, you know what I mean."

When the plane reached its parking place at Fiumicino Airport, Poldi reached into her cleavage and graciously returned her neighbor's well-warmed phone. Then she grabbed her carry-on bag from the overhead bin, wished the pair a successful day, and made a rapid exit.

It would of course be permissible to cock a finger and ask how the devil Poldi, who was on the plump side and had a bad knee, proposed to shake off two fit and bad-tempered young cops in her strappy sandals and leopardskin trousers. But as I have said, my Auntie Poldi possesses an extra gear.

"*Permesso! Permesso!*" Panting, she pushed and shoved and squeezed past the other passengers in the plane, then forged a path across the terminal to the nearest toilets. There she locked herself up in a cubicle, gasping for breath after her brief sprint, and opened—*click, click*—her carry-on.

Soon afterward, when her recent seatmates were roaming the terminal like two stray wolf cubs, they scarcely registered the rather portly nun in the cowled habit and sunglasses who emerged from the ladies' with a black bag and made swiftly for the exit.

Poldi saw the pair gesticulating out of the corner of her eye. Then one of them cuffed the other on the back of the head.

• • •

"Pull the other one!" I exclaimed when Poldi calmly tried to sell me this story. "Where in the world would you have magicked a nun's habit from?"

"Are you disbelieving me again?"

I thought for a moment, then nodded.

With a sigh, Poldi got to her feet and went back inside the house. A few minutes later, when she returned with two chilled Morettis and flopped down on her chair again, she was wearing a black habit.

"Wow!" I said, impressed despite myself. "Where the hell did you get that from?"

"Why, from my past life."

To dispel any misunderstandings, Poldi had never been a nun. She was referring to her previous existence as a costume designer in the film industry. Having kept the best costume from every movie she worked on, she'd built up quite a collection over the decades.

"I sold most of them before I moved here," she explained. "I wanted to dump all my ballast and the money came in handy, but nobody wanted this habit and it was too good to throw away. It's a Gammarelli—finest clerical chic."

She handed me a bottle, and—against my better judgment—I went on drinking.

Poldi had a plan, as you might have guessed. Having deposited her trolley bag in a locker at the main station, she went to a *tabacchi*, where she bought a white touch-up pencil and a Calendario Romano.

"That's a pinup calendar," she explained. "Of twelve young priests. Not in the buff, of course, but they're all as hot as hell."

My Auntie Poldi knew a thing or two about hotness, and the Calendario Romano has long ceased to be a dirty secret. One of the most popular souvenirs from Rome, it's reputed to sell a million copies and has become something of a cult object. The priests it depicts look like top male models in cassocks and are idolized like pop stars.

Where the devil are you?

A text message from Montana popped up. It was his fifth communication that morning, not counting unanswered phone calls. Assailed by a twinge of remorse, Poldi briefly debated whether to reply but abandoned the idea. Better he didn't know anything, she thought. She'd be able to explain it all later, she thought. And then, she thought, he would see how promptly and circumspectly she had acted.

Determined to carry out the operation according to plan, Poldi took a taxi to St. Peter's Square. From there she made her way on foot to the Petrianus Gate, one of the Vatican's few gates, which is situated between St. Peter's Square and the palace of the Congregation for the Doctrine of the Faith. She knew it was much harder to gain access to the Vatican than it used to be.

"The most important feature of the Vatican is its wall," Poldi stated like a tour guide when telling me all this. "Without the wall there wouldn't be any Vatican myth; everyone would immediately spot how boring it is inside. The wall is like a cell membrane separating the permissible from the impermissible. Lots of things are possible *extra muros* — love affairs, debauchery, a discreet double life, you name it — but woe betide anyone who imports them! Oh boy, then they're for it! *Intra muros* is holy ground, that's why."

A few years ago, anyone in suitable clerical attire could shuffle past the Swiss Guard sentries unchallenged and without any permit, but Poldi was chary of relying on that. Times had changed, and she had to assume that the Sister Rita incident would have prompted Morello to tighten up security measures. For German-speaking visitors, however, there still existed an old recourse.

"To the Campo Santo, please," Poldi said in German to the Swiss Guard at the Petrianus Gate.

Behind the gate lay the Campo Santo Teutonico, the German cemetery, which belonged to Italy under international law. Sicily is complicated, but so is the Vatican. This being the case, and because Germans must always have access to this last vestige of the Holy Roman Empire of the German Nation, the young sentry in Renaissance uniform waved Poldi past without demur. Only one more checkpoint, and she would be almost inside the Vatican.

Well worth a visit, the Campo Santo is an enchanted jewel of a place enclosed by a high wall. Interspersed with its palms and strelitzias are old gravestones bearing German names. A place of silence and contemplation, it is also notorious among clerics for the wild parties held in the adjoining theological college.

But Poldi had no time to spare for sightseeing. She still had to get past the two Vatican policemen who were leaning against their patrol car near the cemetery to ensure that no tourists or Bavarian private detectives infiltrated the Holy See. Poldi removed her sunglasses and made her way into the

Campo Santo, which she strolled around once for form's sake. Then she hurried straight over to the Vatican policemen.

"You must help me, *Assistente*!" she told the elder of the pair excitedly in her best Italian, but with a strong German accent. "I've tried, God knows, but I simply can't do it."

The two policemen submitted the odd-looking nun to a brief inspection.

"What's it all about, Sister?" asked the older man.

Poldi gestured wildly at the German cemetery. "*He's* in there."

"Who is?" asked the younger.

She stared at him with a puzzled expression. "You mean you didn't see him? You've been standing here—you *must* have seen him!"

"*Who*, Sister?"

Poldi held out the Calendario Romano and pointed to the cover, which featured a fit young priest whose looks would have equipped him for Hollywood.

"*Him!*" Poldi clutched her bosom and fanned herself. "Padre Adriano from Brescia. I've been following him all morning, God forgive me. *Mea culpa*. I know it's unseemly, but"—she quickly crossed herself—"I must have his autograph. Not for myself, of course. It's for a lay sister who's a friend of mine."

"Of course."

The two men looked amused, she was pleased to note.

"Why don't you simply ask him?"

"I meant to, *Assistente*! I meant to the whole morning, but honestly, what would it look like? I simply can't, that's why I'm asking for your discreet assistance." Poldi held out the calendar and the white touch-up pencil like a sacrificial offering.

The two policemen glanced at each other and the younger one turned away, smirking. The older man drew a deep breath, took the calendar and the pencil from Poldi, and strolled over to the cemetery.

Poldi nudged his junior colleague. "Well, my son, go with him. I'll hold the fort."

Spurred on by curiosity and my Auntie Poldi's determined manner, the younger policeman followed his superior into the Campo Santo. That gave Poldi free rein. Unchallenged, she hurried around the back of St. Peter's into the Vatican Gardens, past the Sistine Chapel, and, through a side entrance, into the Vatican Museum. Without even a glance at the Raphael tapestries, she made her way to the last room of all. There, beneath a portrait of Pope Clement I, was an emergency exit for any tourist who had a heart attack and needed to be evacuated in a hurry. And this old oak door led straight into the Apostolic Palace.

3

Tells of solid preparation, old passages, minor mistakes, preservation of momentum, sightseeing, octopuses, and forty winks. Poldi is in a sudden hurry and makes a new acquaintance. Her nephew, on the other hand, drinks more than is good for him. Poldi suddenly has plenty of time and Montana yearns for a past life. But let's not kid ourselves, leopards can't change their spots.

E r, stop, one moment," I cut in. "Have I missed something? How did you know that?"

"Well . . ." Poldi said evasively, "I have my sources."

"Like some Vatican bigwig, I suppose. The Holy Father himself, maybe?"

That was meant as a joke. I thought it was a good one, so I giggled rather hysterically. Poldi just looked at me, shaking her head.

"All right, what sources?" I asked, still chuckling.

"You're beginning to annoy me, had you noticed?"

"What sources, Poldi?"

"Why, just a book."

"Oh? What sort of book?"

"Well, a novel, a Vatican thriller. You know the sort of thing."

"What!" I stared at her. "You relied on a route described in a *novel?*"

"Why not, for God's sake? It only goes to show you have to take extra care with your research, so your readers can also make use of your rubbish later on."

She cleared her throat—violently, to indicate that I was to shut up for good—and was about to go on when her mobile buzzed and vibrated. She glanced at the display and held it out. Valérie. I instantly got palpitations, but I shook my head.

Poldi needs little prompting in matters of the heart, she simply gets the picture. She not only deleted the call, she turned her mobile off altogether.

"All good?"

My mouth was too dry to answer. I just nodded and took another swig of beer.

"*Forza,* Poldi!"

Click, click, click. The wooden door's old lock presented no real obstacle to a professional with the appropriate precision tool. Like a shadow, Poldi slipped through and climbed the stairs beyond it, which led up to the loggias of the Apostolic Palace. Her plan was to get to the roof terrace and look for some clues there. Pope Francis had left the roof terrace free for his Curial officials to stroll there, so some form of access must exist. That, at least, was my aunt's razor-edged conclusion.

Almost complete silence reigned in the centuries-old Renaissance passages worn smooth by hundreds of thousands of discreet footsteps. There was a smell of cleaning fluids, old timber, coffee, power, and original sin. From behind some closed office doors came the sound of a radio, a copy machine, a sneeze. Poldi only rarely passed priests and Curial officials, who flitted across the ancient flagstones as silently as possible and barely noticed my aunt in her nun's habit. Everything was going according to plan—clicking into place like the beads in a rosary, so to speak. The only little fly in the ointment was that Poldi hadn't the faintest idea of how to get to the papal roof terrace.

"But I didn't worry," she told me. "That's because every operation needs to be well prepared. Good basic preparation is the *A* and *O,* the alpha and omega. All that's needed after that is *I* and *I:* improvisation and intuition. Write that down and bear it in mind for your novel."

In addition, my Auntie Poldi knows a trick that'll get you to your destination anywhere in the world, by the quickest route and without a GPS. I'm not good at it, though the trick is very simple: Ask the way. And keep asking.

Since she now felt comfortable enough in her disguise, she accosted the next priest to come along.

"Excuse me, Father," she whispered respectfully but firmly. "I have an appointment with Monsignor Ottolenghi on the roof terrace, to discuss the organization of the Estonian delegation's ecumenical pilgrimage to Lourdes in October—not an altogether simple matter after the recent scandal, as you'll appreciate—but I think I may have lost my way."

I don't know how she does it—I mean, how can she bring herself to utter such brazen balderdash with such aplomb? The priest, who didn't smell a rat, merely cast an impatient glance at Poldi and curtly advised her to take the lift to the fourth floor, then climb the adjacent stairs.

Bingo! Poldi told herself contentedly.

"*Grazie mille,* Your Reverence!" Giving the priest a somewhat overly coquettish smile for a nun, she hurried off in search of the lift that would take her to the fourth floor.

But happiness is reality minus expectation, and whenever you expect too much of your happiness or think *Bingo!*, reality quickly reasserts itself.

In Poldi's case, this happened when she reached the old, wood-paneled elevator with the trellis door, which came rumbling and creaking down from above. As it did, she heard the voice of Commissario Morello.

"Bloody hell, she can't have dissolved into thin air! I want you to find her, even if you have to lock the whole of the Vatican down and search it."

Who else could he mean but her?

Poldi looked around quickly but could detect no potential hiding place anywhere along the passage, just a lonely trolley stacked with files. She couldn't just burst into the nearest office. The lift came to a stop. Spinning around, she dashed to the trolley, bent low over it, and simply pushed it down the passage. The lift door creaked open behind her and Morello emerged, phone to ear.

"No, I've just come from there. Keep looking!"

Forcing herself not to run, Poldi simply continued to push the trolley along. Out of the corner of her eye she saw Morello dash past her and disappear around the corner. She paused briefly and listened to his rapidly receding footsteps. With a sigh of relief she turned on the spot and was about to wheel the trolley back in the direction of the lift when she heard the footsteps come to a halt, then swiftly grow louder as they came racing back. Poldi had to break into a run after all. Leaving the trolley in the middle of the passage as an obstacle, she gathered up her habit and set off as fast as she could, or rather, as fast as her bad knee permitted. She sprinted along the passage, scooted past the lift, narrowly avoided a priest, skidded across the flagstones, just made the bend, and pelted down the nearest stairs.

"Stop!" roared Morello behind her.

Naturally my aunt ignored that, as she always did when a man tried to lay down the law. It was a kind of red line of hers. She simply hurried on down to the first floor and around the next corner in the hope of somehow shaking off the *commissario* and finding an exit somewhere, or at least a hiding place of some kind.

"Stop!"

She might even have made it, who knows, but the fact is, not even my Auntie Poldi is proof against centrifugal force and the preservation of momentum.

When a door opened just ahead of her and a small party of elderly Curial dignitaries debouched into the passage, she simply had no chance of braking to a halt in time. Although she instinctively tried to swerve when the first purple cassock appeared out of the blue in front of her, her momentum sent her crashing into the little group of men. The cardinals toppled over like pins scattered by a powerfully propelled bowling ball. Poldi positively mowed them down, and while spinning around, she threw up her arms and caught someone under the chin with her elbow. She became aware that a seam in her habit had split under the strain, and groped for some form of support, buried her fingers in a cassock, finally lost her balance, and, taking the cassock's elderly occupant with her, buried him beneath her like an avalanche.

There was a moment's silence. Poldi could hear the blood roaring in her ears, Morello's hurrying footsteps, and the heavy breathing of the man she was lying on top of in her torn habit. His face, which seemed somehow familiar, looked bewildered rather than shocked.

"Good morning, Sister," he said jovially. "Why in such a hurry?"

"Well, I'll be buggered!" Poldi blurted out as the handcuffs clicked shut on her wrists and she recognized Fı lying beneath her in his white soutane.

"No!" I exclaimed, flabbergasted.

"Yes."

"I don't believe you."

Poldi spread her arms.

"You laid the pope!"

She giggled. "Vito put it like that too, when I told him. I couldn't help it."

"Izzat how you met all your sheleb friends?"

"Hey, had one beer too many, laddie? Feeling all right? Would you like a lie-down?"

"No," I croaked loudly, "I'm fine!" And I indicated, with a sweeping gesture, that she was to go on. "Get on with your story. What happened then?"

"Well, then Morello marched me off, as you can imagine. I tried to explain everything, but he wouldn't listen. He simply marched me off and locked me up."

"Locked you up?"

"Yes, the Vatican has a jail of its own, didn't you know?"

. . .

Poldi was still stewing in a small cell in the Vatican police force barracks six hours later. Neither Morello nor anyone else had turned up to interrogate, torture, exorcise, or just ask if she'd like a beer. And Poldi could have used a beer.

Although a nun had silently and with distinct disapproval dumped a bottle of mineral water and two flabby sandwiches down on the table, that was it. The disagreeable creature had also frisked her and removed all her personal possessions. No one else had appeared after that.

Compared to the police cells familiar to Poldi from her wild and woolly days, when she had—not for the first time —slightly overstepped the limits of civil disobedience, this cell made an almost welcoming impression: a little bed with clean sheets, a table, a chair, a washbasin with mirror, a crucifix above the door, a picture of the pope on the bare, whitewashed wall, and, facing it, a framed print of a Madonna icon. And, of course, a built-in stainless steel toilet. The Vatican Gardens were visible through the barred window.

This smallest prison in the world contained only two cells, and they had long been used as storerooms until a few years ago, when the pope's thieving valet had had to be incarcerated there. Their only other occasional occupants were foulmouthed tourists, pickpockets, or women's rights activists, who were briefly housed there before being handed over to the Italian police.

There could be no question of that in Poldi's case, and the longer she vegetated on the narrow bed, waiting for something to happen at last, the more she dwelled on the thought of a cool beer and the minor mistake that had given her away.

"What was it? How did you spot it was me?" she'd asked

Morello as he led her away in handcuffs. The Vatican police-man had simply pointed to the strappy gold sandals peeping out from under her habit.

Such things happen to the best of professionals, she told herself, though she could have torn the wig off her head in annoyance.

Outside, the day wore on. If Poldi hates anything, it's waiting — in fact it comes second only to murder and thirst. Waiting for something or someone has always been my aunt's least favorite activity — sheer torture and brainwash-ing. If she has to twiddle her thumbs, she blows a fuse, hence her lifelong aversion to public transport.

"I realized it could only be an attrition tactic on Morello's part," she told me. "It was meant to soften me up for my forthcoming interrogations."

"Mm, sure, that makes sense. After all, there's little to choose between the Vatican and the Lubyanka."

"Don't be sarcastic. So I had to do something to preserve my sanity — to stop thinking all the time of a nice cool beer and my stupid little mistake."

"So?"

"So," drawled Poldi, "I simply had a nap."

"Seriously?"

"Of course. It's the best thing for your mental health. You can never have enough shut-eye. Besides, I realized my every movement was being recorded by concealed cameras, and I wanted to show Morello he could get stuffed. Taking a nap can also be an act of rebellion, remember that."

And my Auntie Poldi knew a thing or two about naps and acts of rebellion.

However, when nobody showed an interest in her after said nap, she started to worry despite herself.

"Hey!" she called loudly. "You realize the Geneva Conventions apply to the Vatican as well?"

No response.

She wondered whether to go on a rampage, as she might have done in the old days, but abandoned the idea. Images of the Madonna have a moderating effect, even on heathens like Poldi.

"So what did I do to kill time in a sensible way?" she asked me in a schoolmarmish voice.

"Have some more shut-eye?"

"Nonsense. I made a mind map."

"A mind map? You mean . . ."

"Exactly. A visualization of my train of thought. A map of associations, facts, leads, questions, the works—you know. I didn't have much to go on, but it's like making lists: as soon as you start mapping your thoughts, more and more come flooding in until—whoops!—you see the full picture. A mind map is a sort of guide to the subconscious."

"Would you permit me to ask a question, Your Worship?"

Poldi rolled her eyes.

"How. Did. You. Draw. A. Mind. Map. In. Jail?"

"Just think. What do you need for a mind map apart from some gumption? Exactly. You need a blackboard and some chalk. I had a blackboard, i.e., the mirror over the washbasin, and as for chalk, well . . ."

Poldi stationed herself in front of the little mirror, straightened her black beehive of a wig a little, fished around in its woolly depths, and—ta-daaa!—brought out a lipstick. Being an old hand, she had swiftly hidden this there under the nun's nose. My Auntie Poldi could dispense with a lot of things, but never a lipstick, least of all after such a disastrously un-made-up morning.

She really didn't have much to go on. In fact, just the video and what Morello and Padre Stefano had told her. Or rather, what they had left out, because Poldi smelled something of a rat in that respect.

Feeling rested after her shut-eye but also riled by all the waiting, she painted her lips and then began to visualize her thoughts. First she wrote SISTER RITA at the top of the mirror. From SISTER RITA she drew a line down to ROSARIA and another line to POLDI. Although one side was missing—there was no connection between Poldi and Sister Rita, after all—this produced a triangle.

"And a triangle," Poldi told me, "is always good. A triangle is stable, like a three-legged stool, and it's also scientifically proven to be the basic shape of space in the nanosphere, did you know that? However complex a state of affairs or an object or anything else may be, you can always measure the world with a triangle. In a sense, the triangle is the universe's answer to every question."

I let that stand.

Inside this open RITA-ROSARIA-POLDI triangle Poldi now wrote down the few facts she knew, joined names with lines, inscribed bullet points, splashed question marks around, circled words and wiped them out with the towel. Time flew by, and when Poldi had scribbled all over the mirror and the towel was thoroughly impregnated with Rouge Hypnotique, she stepped back and inspected her abstract work of art with a critical eye. Something about it wasn't right. She sat down on the bed and regarded her scribbles from further away. And then she spotted something.

"Well, I'll be buggered!"

"Are you going to ekshplain?" I asked. I was feeling rather the worse for wear by now, I must admit. Totti was snoring beneath the table, and the sitar music and the alcohol were scrambling my thoughts.

"No," said Poldi. "It was just a nudge and a wink from the universe, understand? Just a little tip, maybe just happenstance, nothing more."

She would have liked to take a photo of her mirror, but the nun had confiscated her phone, so she indelibly memorized the mind map with her superbrain and scrubbed the whole thing out. Then, resuming her seat on the bed, she waited patiently and somewhat more contentedly for whatever would transpire.

It was late afternoon before she at last heard voices and footsteps. She glanced quickly at the mirror and tweaked her torn habit straight. A key was noisily inserted in the lock, the steel door creaked open, and a *commissario* appeared.

But not Commissario Morello.

"Vito!" Poldi cried in amazement.

Montana was wearing one of his perpetually creased gray suits and had dark smudges under his eyes, and the deep crease between his eyebrows portended storm-force gusts from the south-southeast. He seemed less surprised than tired and disappointed to see Poldi looking like a disheveled nun.

"Come on, Poldi. We're going."

"How did you find me?"

"Morello called me. You obviously mentioned my name to him last night. I've sorted it all."

"I'm being released? No interrogation or anything?"

Montana drew a deep breath. Poldi could see what an effort it cost him not to bellow at her.

"Because," she explained for the umpteenth time, "the man's a detective inspector and a Sicilian. In other words . . ."

"A sexual force of nature," I said with a sigh. "Yes, I know."

"An emotional volcano too, though. Gray and rough and hard on the outside, but emotional magma is blazing and bubbling away inside. I'd wounded him by going at it alone, I could tell that right away. He was deeply hurt, angry, and sad, all at once. And randy too, seeing me in my torn habit like that. That went without saying, because Sicilians always experience a mixture of emotions. They're a baroque race, and it's just that combination of steel and liquid fire that always makes me go weak at the—"

"Poldi!" I exclaimed.

But Montana didn't explode, he had himself under control. He came in carrying a small bag containing some clean clothes from Torre, put it down beside the bed, and promptly turned on his heel.

"Where are you going, *tesoro*?"

"Get dressed. I'll wait in the office out front. You have to sign some papers."

He closed the door behind him, leaving Poldi thoroughly abashed. She gathered her thoughts for a moment, then lost no time in removing her disguise at last and becoming herself again.

Braced for some rigorous questioning by Montana and Morello, she walked into the office at the end of the passage. To her surprise, however, only Montana and two Swiss Guards were waiting for her there. Lying on the table were her phone, her house key, the Calendario Romano, and the few other little personal effects the nun had removed from her.

"Where's Commissario Morello?"

"He's busy." Montana handed her a form. "Just sign that and we can go."

But Poldi dug her heels in. "I won't sign anything until you tell me what's really going on here. Aren't I to be questioned at all? Any new developments in the case?"

"There isn't any case!" snapped Montana, and the two Swiss Guards grinned. "I had a long talk with Morello earlier. It was definitely suicide. Since then Rosaria has turned up at her family home. Morello interviewed her. Rosaria Ferrari suffers from schizophrenia. After the exorcism she spent several hours wandering aimlessly around the Vatican Gardens. Sister Rita found her there and escorted her to the Sant'Anna Gate."

"So why, pray, did Sister Rita throw herself off the roof of the Apostolic Palace soon afterward?"

Montana drew a deep breath. "She was pregnant. She'd evidently had an affair with some priest outside the Vatican and could see no alternative."

"And you believe that cock-and-bull story, Vito?"

Montana brusquely held out the form. "Sign that and let's go."

Poldi could tell that her beloved *commissario* with the green eyes and gentle hands, her tender fellow voyager on the ocean of passion, her stern but indulgent protector and—yes —friend, was on the verge of a meltdown. Not wanting it to come to that, she signed the three-sheet form plus a nondisclosure agreement. Then she had to hurry to catch up with Montana, who marched out of the office without a word.

"I'm sorry, Vito!" she called after him as she followed him out of the barracks to the car park.

A group of priests turned to look, because my Auntie Poldi was not an everyday sight in the Vatican. She was rarer than a Marian apparition, so to speak.

Montana opened the door of the rental car.

"No, Poldi, you aren't sorry at all, but I . . ." He hesitated. "Oh, it doesn't matter. I'm hungry, how about you?"

"Did you see the video?"

"Morello showed it to me. Believe me, that's the only reason I came to collect you myself." He paused and turned. "Do you find him attractive?"

"What?"

"Do you find him attractive?"

Poldi gazed at her beloved *commissario* across the roof of the car.

"All right, yes, I do find him attractive. He is, too, though not as attractive as you. Medium attractive, let's say. Seven out of ten to your ten out of ten. Is that good enough for you? You don't honestly think I'd have done all this for the sake of a date with Morello, do you?"

Montana got into the car and Poldi hurriedly got in too, before hot Sicilian blood made him simply drive off without her.

"Okay," he sighed after a while, "I can understand why the video upset you so much that you invaded the Vatican disguised as a nun and ended up on top of the pope." He shook his head as they turned into the Via della Conciliazione. "You actually laid the pope! I've been a communist all my life, and I've regarded the Catholic Church as a hostile system to be opposed with all one's might, but *you* laid the pope!" He was laughing heartily now. "Pity there isn't a video of *that*."

Poldi chuckled. "He was very friendly."

Montana turned serious again. "But there's an explanation for everything, and there must be one for what goes on in that video of Rosaria. Maybe she heard you giving an interview or something, who knows? In any event, there's nothing to indicate she murdered Sister Rita."

Poldi knew Montana well enough to know that there was no arguing with him in his present mood.

"Where are we going?"

"The hotel, of course. We were taking a vacation, had you forgotten?"

"Oh no, Vito, far from it!" Poldi exclaimed, surprised and delighted not to be simply dumped at the airport. "Does that mean you aren't angry with me anymore?"

He heaved an audible sigh. "You are what you are, that's all. *Madonna,* I don't always like what you do, especially when you keep secrets from me and flirt with other guys, or when I have to dig you out of some hole or other. But I won't be able to change you, not now. Perhaps you could at least promise me not to do anything stupid for the next few days. I simply need a break. Would that be okay?"

"I promise!" Poldi said fervently. "I swear it!"

"Oh no," said Montana, "better not swear!"

Poldi had changed again and brought us two cool beers. "I realized then," she said, "that Vito truly loves me—that he can accept me just as I am. And also that he's a lot more like Peppe than I'd thought."

"Did that scare you?" I asked.

She put her head on one side and looked at me with interest, as if—just for a change—I'd asked a question that wasn't totally daft.

"Want something to eat? Teresa brought me some *polipo in sugo di pomodoro* last night. I'll cook us some spaghetti to go with it, okay?"

"Don't change the subject, Poldi!" I exclaimed, but she already had.

In the first place, it was evening by now and I was feeling thoroughly famished. Second, if presented with a choice between my siblings and a dish of spaghetti with octopus in my Aunt Teresa's tomato sauce, I'd unhesitatingly—sorry, folks!—choose the latter. I would, even though I've read that octopuses are the smartest and most mysterious creatures ever. Octopuses feel emotions, forge friendships, solve complex problems, and spray humans with seawater because they think they're stupid. Or so I've read. Any one of them is probably wiser and smarter than me, and they're certainly also the most graceful creatures—in fact for some weeks I'd been secretly toying with the idea of having one tattooed on my forearm. So eating octopus pricks my conscience, but I do it nonetheless when it's prepared by my Aunt Teresa. Where her *polipo in sugo di pomodoro* is concerned, not even I can resist my vestigial *sicilianità*.

I saw that Poldi was mulling over my question while cooking. She looked suddenly tired, gave a start when a backfiring moped puttered past outside, and asked me to lock the front door and secure the window overlooking the street. I guessed that the murderous graffiti were preying on her mind more than she was prepared to admit—that, absurd though it sounds, my Auntie Poldi really was slightly scared.

"Did you know that octopuses are highly intelligent?" I asked over supper, trying to make a little light conversation.

"Did you know that smartarses are allotted a special place in hell?"

The rest of the meal passed off more or less in silence. The sky overlooking the courtyard lost its color, the cool evening air became scented with jasmine, children were kicking a football around outside in the Via Baronessa. I was full up and sleepy.

"It's nice to have you back, youngster," Poldi said when our plates were empty. Then, abruptly, "I did feel a bit scared, but what do I always say?"

"Fear is where it's at."

"Exactly, my boy."

We clinked bottles again.

"Anyway, we had a very nice week in Rome, Vito and me. A good mixture of sightseeing, *dolce far niente,* and 'it.' It's a fine place, Rome—filled with ancient energy. Vito positively blossomed there. Even his suit looked a bit less crumpled than usual, and as for his performance in bed . . . If I just say Circus Maximus, you'll know what I mean. It was wonderful to see him stretched out beside me morning, noon, and night, like a Roman god—like a wrathful Jupiter forever ready to transfix me with his thunderbolt. His body resembled a temple of lust centered for all eternity on a single marble column that jutted out powerfully, splendidly."

"Poldi!"

"All I mean is, I noticed how much good Rome did him, if only physically. I'm a sensual person—my body is one big aerial sensitive to the vibes of the world. I also know which button to press to lure the Cyclops into my cave. We very seldom argued, and I hardly ever gave a thought to Rosaria and Sister Rita."

In other words, she thought of little else beyond Rosaria and Sister Rita. Poldi resembles every other predator in the animal kingdom: once her hunting instinct is aroused, it can be switched off only by bringing her quarry down. In golden retrievers and border collies, this is vicariously achieved by savaging a hand towel or a cuddly toy. Not so in my Auntie Poldi's case. Once she embarks on a juicy murder inquiry, she relentlessly presses on until the perpetrator is arrested and brought to book.

Vito Montana realized that too, and Poldi realized that he realized it. This was the perfect prerequisite for a relaxing urban vacation, and for the first few days they made every effort to preserve the appearance, and mimic the activities, of a couple on honeymoon. To cite only a few highlights: pistachio ice creams at Giolitti, window-shopping in the Via Condotti, spritzes in the Via Veneto, *caffè con panna* in the Bar Sant'Eustachio, *pasta cacio e pepe* and *carciofi alla giudia* at Archimede, selfies on the Spanish Steps, queuing up outside the Colosseum, putting their hands in the mouth of the stone *bocca della verità,* snapping Poldi in the Fontana di Trevi like Anita Ekberg in the movie. Poldi liked the Eternal City for its self-confidence and its shoulder-shrugging indifference to the course of history, seasons of the year, archaeological excavations, and abrupt changes of government.

"On one occasion," said Poldi, "I was admiring a wonderful sunset at a petrol station and raved about it to the pump attendant. He turned for a moment, shrugged his shoulders and simply said, *"Era ora."* It was time. That tells you everything you need to know about the Romans."

In Montana's company, everything looked new to her. Pervading Poldi was a nice warm sensation she had almost forgotten, and one that—just for once—did not trigger an impulse to run for the hills. More and more often while walking, she would hold his hand and squeeze it. Montana seemed in like mood. He even started to hum old pop songs, exchanged his gray suit for lightweight leisure wear, and chatted jovially with all the waiters. Poldi was discovering an entirely new side to him. He did some enthusiastic mansplaining in the Forum Romanum, the Pantheon, and the Campo de' Fiori, where surplus vegetable crates were burned in an iron barrel on the spot where, in the Middle Ages, heretics were immolated at the stake. Montana also showed Poldi his old workplace, the Antimafia Commission's headquarters in Via Giulia, and as one who knew a thing or two about nostalgia for the past, she sensed that her lover missed his former job.

On the side, whenever she felt she was unobserved, Poldi searched for Rosaria Ferrari on the internet. In Italy one can take it for granted that almost everyone, from infancy to senility, appears on some social media platform or other. It's simply in our nature to be transmitting incessant, unsolicited, unfiltered items of information about ourselves to the world at large. I myself am no exception, I admit, and it's not surprising: the oldest graffiti in the world are to be found in Rome and Pompeii. There were hundreds of Rosaria Ferraris on the internet, ten of them in Rome alone, but the Rosaria from the video wasn't among them.

So Poldi wrote an email:

Dear Antonella,

I've been thinking. Maybe I can help you after all. And maybe you can help me. Are you acquainted with Rosaria Ferrari?

Please let me know.

Yours,
Donna Poldina

"Eh?" I said when Poldi showed me the email. I was rather smashed by then. Wondering if I'd missed something, I feverishly leafed through my notes. "Where did this Antonella spring from?"

"Wait, my boy. It was a shot in the dark, so to speak, because my mind map had given me an idea."

"But who *is* Antonella?"

"Don't be so impatient, for God's sake!"

Said Poldi, who was the epitome of impatience herself.

She checked her emails almost hourly, but she received no reply to her shot in the dark.

At least, not in the form she'd been expecting.

"The thing is," Poldi told me, "an investigator always has to raise some dust. But because action always causes reaction, the dust blows back at you. That's the only problem with dust: it's treacherous. There's dust everywhere, and you never know when and where it's going to envelop you."

The third evening after the Vatican incident found Poldi and Montana, having had an enjoyable siesta and some afternoon "it," sitting outside a trattoria in the Campo de' Fiori with an *aperitivo* intended to mellow them for the night ahead. They were early by Roman standards. The stallholders were just packing up, and there were plenty of empty tables in the restaurants round about. Suddenly, on the other side of the *campo*, Poldi caught sight of one of the twins from the plane. There was no mistaking him in spite of the designer shades that lent him a reptilian appearance. Poldi recognized him at once by his fluorescent green sneakers. With a pizza box in his hand, he made his way over to an old, unmarked delivery van parked between two vegetable stalls and got in the back.

Galvanized, Poldi waited.

"See that delivery van over there?" Montana whispered. "The white one parked between the vegetable stalls—the one that guy just got into? I may be wrong, but I think I've been seeing it these last two days. Odd."

For her part, Poldi hadn't noticed the van at all. Surprised, she turned to Montana and found that his attention was riveted on it.

"The trouble is," he sighed, "I'm never wrong."

"One of Morello's?" asked Poldi.

Montana merely emitted a noncommittal grunt.

At that moment the van's rear door opened again and the other twin, the one in fluorescent red sneakers, emerged. Closing the door behind him, he set off across the *campo* without glancing in Poldi and Montana's direction.

"*Porca miseria!*" hissed Montana. "How I hate this shit! Stay here!"

Before Poldi could object, he was up off his chair like a rocket and sprinting across the *campo*. She really had to hand it to him. For a man of his age, with a little tummy, the first *spumante* of the evening inside him, and the possibility that he was slightly debilitated by his siesta with her, he was pretty fast on his feet. To begin with, at least, and the sprint was his only chance. He reached the center of the square in a trice. Pigeons fluttered into the air, tourists and stallholders scattered in alarm, dogs barked. Poldi saw Montana slalom around a mound of rubbish and go pounding on with undiminished momentum in an attempt to intercept the man.

The latter had almost reached the Cinema Farnese when Poldi saw him look round, spot Montana, and then dash off in the direction of the Via del Biscione. He was fast too, whereas Montana was already slowing.

The next thing Poldi registered was the van backing out of its parking place. Sure enough, that made something go *click* inside her: hunting mode.

Poldi has a bad knee. We regularly advise her to get it examined by a good orthopedist, but no, she refuses every time. However, what my aunt lacks in mobility she makes up for three times over with chutzpah. Far from attempting to follow the delivery van on foot, she stopped a young man on a Vespa, who was just dropping his girlfriend outside a bar.

"Off, both of you!" she yelled. "Don't budge from the spot, you'll get it back in two ticks!"

Thoroughly disconcerted by the termagant in the faux leopardskin jumpsuit and her intimidating German accent, the youth jumped off his scooter. With the agility of a bareback rider, Poldi straddled the saddle and roared off.

I picture my Auntie Poldi and Montana as characters in a split-screen montage in a 1970s action movie: a dream team composed of two hard-nosed cops pursuing the bad guys across Los Angeles, Miami, or Paris to a heroic brass and *wah-wah*ing electric guitar accompaniment. Both of them are always visible in the montage, grimly and tirelessly chasing the gangsters through sewers, along elevated railway platforms and down escalators, along narrow alleyways, across industrial estates, and past smoldering rubbish dumps. There was one minor difference, though: my Auntie Poldi and Montana weren't twenty anymore. Nor thirty or even forty.

Although the actual chase was less cinematic and confined to the streets and alleyways around the Campo de' Fiori, Montana eventually ran out of puff. Trying at least to keep the man in sight, he chased the fluorescent red sneakers into a courtyard and out again by way of a side exit.

Poldi zigzagged through Rome's rush-hour traffic, narrowly missing strollers and groups of youngsters as she kept up with the delivery van. The latter ignored red lights and one-way streets as it sped — aimlessly, or so it seemed — along the alleyways around the *campo*.

Montana had lost sight of the fluorescent sneakers and given up, bent double and panting. Meanwhile Poldi continued to chase the delivery van along the narrow Via della Corda and back in the direction of the Campo de' Fiori, where it crashed into some flower tubs outside a trattoria and braked to a halt. Uproar ensued.

Poldi pulled up likewise. Rather flummoxed, she saw the twin in the fluorescent red sneakers rush past her. Without sparing her a glance, he ran to the delivery van, wrenched open the rear door, and jumped in. The door slammed shut and the van took off again.

It might naturally be supposed that my Auntie Poldi, being still in full hunting mode, would have resumed the chase at once. But she didn't. Why not? Because before the rear door shut she had caught sight of something that temporarily quenched the thrill of the chase: a stack of cartons bearing the logo PIANTE RUSSO.

4

*Tells of aperitifs, team play and whining, lotus leaves
and utter fools, consistency and appreciation, Latin
lovers and mommy's boys. Poldi assembles a jigsaw
puzzle and receives an answer she doesn't like. Montana delivers an impassioned speech, Poldi's nephew
maps out a route to happiness, and Poldi herself
needs a drink. After a disastrous evening she lays her
cards on the table and Montana turns pale.*

N o!"
   "Yes."
"No!"
"Yes, I tell you."
"Well, I'll be buggered!" I said.

Visibly gratified by my tipsy astonishment, Poldi grinned
at me.

My head was spinning. Lethal graffiti, Indian sitar play-
ers, laced ayurvedic smoothies, exorcisms, murder, my aunt
in Rome, in the Vatican, in jail, a missing woman, a manhunt, heat, too much alcohol, and now—on top of
everything else—Italo Russo.

While I had spent the last few weeks putting on rose-
tinted spectacles and taking them off again every hour, infu-

riated by my mediocrity, my lousy French, and my jealousy, Poldi had once more been living life in the fast lane. I felt old by comparison.

Piante Russo, I should perhaps make clear, is a big nursery near Torre Archirafi devoted mainly to the raising of palm trees. Thanks to infestation by the red palm weevil, which is now worldwide, these are threatened with extinction in Sicily. However, Italo Russo also grows lemon, orange, and olive trees, bougainvillea, hibiscus, strelitzias, and many other Mediterranean plants for the beautification of hotels, parks, and landed estates. It's a really big business. Drive along any of the roads between Acireale and Riposto and you'll see Russo's greenhouses and rows of palm and olive trees stretching away for miles.

Femminamorta, Valérie's little estate, lies like an island in the midst of Russo's property. Piante Russo is steadily swallowing up all the land in the vicinity, and Italo Russo, a feared and respected man, is by far the biggest local employer. Poldi is convinced he's a *capo mafioso,* a Cosa Nostra boss, and has been trying for almost a year to prove this, whereas Russo has been trying to win my aunt over. This dance on the lip of a volcano has yielded no definite results. Poldi accused Russo in public, smashed up his old Maserati, accepted his help, and kissed him—and all with only moderate success. Suspicion trickled off Russo like raindrops off a lotus leaf. Even Montana, for all his jealousy, did not believe in Poldi's theory.

Which was why I said, "I don't know."

"You think it was pure chance?"

I shrugged my shoulders.

"Think."

Easier said than done. Thoughts were rampaging through my sozzled brain like football fans after a lost game. I leafed helplessly through my notes.

"Heavens alive," cried Poldi, rolling her eyes, "how slow on the uptake you are! I'd grasped at once that those stupid twins weren't policemen. For one thing, Morello had no need to put two cops on the plane to watch me—they could simply have waited for me in Rome. And their hands! They weren't policemen's hands, they were callused and covered with the little cuts typical of an agricultural laborer's. And the way one of them kept nodding and clicking his tongue to indicate 'No.' That's as typically Sicilian as *cannoli alla ricotta* and fatalism. No, those were two of Russo's young toughs."

"Or a red herring."

Poldi eyed me with interest. "Well, I never, a spark of intelligence. Why a red herring?"

Have I mentioned that I hate it when she questions me like that? I don't have the exam mentality.

Trying not to slur my words, I said, "A delivery van in Rome with a load of Russo's stuff but not his logo on the vehicle. Doesn't make sense somehow."

Poldi nodded. "But there's one factor you must never forget," she said.

"Which is?"

"That most crooks are total idiots."

And my Auntie Poldi knew a thing or two about crooks and total idiots.

Instead of chasing after the delivery van, she took a photo of the license plate. Detectives used to make a mental note of such things, but that's an outdated and un-tweetable procedure. It occurred to Poldi that Marco had advised her to take some short live videos of herself investigating so that she could post them on the various social media channels he had set up for her. She might be pushing sixty-one, but she always kept her finger on the pulse of the age. On the spur of the moment, she switched her mobile phone to selfie mode, stretched out her arm, straightened her wig a little, and was debating what to tell her fans in breathless tones when the screen revealed that a familiar figure was racing toward her from behind. Well, "racing" would have been an exaggeration. Hastily Poldi pocketed her mobile again.

"What the devil, Poldi?" Montana gasped. "Where did you get the Vespa?"

"Cool it, Vito, I photographed the license plate."

Montana indicated the trattoria's waiters, who were still fulminating about their overturned flower tubs. "Was anyone hurt?"

"No, miraculously enough. It was very foolish of you simply to go running off like that."

"Foolish? *Madonna,* now who's talking!"

"What if he'd shot you? Well, if that performance of yours was meant to impress me, *tesoro*" — Poldi looked at him reprovingly — "it did. Brrrr! You were hot. But foolish. But hot."

Montana started to say something, but he was probably still too out of breath. Instead he merely shook his head and called Morello.

"I bet you didn't tell him what you'd seen," I broke in at this point.

"Of course I did," Poldi retorted indignantly. "I'm a team player, you know that." She sighed. "I told him a bit later on, that's all, because my relations with Russo are a personal matter and I didn't want Vito looking at me the way you were just now. And besides"—she sighed again—"things took on a certain momentum after that."

Once Poldi had returned the young couple's Vespa unscathed plus fifty euros "rental fee" and Montana had shown them his warrant card, they generously forbore to bring charges.

While Montana was phoning, first to Morello and then to his colleague DeSantis of the Rome State Police, Poldi flopped down on her original chair and ordered two double brandies.

"There's a call out for them," Montana reported when he'd finished phoning. "I don't get it. If they weren't Morello's men, who put them onto us?"

Poldi spread her arms. He gave her a searching stare.

"Why don't I like that innocent air, Poldi? Did you know those guys?"

"No."

"Did you spot anything when that one jumped into the back of the van?"

Poldi shook her head. "No, but this incident proves that Sister Rita didn't die of her own free will."

"Why were they watching you?"

"Maybe they were just paparazzi."

"Who mistook us for Harry and Meghan? Come on, Poldi, you can do better than that."

"I don't know, Vito!" Poldi sighed. "I only know what my gut feeling is, and my gut says 'Murder.'"

Montana didn't speak. The brandies came. They knocked them back, and Poldi ordered another round. Montana lit a cigarette, still unspeaking. He downed the second brandy, reached into one of the bowls the waiter had plunked down on the table, and shoveled a handful of peanuts into his mouth.

"And they call this an *aperitivo*!" he growled abruptly. "What a rip-off! Three measly bowls of cheap nibbles. Order a sundowner in Milan and you'll get a whole buffet of *antipasti* to choose from in every bar. They positively outdo each other, the bars do there. Call *this* an *aperitivo*? Even at Cipriani in Acireale they cover the whole table with little goodies when you order a Prosecco. Why can't they do that here? Have we been so screwed up by tourism, globalization, the internet, Brussels, and FIFA? What have we come to? Have we no self-respect?"

Eyeing her lover with concern, Poldi was reminded that Italians—even detective inspectors brimming with virility —have no head for drink compared to Teutonic aunts. One glass is often enough to do the trick, as I so perfectly exemplify. Where Montana was concerned, he had already undergone a certain softening-up process due to protracted sightseeing, afternoon "it," his recent manhunt, dehydration, and frustration.

Montana had raised his voice; now he rose from his chair and shouted, loudly enough for all to hear, "The *aperitivo* is an Italian cultural asset, a vertebra in the spine of our *italianità*! If we abandon that, if this country can no longer produce a decent *aperitivo*, we're up the creek! *Vaffanculo!* Italy's up the creek!"

A momentary silence. Then came thunderous applause,

hoots of laughter, and isolated cries of *"Bravo"* and *"Viva l'Italia"* from the surrounding tables.

Montana resumed his seat and lit another cigarette.

Poldi stroked his cheek. "I love you," she said.

He drew a deep breath. "All I want is a bit of a vacation. Can we manage that?"

"We can," said Poldi, but she wasn't thinking of the vacation alone.

It has to be said that they did really make an effort, during the days they had left, to be simply a couple of mature tourists and turtledoves. But leopards can't change their spots, nor could two such hard-boiled investigators as my Auntie Poldi and Vito Montana. It didn't escape Poldi that her Vito kept checking his mobile phone and made discreet calls from time to time. He became more monosyllabic again, and the frown lines between his eyebrows deepened once more. Poldi refrained from asking any questions.

On the penultimate day of their week in Rome, Montana disappeared for two hours, allegedly to have lunch with some former colleagues. Poldi merely wished him *buon appetito,* because he was obviously following some lead but didn't want to talk about it. She briefly considered tailing him, but decided to seize the opportunity to meet up with an old friend of her own.

"Don't tell me," I said with a sigh. "Sophia Loren."

"No, no, she lives in Switzerland," Poldi said dismissively, as if everyone knew that but me. "And I don't know her *that* well. No, I met Gianna, of course."

I smote my brow. "Of course, Gianna. Er, which Gianna would that be?"

"Why, Gianna Nannini. I've known her for ages. A really dear friend of mine—a soulmate, so to speak. She's spent her life singing songs in opposition to Italian machismo and the Catholic Church and in favor of women's rights. I had a lover at the time, Francesco. A bit thick, but insanely good-looking—an immensely vain, macho womanizer. A traffic cop, of course—I'll show you a photo of him later. I was utterly and completely infatuated with Francesco. Anyway, Gianna did her best to talk me into dumping him and going back to Munich, but I was so besotted and stupid, I wouldn't listen—not until Gianna, out of sheer necessity, wrote 'Latin Lover' for me. That song brought me to my senses, I must admit, and I gave the guy his marching orders."

"I'm making no comment, okay?"

"Believe what you like."

As though in evidence of what she'd told me, Poldi thrust a CD into her monster sound system and turned the volume up full. Moments later, Gianna Nannini was bellowing her contempt for the archetypal Italian male at us and the whole of Torre Archirafi.

Ogni notte cambi faccia, cambi stile,
cambi, cambi, cambi, cambi parole,
Latin lover, Latin lover

Gianna's voice and the guitar riffs grated against my brainpan. I felt dizzy, and my condition was not improved by the sight of my hippie-clad Auntie Poldi, who was dancing in front of me with an air mic, shaking her wig, accompanying the song with obscene gestures, and singing along with it to the bitter end. I admired her all the same, I must admit. My Auntie Poldi! If any of her chutzpah rubbed off on me, there would be hope for me yet.

"So why did you suddenly want to meet your old friend Gianna?"

Poldi hemmed and hawed a bit. "I wanted to ask her something."

"Rosaria's identity?"

"Nonsense. A private matter. I'm not just an investigative machine, I'm a human being as well."

That was a new one.

"What private matter?"

"Private means private!" Poldi retorted indignantly. "I don't have to let you in on everything."

I tapped my notebook. "You know it doesn't work like that, Poldi. Either you tell all or we'll drop the whole thing."

I closed the notebook with a snap. I can be pretty hard-boiled myself.

Poldi heaved a sigh.

"I simply had to speak to someone nice because there was this question suddenly weighing me down like an indigestible dumpling. So I went and had lunch with Gianna at Monte Testaccio—you know, the little restaurant Roberto Benigni likes to eat at—and I told her about Vito. The thing is, Gianna knew Peppe too. My boy, it's been a long day. I think I'm going to put my head down."

She started to get up, but I restrained her.

"No, no, no! What was the question?"

I expected another slap, but she merely looked at me with a strangely cryptic expression I couldn't interpret.

"Why . . . whether I should marry Vito."

"Wow! Awesome, Poldi!"

"What am I supposed to do? When Vito delivered his rant about the *aperitivo,* the question was suddenly there, like an affectionate mongrel you can't shoo away and end by taking home with you."

"And what did Gianna say?"

"Gianna is a very wise, clever woman, and she knows what I'm like. She listened patiently to the whole story from beginning to end, and she also looked at some photos of Vito I showed her."

"Cool. And what did she say?"

Poldi heaved a big sigh. "'No.' Gianna looked me in the eye and said 'No.'"

Happiness equals reality minus expectation, Poldi always says. That applies particularly when you ask your friends, aunts, or parents for advice. The usual result is disappointment. Everything usually ends in disappointment anyway, at least where my own life is concerned.

It had been a long day, and when I got up from my plastic chair I noticed how exhausted and, above all, how sozzled I was. Somehow I tottered upstairs to my attic room, stripped off, and flopped down on the bed just as I was, to wit, naked, sweaty, drunk, and bereft of ideas. I barely managed to check my phone. Three calls and eight texts from Valérie, spread over the day.

Good trip?

Mon Dieu, reply!

Go to hell, then! German idiot!

Sorry ☺ I take the German back ☺☺☺

What did you mean by "bit by bit"?

In my world what counts is consistency and appreciation.

Mon Dieu, these games are so stupid!

The last text was a middle-finger emoji. I turned the phone off.

That night I had a strange dream. I was standing beside a road, high up on Etna, that wound its way across a big old lava field. A fine day, only a few clouds in the sky, and I was alone. But not completely so, because there was a dog on the other side of the road. A friendly mongrel combining elements of border collie, flokati rug, and Totti. It wagged its tail excitedly and barked at me. I didn't understand what it wanted until it called, "Come over here, we must go!"

"Where to?" I asked.

"The beginning!"

"I can't," I said.

The dog grew impatient. "Why not?"

"I have to wait for Valérie."

The dog flapped its ears. "Don't wait! We must leave. Valérie will catch up. Or maybe not, we'll see. But we must make a start."

"On what?" I asked.

"Living!"

So saying, the dog trotted off. I turned to look but saw no one, so I crossed the road and followed the animal, because it somehow seemed to know the score. The route it took was stony and arduous, and I sometimes had to crawl under thorny bushes and through puddles. It was all very laborious, but I continued to follow my shaggy guide because it knew the way.

And then I awoke with an appalling hangover.

I was a bundle of misery with a putrid little soft toy in my mouth and a dwarf grimly beating a tattoo on my cranium. The world was a mishmash of garish colors and overly bright light. And, above all, overly loud noises. Something was rattling and clattering right beside me.

Rolling over with a groan, I dimly made out Poldi seated on the edge of the bed like a troll from the kingdom of the elves. Attired in a fringed, rainbow-colored sarong, she was stirring the contents of a large cup. She looked as fresh as a lily of the valley and smelled like one too. Totti was sitting at the foot of the bed, eyeing me enthusiastically.

"I'm naked," I croaked hoarsely.

"Ah, so it can speak," said Poldi, handing me the cup. "Drink that, it'll do you good."

I didn't budge. I'd have liked to cover my nakedness, but my body had evidently forgotten how.

"Oughtn't you to have knocked and waited till I put something on?"

"Don't be such a prude, my boy. You'll never get a taste of *la vie bohème* like this. Believe me, I've seen more naked men in my life, and in all states of arousal, than you've collected little plastic figures from cereal boxes."

I stared at her. "Er, what . . . I mean, how . . . ?"

"Your mother told me recently. I mean, about your collection in the cellar, which she mustn't throw away because you think they may be worth something someday."

Ouch.

I raised my head.

"I . . . She . . . You mean you phone each other?"

"Yes, regularly, always have. Now drink this."

"Ouch."

I sat up, took hold of the cup, and sniffed it. It smelled vile.

"Something ayurvedic, is it?"

"No, a special recipe. It always got Peppe back on his feet."

I groaned.

"Stop whining and drink up."

When the going gets tough, the tough get going. I pulled myself together and took a preliminary sip. It tasted like my idea of a zombie's breath, and it was as hot as molten lava. My mouth exploded. The pain it inflicted was so overwhelming, I saw stars and the dwarf with the hammer was startled into briefly stopping work. Sweat erupted from every pore. It was all I could do not to spit out the diabolical stuff. I fought for breath.

"What . . . the hell . . . is this?"

"Chicken broth, espresso, lemon juice, almond milk, two ibuprofen, some fennel honey, and plenty of chile pepper."

"Why, Poldi?" I moaned. "What have I done to deserve it?"

She got up off the bed and gave me another look of appraisal. "You needn't feel ashamed of your body. Mind you, a bit of waxing wouldn't hurt."

"Please may I be allowed to die alone and in peace?"

"Come down when you're ready, and don't forget your notebook."

Half an hour later, showered and dressed, I was sitting in front of an enormous omelette and an entirely normal cup of coffee. Poldi's apocalyptic potion was taking effect and my headache had almost gone. Although I felt shellacked, I was ready to get my life back on track. I had also, under the shower, mulled over a three-point plan for my path to happiness and greater self-respect:

1. *Stop whining*
2. *Write a bestseller*
3. *Call Mum and tell her she can throw away those three cardboard boxes*

I had even typed the plan into my phone, because I'd learned from Poldi that there's something magical about lists. I could already sense the magic. My plan seemed to wink at me like a staunchly reliable tour guide. There was a fourth item missing from the list. This comprised things I wanted to say to Valérie, but I'd have a careful think about them all in the near future. They would constitute a longish policy statement designed to prove to her that I was a prize acquisition and more than capable of changing my spots. Bursting with maturity and clarity, it would be a perceptive analysis of our relationship, a warmhearted exposé infused with wry sarcasm and brilliant poetic metaphors. In short, it would be toe-curling, narcissistic rubbish.

Poldi was just lacing her espresso with a hefty shot of grappa, a sight that turned my stomach.

"I called Valérie just now," she remarked casually.

I gulped. "Er . . . What did she say?"

"If you don't call her soon, she said, you can get stuffed. You'd better take your time, though, the state you're in. Never send replies when you're angry, never make promises when you're happy, and never take decisions when you're sad. I want you to tell me the whole convoluted story."

She swigged her alcoholic espresso.

"Er, right now?"

"No, I haven't finished catching you up."

I heaved a sigh of relief. "*Forza,* Poldi!"

On the last evening of their difficult week in Rome, Montana fulfilled his intention of introducing Poldi to his daughter, Marta, who was studying medicine in the city.

I mention this only because, as my Auntie Poldi's crimeographer, so to speak, I'm obliged to be thorough. And for completeness's sake, it must be said that their dinner together was even more of a disaster than Poldi had imagined.

"Why was that?" I asked eagerly when she started to move on.

"Vito was jealous, that's why. We formed an immediate rapport, Marta and I. She took to me at once, called me Poldi, and gave me her phone number. She also said that Vito had told her a lot about me, and how happy she was that he'd found someone new, even if he was an insufferable grouch—an insult she atoned for by blowing him a kiss and telling him '*Ti amo, Papà.*' She went on to say she admired me and wanted to know all about me. A fantastic young woman, Marta. Smart, dedicated, determined, and pretty as a picture into the bargain."

"Not my type, you mean."

Poldi ignored that.

"She was in Uganda with Médecins Sans Frontières, speaks fluent English, and is now learning German. Takes after her mother to look at, but the enthusiastic way she speaks about her work and the furrow in her brow reminded me at once of her father. That pleased me, and Vito was also pleased we took to each other."

"So what was the problem?"

"Marta's boyfriend. She brought her Fabio with her, and Vito can't stand him. No wonder, because this Fabio is a real *mammone*, a prime example of a mommy's boy. A *bamboccione*, a big baby. Natty dresser, twelve years older, no proper job, scion of a wealthy Roman family. In other words, not someone who can use unemployment, economic crises, and exorbitant rents as excuses. A good-for-nothing who still lives at home with Mamma in his early forties and is waited on hand and foot. There are more like him in Italy than in any other country in the world. Whole dissertations have been written on the subject, but nothing changes, because in Italy no one thinks it's odd if you live with Mamma till you get married. Also, this guy Fabio is a smartarse of the first order—has never had a clue about anything but always knows better. Spent the whole time sounding off about politics and railing against German austerity. Kept bullying Marta about drinking too much and interrupted her all the time. Stroked her hand and told her she didn't know what she was talking about."

I had to laugh. "So you tore him off a strip, and that soured the atmosphere permanently."

"Nonsense, boy, what do you think I am? I had to restrain myself, granted, but this was a family matter. What really shocked me was the way Marta took it all lying down. Not only that, but she sang his praises, popped food into his mouth, and fawned on him. Imagine, a smart young woman like that! Still, that's Italy for you. It hurt to see how much it bugs Vito that his daughter is in love with such a twat. What can you do, though? Having children means a lifetime of worry."

Poldi took another swig and lapsed into pensive silence. I thought I glimpsed a hint of moisture in her eyes, but that may also have been because I was still having trouble focusing.

"Poldi?"

"Yes, my boy?"

"Any regrets?"

"About what?"

"You know."

"Ah . . ." Poldi heaved a loud sigh, then dabbed her eyes. She said nothing for a moment. Then, softly, "When you come down to it, you know, I'm probably not the maternal type. And who knows, I might have given birth to a wimp like you. Maybe I should thank my lucky stars."

"I love you too, Poldi."

There are occasions that are beyond saving. They're fated, and that's that. While Poldi was trying to simply ignore the annoying *mammone* and concentrate entirely on Marta, Montana was growing increasingly silent and irritable. Marta, who noticed this, became increasingly silent and irritable herself, with the result that in the end Fabio was the only person speaking. When the bill came, he criticized the meal but graciously permitted Montana to pay.

Montana didn't utter a word on the way back to the hotel. Poldi had never seen him so tight-lipped and depressed, and it exercised her more than his anger—more, even, than thirst and murder. Alarmed that her lover, usually so bursting with strength and passion and *sicilianità,* seemed to have lost his carapace of self-assurance, she clasped his hand.

"Marta's a wonderful girl. It won't last."

"It's been two years," Montana growled. "Her mother idolizes him."

"Believe me, Vito, it won't last."

"I don't want to talk about it, okay?"

"As you please, *tesoro,* but I'm not going back to the hotel with you like this."

"No?"

"No, to a bar. We're both in need of a nightcap. We're still on vacation, after all."

There are occasions that are past saving, so it seems. And then they somehow turn the corner because some fairy has waved her wand—or because one is in Rome with my Auntie Poldi.

Holding Montana by the hand, Poldi zigzagged through the back streets of Trastevere until they came to a little piazza fringed with orange trees. Overlooking it was a church and, across the way, a little trattoria. Mass was in progress in the church, and children were still playing tag despite the hour. It was a good place, Poldi thought. The proprietress of the trattoria had an enormous bosom and severe scoliosis. Aurelia by name, she called Poldi "Gioia" and flirted unashamedly with Montana.

Picturing Montana and Poldi in that enchanted, children- and cat-infested piazza in Trastevere, I see them seated at a table with a checked tablecloth, overlooked by orange trees and sodium lamps, with discreet Italo background music issuing from the restaurant's candlelit interior—all very romantic. I see Poldi in her back-combed wig and Nefertiti makeup, white kaftan with the gold threads, and pink knitted jacket fringed at the cuffs in an almost elfin way. Montana is for once wearing jeans and a midblue shirt, camel-hair jacket casually draped over his shoulders, sunglasses still in his hair. Classical Italo chic always works. At first sight, therefore, they constitute one of those sophisticated couples that have always got together and fallen in love since the founding of Rome. He something in the Senate, perhaps, she a lawyer or film producer. Or so one might suppose. A couple from the upper reaches of Rome society, their children long gone and studying abroad, their apartment with the big roof terrace only a few steps away. To my mind, it's a pleasant image—one that I'd like to preserve, to frame and hang up, so that it would all remain the same forever. That's the way I am. I always want everything to remain as it is. I'm more the Sancho Panza type, whereas Poldi is Don Quixote, and the reality is that the world is full of windmills that keep turning.

"How do you do it, Poldi?" Montana sighed after his second grappa.

"Do what?"

"You know, make a silk purse out of a sow's ear."

"Maybe I'm a good fairy."

Montana lit a cigarette and pointed to the children. "That's Italy for you. We were like that too. It's always been the same. Out in the piazza at all hours, and falling asleep in class. Perhaps that's why I became a cop instead of a lawyer or a doctor. I can't think of much about Italy that's good, but in places like this I know I belong nowhere else."

"Oh, Vito!"

"No, hear me out. I admit I'm jealous. Every father is jealous of his daughter's boyfriend, isn't he? The trouble is, I'm Sicilian as well, fuck it. Know what really depresses me? Alongside that worthless bum Fabio, I feel insignificant. Yes, alongside a guy with a family tree that goes back to the Roman Empire, I feel inferior. Vito Montana from Giarre, son of an agricultural laborer, who couldn't find anything better to do with his life than join the police and somehow claw his way up the ladder. A humble cop from Sicily, that's all." Montana grimly dragged at his cigarette. "And now you can laugh at me."

But Poldi didn't laugh. On the contrary, no one knew better than my aunt, and from bitter personal experience, that even the strongest and most wonderful personalities are haunted by shadows that keep whispering, "You aren't good enough! You'll never be good enough!" Sometimes these shadows manifest themselves as real people and bear names like Maria or Fabio. There is nothing you can do but breathe and carry on. Though you could also have friends who support you. Or a family with whom to barbecue sea bass on Sundays. Or children to take pride in, or parents who are so considerate it's almost embarrassing. Or an aunt who suddenly found you smarter than she'd thought. Or . . . you could solve a murder.

"I know what you mean, Vito," Poldi said gently, taking his hand. "I really do, but the truth is, you're the best, smartest, most incorruptible, obstinate, bad-tempered, toughest

cop I know and have ever known. That's why you must never
—never, you hear?—feel inferior to anyone."

Montana took a sip of grappa and looked at her.

"Why don't you think it was suicide?"

"Who says I still think that? The facts are clear, surely. Or
are they?"

"Don't play games, Poldi."

Poldi drew a deep breath. "Right. For a start, pure intuition. I mean, okay, Rosaria spoke in my voice. That's pretty
creepy in itself, but apparently they're used to that sort of
thing. Even Rosaria's subsequent disappearance wouldn't
warrant such an operation."

Montana nodded.

"Besides," Poldi went on, "Padre Stefano blabbed. I'm
sure Morello assumes that Rosaria pushed poor Sister Rita."

Montana nodded again. "Anything else?"

Loath to lay down all her cards at once, Poldi shook her
head.

"I've done a bit of phoning around," Montana said eventually. "The Vatican State is obliged to hand criminal investigations over to the Italian authorities. Since suicide auto-
matically triggers such an investigation, Morello would have
had to relinquish Sister Rita's body to some forensic department."

"And has he?"

"Yes, but not until two days after her death."

Montana puffed at his cigarette.

Poldi waited.

"I managed to get a look at the pathologist's report. Sister
Rita died of her injuries from the fall. But before that"—he

took another puff — "she sustained a blow to the face. Her nose was broken. The pathologist found bruising typical of a blow on the nose that hadn't resulted from the impact."

Poldi thought for a moment.

"Any other pointers to a struggle?"

"No. But investigations are still ongoing. DeSantis will keep an eye on that."

"It'd be better if *you* kept an eye on it, Vito."

"Except that I'm not in charge here, Poldi."

"What about tissue and fiber traces on her clothing?"

"Hm . . . Sister Rita's body was naked when handed over."

"What!"

"Morello insists she was naked when discovered in the inner courtyard. Nor has her habit been found, he says."

"You believe him?"

Montana shrugged.

"He isn't a bad guy. My gut tells me he's an eight out of ten as a detective. Still, even if he is holding something back, the Italian police can't do much about it. The Vatican's a sovereign state."

"Which means it could block the whole inquiry if it wanted."

"The question is, why would it want to?"

Poldi deliberated.

"It doesn't make sense, Vito. If Morello wanted to hush the murder up, he would hardly have flown to Sicily and sought me out in the middle of the night."

Montana nodded.

"So?"

"There's something else, though."

Poldi had suspected as much. "Rosaria Ferrari. Have you found her?"

"No. Morello admitted to me, through gritted teeth, that he invented the business about Rosaria returning to her family. She's disappeared without a trace. An old friend did me the favor of checking the whole of the Italian residents register and criminal database and comparing them with her picture from the video. Zero result. Rosaria Ferrari is a phantom."

"Well, I'll be buggered!" Poldi exclaimed, finding it hard to suppress her exultation. "A female contract killer!"

Montana gave her a searching look. "Then I'm sure you can explain why a contract killer intending to kill a young nun should undergo an exorcism beforehand, one that was actually filmed, in which she speaks with your voice."

"And after that," said Poldi, thinking aloud, "she strolls through the Vatican Gardens for a while, meets Sister Rita on the roof of the Apostolic Palace, knocks her out and strips her naked, pushes her over the parapet of the terrace, and escapes from the palace and the Vatican unobserved, taking the habit with her. *Madonna,* it just doesn't make sense." A thought struck her. "There are CCTVs everywhere in the Vatican, especially overlooking the gateways. One of them must surely have picked up Rosaria sometime shortly after the murder."

Montana shook his head. "Morello says he's checked all the tapes shot during the hours after the murder. Rosaria— or whatever her name is—doesn't appear on any of them. Of course, she could have left the Vatican in the back of a car and out of shot."

"By taxi, for example."

"Already checked. Negative."

"Hell's bells!" Poldi forced herself to think harder. "What about the delivery van?"

"No trace so far. They're still looking for it."

Poldi eyed her lover suspiciously. His manner struck her as far too calm—as if he were totally uninvolved in the whole affair—and she didn't like that at all.

"*Benissimo,*" she said sternly. "To sum up, it was a planned murder. Therefore, the question is, why did Sister Rita have to die?"

"DeSantis is working on it," said Montana. "But without Morello's help he isn't getting anywhere."

"*Madonna!* Then put a squib under Morello, *tesoro!*"

To Poldi's surprise, Montana shook his head. "I'm out of it. We're flying back to Catania tomorrow morning."

"You mean you're simply abandoning the case?" Poldi exclaimed, puzzled and more than a little disappointed.

"It isn't my case, Poldi."

"Of course it is, whether you like it or not. That's because *I'm* involved. I may even be in danger!"

Montana said nothing for a moment, seemingly thinking this over. Then he said, "No, I don't think that's true. I'm sorry."

That was when Poldi grasped that he was toying with her. That, knowing her as he did, he already guessed she was concealing something from him again. And that she must now come out with it if she didn't want to lose his support. Which she certainly didn't. So she swallowed her reluctance and told her beloved *commissario* about the twins in the fluorescent sneakers on the flight to Rome, and about the cardboard boxes in the delivery van with Russo's logo on them. She wasn't expecting him to faint or turn cartwheels or anything of that nature, but she did at least think he'd display some kind of electrified reaction. A smothered oath, perhaps, or a "Ha! We've nailed that Mafia boss at last! Excellent work, Poldi!"

But all Montana actually said was "Uh-huh."

"Uh-huh? Is that all, Vito?"

"Are you absolutely sure it was Russo's logo?"

"I'm not blind!"

"The door was only open for a moment, and you'd had to slam the Vespa's brakes on hard. At moments of extreme tension, wishful thinking can affect one's powers of perception."

"Goddammit, Vito, it *was* his logo! We can nail that *capo dei capi* at last!"

To her chagrin, Montana merely shook his head.

"Even if it was Russo's logo, that proves nothing. I'll pass the information on to DeSantis. Once the Rome police have found the van, we'll see."

"Vito, pin your ears back and—"

"Unless . . ." Montana cut in brusquely, and she fell silent. "Unless there's something else you've been keeping from me."

Poldi switched to the wide-eyed-innocence mode. "I've no idea what you mean, *tesoro*."

Unfortunately, the wide-eyed-innocence mode is one of the few things my Auntie Poldi isn't good at. She simply burns on too high a flame.

"Morello showed me the towel from your cell," Montana growled in the *commissario* tone of voice Poldi always finds so sexy. "It was clogged with lipstick, and there were traces of lipstick on the mirror above the washbasin. You'd written something down and wiped it off to prevent anyone from seeing it. So for the last time, Poldi, is there anything else you'd like to tell me? Believe me, if I pick up even a hint of a suspicion that you're making a monkey of me again, I'm out once and for all."

Poldi hesitated. Then, with a sigh, she said quietly, "I drew up a mind map in the cell, and it put me in mind of something. It's only a conjecture, which is why I didn't want to discuss it with you yet. There may be nothing in it whatsoever. It may all be pure coincidence."

"Is that what you think it is?"

"No," Poldi conceded.

"So what *do* you think?"

Poldi glanced around. The little piazza had emptied. Mass was over and the children had run along home. A few cats were still roaming around beneath the orange trees, but that was all. Poldi and Montana were the trattoria's last customers.

"I think," said Poldi, "that this case is somehow connected with . . . well, yes . . . with the Black Madonna."

She was about to explain what she meant when she saw Montana's expression and stopped short in dismay. Her beloved *commissario* had turned pale and was staring at her in consternation.

"What did you say just then?" he asked in a strained voice.

"The Black Madonna. I think there's some connection with the Black Madonna."

5

*Tells of the Black Madonna, method investigation,
female stalkers, Capricorns, ignorance, and the two
most important words in showbiz. Poldi puts two
and two together and Montana reacts with obstinacy. Poldi's nephew learns another lesson. She herself suppresses a couple of tears, is abducted, loses
her temper, and then succumbs to vanity.*

The Black Madonna is one of the biggest riddles in
Christian iconography and mysticism. People all over
Europe revere and attribute special miraculous properties to
portrayals and sculptures of the Black Madonna. Famous
Marian pilgrimages involving Black Madonnas—Często-
chowa, Altötting, and Rocamadour, for example—attract
hundreds of thousands of pilgrims every year. No one knows
what color the Virgin Mary's skin really was, of course, and
no one knows precisely how the Black Madonna originated.
The Roman Catholic Church tries to play it safe and ascribes
her dark complexion to centuries of soot deposited by candle smoke, but this does not explain why only the faces and
hands of these figures are blackened. As usual, the truth is a
bit more complicated than it seems. It is probable that a connection exists between the Black Madonna and ancient

female deities. After all, early Christian missionaries had only a male divine creator to offer, whereas the tribes to be converted were often matriarchally organized, worshipped earth mothers and fertility goddesses, and simply didn't warm to the bachelor Christian god. This situation persisted until 431, when the Council of Ephesus paved the way for Marian devotion. Cybele, Isis, Ishtar, Astarte, Freya, Artemis, Demeter, Kali & Co. could simply be cashed in and reinterpreted into Mary. Thus, places where Black Madonnas are revered were probably ancient cult sites.

In Europe, Black Madonnas appeared suddenly and in considerable numbers after the Crusades. They betray remarkable similarities. Nearly all carved from wood, they are portrayed sitting erect and gazing stiffly into the distance, and their fingers are inordinately long.

One can imagine how astonished the Crusaders were to come across portrayals of the goddess Isis in the Holy Land: a young black woman seated on a throne with a child in her arms—one, moreover, that was worshipped under her Egyptian name Mataria, or Mari. These were brought back to Europe as souvenirs, on the assumption that they represented the Virgin Mary.

Other sources identify the Black Madonna with the Queen of Sheba, whose diplomatic mission to King Solomon was the first recorded state visit in history. It was Solomon who quoted her as saying "I am black, but comely" in the Song of Songs.

The Sinti and Roma revere a wonder-working saint named Black Sarah or Sarah la Kâli, who was alleged to have traveled to the South of France as Mary Magdalen's maidservant and carried out missionary work there in the first century. It's a short step from her name to that of the Indian goddess Kali. And that, if not before, is the point at which esoterics exclaim "Aha!" and blithely egg-whisk everything up together.

In any event, the phenomenon of the Black Madonna has still to be fully researched and is consequently a subject popular with fringe scientists and authors of trashy novels.

"I see," I said when Poldi had explained all this in a *tour d'horizon*. "I'd no idea you were interested in Christian iconography."

"Only as part of the investigation, though," she said modestly. "Get this: if you want to understand murderers and form an idea of them, you have to find your way into their world of ideas, scientifically and emotionally. It's called method investigation, by analogy with method acting."

"Oh, is that what it's called?"

"You can take that smart-alecky expression off your face. I call it that because I invented the term. But the Black Madonna has always fascinated me, of course. That's because I can well imagine having turned Solomon's head in a previous existence."

"Don't be daft, Poldi!"

"Nonsense. But forget what I said just now. It was a test. I wanted to see how you'd react."

Poldi seemed suddenly to want to change the subject.

"Why," I asked, trying to get back to the case, "did Montana react to 'Black Madonna' with such dismay?"

"I can't talk about it," Montana said stiffly when Poldi asked him that very question beneath the orange trees.

"Why not?"

"I just can't. *Basta*."

"Because it reminds you of an old case?"

Montana looked at her. "What made you think of the Black Madonna?"

Whatever was eating Montana at that moment, Poldi knew him well enough to realize that he wouldn't discuss the subject. Not right now.

"I had a bit of time to think in that cell," she said, "and that was when it occurred to me. For one thing, because Rosaria quoted from the Song of Songs. For another, one of the twins in the plane had a sticker with a Black Madonna on the back of his mobile phone. And third . . ." Poldi hesitated. "Third, I think Rosaria is familiar to me."

Montana glared at her.

"And you're telling me that only now?"

"I only just realized it," Poldi said meekly. "It was when you said Rosaria probably isn't her real name, and that she's disappeared without a trace."

And then she told Montana about Antonella. It had started the previous autumn, shortly after Poldi had solved her second case in Sicily and some articles about her had appeared in the local press. A local radio station had even interviewed her and asked for some Bavarian comments.

The first email arrived a week later, in October. It was in Italian and littered with spelling mistakes.

Deer Signora Oberreiter (may I call you Poldi?)

To me, writting to you seems orlmost like a miner mirakel! I've always tride so hard to fit in, but it's never really werkd. I'd like to tell you about my speshl kind of intense feelings because I think we're sole-mates. I feel this with my sensitive antennae. I wud like to be like you, Poldi. I feel like a wild mair shut up in a horsebocks when she would rather be gal-loping around free, because the emoshuns that per-vaid me are so intense that I can hardly bare it. But in real life wun has to stifel wun's emotions because they annoy peeple. That makes me so desprit and an-grry, because I'm not a bad purson. On the contrery, I think I'm like the Black Madonna. I think I'm like you, Poldi. Wud you help me to becum like you, deer Poldi?

Yours, Antonella

"Quite apart from her severe dyslexia," said Montana, shaking his head, when Poldi showed him the email, "the woman is clearly disturbed."

"Oh, Vito, who isn't disturbed in this world! I realized I couldn't help her, of course, so I sent her a very brief reply."

Dear Antonella,

I'm sorry, but I can't be of assistance to you. Please seek professional help.

Yours, Isolde Oberreiter

"Let me guess," said Montana. "She went on writing to you regardless."

"She most certainly did." Sighing, Poldi showed him the other emails too.

All couched in the same misspelled language, they became more and more confused and urgent in tone. Many were reproachful and petulant, others imploring or flattering, and every one of them compared the writer to Poldi and the Black Madonna. Poldi never replied to any of the subsequent emails, but Antonella was undeterred. She kept writing that she wanted to become like my aunt and attached photos and press cuttings of her. Poldi found this a bit much, because Antonella had taken the photos undercover. Poldi in the café, Poldi shopping at the supermarket, Poldi with her German nephew at the mineral-water spring in Torre Archirafi.

"What?" I exclaimed, slightly perturbed, when she told me this. "She photographed us together?"

"Why the look of outrage? Am I an embarrassment to you?"

"But Poldi, this is crazy. She was really stalking you."

"Poof!" Poldi said dismissively. "I wasn't worried. I've been in tougher situations, believe you me. Like that time in Munich when I helped Lady Di."

"But why didn't you tell Montana about it?"

"I was just about to, but first I wanted to find out who Antonella was. So I tried to get her home address by way of her email and IP address. I have my contacts, as you know, but it turned out that her emails came from the dark net. Know what I mean? You can't trace anything back to source, it's all completely anonymous. Then, last November, the emails suddenly dried up and I eventually forgot about them. After all, my life was in enough of a turmoil, wasn't it?"

. . .

Poldi told Montana all this on their way back to the hotel. He listened in silence until they were alone in their room.

"All right, so you had a stalker who identified with you and the Black Madonna. But that doesn't explain why Antonella, if it really was her, spoke in your voice during the exorcism and subsequently killed Sister Rita. Nor does it explain why those two guys were watching us. It doesn't really explain anything."

"I know, Vito," Poldi said with a sigh, "but maybe it's a lead all the same."

"Or a coincidence."

"What do you mean?"

Montana eyed her gravely. "This Antonella was quite obviously disturbed. She's probably suffering from some personality disorder. It isn't unusual for women in that state to identify with the Mother of God or the Black Madonna, hence the emails and photos. But it's over, Poldi. She hasn't been in touch since November, you said so yourself."

Poldi became suspicious.

"If that was a subtle attempt to tell me to forget the whole thing, it's completely misfired. What's more, I don't like the look on your face, Vito. I don't like it at all. What's wrong?"

"I'm going to stay on here for a couple of days," he said. "You'll fly to Sicily tomorrow morning and chill until I get back."

"I will, will I?"

"I beg you, Poldi. I mean it. As soon as I know more, you'll be the first to hear, promise."

Needless to say, Poldi felt like obeying her old reflex and giving him a piece of her mind, as she always did when a man tried to lay down the law, but she merely nodded when she saw his expression, because her beloved *commissario* looked so different all of a sudden. His lined, handsome face had taken on a grimly determined expression she had never seen before. And there was another shadow darkening his face that really alarmed her: a sudden look of fear.

That night, when Montana turned over on his side and prepared to go to sleep right away, without indulging in "it," Poldi knew that something was badly wrong. And my Auntie Poldi knew a thing or two about shadows and things going wrong.

Vito Montana isn't the kind of man who can put a brave face on things at the touch of a button. He's no practitioner of levity or outward show, no social butterfly or charming conversationalist. No, the *bella figura* principle doesn't extend that far with him. Montana is a Capricorn, in other words, someone destined to spend his life amid the crags, forever climbing until he reaches the summit and stands there for a moment, resplendent. Born under the most mysterious sign of the zodiac, Capricorns are directly connected to nature's primordial flows. They are earth signs with a backbone of stainless steel, and they always have a plan — which they usually keep to themselves. Although Capricorns can be brusque and dismissive, most of them are friendly creatures; it's just that they have to climb their mountain and can't be bothered with inessentials. They have to keep on climbing, and the steeper the ascent, the better, but once they're up there amid the glacial rocks, where the air becomes thin and lethal ice storms rage, they're the masters of their world. Earth signs are ruled by instinct, Taurines by sensual pleasure, but Capricorns are ruled by primeval forces of nature. In Montana's case by the urge to hunt.

Poldi knew all this. Being a Cancer, a water sign, she is ruled by emotion and defenseless against the tidal forces of the heart, so she admires Montana's strength and the serenity with which Capricorns confront the storms of existence, clambering steadfastly onward up the narrowest of ridges.

And because she knew all this, she didn't kick up a fuss about Montana's demeanor the next morning. He made absolutely no attempt to look bright and cheerful and wore the same grim, worried expression as before. Having walked her to the taxi, he enfolded her in a tight embrace.

"You made me a promise," he said softly.

Poldi nuzzled his neck, inhaling the scent of his aftershave and skin as if for the last time.

"Don't worry," she sniffed, and, as ever when she uttered those words, they concealed a lie.

In the taxi to the airport she wiped away two little tears. Not that you would think it from her robust Bavarian appearance, my Auntie Poldi cries easily, especially when having to say goodbye to people. Poldi has often had to say goodbye. To numerous lovers and dear friends, to my Uncle Peppe, to her parents, to two unborn babies, to Tanzania, to so many dreams of happiness. Every farewell has meant leaving a little bit of herself behind, and it sometimes surprises me she's still here at all. But she is. It's not only miraculous that my Auntie Poldi is still here, it's a universal boon.

However, it has to be admitted that the previous week had been a challenging one, even for a woman as emotionally strong as my aunt: incarceration, sex, family, a car chase, clues, and, last but not least, a lover with a dark secret. Not to mention a close woman friend's "No," which was still giving Poldi food for thought. So it was perhaps hardly surprising that she had a moment of weakness in the taxi.

"Everything all right, signora?" asked the cabbie.

He was wearing sunglasses, but Poldi could tell he'd been watching her the whole time in his rearview mirror—not that this prevented him from slaloming through the Italian capital's traffic as if the zombie apocalypse had broken out. Poldi guessed him to be in his late twenties. He was wearing jeans and an unironed T-shirt, and his hair was as tousled as if he'd just got out of bed. He looked like an overgrown student.

"*Tutto bene,*" said Poldi, blowing her nose *con brio*. "Would you mind keeping your eyes on the road?"

"No worries, signora, I'm a multitasking expert. Hey, don't I know you? Are you a famous actress or something?"

"Sorry to disappoint you, but no." Slightly flattered despite herself, Poldi tweaked her wig straight and asked, "What gave you that idea?"

"Well, the paparazzi behind us."

Alarmed, Poldi turned to look. Through the rear window she saw two familiar figures weaving their way through the chaotic Rome traffic on motorbikes. One of them had just stalled his engine; the other was arguing with the car driver alongside him.

"Well, I'll be buggered!"

"Don't worry, signora," the cabbie called cheerfully. "They're not up to much, you can tell that right away. Want me to get rid of them, or should I let them close up for a few photos?"

"It would be really wonderful if you could shake them off, young man. What's your name?"

"Pasquale, signora. Maybe you'd better buckle up."

Poldi never buckles up, for ideological reasons. "Compulsory seat belts," she once told me in all seriousness, "are like compulsory helmets. They're just a way of exploiting and suppressing the masses." Although that attitude could be summarized as free death for free citizens, Poldi is an implacable libertarian.

Pasquale slowed to a halt at some lights that were just turning amber. Poldi saw the twins worming their way once more through the congested traffic. When the lights went red, Pasquale suddenly stepped on the gas and, horn blaring, tore across the road junction. He nipped through a gap between two cars and made a sharp left.

Poldi buckled up after all.

Pasquale drove like a maniac. Even Poldi had never encountered anything like it. In contrast to his scruffy, rather sleepy general appearance, he changed gear, accelerated, braked, and drifted like a professional rally driver, looking as relaxed as a farmer on his tractor. Poldi lost her bearings, but it struck her that they certainly weren't heading for the airport anymore. Whenever she turned around she could still catch a glimpse of one of the twins, who clearly wasn't that stupid. Pasquale kept his cool. He roared at top speed into the handsome, middle-class district of Monteverde Vecchio, zigzagged left and right down some side streets, then slowed to a halt in a quiet avenue shaded by tall plane trees and pulled up, with his engine still running, in front of a gateway.

"Go straight across the courtyard. I'll wait for you at the exit on the far side, then we'll be shot of them."

Poldi, her suspicions suddenly aroused, hesitated. The whole situation somehow struck her as rather stage-managed. She noticed only now that Pasquale had never turned his taxi meter on.

"You aren't a cabbie at all, are you, my little Fangio?"

Pasquale turned to look at her. "You must hurry, signora. Cross the courtyard and we'll meet up on the other side."

Me, I might have soiled my pants in the circumstances, but Poldi wouldn't have been Poldi if she'd let herself be intimidated so easily. Thoroughly cool and *bella figura*, she unbuckled her safety belt, got out, and even took a moment to straighten her wig. Outwardly she was completely calm, but her highly attuned senses were now switched on to receive. My Auntie Poldi resembled a lioness about to pounce. Okay, a rather elderly lioness in a wig.

She was expected.

"You!" Poldi exclaimed, rather disappointed to recognize the man waiting for her in the courtyard. "What's the meaning of this charade?"

"There was no alternative," said Commissario Morello. "You were in good hands, though. Pasquale is my best driver."

"Who do the twins belong to?"

"We don't know yet, but we're working on it. Follow me, please, we have only a narrow time frame."

"I have to catch my flight to Catania."

"Don't worry about that, we'll take care of it."

Without further explanation, Morello led the way into the side wing of an unpretentious nineteenth-century building that might once have been designed to house Italian civil servants. Poldi followed the *commissario* upstairs into a pleasant apartment with a parquet floor, a large library, and furniture from the sixties. It smelled of dust and coffee. The drawing room Morello ushered her into had big windows overlooking the street. The shutters were closed, but the light that filtered through the louvers was sufficient for Poldi to instantly recognize the two men waiting for her in there.

"Well, I'll be buggered!"

"I beg your pardon?" snapped Padre Stefano, who was standing in the gloom a little to one side.

The other man advanced on Poldi with his hands out-stretched. He was shorter than Poldi remembered.

"What a pleasure to make your acquaintance at last," said the pope. "May I call you Donna Poldina?"

"No!"

"Yes!"

"No!"

"Goddammit, d'you think I'm making all this up?"

I tried to imagine it like a scene from a movie that suddenly freezes, enabling me to enter the set like an invisible spectator. I picture a dimly illuminated *salotto*, old furniture and lots of books, dust scintillating in the air, tremendous tension, the whole scene overlaid by some ancient secret and peopled by figures resembling men in a board game: the pope, Padre Stefano in the background, Commissario Morello near the door, and, in the midst of them like some exotic creature from Mars, my Auntie Poldi in a psychedelic, off-the-shoulder, Romany-style dress composed of a hundred colorful scraps of material, each of which, if able to speak, could tell a colorful story. Time stands still, nothing moves. I picture myself crossing the creaking parquet floor and taking a good look at everything. I mean, how often can one get that close to a pope?

"You had a date with the pope?"

"Well, I wouldn't call it a date, exactly. More of a discreet, informal meeting in private, if you know what I mean."

"And what was on the agenda?"

"Good God, how dense you are! The Black Madonna, of course."

I hurriedly leave the *salotto* to allow the movie to continue.

"Please excuse this unusual procedure," said the pope, shepherding Poldi over to an armchair, "but I wanted a quiet word with you. Do sit down. Coffee?"

He made a thoroughly relaxed, positively jovial impression, which was more than could be said of the other two men. Commissario Morello and Padre Stefano were on edge, Poldi could clearly sense that. She inferred from the priest's presence that despite his efforts to melt into the background, he was more important than she had supposed. So she remained on the qui vive, seated herself where she could see all three men, and accepted the offer of a coffee.

"That's a lovely dress you're wearing," said the pope, sitting down likewise. "It reminds me of my home."

"Thank you."

"I use this apartment occasionally for informal meetings," the pope went on. "Inside the walls of the Vatican, confidentiality is a problem, if you know what I mean. I'm afraid we don't have much time, either."

"I'd like to apologize most sincerely for bumping into you the other day," Poldi began.

The pope laughed. "Forget it. Perhaps it was a divine dispensation, because otherwise I wouldn't have heard about you and that terrible business with Sister Rita."

He cast a quick glance at Morello, who was hovering uneasily in the doorway.

The silence was suddenly punctured by a mobile phone. It sounded like the groan of someone in torment. Padre Stefano hastily felt in his trouser pocket and turned it off.

"My apologies."

"Commissario Morello didn't want to trouble me with the affair," the pope went on, "but after our little collision he told me everything, so now I'm in the picture."

Poldi took a sip of coffee. "Why am I here?"

The pope's expression was grave but amiable. "Because I'd like to request your help, Donna Poldina. Unofficially, of course. I'm sure you'll understand that this conversation never took place. Once Commissario Morello and Padre Stefano had informed me about the incident that occurred during the exorcism of Rosaria Ferrari—we know that that isn't her real name—and about Sister Rita's death, I made some inquiries about you. That is how I learned that you're a remarkable detective with a no less remarkable past."

"What exactly do you mean by that?"

The pope smiled. "All that matters is that you're a very talented private investigator with a peculiar personal involvement in this case."

Poldi thought this sounded too convoluted.

"But what do you actually want of me?"

"I'd like to employ you to recover something of great importance to the Vatican." He paused for a moment, eyeing Poldi intently. "The Lost Madonna."

Who would have thought it?

Poldi wasn't really surprised. She donned her poker face and crossed her legs.

"Can you give me some context?" she asked casually, every inch the unimpressed professional sleuth.

"For that I'll have to go back a bit," said the pope. "We're still getting to the bottom of the plot that directly and indirectly led to my predecessor's retirement. The Vatican still functions like a medieval royal court. There are certain networks that pursue opposing objectives and form unwelcome alliances with other networks extraneous to the Vatican."

"In other words, the Mafia," Poldi said drily.

Morello coughed. Padre Stefano started to apologize for her but this time restrained himself.

"Evil has many names," said the pope. "As I'm sure you're aware, the previous pope's retirement was connected with a breach of trust on the part of his valet. Personal and confidential documents were leaked to the press, and things were stolen as well. Very valuable things. Most of them were found in the valet's apartment, but one particular object was not. An extremely important object. The valet claims to know nothing of its whereabouts, and all our efforts to recover it have hitherto proved unsuccessful."

"The Lost Madonna," whispered Poldi.

"To be more precise, a priceless wooden statuette of a

seated Madonna with a dark face—a Black Madonna. Scientists have dated it to the first century. Originating in Jerusalem, this figure was brought to France in the late Middle Ages by a crusader named Hugues de Payens. Initially in the possession of Bernard of Clairvaux, it was later taken to Avignon and from there to Rome."

"What makes this figure so exceptionally valuable?" asked Poldi.

"It's one of the earliest pieces of evidence relating to the early Christian communities in the Holy Land," said the pope. "And it's a statue of the Virgin. The figure is of great spiritual value to the Church." The pope continued describing the statuette in detail.

"What nonsense!" Poldi barked in Bavarian. Then, reverting to Italian, "I can kid myself, I don't need anyone else to do it for me. I'll ask you again: Why is this figure so important that you're desperate enough to employ a crazy old crone to get it back?"

"I apologize on her behalf," muttered Padre Stefano.

The pope turned to Morello.

"We're anxious to get at the network that has stolen the Black Madonna," said the *commissario*. "We believe that it was also behind the plot against the Holy Father emeritus. There are indications that the Black Madonna is still in the network's possession."

"And I'm supposed to kick up a bit of dust and act as your bait, so you can strike when the time is right."

More apologetic noises from Padre Stefano.

"We would, of course, recompense you generously for your efforts," said the pope.

"Money doesn't interest me," Poldi said firmly.

A little brusque, perhaps, because she was feeling piqued. No, not just piqued. My Auntie Poldi was overcome with fury when it dawned on her that she had once more blundered into a male trap—when she realized that she was sitting in a room with three men who had abducted her and made her a bizarre offer without coming clean. What was more, they naturally expected her to accept it with cries of delight and without reading the small print. Men had tried to smother her free will all her life, to change her and mold her into their own ideal. Men had always expected something of her. They'd wanted her to be thinner, quieter, gentler, more sensible, less rebellious, less clingy, more conservatively dressed, more affectionate, more diplomatic, more ambitious or less, more emotional but not too much. Men had tried to dominate her life just as they ruled the world.

"Whodunnits are just the same!" Poldi told me fiercely. "In them, women just pass muster as sexy sidekicks and murder victims—you can read that in every set of crime statistics—and sometimes as demented murderesses, but seldom as detectives with brains and humanity. And if they *are* allowed to be detectives, they're ridiculous, nymphomaniac old fruitcakes."

"Er, for instance?" I stammered.

Poldi calmed down. "Forget it," she said, and resumed talking about the case.

"Very creditable of you, Donna Poldina," the pope said mildly. "So what *would* interest you? There are many arrangements we could make."

"You can arrange to kiss my arse, the lot of you!" Poldi

barked in Bavarian. "That's to say," she added in mellifluous Italian, "no thank you, I'm not interested."

"Because there's something you should remember," Poldi told me, breaking off again at this point. "What are the two most important words in showbiz?"

As usual when put on the spot, I wavered. "Er . . ."

"'No thanks.' Make a note of that! No thanks, I don't need the part if I have to go to bed with a scumbag like you. No thanks, for that measly fee I could sell flowers in the street. No thanks, I'm not desperate enough to sign the first book contract I'm offered. Get it?"

"Okay . . . But what if I *am* desperate enough?"

"Then you need a hard-as-nails agent with charm." Poldi tapped her bosom. "By the way, made any progress?"

"Er, in what respect?"

"What we discussed. I mean, you recording my cases as a kind of ghost writer."

"No thanks!"

An awkward silence reigned in the gloomy *salotto* of the Monteverde apartment.

Poldi got to her feet. "Well, many thanks for the offer, but I don't want to miss my flight to Catania."

She put out her hand. The pope just looked at her mildly and didn't move.

"This is when men usually start threatening me—telling me I'm making a big mistake," said Poldi.

The pope smiled. "I respect your decision, Donna Poldina. The assignment is tricky, complicated, probably impossible, and certainly very dangerous."

Direct hit.

Poldi sat down again. "You really take the cake," she said.

"I'm just a simple man with a difficult task to accomplish."

"And I'm not on board yet. I think you're still keeping something from me."

Morello cleared his throat in the background.

The pope looked at Padre Stefano, who came hurrying over.

"Excuse me, Holy Father." He fished out his mobile, tapped the display a few times, and handed the phone to his lord and master. "Simply press Play, Holy Father."

The pope passed the phone to Poldi. "You already know the video. What you don't know is how the session ended. Just press Play."

Poldi had guessed as much. She watched the video of Rosaria's exorcism again, this time to the end.

"I understand," she said thoughtfully, handing the phone back to the pope.

There was a renewed silence.

"Will you accept the assignment, then, Donna Poldina?"

Poldi shook her head. "No, but if I happen to come across the Black Madonna in the course of my investigations, I'll let you know."

"Unacceptable," said Morello from his post in the doorway.

The pope made a placatory gesture in his direction.

"We can live with that, Donna Poldina." He jotted down a phone number on a slip of paper and handed it to my aunt. "Don't hesitate to call me if you need assistance."

He rose and held out his hand. Poldi briefly debated whether to curtsy and kiss his hand or the Piscatory Ring, but that would have been going too far for her. She simply shook his hand.

"Thank you, Donna Poldina. This may be the start of a wonderful friendship."

Poldi felt she might just have concluded an agreement with no get-out clause.

A Brief Intermezzo

"Isolde, release your hold on Rosaria's body!" the exorcist went on unctuously, unimpressed by her Bavarian outburst. "Release Rosaria, Demon Isolde, and go back into the jaws of hell!"

But the demon seemed disinclined to comply.

"She must die!" growled Rosaria. "She must crrroak!"

She followed this up with a few juicy curses involving saints and defecation.

"Depart, demon!" intoned Monsignore Amato. He sprinkled the woman once more with holy water and recited Saint Antony of Padua's prayer of exorcism: "Behold the Cross of the Lord! Begone, all evil powers! The Lion of Judah, the Root of David, has conquered! Alleluia!"

Several voices, off: "Alleluia!"

Rosaria rolled her eyes and frothed at the mouth.

"Your pardon, *monsignore*," said a soft voice from out of shot. "Please ask Rosaria who it is that must die."

Clearly irritated by this interruption, the exorcist turned to the camera and made the "little crown"—the age-old

Italian gesture that either underlines what has been said or simply poses the indignant question *"Ma che cazzo vuoi?"* or "What the hell do you want?"

Monsignore Amato readdressed himself to Rosaria. "Tell me, Isolde," he boomed in a commanding voice, because naming a demon is a way of pinning one down, "who is it who must die?"

"The Black Madonna!" rasped Rosaria. "She must die! She sits on her ebony throne and accepts the worship of her false servants." Rosaria emphasized her words by spitting in all directions. "I know all their names! I know them all!"

Monsignore Amato was asked another whispered question by someone out of shot and promptly passed it on to Rosaria.

"Tell me the names of her servants, Isolde!"

Spitting, grunting, gasping—Rosaria's repertoire was extensive.

And then, in broad Bavarian, "You can kiss my arse, you cowled cunt. I'm not answering any questions unless you ask me nicely and make it worth my while." She rubbed her finger and thumb together. "Come through with the moolah, otherwise no dice, get it?"

The exorcist turned to the camera again and made the "little crown" with both hands, this time as a sign of helplessness. He probably mistook Rosaria's Bavarian for some dialect spoken by the denizens of hell. The camera panned. Sister Rita and the other shoulder-shrugging nuns were also at a loss.

"*Basta,* that's enough," the exorcist said off-screen. "We'll leave it at that."

When the camera picked him up again, he was making the

sign of the cross over Rosaria. He muttered a quick prayer and patted her gently on the head. Instantly she relaxed, heaved a big sigh, and opened her eyes.

"What's happened? Why are you all looking at me like that?"

She peered around, puzzled and rather perturbed.

"Everything's fine," the exorcist told her in a friendly bass that would have graced a radio announcer. "Don't worry."

The nuns helped Rosaria to sit up and handed her a glass of water. The camera zoomed into a close-up of her face.

"Do you remember anything?" the exorcist asked amiably.

Rosaria timidly shook her head.

"You spoke of the Black Madonna."

More puzzled head-shaking.

"What Black Madonna?"

"I'm sorry," said Monsignore Amato off-screen. "Does the name Isolde Oberreiter mean anything to you?"

Rosaria blinked a little, looking straight at the camera.

"No, I've never heard it before."

6

Tells of lies, life experience, and the POLDI. But also
of the Risorgimento, brood-carers' reflexes, Padre
Paolo, the sad signora, twenty-four thousand kisses,
and love and letting go. Poldi discovers some incon-
sistencies and impresses her nephew. He puts on
speed and earns himself a slap. No, two slaps. Poldi
convenes a team meeting and loses a friend.

There are things between heaven and earth that cannot
be explained and simply defy reason. But there are
also plenty of things which, with a little experience of life,
can easily be detected. Lying, for instance. I don't know how
she manages it, but my Auntie Poldi possesses this built-in lie
detector. From posture, moist hands, twitching eyelids, tone
of voice, air pressure, time of day, and a thousand other tiny
details that normal individuals like me would never register,
my aunt's superbrain takes only nanoseconds to compute
the POLDI, or Progressive Oberreiter Lie Detector Index.
This is a probability value index for determining the extent
of a lie between zero and a hundred. Or so I imagine. (I studied statistics, but not much of it stuck.) Anyway, zero indi-
cates that the subject has told the whole truth, congratulations! A hundred means the subject has lied like a trooper

and thinks you're stupid. The algorithm on which the POLDI is based is incredibly complex—logarithmical and even more complex than that of an online dating agency.

Most people are quite unaware what utter nonsense they talk. There's a gray zone to the left and right of normal—if someone wavers on the scale, you can't call it a deliberate lie, Poldi told me. In Rosaria's case, however, Poldi felt absolutely certain, despite the limited amount of data, that her POLDI registered a whopping 95.7 percent.

"Did you see that?" she quizzed me once more after showing me the whole video.

Caught on the wrong foot yet again, I said, "Yes, of course. Er, what do you mean?"

"Did you see it or didn't you?"

"Give me a clue, Poldi," I entreated her.

"Jesus, even a blind man could see it! Just look!"

She replayed the end of the video from the moment Rosaria could be seen in close-up.

"See it now?"

I shook my head in despair, feeling very stupid.

"Watch her eyes!"

Poldi showed me the end of the video again. And then I saw it!

The human body is a miracle of nature, but we never have it fully under control. I'm a perfect example where ball games and handwriting are concerned. However, quite different things go on in the brain's processing operations. Depending on which area of the brain is active, our eyes move sometimes in one direction, sometimes in another. These are reflexes we simply cannot control. If you know whether a person is left- or right-handed, you can tell quite a lot about their brain activity from brief movements of their eyes. This is taught in every management seminar.

The way in which Rosaria took the glass of water told Poldi that she was left-handed.

When the exorcist asked her if she could remember anything, she briefly looked down and to the left. To Poldi this was a clear indication that Rosaria was conducting an interior monologue and was, with a fair degree of certainty, remembering something.

When Padre Stefano, out of shot, asked Rosaria about the name Isolde Oberreiter, her eyes briefly swiveled upward and to the left. To Poldi this was a really definite sign that she was visualizing something. Moreover, she blinked, and blinking is always a sure sign of something.

"Aha," I said.

"Hang on, the best is still to come. Rosaria wasn't in a trance at all, not at any stage."

"Really not?"

"Good God, you should have noticed that, at least! No, she was fully conscious the whole time. She gave that exorcist the runaround."

"What convinces you of that?"

"She made a crucial mistake," Poldi said triumphantly. "That was when she asked for money in my voice. She overdid the Bavarian—I just don't speak like that. Besides, a real demon would have known that money genuinely doesn't interest me. You know why."

"Because money equals negative energy."

"Too right! And what did I conclude from that?"

"That you aren't a demon."

Poldi gave me a look. "Right, that's it for today."

"What? You can't stop halfway through."

"With my life and my story I can do what I damn well like, so get that into your head. Anyway, I'm not in the mood anymore." She rose with a groan. "Besides, I still have to go to Femminamorta. Want to come?"

"What, now? To Femminamorta?"

"No, you dumb cluck, to Timbuktu! Of course to Femminamorta. While the pair of you were indulging in *amour fou* in Frogland, I paid the place a daily visit to check that all was okay there. Well, are you coming?"

Valérie's small country estate, Femminamorta, is less than ten minutes by car from Torre Archirafi. Poldi wrote off her old Alfa Romeo last year, but she still has the lovely old Vespa PX that Cousin Marco tarted up for her, adorning it with lavish ornamentation and miniature scenes from her criminal cases like a *carretto siciliano*, a Sicilian donkey cart. The trouble is, she hasn't had a driving license for years, so I enjoy being able to ride such a cool Vespa around the locality and show off a bit. Now, however, I quailed at the thought of having to ride it with Poldi on the back. Or, worse still, of sitting on the back myself while she roared along the Provinciale like Valentino Rossi on speed, and all without a license or a helmet.

"Do you . . . do you think there's enough room for us both on the Vespa?"

Feeble attempt.

"Vespa be buggered! We'll take my new official car."

"Official car?"

With a sweeping gesture, Poldi produced an old Fiat key from an oddments bowl.

At the end of the Via Baronessa, parked up against the

wall in the shade, was a jewel of an old Cinquecento, a re-stored Fiat 500 with new pistachio-green paintwork, a little folding roof, and a rally stripe in the Italian national green, white, and red extending the full length of the vehicle. The bonnet of this lovable little fireball displayed Poldi's new logo, and on the doors, in cheerful acid yellow, was that of Radio Galatea 95.2. This was one of those stations that broadcast incessant commercials occasionally interrupted by good-mood pop music and the high-speed gabbling of eternally jovial presenters. All in all, the car was about as inconspicuous as . . . well, as my Auntie Poldi herself. Why was I surprised?

"Like it?"

"It's a dream," I whispered in awe. "Where did you get it?"

"Well, I'm now involved in a joint venture with Radio Ga-latea," Poldi explained. "They sponsored me the car. All I have to do in return is drive around the neighborhood and be visible. It's what's called a win-win situation."

"No, Poldi, it's called plain stupid. Detectives don't drive around *visibly,* that's not the way they work."

"You don't know the first thing about genuine detective work!"

"Besides, you don't have a —"

"God Almighty!" she snapped. "I don't need a license to drive around locally and go to the supermarket. Besides, I've got you."

She handed me the key.

I stood there, momentarily at a loss. To be honest, could I really afford to open my trap? I was just an aimless, tempo-rarily broken-hearted would-be novelist. Okay, now that I'd tried to dissuade my Auntie Poldi from drinking herself to death, I wore brightly colored shirts and had started to smoke. I had driven a Maserati, witnessed miracles, and been almost blown up and riddled with bullets. So who was I to hesitate when the call of the wild and the windmills rang out once more? Sancho Panza, that's who. But what was it Poldi always said? "Fear is where it's at." At least I'd get a chance to tootle around in my dream car. A car so heart-rendingly cuddly, it positively brought out one's brood-carer's instinct. An eighteen-horsepower icon of the Italian lifestyle. Vintage on wheels. The steering was spongy, the stick change hit-or-miss, and the ride better left unmentioned.

Poldi and I sat squeezed together, practically on the ground and sensitive to every little stone on the road, enclosed by a bit of sheet metal, deafened by the rattle of a two-cylinder, in-line engine. Totti sat behind us and farted. It felt like a ride on an overheated, stinking sewing machine. Eighteen h.p. is a joke, of course, but driving along Sicilian roads in an old 500, with the folding roof open and the windows wound down, one might as well be atop a rocket about to leave the launch pad: pure vibration, borderline physical stress. It was glorious, and the best thing was, Poldi didn't keep urging me to put my foot down this time. Instead she turned on the radio. Radio Galatea 95.2 bombarded us with "24000 baci" by Adriano Celentano, and we sang along with the old sixties classic:

Con ventiquattro mila baci, cosi' frenetico è l'amore
In questo giorno di follia ogni minuto è tutto mio.

The song had only just ended by the time we reached Femminamorta.

Femminamorta isn't a town or village but an enchanting country house which Valérie's eighteenth-century Bourbon ancestors, the Raisi di Belfiores, built for the grape harvest. Constructed of volcanic rock, its thick walls enclose a huge wine press and a cellar lined with barrels the height of a man. There are around twenty rooms, including bedrooms, reception rooms, and a small chapel. During the grape harvest the baron resided upstairs with a view of Etna, as befitted his rank, while the grape-pickers toiled away below, cooking, eating, and praying in the most abject conditions. The pinkwashed house with the old sundial and the big bell stood empty for a hundred years, together with its contents, after a bit of plaster fell from the ceiling during an earthquake and caused Valérie's great-great-grandfather and his family to abandon it in a hurry. The sleeping beauty was somehow forgotten thereafter. The Raisi di Belfiores owned masses of farms, palazzi, and landed estates in those days, so a small estate like Femminamorta counted for little.

In 1861, however, the Risorgimento brought an end to the Kingdom of the Two Sicilies and Bourbon rule. Garibaldi crossed over to Sicily with a force of irregulars, shot a few random barons, and summarily declared himself the island's dictator, though he had to retract that soon afterward. United Italy briefly became a monarchy and then, finally, a republic. What remained of the Bourbons were some melodious place names and a few scattered families still in possession of enough landed property for none of them ever to have to work even three generations later. When money became short, they simply sold a bit of land or a palazzo. In the following century and a half, nearly all of them were fleeced by a new generation of middle-class businessmen,

unscrupulous adventurers, and *mafiosi,* who brazenly did-
dled them out of their land and estates.

No one knows who gave Valérie's house its strange name,
but Sicily abounds in bizarre place names, especially ones
associated with female misfortune. But Femminamorta,
with its faded pink walls and gate flanked by stone lions, is
less a place of misfortune than an oasis infused with age-old
positive energy. The soil there is exceptionally fertile, so it's
no wonder Italo Russo has been making Valérie offers for
years. She has steadfastly refused them so far. It's almost impossible to talk Valérie into or out of anything, because—
who would have guessed it?—she's a Capricorn too.

It was sheer curiosity and love of adventure that prompted
Valérie to move to Sicily after her father's death, bone up on
land management, and cultivate palm trees, lemon trees, and
avocados on her patch of land with the help of two old agricultural laborers. On the side she runs a small B&B which,
in some magical way, attracts the weirdest guests without
benefit of website or advertising.

My stomach churned as Poldi and I drove through the
bougainvillea-smothered gateway with its twin stone lions,
and I felt like turning back at once.

Okay, here's the abridged version. I had first met Valérie a
couple of months ago and spent two tempestuous weeks
with her in a magic bubble remote from the rest of the world.
Then she had flown to Paris "to see to a few things." A few
days later, when her texts cooled and became more monosyllabic, when the endearments ceased, as did the dirty talk,
which I admit I'd enjoyed, I spontaneously flew to Paris to
surprise her. One oughtn't to do these things, I know, but it's
tormenting to be so infatuated. At least, it is for me. Any-

way, it transpired that Valérie's "few things" had a name: David. Her ex-boyfriend or kind-of-still-boyfriend or whatever. She had told me about him as if speaking of some almost-forgotten sorrow in the far distant past. You like to hear that when you're in love and believe yourself to be the cure for all sorrow. The reality, however, looked different. David was an extremely attractive photographer with roots in the Near East. Twenty years older, virile, smart, well-read, successful (naturally), charming, five-days-bearded, and incredibly passionate, he even—just for fun—played occasional gigs with a jazz band. The reality named David had been overseas for a long time; now he was back. Word of honor, he also owned a superb studio apartment on the Île Saint-Louis in the heart of Paris in addition to his pied-à-terre in New York. Because, of course, David had commissions to fulfill all over the world, lived out of a suitcase but didn't need much, just his camera, jeans, T-shirt, and a packet of Gitanes. In short, David was the living embodiment of an irresistible French artist. Me, by contrast: a total zero. I should have packed and left, but I stayed on. The thing is, I can also be a bull terrier. My latest adventure with Poldi had lit a little flame of self-confidence, and I wanted, at least for the first time in my life, to fight for something that was important to me. I stuck it out in a shitty hostel for a while, doggedly learned French, switched to Gitanes, took incredibly artistic photos of Paris at dawn, and spent my nights hatching plots *alla siciliana* to murder David. A great time it was not.

But worse was to come. It always does—with a vengeance, just when you think you're over it.

When we made our way into Valérie's neglected garden

with its old palms, avocados, and hibiscus bushes, she was sitting in the shade of a palm tree, typing something into her mobile phone. She looked engrossed in her thoughts and very beautiful. I think my heart missed a beat.

Little Oscar with the underbite came to meet us, yapping ecstatically. Unable to decide which of us to jump up at first, he rolled in the grass for sheer delight at seeing us again, and Totti did likewise. Poldi bent down and gave the little mongrel's tummy a good tickle.

"Who's a good boy, then? Did you miss me, you little fleabag, you? Yes, yes, that's right, good boy!"

This commotion jolted Valérie out of her reverie.

"*Mon Dieu!*" she exclaimed on catching sight of me.

"Damn it, Poldi," I hissed, "you tricked me!"

"Pull yourself together, boy!" Poldi marched over to her friend Valérie like a thundercloud bearing down on Lake Como. "In fact," she went on in Italian, "pull yourselves together, both of you!"

"*Mon Dieu*, why didn't you warn me, Poldi?"

"Because I didn't want to hear any excuses, that's why. And because the two of you are going to settle this, here and now. I shouldn't really care two hoots what's happened between you, but the trouble is, one of you is my nephew and the other's my friend. I've lost too many dear ones in my life, and I've had enough of it. I'm not losing either one of you because of some bloody stupid love affair. There are worse things, God knows, than being nobody's sweetheart. There are worse things than partings, broken hearts, and jealousy, so the pair of you are going to behave like grown-ups and have a talk. Hit each other over the head, for all I care. Whether or not you become an item is beside the point, but kindly get on together and be friends again."

"Hey, Poldi, it doesn't work like that," I protested. "You can't provoke an argument and preempt the result."

"*Mon Dieu,* he's right for once."

"What do you mean, 'for once'?"

Poldi threatened us both with a raised forefinger. "Don't disappoint me!" she snarled in a tone of voice I'd never heard before, and she marched back to the car, leaving us to ourselves.

"Er . . . ha-ha, well, that's Poldi for you!" I exclaimed, hoping to lighten the atmosphere a little. I rubbed my hands together as though preparing to dig up the garden.

Valérie didn't speak, just looked at me.

I cleared my throat.

"When did you get back?"

Her response was a stinging slap on the cheek that made my ears ring. I wondered what it was about me that had lately kept earning me clouts on the head.

"Ow, that hurt!"

"Want some wine?"

"No. If we're going to take this seriously, perhaps we ought to—"

Smack! Another slap.

"Want a glass of wine?"

"Yes, very much. I mean, it's after midday and I've almost got over yesterday's hangover."

In hindsight, I picture our heart-to-heart as a scene from a French movie. Filled with drama and passion, in other words, but the truth always looks different—where I'm concerned, at least.

And because the whole disaster with Valérie, like everything in my life for the past year, has always been somehow connected with my Auntie Poldi, and because I want to be a reliable and credible chronicler of her adventures who sticks to the facts and the chronological order in a strictly neutral way, I must break off at this incredibly emotional moment and return to Poldi. She told me everything just as I put it down on paper, and I swear I'm not inventing anything. Life tells the most incredible stories in any case, as everyone knows, and in my Auntie Poldi's case I couldn't possibly invent everything. Certainly not the business with Antonella. Or Rosaria. Or Maria.

But I'm getting ahead of myself.

When Poldi returned to Torre Archirafi from Rome, her first official step was to convene a team meeting. I remember it well, because I was still there looking after the house when she got back. It was during this period that I had got to know Valérie and set my life ablaze. It was hardly surprising, therefore, that I was itching to tell Poldi about my latest romantic developments.

"Well, how was it?" I asked brightly. It was more of a rhetorical question.

"Very nice," she replied absently, trundling her suitcase into the bedroom.

This taciturnity should have made me smell a rat, but I was too focused on myself.

"I've something to tell you," I said. "You'll never believe it!"

"Later, my boy, okay? I'm a bit woozy after the flight. Would you be sweet enough to make me a coffee?"

"Is Montana giving you trouble again?" I asked suspiciously.

"No, everything's fine."

And she disappeared into the bathroom without more ado.

I went off to the kitchen, feeling stopped in my tracks. I could hear Poldi calling someone in the bathroom. While the *caffettiera* was bubbling away, I crept back and listened at the bathroom door. I couldn't hear much, but I did pick up the words "team meeting," "vestry," and "right away." This galvanized me, because something was obviously brewing, and after our last adventure I regarded myself as a regular player on Poldi's team.

The other two regulars were Padre Paolo, Torre Archirafi's parish priest, and sad Signora Cocuzza, proprietress of the café bar in the piazza. Both were Poldi's age, and both have been associated with her for nearly a year now in a kind of conspiratorial friendship. They're partners in crime, as it were.

The padre is a positively stereotypical example of the chain-smoking, eternally angry Sicilian with a deep-seated mistrust of almost everything north of the Tyrrhenian Sea, the Vatican included. And he's a communist too, because in Sicily you're either a Catholic or a communist. Or both. But a passionate one, that's the main thing. And passion is something one really can't dissociate from Padre Paolo. His massive frame is intimidating enough in itself. He could have been a professional heavyweight boxer. He uses every Mass he holds in the enchanting little church of Santa Maria del Rosario to deliver tirades against capitalism, the internet, the USA, unprotected sex, divorce, scratch cards, fast food, the Mafia, corruption, plastic waste, Italian politicians in general and the Northern League in particular, knockout drops, Goa parties, the overfishing of the Mediterranean, war in any form, the dire state of Italy's social and educational systems, climate-change deniers, charlatans, thimbleriggers, idlers, bullshitters, mommy's boys, SUVs, smartphones, Sunday-opening supermarkets, envy, lust, and a host of other things. Padre Paolo can always find some cause or other to back, and ever since he's known my Auntie Poldi, women's rights have been on the agenda. His parishioners generally ignore such things, of course, but it has to be said that his church is full every Sunday. Sicilians love drama, and rhetorically well-packaged anger always has a palpable effect. Padre Paolo can be an insufferable grouch, but he's certainly more than just a priest and a communist. I think he's a great humanist and European.

Signora Cocuzza, on the other hand, is a mystery to me. She's simply sad. I've only ever seen her smile once, and she never speaks to me. Mute and colorless, she spends every day sitting behind the counter in the little café bar she runs with her two sons. An almost translucent little figure, she seems to have to cling to her cash register so as not to be blown away by every breath of life in her vicinity. Her sons, by contrast, are surprisingly sturdy fellows, and they make the second-best pistachio ice cream in the world. The best pistachio ice still comes from the Caffè Cipriani in Acireale. Mind you, Uncle Martino says I don't know my arse from my elbow and the best pistachio ice is sold by a bar in Ragusa. But I'm digressing again.

Nobody knows the reason for Signora Cocuzza's leaden sadness, but nobody ever talks about it. Least of all the signora herself. Her friendship with my Auntie Poldi has thawed her out a little, and she's even reputed to have smiled a couple of times, but that's as far as it goes. All Poldi told me was that the sad signora was a whodunnit fan and an extremely sensitive person.

The signora probably responded as most people do when Poldi comes whooshing through their lives like a hurricane of joie de vivre, drama, danger, and Bavarian warmth: the fug gets blown away, the windows fly open, the world widens once more, and everything seems to smell of pork chops and promise. My Auntie Poldi always leaves chaos in her wake, a wonderful trail of destruction, an escape route from all the ballast we've been hauling around the whole time—all the garbage of offended egos, narrow-mindedness, possessiveness, circumstances beyond our control, and things of no significance to us. Anyone who has ever been buffeted by this storm wind named Poldi knows that life means loving and letting go.

But not even Poldi had been able to dispel Signora Cocuzza's sadness altogether. The signora was forever haunted by some nameless shadow from the past, and without a name we're powerless against our demons, as everyone knows. And Poldi knew a thing or two about shadows from the past.

So, as I already said, Poldi convened a team meeting with the padre, the sad signora, and me. Or so I'd supposed. Over coffee, however, she let off a bombshell.

"Don't be cross with me, my boy," she said as she laced her espresso with a big slug of grappa, "but I must be off again in a moment."

"Did I hear something about a team meeting?"

"Yes, I'm having a quick get-together in the vestry with the padre and Signora Cocuzza. You can tell me everything when I get back."

"You mean . . . you're having a team meeting . . . without me?" I asked in bewilderment.

"Yes, sure, why not?"

I'm used to being ignored, and—yes, I admit it—I still don't have my offended ego under control. I simply stared at Poldi, turned away without a word, and went upstairs to my attic room to pack.

When I came down again, carrying my rucksack, Poldi was waiting at the foot of the stairs.

"What's all this, then?"

"I'm moving in with Valérie for a bit. Cheerio."

"Why with Valérie?"

I could have said, quite casually, "Why do you think? We're our own team now. Pay us a visit sometime."

Yes, I could have. But I didn't, because it's always the same with me. Whenever something's important, or whenever I want to go on with my novel, my mind goes blank. My speech center spontaneously empties and all the words in my head go *phut*. It's only later that I think of all the cool and witty bons mots I should have uttered. Usually just before going to sleep, and they're naturally gone the next day.

So I merely opened and closed my mouth a couple of times, like a stranded fish, and left the Via Baronessa. I heard nothing more from Poldi after that until I was called back from France and she finally brought me up to date.

And so, while I flounced off to Femminamorta in a huff, Poldi hurried into the church to see her friends. For discreet conversations out of earshot of the inquisitive, they always used the vestry.

When Poldi came in, Signora Cocuzza was nervously sipping an ice-cold almond milk. The padre was shoveling *gelato* into his mouth with a tiny plastic spoon in his massive paw and intermittently puffing at the cigarette that smoldered in the ashtray beside him. He was making every effort to look dispassionate. Not so the sad signora.

"Is it another murder?" she whispered excitedly, even before Poldi could sit down. Her sunken cheeks were bathed in a rosy glow. "*Madonna*, Donna Poldina, it never stops with you. You positively attract dead bodies."

"Steady, *mes enfants*," Poldi said breathlessly, mopping her moist brow. "First I have to come to terms with the fact that my nephew has clearly become infatuated with Valérie."

"No!"

"Yes."

"So there isn't any murder?"

"Yes, that too."

"Thank God!"

"Signora!" thundered the priest.

The sad signora crossed herself and muttered a half-hearted apology—halfhearted because murder inquiries acted on her like an elixir, and she yearned for the next case like a junkie craving her next fix.

"A young nun named Sister Rita was thrown off the roof terrace of the Apostolic Palace," Poldi reported.

"No!" That was the priest this time.

"Yes."

"No!"

Poldi rolled her eyes.

"The presumed perp, identity unknown, has gone on the run, but before that she underwent an exorcism during which she spoke in my voice. That's why I've been caught up in the whole shemozzle. Russo is also connected in some way, and there's something else involved as well. That's why I need your help." Poldi drew a deep breath and eyed her friends in turn. "What do you know about the Black Madonna?"

And at that moment, Poldi told me later, she became aware of a drastic change. The temperature plummeted, gears ground to a halt, a door slammed shut. She saw all the thrill of the chase, all the look of excitement and the rosy glow in Signora Cocuzza's cheeks become extinguished in an instant. It was as if someone had thrown a switch. Her face tightened, hardened.

Poldi was dismayed. "What is it?" she asked.

The priest, who had also noticed, looked a trifle taken aback.

"Why do you ask that?" the sad signora asked in an expressionless voice.

"There are, er . . . indications that the Black Madonna may hold the key to the murder motive," Poldi said vaguely. For the moment she preferred to keep quiet about her apostolic mission.

"Can't you be a bit more specific?" the priest grumbled.

But Poldi wasn't listening. All her attention was focused on the sad signora, whose face had now completely closed up like a Sicilian window at midday.

"I know nothing about a Black Madonna," she said brusquely.

It seemed to be costing her a great effort to preserve her composure. She was looking almost . . .

Shaken, thought Poldi. "What's wrong, my dear?"

"Nothing." Signora Cocuzza mustered a faint smile and

straightened up a little. "I simply know nothing about any Black Madonna."

Silence pervaded the vestry like an unpleasant smell. Then it was broken by a soft *ping*. The sad signora had received a text message. When she looked at the display, Poldi saw her eyes lose their last vestiges of animation.

"There are lots of Black Madonnas," the padre pontificated in his deep bass voice, to break the silence. "There's one in Tindari. And another in, er . . . Oh well, perhaps there aren't all that many. But some. Anyway, most of them are black only because of the candles . . ."

The sad signora rose abruptly.

"Forgive me, but I must get back to the bar. We're very busy today."

Before anyone could object, she turned and left the vestry.

"Good Lord," growled the padre, "what's eating her today?"

Poldi laid a hand on his arm.

"I'll see to her. The thing is, Padre, I want to discover why Sister Rita had to die. I know she was young and pretty and rather too flirtatious, but that's all. I'd like you to find out who she was before she entered the order and where she came from — simply everything. Dig deep, but please be discreet. Can you do that for me?"

The padre saluted. "I'm on it already, Donna Poldina."

"Thank you, Padre."

Poldi gave him a smacking kiss on the cheek and hurried off after the sad signora.

It's only a short walk from the church of Santa Maria del Rosario to the Bar Cocuzza, but Poldi put on speed and reached her friend just before she got there.

"Wait!" she said, grabbing her by the arm. "What's the matter with you?"

The sad signora looked at Poldi with an expression as bleak and overcast as a November morning in Iceland.

"Nothing," she said dully. "I'm feeling a bit tired, that's all. Please let go of me."

Poldi continued to grip her arm.

"Why are you so scared of the Black Madonna? What was that text message you received just now?"

The sad signora heaved a sigh, and Poldi could have sworn that it encapsulated all the unhappiness in the world. She hesitated for a moment, then looked Poldi straight in the eye.

"You know, Donna Poldina, some things are better left alone. I tell you this because you're German and new here and I'm very fond of you. That's why I hope you'll grant a request made between friends. Could you see your way to doing that for me?"

"What sort of things do you mean?"

Again that sigh.

"Drop this case, Donna Poldina. I know how hard for you that would be, but I'm asking you as a friend."

"I'm sorry, my dear, but you know I can't do that."

A last sigh. Then, with a strength of which Poldi would never have believed her capable, the sad signora wrenched herself free, stiffened, and said in a hoarse but determined voice, "Then I'm afraid I can't be your friend anymore, nor will you be welcome in the bar from now on. Good day, signora."

Dismayed and dumbfounded, Poldi stared after her frail little friend as she made her way, slightly unsteadily, into the bar. As the glass door opened, Signora Cocuzza was greeted by a gust of cool air that came wafting out into the April afternoon, laden with the scent of vanilla, almond blossom, coffee, and freshly fried *arancini*. It was as if the sad signora had finally left our world of eternal sorrow and entered another, brighter realm. An invisible fist seemed to tighten around my Auntie Poldi's heart, because as the door closed behind the sad signora, it felt like forever. Like a farewell. No, worse still, like a little death.

7

Tells of Easter and regulations, unicorns and matcha tea, stability and temptation, pompompom, vodka, and "it." Poldi plans to get rat-arsed and receives a visit from a ninja. She enters into a risky deal, feels rejected, receives another unexpected visit, and learns that Montana is feeling rejected too. This leads to a moment of madness and a disastrous provisional outcome.

Easter was approaching, Palm Sunday just around the corner. Even though she wasn't a great churchgoer, Poldi usually found Holy Week a nice, cheerful time filled with promise. A time for colorful, noisy processions, family outings, and pretty dresses. A time for reopening resorts where you can buy designer shades and a new bikini for the season. A good time for falling in love and making plans. Holy Week was like a shot from summer's starting pistol.

But this time: a tight-lipped Montana, an offended nephew who'd stormed out of the house, and a lost friend, and all within a few hours. No mistaking what that meant: utter disaster.

Despite her veneer of Bavarian stability, Poldi is always treading on thin ice, always walking the knife edge between joie de vivre and melancholy. She has simply lost and been forced to let go of too many people dear to her heart.

My hurt, resentful behavior was attributable to my hormone levels, and that, as Poldi knew from experience, would sooner or later—in my case, sooner—adjust itself. The same went for Montana's taciturnity. He would start talking again, likewise sooner rather than later.

But the Signora Cocuzza situation was really getting Poldi down, it has to be said. She only just made it to the supermarket to stock up on three bottles of vodka, then returned, exhausted, to the Via Baronessa to have a quiet think. And for a quiet think Poldi needs three things: peace, hard liquor, and "it." Although this may sound self-contradictory, it's in the nature of exceptional people to have exceptional needs. Poldi, for example, is a person who blazes fiercely, who is almost consumed with passion and zest for life. When emotional upsets supervene, stability goes out the window. That's why Poldi needs intoxication, either alcoholic or erotic, in order to come down to earth. In order to quench her fire, so to speak. Or simply to quench herself, because that had always been her Plan A: to drink herself to death in comfort with a sea view. But life, as we all know, is what intervenes just when you're making plans, so Poldi had provisionally switched to Plan B. This entailed solving a few murders first, making some friends, and occasionally screwing a handsome police inspector. But now, from the look of it, she needed a Plan C, and for that she needed to think. And because Montana's animal lust wasn't readily available, she would have to get rat-arsed. It was only logical.

But something intervened again. When Poldi opened her front door laden with three bottles of vodka in a plastic bag, she heard the clatter of crockery and the sound of water running in the kitchen. Assuming that her nephew had returned, filled with remorse, she strode into the kitchen to give me a piece of her mind.

"Well, I'll be buggered!" she exclaimed in surprise when she saw who her visitor was. "What on earth is that get-up?"

Death was carefully and very thoroughly washing up a solitary Japanese tea bowl from my aunt's collection. He might as well have been polishing an apple. He kept the water running, used vast quantities of detergent, and dried the cup repeatedly betweentimes.

His brand-new look consisted of a traditional black ninja yoroi with cowl. It was rather threadbare and stained, as if he'd already worn it for hundreds of years. It also smelled sweaty and musty, like the cellar of an old house. Death even had a katana sword on his back, but his scrawny, decrepit physique was far from genuinely intimidating.

Poldi noticed at once that his clipboard with the list on it was lying facedown on the kitchen table. This reassured her a little, because, although she had become used to Death's fleeting visits, they still gave her an uneasy feeling.

"I was going to make myself some tea," he said apologetically. "Would you like some too?"

Poldi ignored this. Death indicated the vodka bottles. "Is that such a good idea?"

Poldi laid the bottles aside, turned off the tap, and relieved Death of the cup. "It's clean! Besides, in Sicily we don't waste water."

"There are germs everywhere. No one wants to catch their death." The visitor paused, looking at Poldi expectantly. "Well, how was that for a joke?"

Poldi sighed. "So-so. Four out of ten."

"Thanks, that's good to hear. I wouldn't want anyone dying of laughter." Another brief pause. "How about that one?"

Poldi merely sighed.

"The thing is," said Death, "I'd like to make a more relaxed impression—inspire more confidence. What do you think?"

Poldi pointed to the katana. "Then first you'd better work on your outward appearance. First impressions count."

"Oh, this is just a traditional thing. Blades have lately been reintroduced as part of our official uniform. It's all giddy-up or whoa where I come from, you've no idea. First it was okay to dispense with a blade, but now it's scythe, sword, or ax again. The personnel department keeps changing our order of dress—it's harassment, pure and simple. The top brass don't care, of course, they spend all their time in strategy meetings while we on the operational side have to implement the whole transformatory process. Do you have some matcha tea?"

Poldi pointed to the sofa in the next room. "Have a seat."

Glancing regretfully at the vodka, she made some tea. Death nursed his Japanese tea bowl like a Zen master, Poldi used a coffee mug. She ignored her cheesy-smelling acquaintance's disapproving expression and laced her matcha with vodka after all.

"May I ask you a personal question?"

Death took a noisy sip of tea from the little bowl.

"Slurping is the done thing," he said apologetically, seeing the look on Poldi's face. "Of course. Shoot."

"Do you sometimes have doubts about your job? I mean,

where murder victims or war casualties are concerned, or children, or geniuses who might have changed the world?"

Death thought for a moment, then shook his head.

"I've been doing this job for half an eternity. To start with, yes, I sometimes found it hellishly difficult. The mass extinction in the Cambrian period, for instance. I disliked that because so much of what died out was beautiful. The unicorns and dinosaurs made me wonder, too. *Must they really bite the dust?* I asked myself. You can get used to anything, though. The plan isn't perfect, but by and large it works."

"Unicorns?"

Death chuckled softly. "That was an eight out of ten at least, you've got to admit." He bumped fists with Poldi.

"Why are you here?"

"Er, tea break? I always feel half dead in the afternoon."

"Nought out of ten!" sighed Poldi before Death could ask. "Well, is my time up? I don't care if it is, I've had enough."

"Always this eternal mistrust on your part," Death complained. "It hurts my feelings."

"I mean it. I've had my fill. I lost a friend today, and do you know why? Because I'm the way I am, that's why. Because I'm egotistical. Because I have to poke my nose in everywhere. Because I attract misfortune like a sort of black hole. But I don't want to be a black hole anymore, understand? I'm Poldi! I'm just a human being, nothing more."

Death sipped his tea.

"Well, say something, for God's sake!"

"It isn't time yet."

"Bugger that! Do a bit of hanky-panky with the date on

the list. Go on, for friendship's sake! I want my Plan A back, and then *basta*!"

Death carefully deposited the old tea bowl on a little side table. The clipboard appeared in his hand like magic.

"Hm," he said, "from the look of it, there'll be no need for any hanky-panky."

Poldi felt suddenly queasy. "Meaning what?"

Death cleared his throat. "I already indicated to you that . . . that because of standardizations in the universe's project flow, and for reasons of transparency vis-à-vis the shareholders, certain, er . . . rectifications in the structure of destiny have been introduced. These are intended, among other things" — he cleared his throat again — "to lead to an improved outcome by means of individual lifetime adjust-ments."

"Yes, I remember," Poldi said grimly. "You said I didn't have much longer. *Carpe diem,* that's what you said."

"True." Death shrugged.

Poldi drew a deep breath. "Well, I'll be buggered. When?"

"Your sixty-first birthday. Heart attack, very quick. Sorry. That's why I'm here. I thought you might like to do some-thing nice in your last two and a half months. A world cruise, perhaps?"

"Two and a half months?" Poldi whispered in dismay.

"Yep."

She struggled for composure. "And that's final?"

"Very well put. Yes, pretty final."

"Quite sure? No mistake?"

"Listen, Poldi. I—"

She checked him with a brusque gesture. "I must have a little think."

But, not unnaturally, she found it impossible to frame a single clear idea.

"What if I wanted a little more time?" she blurted out. "I mean, er, purely theoretically, what if I asked you to engage in a bit of hanky-panky after all? For friendship's sake?"

"Ah, no, Poldi, it doesn't work like that. You're really putting me on the spot, now of all times."

"I know," Poldi said meekly. "More tea?"

Death looked at her. "Let's assume I said, 'Okay, Poldi, if you stop doing this or that, you won't have to die on your birthday.'"

"'This or that' meaning what?" she asked in a low voice.

"Something very important to you, anyway. Would you give it up in order to live a bit longer? Even if you didn't know how much longer—maybe just a day?"

It started to dawn on her what he was getting at.

"And what if I'd simply wanted a bit more time?"

"Everything has its price, Poldi. Sorry."

"For God's sake, yes!" Poldi burst out. "All right, I'll stop drinking. I can do it!"

"Okay," said Death. "Assuming, purely theoretically—"

"Of course!"

"—that I could fix it. Well, because the Lifetime Assessment Bureau is just being reorganized and I may know a female colleague who, er, would do me a favor. So let's assume I could obtain a new deadline for you . . ."

"Yes, what then?" Poldi asked hoarsely.

Death stiffened a little. "It would come with a few conditions."

"What do you mean? Where did these 'few conditions'

spring from all of a sudden? Let me tell you something, my friend: I'm going to—"

"Shut your trap, Poldi!" roared Death, and the whole house shook as if smitten by an earthquake.

Poldi gave a start. She had never known him to behave like this before. He got up off the sofa and loomed over her, looking suddenly quite frightening in his ninja outfit. Taller too, it seemed to her, and his voice sounded far deeper than usual. The house shook at every word. He drew the katana from its scabbard and flourished it menacingly—*whoosh, whoosh, whoosh*—in front of her.

"This is the deal!" he bellowed. "On your birthday I shall come to fetch you, unless you manage, in the next two and a half months, to abstain from investigation, drink, and 'it'!"

"What? Are you mad?"

Whoosh! Back in his usual scrawny persona, Death was sitting beside her on the sofa once more. He spread his arms apologetically.

"Oh yes, and you mustn't speak to the sad signora. If I catch you breaking even one of my conditions, your birthday will mean curtains."

Poldi fanned herself for a moment, then glared at Death resentfully.

"This isn't a deal, it's extortion. I'm not playing. Let's forget all about it."

"No," said Death, "we won't. Sorry, you've already signed." He showed her an illegibly handwritten agreement with Poldi's signature at the foot. "The deal stands, Poldi."

"Bugger that!"

Poldi tried to grab the document, but Death was too quick

for her. Lithe as a ninja, he snatched the clipboard away and hugged it to his chest like a treasured possession.

"You tricked me!" Poldi hissed. "You planned this, didn't you?"

She went to take a gulp of her tea laced with vodka, but Death raised his finger warningly.

"Better not." He got up off the sofa. "Thanks for the tea," he said amiably. "See you around, and don't forget: stay nice and clean—I'll be checking on you. Cheers!"

When Poldi awoke on Palm Sunday with her head buzzing, having brooded for most of the night, she became aware of the full extent of her dilemma. Whichever way she looked at it, she was trapped. She had always imagined she would arrange her demise with the freedom and self-determination that had marked her whole life. She had wanted to depart in a thoroughly pleasurable manner, but Death had now put a spoke in her wheel.

By noon Poldi had, in quick succession, passed through the seven phases of shock that ensue on life-changing events. Everything usually began with a presentiment, and that Poldi always had when Death came visiting—and no wonder. Then came alarm and disbelief that this time things were really serious. Then anger, first with Death and then with herself, for having been so royally conned. After that came the phase of resignation, because two and a half months would be over in a flash but were long enough for her to snap and do something stupid. For Poldi had realized something during the night: she had no wish to die. Well, not yet. She loved this life, however screwed up and onerous and unfair and filled with farewells it might be. That was on the one hand. On the other, detection, drink, and "it" were simply integral to her life—those and friends whom she could care for and sometimes be admired by. What was a life bereft of all those things worth? That had been the melancholy phase, when realization dawns that one's old life must be relinquished. It was followed by the phase of acceptance, solutions, and curiosity. Looking on the positive side, Poldi found two and a half months' abstinence manageable—a kind of Lent, so to speak. When it was over, she would be able to live it up again for an indeterminate period. All right, so she would have to drop the case of the Black Madonna. She would have to find pretexts for keeping Montana at arm's length in the immediate future. She would also develop a thirst, a monumentally awful, unbearable, excruciating thirst. In the end, though, she would live a while longer and might even win her friend back.

Okay, she told herself resolutely after her first cup of nonalcoholic coffee, buoyed up by the final phase of newfound self-confidence, *let's have a go. I can cut it, buddy, you see if I don't!*

It was a hard time. Poldi managed to call off Padre Paolo and fend off Montana when he got back from Rome two days later. Both were naturally miffed. She also refrained from paying Russo the visit she'd planned, to sound him out about the delivery van and the twins in fluorescent sneakers. From now on, on her solitary walks along the promenade, she always steered clear of the bar in the piazza and, hard as she found it, avoided bumping into the sad signora. Severing communication with me she found easier because I was obviously in an altogether different movie. Poldi was surprised to discover that the first few days of teetotalism were easier than she'd thought, and the same went for sexual abstinence. There was something almost sacramental about this brief spell of celibacy—a kind of purification that only intensified her sense of anticipation at the thought of Montana's wandering hands. Just as long as he didn't get the wrong idea.

"Have you met someone?" he was quick to ask her on her fourth day of resistance.

"Don't talk nonsense, Vito," she said, stroking him gently on the cheek. "I'm not in the mood right now, that's all."

This was a lie. Poldi couldn't have been more in the mood. She had only to catch a whiff of Montana's aftershave to go hot all over. When she glimpsed the hairy chest beneath his shirt, she was inundated with lust. The sight of his little tummy or bottom made her head swim. And when he drew her to him with his big hands and she felt his Olympic arousal, all she wanted to do was rip the clothes from his body and hers. It was no good, though, because Death would always be somewhere nearby. And so, with a heavy heart, Poldi extricated herself from Montana's embrace and, sighing, pushed him away.

"Or is it some form of revenge or blackmail? What's wrong, Poldi? Tell me."

What could she have said? She could only hope Montana's love for her was strong enough to survive this dry spell. Looking over his shoulder, she could see Death holding up a sort of ice-skating scorecard. Five point seven. An average performance, it was clear.

What Poldi found very hard was the ban on communicating with Signora Cocuzza. It gradually dawned on her that her sad friend's violent reaction might have something to do with the reason for her sadness. This was another mystery Poldi wanted to solve, but that was just what she couldn't do. She would have liked at least to personally assure Signora Cocuzza that she was off the case. She had asked Padre Paolo to tell the signora and was hoping every day for a little sign. But the sad signora remained silent.

What Poldi found hardest of all, though, as may be imagined, was having to desist from investigating, because she couldn't stop thinking about Sister Rita's murder and the pope's Black Madonna mission. However, she pulled herself together. She checked her emails when she felt she was unobserved, but she had never received a reply from her stalker, Antonella.

On one occasion Death caught her at it. Suddenly materializing in the inner courtyard, he silently but with distinct disapproval held up the scorecard again. Four point three. A very poor performance, very thin ice. Poldi's blood ran cold.

"Jesus wept," she grumbled. "Surely I can check my emails occasionally?"

"It's up to you, Poldi," Death told her with a shrug. "I'm simply transmitting intermediate results. You'll get the global assessment on your birthday. Anything under nine will be a deal-breaker. Sorry."

Poldi tried some belated haggling. "Let's call it eight, okay? That'd be only fair. After all, the whole thing's very subjective, don't you think?"

Death just gave another regretful shrug. He was now making surprise appearances and brandishing his scorecard every day. At first it seemed like a game, but it became ever clearer to Poldi that the situation was serious. That the clock was ticking. That her time was running out.

Nevertheless, her score rose during Holy Week to seven point three. Poldi resolved to score a straight ten point zero —to make up for any future falls from grace.

She began by switching from Prosecco, beer, grappa, etc., to ayurvedic smoothies. When her thirst became too much —when she experienced the shakes and her first hallucinations—she engaged in the kind of meditation procedure she'd practiced during her wild youth in Munich. It took the following form: Poldi sat cross-legged on the sofa (the lotus position was out because of her bad knee) and smoked a spliff with rapt concentration. Death had said nothing about cannabis. The spliff was an antidote to thirst; the trouble was, it made her feel randy. However, she soon found a cure for that: the flexible little gizmo in the drawer in her bedside table. This she covertly employed beneath the bedclothes, hoping that Death would have the decency not to monitor her behavior there. Poldi always visualized Montana for the first few nights, but after a day or two she fished out her photo albums of stalwart policemen from all over the world. It was also possible that a certain *commissario* of the Vatican police may have insinuated himself into her thoughts from time to time. According to my Auntie Poldi's definition, though, that wasn't really sex.

To take her mind off things, Poldi went mushroom-picking on Etna with Aunt Teresa, Uncle Martino, and Totti. The combination of peaceful natural surroundings and hysterical collecting bug had a calming effect on her. Uncle Martino drove high up, as far as the first lava fields, and as usual he drove the car over terrain so rough that it eventually bottomed out and would go no further. Then the doors flew open and Totti leapt out, followed by aunt and uncle with their baskets, and away they went.

Because mushroom-picking with Martino and Teresa is a serious business. You don't just amble along, bending down occasionally to pick a plump *porcino*. What matters to mushroom-picking professionals is results, of course, and that means picking the biggest possible quantity, size, and variety in the shortest possible time. Besides, it mustn't be forgotten that Aunt Teresa and Uncle Martino have been fiercely competing with their neighbors and best friends, the Terranovas from downstairs, since time out of mind. The moment when the two couples meet over a bottle of wine to compare their hauls is a pitiless ritual marked by triumph or disgrace. At the same time, it's the finest example of sportsmanship I know.

Poldi, who couldn't have cared less about all this, simply relished the silence and fresh air halfway up the mountain. Armed with her little basket, she made her way to one of her favorite places, a spacious clearing not far away. "Clearing" isn't quite the right word. A patch of greenery, an oasis in the midst of a solidified stream of lava, it protrudes from the ground like a little humpback. I actually know the spot myself. It's an enchanted old place Uncle Martino discovered many years ago on one of his expeditions. Silence seems to rise from the ground like a mist, and the lava bulges up all around as though it dared not go any further. The ground is completely covered with soft, thick moss, probably the product of centuries. Growing on the edge of the clearing is a ring of gorse and a little, gnarled old oak tree, and in the middle is a weatherworn boulder of shiny basalt, flat on top and wide enough to picnic on. It's as if ancient earth magic had provided a table here for trolls and giants. This is one of the hot spots of positive energy with which Sicily is so richly endowed, and in which, with a little patience, the universe will answer your questions.

Poldi could hear a soft, monotonous *pompompom* in the distance. Not an unpleasant sound, it was a kind of drumming that reminded her of a self-discovery trip she'd made to the Hopi tribe.

On reaching the clearing soon afterward, she saw a short-legged, elderly gentleman standing beneath the oak tree. He was staring pensively into the distance and beating a flat Native American drum. *Pompompom, pompompom.*

Poldi took a moment to absorb this peculiar sight and then went over to him.

"Good morning."

The man stopped beating his drum and smiled at her.

"Good morning, signora."

"May I ask you something?"

"But of course, signora."

"Why are you doing that?"

"Does it bother you?"

"No, far from it. I'm curious, that's all."

He nodded and appeared to cogitate.

"I'm activating the Mother Earth Snake," he said eventually.

"Really? Why?"

The man with the drum seemed to cogitate again.

"Fundamentally, signora, it's a therapeutic process."

"I see, and who or what is the Earth Snake healing?"

He made an all-encompassing gesture. "The forest, the trees, the mountain. Sometimes me, sometimes the earth. You too, perhaps."

"Hm," said Poldi. "But why here, of all places?"

The man shrugged his shoulders. "Because there's something asleep here," he said shyly. "Something good. And old. I can sense it."

Poldi had a soft spot for friendly oddballs. The man's name was Mezzapelle—a rather odd name in itself, but one she found somehow appropriate. Originally from Trapani, he had spent his retirement activating the Earth Snake all over Sicily, that being his modest contribution to the healing of the world.

Cheered by this encounter, indeed possibly healed to a limited extent, Poldi rediscovered her liking for life's little pleasures in the next few days.

She accompanied Aunt Luisa to Lido Galatea, a smart establishment where she was interviewed by Radio Galatea 95.2 and invited to deliver a few pithy remarks in Italian and Bavarian. Poldi spent a lot of time with the family at this period. She played rummy for hours with Aunt Caterina, helped her in the garden, and got Marco to work out a comprehensive brand concept for her.

But she no longer planned to open a detective agency. She wondered every day if it wouldn't be wisest—provided she outlived her birthday—never to investigate another case, never to poke her nose into anything again, and to simply consign her hunting instinct and her vanity to the lumber room of old whimsies for good and all. But—you've guessed it—Sicily is complicated, etc.

. . .

The first signs that something is going catastrophically wrong are always so subliminal, isolated, and silly in themselves that for a long time you ignore or dismiss them as unimportant mood swings. Even though the little warning bell of intuition is already tinkling, you initially fail to spot a partner's lies and concealments. For instance, when a mobile phone is suddenly turned off or muted but checked more often than usual. When your text messages no longer end in a row of heart emojis. When your partner looks abashed, as though caught doing something impermissible. When you lie beside them in bed, not daring to ask what's wrong. When a sarcastic but affectionate cliché becomes affectionate no longer. When love itself becomes a cliché.

Or when your neighbors suddenly avoid you. You don't notice this at first, but you do in the end. It struck Poldi that no one was coming to ask her to do a little private investigating or bring her Tupperware boxes of homemade *caponata* or *parmigiana;* that Torre Archirafi was falling silent, very silent. It was a positively hostile silence. Signora Anzalone from next door merely waved back, and only when Poldi persisted in waving to her. Signor Bussacca from the *tabacchi* no longer chatted to her. After a week Poldi could no longer ignore the fact that she was being shunned by the little town that had become her home—that a rift had opened up, and it cleft her heart in two.

It was at Easter, of all times, that there occurred a disastrous concatenation of events which thoroughly compromised Poldi's prospects of outliving her sixty-first birthday. I still find it hard to imagine how everything came to pass. Even Poldi could no longer recall the exact sequence of events when telling me about them later. All she was quite certain of was that it had all begun on Good Friday, when —*ding-dong*—Padre Stefano appeared at her front door.

"What are you doing here?"

"My apologies. I, er . . . come from Linguaglossa and always spend Easter here with my mother, so I thought I'd take the opportunity to . . ." He cleared his throat.

"Would you like a coffee?"

"Only if it isn't too much trouble."

Poldi just shook her head. She had started to turn away when the priest pointed to the outside wall.

"How long has that been there?"

Poldi, who hadn't yet left the house that day, came outside to see what he meant. It was a respray of the original threat: POLDI GO HOME!

It rent her heart, not that she would ever have admitted as much, but she kept her composure admirably. "It must have been done during the night," she said. She seated Padre Stefano on the sofa and plied him with coffee and almond biscuits. She could see Death sitting outside in the courtyard, clipboard ready to hand on the table. He was picking his toes with a dispassionate air.

"I trust that unfriendly injunction has nothing to do with your investigations, Donna Poldina."

"I'm not doing any investigating these days," Poldi said stiffly.

"I'm sorry?"

"I've given up, you can tell that to your boss and Commissario Morello. Personal reasons."

"Oh, how regrettable." The priest lapsed into silence for a moment.

His mobile phone hummed like a monster insect from outer space. He hastily groped in his pocket and turned it off.

"A pity, I would have liked to assist you in your investigations."

Poldi saw Death reach for his scorecard.

"I'm sorry, my decision is final."

Death gave her eight point four.

"I understand," said the priest. "Well, I shall have things to do here for the next week or two. May I look in on you now and then?"

"If you must, Padre."

Soon after she had shown the ill-shaven priest out, Poldi went to the storeroom and fetched the bucket containing a residue of house paint. She took a photo of the graffito and then painted it over. Even after three coats, however, POLDI GO HOME! continued to show through like a distant echo.

That afternoon the same thing happened.

Ding-dong. This time it was Italo Russo, inappropriately dressed for Good Friday in black chinos and a black polo shirt. He was accompanied as usual by his two German shepherds, Hans and Franz. Before Poldi could yell, "Gerrout, you goddamned brutes!," they stormed past her into the house, tongues lolling, and inspected it from top to bottom like a couple of cops on a drugs bust.

Poldi had no choice but to invite Russo in. He came straight to the point too.

"Are you in difficulties, Donna Poldina?"

"What gives you that idea?"

"One hears things."

A wishy-washy question-and-answer game like that can go on forever, but Poldi wasn't in the mood for games.

"I know you're involved!" she told him angrily.

She itched to quiz him about the twins and the delivery van, but Death was back in the courtyard, pensively nibbling an *aranciata*.

"I'm not your enemy, Donna Poldina, you know that. If you're having problems here in the locality, I can take care of them. People trust me. These things can all be sorted out." Russo took Poldi's hand and bent forward. "One good turn deserves another."

The dogs came scampering downstairs and out into the courtyard, where Death was sitting with his lemonade. He hissed when they came too close. Poldi saw Hans and Franz give a start and return to their lord and master, whimpering, with their tails tucked between their legs. Death gave Poldi a wave.

Poldi withdrew her hand. "What are you really getting at?"

"Well, I happen to know that you're looking for a certain Madonna statue. I've an idea who your employers are, but I represent a small group of . . . investors, let's say, who are also interested in that statue, and—"

"Get out!" hissed Poldi, because Death was reaching for his scorecard again.

Russo looked puzzled.

"Are you feeling all right?"

Poldi strode along the passage to the front door and flung it open.

"Out!" she yelled, and watched with satisfaction as Hans and Franz fled from the house in a panic.

Russo remained as unruffled as ever. He made a leisurely exit, then turned to face her.

"I'm always here for you, Donna Poldina."

162

. . .

That evening Poldi heard the little Good Friday procession, complete with local brass band, making its way along the Via Baronessa. The whole of Torre Archirafi was afoot, led by Padre Paolo holding the monstrance on high. The air was filled with alleluias, discordant singing, and childish laughter. Poldi didn't venture outside or even look out the window.

She felt excluded—and felt like getting rat-arsed—but ended up merely lying stoned and sleepless on her bed.

The next day, Holy Saturday, the threat was back on the wall: POLDI GO HOME! Poldi went and got the bucket of paint again, guessing that it wouldn't be the last time she had to do so. When she had finished, a young Indian man with a sitar case on his back was standing beside her.

"I could do that for you the next time," he told her in English. His friendly manner implied that such threats were the most normal thing in the world and about as intimidating as an autumn leaf. It was an attitude that appealed to Poldi.

The young man, whose name was Ravi, was looking for a job. Because Poldi really was in need of a little help and she trusted her knowledge of human nature, she showed Ravi where the paint was and drove off in search of some peace beside the sea. Ravi was welcome to loot the house—somehow, she suddenly couldn't have cared less.

She drove to Praiola, her favorite little beach not far away, where the water is clear and cobalt-blue and the shore consists entirely of rounded volcanic pebbles that look like fossilized dinosaur eggs.

Once there, Poldi dunked her feet in the water and tossed a little dinosaur egg into the sea in memory of Peppe. Folding her hands on her chest, she bowed and said softly,

"*Namaste,* life!" And then, "The rest of the world can kiss my arse!"

The symphony of the waves soothed her. Seated on the canvas stool she'd brought with her, she watched them breaking sluggishly on the shore. For Poldi is a Cancer, a crab, a creature of transition and constant change, always on the edge, always at home somewhere between two elements at the point where land and sea meet.

Near noon a figure approached her. Recognizing Montana from a long way off, Poldi watched him picking his way toward her over the boulders.

He sat down beside her and started to say something, but she took his hand and said, "Ssh! First, just listen to the sea."

Montana lapsed into silence for a moment, but he couldn't keep it up.

"Are you terminally ill or something? I'm worried about you. What are you keeping from me?"

Poldi looked around. Not a sign of Death anywhere.

"I've stopped drinking. It's a bit sexually offputting, *tesoro,* that's all."

"Are you still on the case?"

"Seriously not, and that's final."

Montana looked relieved.

"Good. Neither am I. I . . ." He cleared his throat. "I've been sent on leave."

"What? Suspended, you mean? Why?"

"An old story. I can't talk about it."

"Why not?"

"*Madonna,* because it would put you in danger!" Montana's sudden outburst made Poldi jump.

"Because of that business in Rome, you mean? Come on, say something!"

"No, Poldi, you first. What's the matter?"

What could she tell him? That she'd made a really stupid bargain with Death? She said nothing, merely squeezed his hand tighter.

"Just trust me, Vito, please! Everything's going to be fine."

Montana stared at her in bewilderment, as if she'd just fobbed him off with some consolation candy. Smiling mirthlessly, he withdrew his hand and rose. After struggling for words, all he said eventually was "Marta sends her regards."

And he strode off.

Death, leaning against Montana's Alfa, showed Poldi an eight point nine. She felt like bursting into tears.

When she got home, Ravi was sitting in the inner courtyard playing his sitar. He hadn't ransacked the house—in fact he'd cleaned the kitchen and bathroom. He stopped playing when Poldi came in and got to his feet.

"Sorry, I was just taking a break."

"Please go on playing," said Poldi. "It sounds so lovely."

So Ravi played her a few more ragas before discreetly taking his leave.

Poldi asked him to come back after Easter, complete with sitar. They bowed and said *"Namaste!"* to each other, and because a freshly cleaned house always reconciles one a little with the universe, Poldi got through this evening too without drinking.

She also managed somehow to survive Easter Sunday. That morning's message on the wall was simply DIE! She didn't bother to paint it over.

Poldi drove to Aunt Caterina's, where the whole family traditionally meets for a lunch to which everyone makes some contribution, where the table groans beneath delicacies, and where all are loved for themselves — just as long as they eat with appetite. It's my favorite get-together, actually, but at that stage I had nothing better to do than quarrel with Valérie.

The aunts spotted Poldi's disconsolate state of mind right away, of course, and went at once to Code Red, because whenever Poldi suffered a melancholic relapse they feared the worst. The three of them nagged her until she told them about the menacing graffiti, whereupon Aunt Teresa insisted that Poldi move in for a while with her and Uncle Martino. This suggestion Poldi naturally rejected outright, refusing to be driven from her home. Aunt Luisa, for her part, offered to move to Torre as a sort of personal protection officer, and also to discreetly assist Poldi with her inquiries. Poldi just managed to fend off this suggestion as well. What she failed to fend off was Totti, because Uncle Martino insisted on at least lending him to her for a while as a guard dog.

At any rate, Poldi was now, on top of everything else, saddled with a good-natured but pestilently malodorous animal. Perhaps that was the straw that broke the camel's back — Poldi couldn't really explain it to me. The fact is that she knocked off the three bottles of vodka that were still tucked away in the kitchen.

When she awoke with a mental blackout of the night before at noon on Easter Monday and tottered into the kitchen, groaning, to concoct her special hangover cure, she found a note in spidery handwriting stuck to the fridge: "Two point four."

If a person is to change course and survive the preliminary rounds, disastrous intermediate results of this kind call for resilience. It's true that at this stage Poldi still had several weeks to go to her birthday and the "deadline," and that this might have been sufficient for her to do nine point zero and make it into the next round. But it's also true that Antonella telephoned her.

8

*Tells of failure and petits fours, of killer remarks
and love, of wild mice, neglect, transparent envelopes, and Black Madonnas. Poldi's nephew abne-
gates first and then steps on the gas. Poldi is sent
another note and earns respect. She makes
Antonella's acquaintance at last, but something
again intervenes. Brrrooom, to be precise.*

F ailure," Poldi is fond of emphasizing, "is always breathing down our neck. Every success is merely the outcome
of a series of failures, so bear that in mind. It applies to
everyone — investigators, lovers, and authors of trashy novels included."

I could have devised that maxim myself — all except the
bit about success, because I know a thing or two about failure. In my case, failure always sits up front behind the wheel.
Which is to say that things weren't going well between Valérie
and me at our first reunion since France. I mean, we'd had
some magical moments, and that *had* to signify something.
Perhaps, I sometimes thought, *you're just an uptight control
freak who simply isn't made for drama and erotic passion.*
Besides, misunderstandings were preprogrammed thanks to
my clumsy Italian and my lousy French. I talked my head off,

which is always counterproductive, and all I gathered was that Valérie was somehow between two stools. She no longer knew what she wanted, because scarcely had I come into her life when—ta-daaa!—David popped up like an internet banner ad that you can click off as often as you like but that still reappears again and again. I called him Petit-Four David, because he kept throwing her emotional tidbits to which she responded mistrustfully but eagerly, as though starving. He resembled a comet that circles its sun in an elongated ellipse without ever coming close enough to burn up. David was the thorn in Valérie's heart, the unanswered question, the eternal disturber of her equilibrium.

But let's not delude ourselves, the second hardest thing is to realize that we can never change anyone. Only ourselves, but that's the hardest thing of all, and we usually prefer not to. I do, anyway. What I did want, though, just for once, was to be better than my Auntie Poldi at one thing: letting go. I didn't want her to lose another woman friend on my account, so I tried at least to be self-sacrificing.

"In that case, let's just remain friends," I said feebly, feeling immensely self-sacrificing and mature, like a character in a Hollywood movie in which a couple who were made for each other have to spend half a lifetime apart before reuniting in their twilight years.

"Go to hell!" Valérie hissed angrily. *"Mon Dieu!"*

We were going in circles, and red wine never helps. I wanted to ask what she meant, but she abruptly changed the subject.

"I'm worried about your aunt."

"Eh? Why, exactly?"

"I think she's in real trouble."

"Oh, it's just a tempest in a teapot. Poldi has everything under control."

Valérie stared at me.

"*Mon Dieu*, what has to happen before you take off that supercool mask of yours?"

"Er, meaning?"

"What if she died tomorrow? Is 'eh?' and 'er' all you'd say then too?"

A car could be heard driving into the courtyard on the other side of the house.

"What are you expecting me to do, actually?"

"*Mon Dieu!* I'm expecting you to look after her! Got that?"

"And who's going to look after me?"

"I mean it. I don't want to lose either Poldi or you, so stay with her and take care of her."

The scales finally fell from my eyes.

"So you want to get rid of me, is that it?"

"What nonsense!"

Just at that moment, as if on cue, Petit-Four David came out into the garden with one of those cool aluminum cases for holding photographic equipment in each hand.

He said a cheerful hello in French, calling Valérie *chérie*, gave me a casual nod, and indicated that he was going to take his stuff inside. He gave the impression he had always lived there. Like the master of the house, so to speak.

"What's he doing here?"

Valérie ran her fingers through her hair.

"David wants to work on a project here. Maybe it'll be better if we don't see each other for a while. I need a bit of time, okay?"

Two killer sentences from hell—just what a man likes to hear!

"Friends, then?" she asked.

I nodded. "You took the word out of my mouth."

She gave me a farewell hug, but it was one of those get-going hugs.

And because loving means letting go, I went. Without more ado, I plodded through the gateway and headed back to the road along the unsurfaced track that led past Russo's tree nursery.

I don't know how I managed it. I had no strength left, I was so overwhelmingly lovesick. I didn't just feel thin-skinned, I felt completely flayed, raw and filled with self-pity. Everything hurt. I wasn't myself anymore. All I wanted was to cease to exist—to evanesce, if that were possible. In Korean there's a word for a particular form of profound unhappiness: *han*. It's a kind of world-weariness, an overwhelming sense of helplessness, a revenge one can never take, a sadness of the soul so great that it evokes no tears, a knot in the heart that never unravels and is capable of destroying one. It was an emotion that only Koreans and my Auntie Poldi can really experience, but even I, at that moment, felt something akin to *han*.

But happiness, Poldi says, is never anything but a decision. So I resolved, on that short walk back to the road, to take a leaf out of her book and finally become a phoenix myself. To straighten out my life and not go to seed, to stop whingeing and be a better person than I was now. And while I was at it, I also resolved to let go of my ego and be there for Poldi and look after her, come what may.

On reaching the road, I called her and asked her to pick me up.

During the fifteen minutes it took her, I came to realize something strange about my emotions. It was that I no longer felt stunned or floored or anything, but relieved of a burden I'd been carrying around half my life: cry-babyism.

"Did you have a row?" Poldi asked suspiciously when she picked me up.

"No, everything's fine. Move over, I'll drive."

She stared at me.

"Are you kidding me?"

I drew a deep breath and returned her gaze.

"We're now going to solve this case."

"Did I heard you say 'we,' laddie?"

I grinned at her.

"Like it or not, Poldi, you're stuck with me. Now shift your butt, we're going to La Grotta in Santa Maria la Scala. I need a *pasta al nero,* and I want to hear how things went with Antonella."

From Femminamorta to Santa Maria la Scala is almost exactly eight kilometers. It isn't a busy road but narrow and winding, scarcely wide enough for two cars to pass each other. Oncoming lorries present a problem, not to mention motorcyclists and mountain bikers. Moreover, most of the old road is enclosed by high lava rock walls, so it's advisable to drive slowly and sound your horn before every bend if you want to reach your destination unscathed. No problem in a Fiat 500, one would think.

With the hood down and Radio Galatea 95.2 turned up

full, we puttered leisurely along. There was hardly any traffic, and we had just passed Pozzillo when I heard a sound behind us, a deep, ominous sound like that of an approaching thunderstorm. Looking in the rearview mirror, I saw a truck. One of Russo's usual palm transporters, I thought at first, but then I saw that this one looked somehow different. Black and dirty, with reflective foil stuck to the windscreen to keep the sun out. Before I had a chance to think, it was tailgating us and blowing its horn—a sinister, menacing sound resembling the roar of a wild beast.

"Hey, what's he playing at!" I exclaimed.

Poldi glanced over her shoulder.

Turning to face the front again, she said, "Step on the gas, boy. Give it all the old crate's got!"

And she fastened her seat belt.

I was just going to ask what she thought the driver was doing when the truck rammed us from behind. I uttered a yell and the little Fiat leapt forward and briefly lost traction. In spite of the spongy steering I regained control of the car somehow and just managed to avoid grazing the nearest wall.

"Shit! What's he up to?"

"Step on it, laddie!"

Easier said than done. I floored the gas pedal, but the old Fiat seemed wholly unimpressed and did not accelerate at all. The truck fell back a little and then put on speed again. Engine roaring and horn blaring, it rammed us again, more violently than the first time. The Fiat swerved. I spun the wheel.

"Don't brake!" cried Poldi. "Keep your foot down!"

We briefly went over onto two wheels and I thought we would overturn, but the Fiat engineers had evidently constructed a self-righting miracle, because our cute little car dropped back onto four wheels. I got it under control, we careened into the next bend, and I thought we might now be able to shake the truck off.

But the driver must have been a rally pro, because he roared around the bend at an undiminished speed. Hearing a crash behind us, I looked in the rearview mirror and saw that the truck had swerved, grazed a wall, and half demolished it. It simply sped on regardless, however, and it was soon back nudging our rear bumper and pushing us along in front of it like a toy. I no longer doubted that the driver intended to squash us against the nearest wall or the next oncoming vehicle. *Bang!* He rammed us again and continued to push us along.

I'm not a particularly good driver. I enjoy driving around —preferably on the slow side, but that had ceased to be an option. I coaxed all the speed I could out of the Fiat and tried to keep us in the middle of the road. It was a miracle we met no oncoming traffic, but that—purely statistically speaking—would soon change.

The truck accelerated.

I realized I was bound to lose control of our gallant little vehicle sometime, and that I'd be unable to keep my promise to take care of my Auntie Poldi. Nevertheless, I did have one advantage: I knew the road. I had driven it hundreds of times, usually engrossed in my thoughts, but I knew every bend, every fig tree, every rusty refrigerator dumped on the verge, and every almost invisible farm track that led off the road. I knew there was a gap in the wall just before Stazzo, where one of these farm tracks led to a lemon plantation. The spot was easily recognizable from a faded poster advertising the services of Mago Rampulla, clairvoyant and fortune-teller.

And then I saw the poster. We were speeding straight toward it.

At that moment, I think, my brain switched to autopilot or my reflexes took over. In many German fairgrounds there are old-fashioned timber-built roller-coasters called Wilde Maus. The Wild Mouse looks innocuous enough, but it's scary because the little cars turn ninety degrees at full speed. It's terrifying, but I can't help it: whenever I see a Wild Mouse anywhere, I have to go for a ride. And to be honest, what is a Fiat 500 if not a Wild Mouse?

Just before we reached the gap in the wall I swung the wheel over. In response to this surprising maneuver, the Fiat reacted with little delay. It made a ninety-degree turn at precisely the spot where the farm track led off to the right. Taking my foot off the gas at once, I spun the wheel somehow to get the car under control and we jolted our way into the plantation, where we grazed a single lemon tree. I could hear the truck thundering on without stopping.

Silence reigned for a moment.

No, that's wrong, because Radio Galatea 95.2 was just playing "Surfin' Safari" by the Beach Boys. I was panting, Poldi was panting. I killed the radio and turned to her.

"You okay?"

A trifle pale around the nose, Poldi smiled and laid a hand on my arm. "Not bad, my boy. Not. Bad. At all." She straightened her wig in the rearview mirror. "I could do with a bite to eat. How about you?"

"Er, and the truck? What if it comes back for us?"

"I don't think so. We'll be left in peace for today. Besides, we must get on with my backstory. After all, the two of us still have something to do."

"Er, like what?"

"Hello?" Poldi gave me a look. "Like solving the case, of course."

And while I maneuvered our gallant and slightly battered Wild Mouse out of the lemon trees, still feeling rather shaky, I must admit, she went on talking. She told me of the sad signora's curious behavior, of her pact with Death, her depressing Easter, and the moment on Easter Monday when her land-line phone rang.

"Pronto," said Poldi, employing the usual Italian response.

Unknown number.

"Antonella here."

The words sounded harsh and metallic, as if the connection was bad or a voice changer had been switched on.

"Antonella, at last!" Poldi exclaimed after a moment's surprise. Despite her hangover and the note on the fridge, all her senses were instantly on the alert. "I was afraid something might have happened to you."

"Don't talk nonsense, Donna Poldina," rasped the voice. "I know exactly what you want. You want to screw me over, that's all."

In spite of the distorter, which had clearly been turned on, Poldi thought she recognized the voice so close to her ear. It seemed almost familiar, but she couldn't think from where, so she decided to stall.

"I only want to talk to you, Antonella."

"You cold-bloodedly rejected me, Donna Poldina. You threw me away like rubbish, and I had so much to offer you. I'm like you. I'm the sun. I'm beautiful."

"I'm sure you are, Antonella."

"You don't deceive me, Donna Poldina. I can tell from your voice you're lying. You're no better than the rest. You don't understand people who feel as intensely as I do."

"Why did you call me, Antonella?"

"That's right, keep the caller talking so the tracer can kick in. How many of those swine are sitting there with you? Two? Three? Or just the good-looking *commissario* you never wanted to introduce me to?"

Antonella fell silent. Poldi remained silent too. The line crackled, and she could hear Antonella breathing. She looked over at the note on the fridge.

"I should hang up now," she said with a weary sigh. "All the best, Antonella."

"Wait!" Antonella was breathing heavily. "I must give you something."

"Like what?"

"Good God, don't be so naive!"

Poldi was galvanized. "You mean you have it?"

"I've had it for ages, but it's a threat to my existence, that's why I want you to have it. Then I'll disappear for good."

Poldi was finding the situation altogether too convoluted for her taste.

"Why trust me all of a sudden, Antonella?"

"I don't trust you in the least, Donna Poldina. I would have trusted you if you'd been more sympathetic, but you were focused on yourself alone. The Black Madonna leaves me no choice, though, so listen carefully . . ."

After Antonella had told her when and where to meet her and hung up, Poldi continued to hold the receiver in her hand for a while, as though some last little piece of information had lodged in a crack and might seep out of it.

Still staring at the note on the fridge, she thought of her birthday, of Montana, of the late Peppe, of the Black Madonna, Death, and Signora Cocuzza. And she came to a decision.

"Bollocks!"

With a resolute gesture, she snatched the slip of paper reading "2.4" off the fridge, crumpled it up, and tossed it away.

"Now pin back your ears, Death!" she shouted at the top of her voice. "When my time's up, so be it, I don't care. That's because I'm Poldi, you hear? I don't let anyone dictate how I live. You can come for me on my birthday, buddy, but by then I'll have solved this case, I promise you. And I'm going to booze to my heart's content if I feel like it! *And* screw anyone I want! Because that's the way I am. Because otherwise life wouldn't be worth a damn . . . *Namaste*!"

True to her favorite mottos, "Moderation is a sign of weakness" and "Always overdress," at three o'clock on the dot she appeared in Catania's Piazza Duomo wearing a mallow-colored skirt with floral appliqués, an apricot blouse, a floral headscarf, huge sunglasses, and cream-colored court shoes—a thoroughly vernal and Easterish get-up, in other words. Casually, casting unobtrusive glances in all directions, she strolled around Catania's famous landmark, the fountain with the obelisk and the little black elephant.

A clear blue April sky discreetly stippled with bouffant cumulus clouds, the cathedral, the elephant, and, at the end of Via Etnea, the distant shape of Etna still mantled with snow. A kitschier postcard subject could not be imagined.

"I've always known," said Poldi, digressing abruptly, "that I lived beside the elephant fountain in an earlier life. Elephants always were my favorite animals, and they made a splendid sight in Tanzania."

"Aha," I said, rather thrown by this hiatus in her story.

"Did you know that it brings everlasting happiness if you kiss that elephant on the bum?"

"What? You couldn't get to it, you'd break your neck climbing up the plinth. Everlasting happiness my eye!"

She cast her eyes up to heaven. "That's what's called an ironic metaphor—bear it in mind for your novel. Hey, prize question: What would you do if God told you, 'If you climb up there and kiss that little elephant on the bum, I'll grant you everlasting happiness, but there's a fifty-fifty chance you'll break your neck'?"

I stared at her.

She nodded. "See? That's the difference between you and me."

Italian families traditionally spend *Pasquetta,* or Easter Monday, going on little excursions or walks to drum up an appetite after the gluttony of Easter Sunday. Consequently, the piazza was thronged with dolled-up Italian families and less dolled-up study tour Germans in three-quarter-length trousers and functional clothing. Outside the pavement cafés facing the cathedral, waiters hurried from table to table laden with *granite di mandorla, brioche, gelati, cornetti, arancini, cannoli di ricotta, babà al rum,* ice cream cakes, coffees, spritzes, lemonades, and freshly pressed juices in such profusion one might have assumed that paradise began at the counters just inside.

Poldi briefly debated whether to wait for Antonella over a coffee and grappa, but decided to adhere to instructions. Graceful as a diva from a fifties movie, she tweaked her skirt into place over her knees, enjoyed the looks she attracted, and flirted with a mustachioed traffic cop wearing an immaculate uniform and—in celebration of Easter Monday —a white tropical helmet.

So she may have been a trifle distracted—these things happen even to the best of professionals—because she suddenly found herself confronted and stared at by a little girl not much more than eight or nine years old. The girl was wearing a plain pale-blue cotton dress and did not seem to belong to one of the Roma families in the square.

"Hello," Poldi said amiably. "Who are you?"

"Are you Donna Poldina?"

"Why? Would you like to take a selfie with me?" Poldi asked, feeling flattered.

The girl shook her head and put out her hand. "I'm to give you this."

It was a slip of paper bearing an address and the words "Pandolfino button."

Before Poldi could ask the little girl who had given it to her, she ran off across the piazza.

Poldi jumped up and looked around. It dawned on her only now that she must have been under surveillance the whole time, and she cursed herself for not having taken more care. No use crying over spilled milk, though. Checking the address on her mobile phone, she was faintly uneasy to discover that she had to go to Librino.

Librino is a district near the airport in the southwest of Catania, a housing estate consisting of soulless blocks of flats devoid of greenery. Cheaply and hurriedly constructed on the edge of the city during the seventies building boom, it exemplifies the greed, corruption, and degeneracy of a whole generation of politicians, civil servants, and building contractors. It was planned in such a comfortless and dehumanizing way that it couldn't fail to become a hotbed of decay, neglect, and crime. Anyone growing up there is out of luck, has little schooling and no work. All that remains is the Mafia, which recruits its *picciotti*—its young toughs—from there.

There are suburbs like Librino all over the world, and they all fulfill the same purpose: they enrich their builders and impoverish as many of their residents as possible, because even though their victims' shame at their own poverty occasionally spills over into rage and public disorder, they form a solid base for populist parties that invariably promise them everything and never keep their word. It's a system that has always functioned admirably.

So it was no wonder Poldi felt a little apprehensive in her Easter outfit as she rode her brightly painted Vespa around the run-down apartment houses in search of the address on the slip of paper.

The universal state of decay was shocking. Mounds of garbage lined the streets; some of the high-rises stood empty and looked as if they'd been bombed. In one locality replicas of them were under construction. They already looked half dilapidated. Looking for street signs was a waste of time.

Rather disoriented, Poldi cruised around in search of someone she could ask for directions, but the streets were deserted save for some youths on mopeds who followed her for a while, eventually drew level, and hemmed her in like an escort of outriders. Guessing what would happen now, she wasn't frightened, just angry that her meeting with Antonella would probably fall through.

The youths on their mopeds drew even closer.

"Pull over!" called the one on her right, and he spat into the roadway.

Poldi pulled over, but she remained seated on the Vespa and kept the engine running.

The youth who had stopped her sauntered over, spitting again as he came.

"Nice Vespa," he said in a strong Sicilian accent. "I like it."

"Good for you, sonny," said Poldi. "Happy Easter."

The youth smirked at his pals, snorted, and spat.

"Kill the engine and get off."

"Oh no, sonny, you'll have to lift me off first."

In a trice the youth had a knife in his hand and was holding it under her nose. "Get off, I said!"

But he was reckoning without my Auntie Poldi. Quick as a flash, she twisted the knife out of his hand and used her other hand to give him a resounding slap in the face.

"I'll do nothing of the kind, you lousy little turd!" she yelled at him in broad Bavarian. Then, turning to the others, "And now push off, the lot of you, or you'll regret it!"

It was always worth a try. The German language, especially when laden with Bavarian dialect, has a thoroughly deterrent effect in Sicily.

The youth stared at her in bewilderment. His pals looked equally flummoxed.

Poldi was about to ride off when her assailant said haltingly, "Are you by any chance . . . Donna Poldina?"

"Yes, I most certainly am."

His face cleared in an instant.

"Hey," he called delightedly to his pals, "it's Donna Poldina, the crazy detective!"

"Eh? The one on Radio Galatea?"

"That's her!"

Poldi now paid something of a price for having listened to the station so seldom. She was promptly surrounded by the youngsters, who got out their mobile phones and took excited selfies.

"What?" I exclaimed, breaking in on Poldi's flow of words. "How come they called you 'the crazy detective'?"

We were sitting at a table outside my favorite eating place, the little La Grotta in Santa Maria la Scala, which serves excellent *pasta al nero* and the world's best seafood salad.

Poldi, sipping some ice-cold white wine, looked rather embarrassed.

"Well, they'd made a sort of compilation, a crude mix of remarks of mine they'd recorded at the lido, and they broadcast it regularly between records. Just stupid gibberish in Italian and Bavarian. Meaningless, the whole thing, but not bad all the same. A bit of hip-hop or rap, and always preceded by a little jingle: 'A rap on the international situation by Donna Poldina, the crazy detective!'"

I was mystified. "And you lent yourself to that?"

"I thought I was just being interviewed, damn it!"

I grinned maliciously. "No, Poldi, vanity got the better of you."

"A little respect, please, I'm still your aunt!" She drained her glass. "Besides, every cloud has a silver lining, remember that. I naturally kicked up a hell of a fuss, and the radio station ponied up the Fiat 500 in compensation."

Poldi was understandably thrown for a moment when she learned of her newfound celebrity as a crazy, rapping detective, but she knows how to make the best of any situation, even if she has to overstep the mark occasionally.

"What's your name, sonny?" she asked the spokesman of the little gang.

"Saro."

Poldi showed him the address on the slip of paper. "Do you know where that is, Saro?"

Saro glanced at the address and looked at her suspiciously.

"Why do you want to know?"

Poldi is quicker on the uptake than most.

"You look to me like someone with his head screwed on, Saro. Someone who doesn't let himself get suckered, am I right?"

Saro snorted, spat, glanced around at his pals, and nodded.

"So I'll be honest with you, Saro . . ." Poldi paused and spat in the interests of street cred. "I want to sucker someone. It's a joke for Radio Galatea, understand?"

I don't know how she manages it, but the most brazen lies pass her lips with consummate ease and people believe them.

In any event, five minutes later the youngsters had guided Poldi to a twenty-story high-rise. Having parked her Vespa behind a skip, she inspected the building and its entrance from a distance. From the way the youths crouched behind her in the lee of the skip, they weren't unacquainted with such games of hide-and-seek.

"You'll stay here and keep an eye on things," Poldi told Saro, giving him her phone number. "If you see two guys in fluorescent sneakers, call me at once, okay? They're twins, so they're easily recognizable."

"What's in it for us?" Saro grumbled.

With a sigh, Poldi reached in her handbag and produced a fifty-euro note.

"And there'll be another fifty when I'm through."

"You aren't planning to kill or kidnap someone, are you?" Saro demanded. "That'd cost more."

Poldi gazed at him sternly.

"You're no fool, Saro, but I'm worried about you, very worried. No, I'm not planning to kill or kidnap anyone. I want to conduct an interview, that's all, but I don't want to be killed or kidnapped myself. How does that strike you?"

Saro snorted. "*Beh!*" He spat. "But if you aren't back in an hour, we scoot. With your Vespa."

Poldi emerged from behind the skip.

The flat was on the ninth floor. The lift was kaput, of course, so she dragged her bad knee up the stairs, flight after flight, and took a short breather on every landing. The whole building stank of garbage and urine. From the flats she passed came the sound of televisions turned up loud, quarreling couples, bawling children, and thudding bass notes.

The few residents she encountered eyed her suspiciously but flitted past without a word.

A quarter of an hour had elapsed by the time Poldi rang the Pandolfino bell on the ninth floor, and no one came to the door. She listened and rang again. Nothing. Not a sound, no footsteps, no reaction at all.

What a lousy, depressing last Easter I'm having, Poldi thought disconsolately. She considered simply turning around and getting thoroughly drunk at home.

But then she tried the handle and—*click*—the door opened.

In movies the tough heroine always enters an apartment gripping her automatic in the regulation two-handed manner and accompanied by her partner, whom she trusts implicitly. She skirts the wall, glancing into every room, gives a hand signal, and presses on until all hell breaks loose. Such is the usual form, but at that stage I was still in France and Poldi was unarmed.

She cautiously pushed the front door open and tiptoed along a short passage flanked by the bathroom and kitchen.

"Hello? Antonella?"

No reply.

But by now Poldi guessed what awaited her at the end of the passage. She crept past the kitchen and bathroom into the main room of the studio. Antonella was lying on a mattress in the corner. Poldi knew at once that it was Antonella, even though she was lying in a strangely contorted attitude, with her face half buried in the grubby bedclothes. She was wearing the patterned tracksuit from the video. Poldi saw at a glance how she had died. The back of her head had been staved in, and the pool of blood around it had not yet congealed, which implied that her murder was very recent. Poldi promptly visualized all the neighbors she'd passed on the stairs and cursed herself for not taking careful note of their faces.

When visiting the scene of a crime, Poldi once told me, it's only gradually that you become aware of all the details. The sight of someone who has been beaten to death, strangled, stabbed, or shot is always a shock that initially claims your full attention. Apart from the corpse, Poldi was only marginally aware of the stench of garbage and the shabby décor, the full extent of the squalor, the piles of unwashed clothing, the bulging trash bags and stacks of pizza boxes, the heaps of newspapers—in fact all the junk and plastic gewgaws Antonella had accumulated over the years.

Antonella had been a hoarder, no doubt about it, and her flat was so clogged with clutter that Poldi failed to notice Death sitting on the sofa until he gently cleared his throat. Still sporting his silly ninja outfit complete with sword, he was holding his clipboard on his lap and carefully filling out a series of forms, the multicolored carbon copies of which he neatly tore off along the perforated lines and inserted in various plastic envelopes lying beside him on the sofa.

"Almost finished," he said without looking up. "This paperwork is killing me. A new form comes out every year. We filed away the dinosaurs all in one go, but these days head office wants every single death documented in umpteen copies. It's purely a job-creation measure, of course, because the whole administrative apparatus has become so bloated in the last five thousand years, you've no idea. One department doesn't know what the other is doing, and the result is that innumerable lost souls are log-jammed in limbo. What do you think is the current waiting time for a normal reincarnation date? I'll tell you: two thousand years plus! I'm not joking. In the case of guardian angels it's almost ten thousand. And digitization is out, obviously! Insufficient resources, they say. Why mess with success, they say. Fine, until the system runs full tilt into a brick wall and we have to shut down completely. I'd like to see what head office does then." Death looked up at last. "Do sit down."

He brushed aside a couple of see-through envelopes and patted the vacant cushion invitingly.

Poldi sat down.

"When did she die?" she asked softly.

Death glanced at his list. "Twenty-one minutes past three."

"That's less than twenty minutes ago."

"Yes, and that's why I'm still sitting here with the paperwork, as you can see."

Poldi gripped Death by the scruff of the neck and shook him violently.

"Hey, what are you doing?"

"Are you listening to me at all? A person has been brutally murdered, and you're filling out forms. Have you no heart?"

"I'm only doing my job, Poldi," wailed Death. "You know that. I'm only responsible for transfers. Don't shoot the messenger!"

She let go of him and drew a deep breath.

"All right," she said, controlling herself with a supreme effort. "I want to know who did it, and no excuses. Don't plead regulations or I'll flip my lid!"

"Okay," Death said with a sigh. "Just this once, Poldi. Because it's you."

And he told her a name.

"No!"

"Yes!"

"No!"

"Hell's bells, why do you never believe me?"

Having consumed a plate of pasta in squid ink, a heavenly seafood salad, and a small sea bream from the grill, I felt as if nothing more could shake me.

Although I was still haunted by the recent attempt to kill us, my little Wild Mouse maneuver had also left me with a kind of adrenaline high. I felt like a motor-racing god, a rally genius, a speedster. I would be employable anytime as a getaway driver.

All that slightly dented my sense of well-being was a little pang of conscience with respect to the octopus sauce, and I wondered if I was really ready for an octopus tattoo if I was still so fond of eating those wonderful creatures.

And then Poldi pulled this one on me!

"You mean that's it?" I exclaimed, disappointed. "He told you the name of the murderer and that's all?"

"Murderer or murderess, I don't recall which."

"Come on. Did he tell you a name or didn't he?"

"He did!" said Poldi. "I remember that distinctly, but not the name itself, because everything suddenly went haywire. All I know now is, the name got stuck somewhere inside me and wants out. It's sort of connected to my mind map, understand?"

"You're shitting me, Poldi."

"God give me strength! Haven't you caught on yet? It's a metaphor for the subconscious, if you know what that is."

I'm not a complete fool.

"So what you're saying," I summarized, "is that all the clues pointing to the murderer or murderess were already subconsciously known to you, but you couldn't place them?"

"*Cento punti*, my boy. The suspects had already been narrowed down, but I didn't realize that until later, using POLDI."

"Er, just a moment . . . You know who it was?"

"Yes, of course, what did you think?" She sighed. "All we have to do now is prove it."

"You said 'we,' Poldi."

"Silly of me, wasn't it?"

"Well, I'll be buggered!" Poldi exclaimed, looking stunned. "But why?"

Death shrugged. "I've no information on the subject, you know that." He made a theatrical gesture that embraced the whole of the late Antonella's room. "*Voilà!* You're the detective. Oh, and by the way . . ." He reached behind him and brought out his scorecard, which he held under Poldi's nose: zero point zero. "Just saying."

Poldi ignored this. She was too busy taking a closer look at the room.

"Well, I'll be buggered!" she said again.

For her attention had been caught by several objects in the accumulated rubbish that were not consistent with the image of a squalid hoarder. The first was the neatly dressed wig on a wooden stand on the windowsill. Almost the same model as Poldi herself wore, real black hair plumped up into a beehive. Beside this, looking like a strange little altar, were various Madonna figures of every size in wood, plaster, or plastic, all their hands and faces black. Then there was the collection of photo and press cuttings on the only bare wall facing the sofa. Going closer, Poldi saw that nearly all the photos were of herself, and that they had been secretly taken by Antonella over the last few months. Many seemed to have been taken at such short range than Antonella must have been standing within arm's reach. Poldi couldn't understand why she had never noticed the woman. In addition, there were photos of Montana, me, the aunts, sad Signora Cocuzza, and Padre Paolo. Antonella had clearly kept Poldi and her surroundings under surveillance for months on end. But what really took Poldi's breath away was the rest of the photos, which showed her home from the inside. Her décor, her knickknacks, the antique muskets on the wall, open kitchen cupboards, the inner courtyard, her bedroom and wardrobe, my own bedroom in the attic. Antonella had even taken a selfie seated on Poldi's sofa, wearing a wig and one of Poldi's dresses, the red one with the white polka dots.

When Poldi turned away from inspecting the photo gallery, the sofa was unoccupied and all was silent, very silent, as if the world were frozen with terror.

Making her way around Antonella's dead body, Poldi discovered a number of familiar objects among her conglomeration of rubbish: a coffee cup bearing Munich's coat of arms, a Hacker-Pschorr beer tankard, an old corkscrew with the vine-wood handle, a small enamel box containing seashells, a decorated plate that had belonged to her parents, a gold chain with coral pendants, a handbook stolen from the Abu Dhabi Hilton, a floral summer dress, a pair of sandals, even some underwear. All things of no great value which Poldi had missed at some stage without remembering how or when they had disappeared—as is the way with the things we accumulate and take through life with us; some of them seem to vanish without trace, often without our noticing. From the look of it, Antonella had repeatedly gained access to No. 29 Via Baronessa and purloined little personal possessions.

Swallowing hard, Poldi used her investigative scanner vision to look around for clues and leads, conscious that the smallest detail might be important. This was no easy task, because there were plenty of details in this hoarder's paradise. Her eye was caught again by the wall with the photos on it. It would soon be time to notify the police, so she took one photo of the whole wall and a series of detailed shots.

With a groan, she went down on her knees beside the corpse and forced herself to inspect the head wound. It looked really nasty. The skull had clearly been shattered with a heavy, sharp-edged object. Poldi had been unable to detect any signs of a break-in, which is always a pointer to the relationship between victim and perpetrator.

"Why, Antonella?" whispered Poldi, as if there were still a chance that the dead woman might open her eyes for the last time and answer her. "Why?"

But Antonella remained silent.

Instead, Poldi's mobile phone rang.

"*Pronto?*"

"Donna Poldina? It's me, Saro."

"I'm going to need a bit longer in here, Saro," Poldi told him with a sigh.

"That may not be a good idea, Donna Poldina. Two guys

in fluorescent sneakers have just gone into the building. They look like twins."

Poldi stiffened. "Thanks, Saro. Call the cops and then beat it! I'll pay you later."

She hung up.

She had no chance to do more. She simply couldn't get up off her knees before she heard the sound behind her. Not a loud sound, but menacing, powerful, malevolent, and nerve-racking.

BRRROOOM!

It sounded like the distant trumpets of an evil army.

And again: *BRRROOOM!*

Poldi gave a start and made another attempt to get up.

For one thing, however, she was hampered by her bad knee, and, for another, a hand was already clamped across her mouth from behind.

She felt a sharp pain in her neck. It seemed to squeeze all the light out of her world and plunge her into a colorless abyss.

BRRROOOM!
BRRROOOM!

9

Tells of clues, policemen, the Black Madonna (of course), mentors, mass manufacture, and Pirate's Dice. Poldi is in a fix again. Her nephew gets the bit between his teeth and learns something about applause and humility. Poldi is ostracized and again has plenty of time to think. She receives definite demands to advance a certain deadline, together with good news and bad news.

*B*rrrooom?" I chuckled, rather at a loss and still keyed up, when Poldi demonstrated the sound à la beatbox.

"Don't you know it? Of course you do. Wait, I'll show you."

She fished out her laptop and showed me a video from the internet, a compilation of scenes from various action movies. Underlying them all was the same sound effect, which I now recognized too: a menacing, nightmarish, synthesized *BRRROOOM!* that pierces you to the marrow and in Hollywood blockbusters almost invariably portends disasters of all kinds, extraterrestrial in particular.

"What was making the sound?"

"If I knew that, I'd be the wiser."

"And where did it come from all of a sudden, the hand holding the hypo of anesthetic?"

"I don't know," she admitted. "Maybe I should have taken a closer look in the bathroom and kitchen. Failure is always breathing down one's neck, not that I need to tell *you* that."

A lone thought stumbled rather forlornly through the desert in my brain.

"Tell me, Poldi . . . When that woman called me in France a few days ago, mimicking your voice . . . was Antonella already dead by then?"

"*Cento punti,* my boy. You were paying attention."

"Yes, but who was it? I mean, someone commits a murder, and they also very conveniently have some anesthetic handy? And don't give me the 'There are more things in heaven and earth, Horatio'!"

Poldi sighed. "Patience."

The first thing Poldi registered, when the world gradually took on color again, was that she was lying on the sofa. She sat up with a groan but immediately felt dizzy, so she lay back and drew several deep breaths. Only then did she make another attempt. Nice and slow. Her head was buzzing worse than it did after a binge. Sitting up at last, she saw to her surprise that the general situation was unchanged. Antonella's dead body was still lying on the mattress in front of her. That apart, she appeared to be alone.

"Hello?" she croaked experimentally, but there was no reply.

Still rather dazed, she felt the puncture wound in her neck and wondered why she hadn't been killed, just knocked out and left where she was. On the other hand, she wasn't due to die until her birthday.

Only explanation: the killer had wanted to vamoose without being identified or committing another murder.

She wondered what that could mean, but she didn't get very far with her deliberations, because at that moment she saw she had blood on her hands. A lot of blood. And there was more blood on her clothing.

Staring at her hands and her pretty Austrian petticoat outfit, Poldi emitted a cross between a squeak and a whimper. Panic-stricken, she wiped her hands on the petticoat, drew a deep breath, and yelled at the top of her voice.

"HEEEEELP!"

As though on cue, the front door, which was already ajar anyway, was kicked open. Poldi heard pounding footsteps and a tense voice shout, "Clear!" And again, "Clear!" Then, like a pair of Dobermans let off the leash, two strapping young carabinieri dashed into the living room with pistols drawn. They came to an abrupt and simultaneous halt at the sight of Poldi and the corpse.

"*Madonna mia!*" gasped one of them, crossing himself.

"Who are you?" demanded the other, and he pointed his gun at my aunt to preclude any misunderstandings.

A standard situation for Poldi, actually. She raised her blood-smeared hands and was about to essay an explanation when the front door was kicked in again.

The carabinieri spun round.

From the passage came the sound of pounding footsteps and tense, successive cries of "Check!" Then two tubby members of the State Police rushed in with pistols drawn, almost colliding with their colleagues from the competition. They stopped dead, caught sight of the corpse, exclaimed

"*Madonna mia!*" and crossed themselves. A triple shock: a murder victim in a pool of blood, the perpetrator alongside, the competition in situ.

Rather overwhelmed by the situation, all four public servants froze.

"It wasn't me this time!" cried Poldi, still holding her bloodstained hands in the air.

The four policemen naturally took this as a confession of some earlier misdemeanor, but all she had meant was that this time she hadn't inadvertently called both emergency numbers, 112 and 113. The former belongs to the Carabinieri, the latter to the State Police.

Policing in Italy is handled by a number of different forces that are partly intended to keep each other under control. The trouble is, this democratically shrewd system leads in practice to a bloated administrative setup and uncertainty regarding spheres of responsibility. In short, carabinieri and state police can't stand each other. This is due among other things to the fact that carabinieri are traditional targets for derision and mean jokes characterizing them as intellectual boobies. The truth, as ever, is more complicated.

Poldi already guessed that the usual argy-bargy—the duplicated questions and bickering about jurisdiction—would soon begin. In order to shorten the proceedings a little, she wanted to deliver a brief explanation of the situation. Before she could utter a word, however, the four policemen lowered their guns and exchanged salutations.

"*Ciao*, Salvo. Happy Easter."

"Happy Easter, Luca!"

"How's tricks, Gianni?"

"Is your daughter better, Tano?"

"She's fine, hardly coughing at all now."

Poldi looked on in astonishment as the four men kissed each other on both cheeks and slapped each other on the back like old pals meeting on the beach of a Sunday.

"Okay, what have we here?" the tubby policeman whose name was Gianni asked brightly.

He looked around the room, paying no more attention to Poldi than he would have to a piece of furniture.

As though in response to a word of command, all four men pulled on latex gloves.

"Female person, early forties," the carabiniere named Tano said in a businesslike tone, bending over Antonella's body. "Severe cranial injuries inflicted with a heavy object, I'd say. Time of death? At a guess, an hour ago." He looked at his colleagues.

The other three glanced at the corpse and nodded.

"The deceased appears to have been killed where found," the carabiniere went on matter-of-factly. "Female suspect still at the crime scene. Has blood on her hands and clothing and has already made a partial confession."

"Just a minute, guys!" cried Poldi, but no one was listening.

"Makes a slightly confused impression," his colleague Salvo amplified. "May have taken drugs and is, judging by her accent, a foreigner."

"Hellooo?" Poldi put in loudly.

The state cop made a soothing gesture. "We'll get to you in a minute, signora. Please be patient for a little longer." He turned to his carabiniere colleague. "Would you mind, Salvo?"

"Of course, Gianni."

All four of them would have earned stars for courtesy and

professionalism. With absolutely no demur and no arguments over hierarchy, Salvo stationed himself at the living room door. The others looked as cool and experienced as heart surgeons performing an appendectomy.

Poldi, who really did have plenty of experience with policemen by now, had never witnessed anything like this display of cooperation. She didn't like it somehow—not in the least. She decided to leave, but no sooner had she started to get up than Salvo forced her gently but firmly down on the sofa.

"Please remain seated, signora, or I shall have to cuff you."

"Kindly call Commissario Montana of the Polizia di Stato in Acireale," Poldi told him. "He'll soon dispel this little misunderstanding."

The four policemen ignored this. Three of them were looking at the photo wall and comparing the pictures of Poldi with the original on the sofa.

She was beginning to feel uneasy. When the trio who had been obscuring the photo wall stepped aside, Poldi gained the impression that something about it had changed. To make quite sure, she took her phone from her bag. It was scarcely in her hand, however, before Salvo took it off her, inserted it in an evidence bag, and put it in his pocket without a word.

"You're making a mistake, *Brigadiere,* believe me."

"How about this for the murder weapon?" asked Luca, the other state cop.

All four policemen focused their gaze on an object on the windowsill. Poldi couldn't see it properly because Luca was standing in the way. She saw them nod in agreement, but that was all.

"The weight and size are about right," said Gianni. "The object displays bloodstains and smears of brain tissue." He looked at his colleague Tano. "*Beh!* How are we going to handle this? Do you want the case, or shall we take care of it? You were here first, so it's up to you."

The carabiniere shrugged his shoulders. "It's all the same to me, but we've got a few men off sick. You're welcome to the case."

"*Benissimo,*" said Gianni. "In that case, we've gone as far as we can here, so we'd better call the cavalry. What do you think?"

Nods all round.

Luca stepped aside to call forensics and homicide.

Poldi at last saw the relevant object: Antonella's wig. Or rather, the carved wooden stand over which Antonella had draped it. Poldi had paid little attention to it during her inspection of the room. Now, however, she saw what the stand really was: a fifteen-inch Black Madonna.

"No!"

"Yes!"

"No!"

"Know something, sonny? You're starting to bug me."

"Don't take it amiss, Poldi, but I'm beginning to think you're going over the top. Not only does the Black Madonna suddenly reappear, but it has to be desecrated as a murder weapon. Seriously?"

"Yes, goddammit! You only find that hard to believe

because you, in your stuffy little ivory tower, have absolutely no feeling for the intricacies of the universe and the secret ebb and flow of human destiny."

I put my fingers in my ears and fluttered my lips like a horse.

"All right," Poldi went on, unimpressed, "so you haven't had the magnificent mentors I had. You do have me, but *my* great mentors equipped me for life with the three invaluable 'alwayses.'"

"So tell me, Poldi," I said with a sigh. "I'm lucky enough to have *you,* but who were the great mentors in *your* life?"

"Why, Vivienne Westwood, Simone de Beauvoir, and Tina Turner, of course."

I tell you, these things trip off her tongue with such fluency, I bet she could outsmart her POLDI—her own lie detector. She didn't even blink.

"What I learned from Vivienne," she went on, "was 'Always overdress.' Back in Paris when I was very young, Simone told me, 'Everything always seems impossible until you do it.' As for that nutcake Tina, she told me, 'Always expect the unexpected.'"

"Okay. So what happened then?"

"Why, then they remanded me in custody on suspicion of murder. My DNA and fingerprints were all over the place, I was present at the crime scene at almost the time of the murder, and Antonella had been stalking me, which was a first-class motive. The magistrate in Catania, a Dottore Marino, didn't hesitate."

As may well be imagined, I spent a sleepless night after such an agitating day. There was something disturbing, terrifying, about the idea that someone with a perfectly impersonated voice had ordered me back to Sicily in order to kill someone. I had never believed in demons or anything of that kind, but after hearing Poldi's account, which wasn't very reassuring, I suddenly didn't feel so certain anymore. I was dog-tired but pumped up at the same time.

Because it's the best way of sending myself to sleep, I opened my laptop and, after not writing for several weeks, resumed work on my family saga.

I could feel them, the adjectives. They whirled around inside me, snarling and clamoring like chained demons. Impatient, tender, sensual, comical, puzzling, sophisticated, supercool, bestsellerish adjectives, they were all in urgent need of an airing.

Some of you may perhaps remember: Barnaba, my great-grandfather and the hero of my epic, had emigrated as a young man from Sicily to Munich in 1919, on orders from the Devil. He had withstood innumerable distressing ordeals and hardships and, with the help of his mysterious aunt and mentor Pasqualina and the preternaturally beautiful Cyclops Ilaria, built up a fruiterer's empire. He had also risen to become the boss of a certain organization that, operating in a kind of legal gray area, carried on a flourishing import-export business. Barnaba had sired countless children in Catania and Munich, both in and out of wedlock, among them sickly Federico and brawny Walter. Together with Pasqualina, he had—among many other things—discovered Atlantis, found the treasure of the Knights Templar, cracked the Enigma code, and paved the way for the Allied invasion of Sicily. Finally, in a shattering and emotionally draining showdown, he had died in a hail of bullets fired by his envious competitors.

I was naturally aware that Barnaba's heroic death would come as an almost unbearable shock to my readers, but I couldn't help that. The plot had long ago developed its own nerve-racking dynamic and was mercilessly driving me on.

In any event, it is now 1945. The war is over, Germany lies in ruins, and the black market is booming. American GIs patrol the streets of Munich, chewing gum, dancing to swing, and doling out chocolate. I made a note to research this turning point in history more thoroughly at a later stage and bring it to life again in rich and colorful language. I could almost see it in my mind's eye: great cinema, real Hollywood material.

After the death of his unique and irreplaceable parent, my grandfather, the frail and sickly Federico, continues to make ends meet as an alteration tailor in Westermühlstrasse. He very seldom goes out, being allergic to sunlight, and suffers constantly from the föhn and the umpteen vague ailments that have turned him into a hypochondriac and convinced him he is soon to die. Or so I imagine. Walter, by contrast, is an ultrafit, ultra-Bavarian toughie who earns his living as an assistant to the Munich protection racket. He seems to display a certain talent for the business and goes about his rough manual labor with touchingly childish enthusiasm and considerable imagination. He simply has a feeling for human anatomy and the innumerable varieties of pain that can be inflicted on it.

The previous three years have been really hard on the dissimilar half-brothers, but being thrashed almost daily by their father's enemies has welded them together. They owe their survival to the intervention of their great-aunt Pasqualina and a protective spell cast by the preternaturally beautiful Cyclops Ilaria. Dissimilar though the half-brothers seem, they take after their father in two respects: virility and irascibility. They're Sicilians, albeit only half so in Walter's case. Even sickly Federico is endowed with impressive, voracious *sicilianità* and, with Walter's fraternal assistance, learns to assuage it regularly at certain establishments. However, Federico remains shy in matters of the heart, is distressingly teased by girls, and longs to be put out of his misery by a *grand amour*—or by his next attack of asthma. Meanwhile, Pasqualina teaches the brothers how Sicilian fury can be turned into success in business. Now that the war is over, she maps out a golden future for them in which, with fiery *sicilianità*, entrepreneurship, and a certain flexibility in their choice of expedients, they will be able to achieve great things. And after three years of pain and hardship, the brothers really are very, very angry. So . . . no sooner said than done.

From now on Federico produces smart bespoke suits for war profiteers and American officers and fashionable evening dresses for their fräuleins, while Walter roams dark, bomb-gutted Munich with garrotes, knuckledusters, and a list of names given him by Pasqualina, settling certain debts and rearranging the balance of power in the city's black market. Through Pasqualina he also obtains contracts from foreign secret services that likewise have debts to settle in chaotic postwar Germany, and are dependent on reliable local outworkers who ask no questions.

My grandfather Federico's elegant tailoring is soon so highly esteemed by the U.S. authorities that the acquisition of cigarettes, nylon stockings, soap, and other luxury articles no longer presents a problem, and the brothers, with Pasqualina's assistance, attain the higher reaches of the black market. They also invest in the entertainment business and open two discreet nightclubs, the Bar Amore and the Fräulein Darling. Recruiting young and willing staff is no problem these days. The job of selecting and training the girls is naturally reserved for the bosses, Federico and Walter being experts in that field. While ordinary Germans subsist on maize gruel, the brothers are soon sporting smart suits and quaffing bubbly. This wonderful period of reawakening and recovery, which continues undiminished after the currency reform, could have led to a happy ending if the situation hadn't been so complicated, as usual, and if something hadn't intervened.

Besides, I felt it was getting to be time for another firecracker—a complete surprise, but one that was wholly consistent with the storyline and characters: a turning point that would mark the beginning of the end. And what could be more suitable for this than an unrequited passion? I imagined Federico falling hopelessly in love with Valeria, the incredibly beautiful and mysterious daughter of a Russian oligarch. (Note to self: Were there any oligarchs at that period? If not, leave it anyway. Sounds good and no one'll notice.) Valeria hails from an ancient Russian family of royal blood, is two heads taller than Federico, and her beauty and passionate nature exceed all bounds. Raphael, Titian, and Botticelli would have gone mad about her. Federico showers Valeria with expensive gifts, warbles nightly serenades beneath her window, and starts learning Russian. He even gives up his visits to the Bar Amore and the Fräulein Darling. All to no avail. Although Valeria takes pleasure in the shy, sad-eyed little runt of a Sicilian and particularly enjoys being plied with gifts, she refuses his entreaties even when certain rumors about the brothers' legendary virility come to her ears. Why? Because Valeria is betrothed to a pockmarked, unintelligent, impotent Uzbek clan chieftain and gangster named Darkhan Davidov, who lives on a diet of minced ass's heart, raw garlic, and sour mare's milk. (Note to self: At least 3 pp. on Darkhan's vile and repulsive personality.) A contract killer and torturer of the worst sort, Darkhan operates internationally and is a danger to world peace. He has to be eliminated, if only for Valeria's sake, but Federico and Walter, although not inexperienced in these matters, simply can't lure him into a trap. Being the son of a rainmaker, Darkhan is used to working with black magic, which is why Valeria fell prey to him. The half-brothers' businesses suddenly go downhill, Federico's gifts to Valeria threaten to ruin him, and the Bar Amore and Fräulein Darling burn down in quick succession.

Vitus Tanner, the Munich detective inspector, archenemy of Barnaba and former lover of Pasqualina, recovers from his insanity and proceeds to investigate Pasqualina and the brothers. He even succeeds in remanding Pasqualina in custody on a far-fetched charge, but an army of international shyster lawyers gets her out within a week. She does, however, have to assume a new identity and go into hiding. It is only thanks to Federico's courageous intervention that she escapes assassination by truck soon afterward. (Note to self: Will require a lengthy action scene to be choreographed in excruciating detail at a later stage.) I was already looking forward to this.

Darkhan is in league with the powers of darkness, so the brothers' Sicilian fury avails them nothing. Federico and Walter are eventually compelled to sell off the family's thirty-room palazzo in Catania for far less than it's worth and send the entire clan, siblings, cousins, aunts, uncles— even Federico's mother, sad Eleonora—to the poorhouse. A really tragic episode, I only sketched it in for the moment, intending to flesh it out later in a dark, raw style entirely consistent with Italian neorealism. I could already imagine the literary critics' delight at the elegance of this stylistic tour de force. Eleonora, who hasn't seen any sunlight for over twenty years and has lived exclusively on candies and *cannoli,* suffers a heart attack on being led out of the house and dies en route to the hospital.

Maddened by unrequited love and feelings of guilt, Federico makes a pact with the Devil in which he promises him his firstborn son if business picks up and Valeria yields to him. To break Darkhan's devilish spell, Pasqualina sets off for Tashkent to find the Black Madonna, the source of Darkhan's magic—a relentless race against time. I panted while writing. My novel was developing into such a mad gallop, I felt dizzy. I was the god of adjectives, the prince of dramatic twists and turns: I was in the zone!

In the morning I filed the whole of this section under crapo7.txt.

It was still very early. The sun was just rising as I sat down on the roof terrace with a cup of coffee and a cigarette. The house and the street were so hushed, I could hear the whisper of the waves. This was my reality, the only one I had, so I would work with that reality as well as I could, not expecting anything more. Apart, of course, from the unexpected.

"Know what you need?" Poldi asked gently when I told her over breakfast of my desperate nocturnal effusions.

I could think of at least twenty things off the cuff, but I shrugged.

"Humility," she said. "You've hardly started, and already you're thinking of the applause."

"But artists live on applause."

"Whatever gave you that daft idea? Applause is just the cherry on the cream cake of success. Sweet, but not filling. Addictive at most. Besides, applause is worth zilch if it comes from the wrong source, so bear that in mind. Writing is the same as living. You may love writing, but writing doesn't love you back. That's because it's indifferent to you. But if you're hardworking and modest and display some humility, writing can prove extremely generous. It's just a question of letting go of your ego, making other people happy, and making yourself happy in the process. That's what's called mindfulness."

"Does the same apply to investigation?" I countered.

Poldi's expression suggested that I had put my finger on a sore point.

"It certainly does, sonny," she said with a sigh. "That was my Achilles' heel. I lacked humility because the applause I earned for the last three cases went to my head a little and I was consumed with vanity. That's why I got drawn into taking personal charge of the Black Madonna affair. I wanted to show everyone what I'm made of — Vito, Morello, the pope, the sad signora, Death, and you too. Yes, I wanted to impress everyone. But things like that always backfire. While I was on remand, I realized that that was my Achilles' heel, my hubris. *Namaste.*" She folded her hands on her bosom and inclined her head, then sipped her coffee in silence.

"Poldi?"

"Yes, my boy?"

"You're the most modest, big-hearted, and passionate person I know, you really are. But humility isn't your strong point, honestly it isn't."

"How do you mean?"

"It's not sexy."

Poldi grinned at me. "It isn't, is it? No, the world can kiss my arse. I'm Poldi, and while there's still breath in my body, I'm going to live it up till the sparks fly!"

"*Forza*, Poldi!"

Poldi was interviewed at police headquarters in Catania by a young and ambitious *commissario* whom she had seen at the crime scene shortly before. Having told her how incriminating the evidence against her was, he naturally expected her to make a full confession. But Poldi, who had decided to say nothing for the moment apart from "I did not kill Antonella!," demanded to speak to a lawyer. The *commissario* handed her phone back and permitted her one call. Poldi wondered whether to inform Montana, but then she called quite a different number.

"Donna Poldina! How nice to hear from you."

"I have the Black Madonna. That's to say, I did have it, but it's now . . . well, in a safe place, at least."

"Oh! You really are the best."

"Thanks, but I'm afraid the situation is complicated."

She briefly described the fix she was in.

"I understand," said the pope. "We'll take care of it. Better say nothing at all for the moment."

Poldi was taken before the magistrate and then consigned to the handsome old jail in the Piazza Vincenzo Lanza in central Catania, which might from the outside be mistaken for a normal nineteenth-century office building.

Soon afterward, Poldi was seated on a bed in a cell that looked almost identical to the one in the Vatican, thinking of Antonella. She reproached herself for not having replied sooner and more sympathetically to the woman's emails, and wondered how her life could have gone so wrong that it had had to end in such a way. Clasping her hands together, she bowed and asked the dead woman's forgiveness.

Three hours later she was taken to an interview room. Waiting for her there was a young lawyer named Dottore Bonacorsi, who smelled pleasantly of figs and wore a small cross in his lapel. He handed Poldi a packet of biscuits and a bag containing some toiletries and asked her to give him her version of events. He listened to her in silence, his sole reaction a periodic frown.

"I shall see to it that they take a blood sample from you, signora, but I fear it won't prove anything. The evidence against you is strong, alas."

"I didn't kill Antonella," Poldi said quietly. "They're trying to pin a murder on me. Don't *you* believe me?"

Bonacorsi gathered his papers together.

"Keep calm, signora. Is there anything you need?"

A beer would be good, thought Poldi, but she said, "Please inform my family, or they'll be worried."

"Of course."

Bonacorsi shook her hand and departed, leaving behind a scent of figs.

Poldi felt sick.

She was forced to spend a whole week on remand—a week in which she was repeatedly grilled. It was no fun, but my Auntie Poldi managed to display the full extent of her mental strength and persisted in remaining silent. That one seemingly interminable week gave her time to reflect on a lot of things. On life, death, Antonella, the sad signora, and herself. And on the detail that had disappeared from the photo wall, but without her phone she couldn't check that.

Poldi's only visitor during that week was Bonacorsi, who brought her *biscotti* and, on the second day, some worried letters from the aunts and an offer from Uncle Martino to infiltrate the jail and free her. On the third day Bonacorsi gave her a sitrep on the progress of inquiries. Things didn't look good.

"Your fingerprints are everywhere and your presence at the murder scene accords with the time of death. Then there's the blood on your hands and clothing, and fibers from your clothing have been found on the corpse. You were the only person seen and heard by the dead woman's neighbors. Antonella stalked you, you went there to question her, there was an altercation, and you lost your temper. Anyway, the district attorney's office thinks it's an open-and-shut case. I've already seen the indictment."

"Really?"

"Yes, that surprises me too. Certain people are in a very great hurry. Oh, and another thing: the Black Madonna used to kill Antonella Pandolfino wasn't the original. Fortunately."

"What!"

"It was a replica," said the lawyer. "Not a particularly brilliant one, but not badly done."

• • •

I still find it hard to imagine my Auntie Poldi in jail. I like to picture her wearing the sort of orange jumpsuit familiar from TV prison series. I picture her having to hold her own against the other prisoners and survive fierce punch-ups, all of which she naturally wins, thereby earning respect and making her the leader of the inmates. And then she organizes a revolt against the sadistic wardresses.

But reality always looks different. Just sad, usually. The prison was rather small, the other women were at most serving short sentences for theft, and the majority of them made an apathetic and disconsolate impression. Poldi did notice some little cliques of inmates casting surreptitious glances at her during cigarette breaks, but no one came over to hit on her, no one picked a quarrel or even spoke to her. When she experimentally strolled over to one of the groups, the women just turned away and scattered.

Afterward, when Poldi was returned to her cell, she found a noose lying on her pillow. This convinced her that she really was in deep trouble, that this time she was up against powerful people who could pin a murder on her, expedite indictments, and intimidate women prisoners. People who wanted her dead, sooner rather than later, without getting their hands dirty. Poldi's first thought was Russo, but then she discarded it.

"Really?" I put in when Poldi was telling me about her time in jail. "Why? I mean, you always say you'd put nothing past him — that he's a crime boss and so on."

"True," Poldi conceded. "But look, Russo may be a *capo*

mafioso, but he's already had umpteen opportunities to get rid of me, right? Besides, this way of going about things just isn't him—it isn't his style, understand? I told myself that whoever was playing this nasty game with me was scared. And Russo certainly isn't scared. What do we deduce from that?"

"That the murderer or murderers of Sister Rita and Antonella were afraid everything could blow up in their faces?"

"*Cento punti*, my boy! And that could only mean I was hotter on their heels than I'd imagined."

On the second evening a razor blade was lying on her pillow. Death was sitting beside it with his clipboard, smiling broadly at her. He had exchanged his ninja costume for his rather shapeless leisure outfit: a pair of overly baggy black trousers and a black hoodie. Completing his attire were some worn-out black clogs and black wool socks with a death's-head pattern.

Poldi waited until the cell door had been locked behind her.

"What's that doing there?" she demanded.

"It was there when I arrived, but you can ignore it. Your deadline is fixed, after all."

"Then why are *you* here?"

Death held up a plastic mug and shook it. Dice could be heard rattling inside.

"A bit of a diversion? A game of Pirate's Dice, perhaps?"

"Pirate's Dice is a drinking game. Anything to drink around here?"

"No," Death said with a sigh. "But Pirate's Dice is the

only game that falls more or less within the compliance regulations. Well?"

He shook the mug again.

"What would we play for?"

Death heaved another sigh. "This cost-benefit mentality hurts my feelings, honestly it does. Can't we just play?"

Poldi made a dismissive gesture. "Boring."

"True. Okay, let's say this: if you've won more games than me by the time you're released, I'll tell you what was missing from Antonella's flat when you regained consciousness."

"No, I want the murderer's name again."

"Forget it, Poldi. My game, my rules."

Poldi drew a deep breath and sat down on the bed.

"In that case, sonny, prepare to take a beating."

I really like playing Pirate's Dice, but I hardly ever win because people can always tell when I'm bluffing. I don't have a hope when I play against my Auntie Poldi. Poldi didn't exactly invent the poker face, but she has her POLDI, her lie detector index. She always knows when you're bluffing, and Death could sense that.

In spite of his hoodie, she never lost sight of his colorless eyes when he peeked beneath the mug and made his bid, so she easily won the first few games. Then Death smelled a rat and kept his face under control. After that the game became an epic battle between two ruthless gamblers of equal skill. They played half that night and on each succeeding night, with Death keeping the score. When Poldi was unexpectedly released from custody after a week, she was leading 302–298, so Death kept his promise and delivered.

· · ·

I hadn't really expected Poldi to tell me right away what was missing, but this time, without more ado, she showed me the photo she'd taken of the wall in Antonella's flat, together with one of the same wall taken by forensics, a print of which Montana had obtained from some old contacts of his.

"Spot it?"

I looked closely at the two photos, comparing each with the other in turn, but for whatever reason, the resolution or the numerous details, I couldn't detect it.

Poldi tapped the edge of her photo impatiently and blew it up a bit.

"There! Now do you see?"

I made out a framed black-and-white photo that clearly didn't belong to Antonella's stalker's picture gallery. It showed a group of twelve people standing in front of a building. They were drawn up in a semicircle with their hands loosely clasped, possibly folded, in front of them. Most of them were women. They did not look particularly happy, but were gazing at the camera with grave, mistrustful expressions. A man was standing one pace in front of them, like a choirmaster. I did in fact assume they were a choir, because they were uniformly dressed, the women in plain white cotton smocks, the two men flanking the picture in white trousers and collarless white shirts that reached below their waistbands. I could also detect that the photo had acquired a crease that rendered the face of the man in the middle unrecognizable. Nothing else struck me, apart from the fact that this photo was missing from the forensics print.

"Well, what do you think?"

"They could be a choir or something."

"Not bad. The question is, what sort of choir and where's

the building behind them? I didn't catch on either, not right away."

I looked at Poldi.

"First things first, though. Why did they suddenly release you?"

Bonacorsi had some good news and some bad news for Poldi. The good news was, the evidence wasn't sufficient to warrant a charge of murder. This was because, to Poldi's great surprise, Saro had gone to the police and provided her with an alibi for the time of the killing. The bad news was, Poldi was still under suspicion and would be released only on condition she did not leave Torre Archirafi until the case was wound up.

"What? They're putting me under house arrest?"

"It does sound strange, I know," Bonacorsi conceded. "Especially as it'll be hard to ensure you're observing the condition. But that's not all . . ." He cleared his throat before coming to the really bad news. "They're instituting deportation proceedings against you."

"*What?*" Poldi said, thunderstruck. "But they can't!"

"Yes, technically they can. EU citizens who have lived in another EU country for longer than five years can't be simply deported, even after committing a crime, but you haven't been resident in Italy for that length of time."

"I haven't committed any crime!"

"We'll lodge an appeal. I get the impression they want to get rid of you as fast as possible."

"No, someone wants to neutralize me. Can you block the deportation or postpone it somehow until my birthday at the beginning of July? Could you manage that?"

"I'll do my best, but I can't promise anything."

Bonacorsi escorted Poldi out.

Montana was waiting outside the jail in his Alfa. Poldi thanked Bonacorsi and hurried over to her *commissario*. Before he could utter a word, she flung her arms around his neck and kissed him passionately, burying her fingers in his graying hair and breathing in the familiar and beloved scent of cigarettes and aftershave.

"I love you, Vito," she gasped. "I'm sorry I gave you the elbow. I want you, and I've wanted you the whole time. Let's go home, let's drink and smoke and make love till the cups rattle. And when we can't anymore, let's solve this case together and bust these people's balls. How does that sound?"

"Sounds like a damn good plan," growled Montana, and he started the engine.

10

*Tells of sex and the Black Madonna, but also of
whores, total idiots, and silencers. Poldi has an awful
suspicion and tries to break through a wall of silence. Padre Paolo has not been entirely idle in the
meantime, so Poldi and Montana begin to see how
everything could fit together. It doesn't do them
much good, though, because soon afterward . . .*

I still find it hard to imagine Poldi and Montana having
sex. It's nothing to do with their age, but Poldi is my aunt
and I find that inhibiting somehow, I admit. But sex is as
much a part of Poldi's life as booze, the thrill of the chase,
melancholia, joie de vivre, and her wig. And the wig was all
she kept on when she got back to Via Baronessa with
Montana.

Parked outside the house was her Vespa with a note attached to it: INNOCENT! Poldi felt touched. Suddenly not as
worried about Saro as she had been, she resolved to take him
his other fifty euros in the near future. But first things first.

Poldi and Montana just managed to shut the front door
behind them before falling on one another like animals, it
being hard to say who was the lamb and who the lion. I picture them panting, chortling, and stumbling around as they

tore each other's clothes off. Anyone might have thought Poldi had spent not a week but the last ten years in solitary confinement—Montana too. The phoenix tattooed on Poldi's left breast spread its wings and positively fluttered with joy as Montana took hold of it and, scarcely were they inside the house, started to taste the fruits of paradise. With an elfin little squeak, Poldi twisted away, scampered into the bedroom, and exultantly threw herself down on the bed. Snorting like Zeus in the guise of a bull, Poldi's beloved *commissario* drew himself up in front of her, together with his gigantic, throbbing, marble pillar of Hercules. He emitted a primal, lustful bellow that reverberated along the Via Baronessa to the church, where it made the bells respond with a sensual little *ting* of their own. Poldi, for her part, purred like a wildcat, and away they went. Montana swooped on her like the eagle on Prometheus. Then, mutating into Poseidon armed with his trident, he leapt into the raging sea, parted the storm-tossed billows, surrendered to their embrace, and was sucked down into their darkest depths, to where the earth's crust breaks open, glowing magma erupts, and continents are cleft in twain. Yes, that's how I imagine them: like two no longer youthful continental plates forever sliding over and under each other in such a way as to generate catastrophic earthquakes and tsunamis of lust. Because when I imagine my Auntie Poldi and Vito Montana having sex, I do so with a vengeance, picturing it as a Götterdämmerung complete with thunder and lightning, a monumental, shameless, greedy, harsh, and tender coming-together.

Montana went to sleep afterward, which was understandable.

Later, when he woke up, Poldi handed him a beer and a cigarette.

"Who'll go first?"

Montana looked at her. "You."

Drawing a deep breath, Poldi told him as succinctly as possible about her encounter with the pope, Signora Cocuzza, Antonella's phone call, her trip to Librino, and her discovery of Antonella's body. She ascribed her celibacy to the fact that Signora Cocuzza's hostile attitude had shaken her to the core — so much so that she had given up everything: investigating, drinking, and "it." Which was more or less true.

Montana simply listened.

"I had a lot of time to think," Poldi went on. "I thought the penny would drop at some point and I'd see the light, but I simply don't get it. I simply can't make sense of it. What's the connection between Sister Rita and Antonella? Why did she have a copy of the Vatican's Black Madonna? How does it all fit together? Where do I come into it? Why did you suddenly act so weird, and why did Signora Cocuzza stop being my friend when I mentioned the Black Madonna? Why is someone spraying threatening messages on my house? Why is someone trying to pin a murder on me and boot me out of the country? Who are those twins? What is Russo's connection with them?"

"Forget Russo," said Montana. "He has nothing to do with it."

"How can you be so sure?"

"The delivery van was found. The twins had stolen it. It was pure chance Russo's cartons were in there."

"You don't believe that yourself!"

"Forget Russo. May I speak now?"

"Go ahead!"

"It's no wonder you can't join the dots. You're missing the key to everything, and that key is the Black Madonna."

Poldi bent over him. "Are you joking?"

Montana was looking thoroughly serious.

"But I'm not talking about the wooden figure the Vatican is after. I've also been after a Black Madonna. I've been hunting it for nearly thirty years."

"What is this, Vito? Why have you never told me about it?"

"Because I've been out of the running for years, and because the Black Madonna I'm after isn't a wooden figure."

"So what is it?"

Montana drew a deep breath. "An organization."

And then he told her.

"In the mideighties I was in the Organized Crime Section of the State Police in Rome. Those were the years when the Cosa Nostra under Totò Riina was waging a blood war against the state and Italian civil society. The years in which heroic public servants like Borsellino and Falcone and many others were murdered. But it was also a time when the Sicilians got fed up with the Mafia and took to the streets, and when many members of Mafia families had had their fill of murderers and testified against them. But the Mafia wasn't alone in waging war on the Italian state. We had evidence of a secret neofascist organization that had been systematically staging terrorist attacks and blaming them on the Communists and the Red Brigades in order to foment fear of terrorism and left-wing members of the population. This procedure later became known as the 'tension strategy.' We discovered that said organization called itself Madonna Nera. There were also indications that Madonna Nera maintained links with Masonic Lodge P2 and high-ranking government representatives—even with the Vatican. We had some names, but we couldn't prove anything. In 1992, when the Antimafia Commission was set up, I joined it with orders to trace the links between Madonna Nera and Cosa Nostra. I mean, I was young and ambitious and I genuinely believed we could purge the country of all that filth."

Montana sighed and puffed at his cigarette.

"I was so naive. Anyway, to cut a long story short, one day a soft toy appeared in Marta's pram—a bunny rabbit, and she was already chewing it. I at once had it examined. It contained a hand grenade—a warning, nothing more, but I tucked my tail between my legs and got myself transferred to the homicide squad in Milan. Well, what do you say now? So many splendid people risked their lives, and I buckled at the first threat."

He drained his beer.

"Go on, *tesoro*," Poldi said softly.

Montana was looking really agitated. He needed another whole cigarette before he could continue.

"The trouble is, a murder inquiry years later turned up a connection with a senator whose name had cropped up during investigations into Madonna Nera. When I started probing a bit deeper into the case, they came for me. One day the anticorruption unit found twenty thousand euros in the boot of my car. Then they sidelined me. I spent two years fighting for my reputation. It destroyed my marriage, among other things, and it almost destroyed me. In the end the case was dropped and I was transferred to Acireale. And then I met you. We solved three murders, we went to Rome, we were watched, the Black Madonna came back into my life, and I had only just made a few inquiries when I was taken out of circulation again. But this time I'm not going be brushed aside like a troublesome insect—this time I'm going to finish them. Are you with me, Poldi?"

She kissed him.

"You do ask some pretty dumb questions, *tesoro*."

"I mean it. They're powerful people and they're still active. They've been holding Italy for ransom for decades. They're vampires. To be honest, I don't think it's possible to destroy such organizations completely, but we might be able to give them an almighty kick up the backside."

"Why didn't you tell me all this in Rome, or on the beach the other day?"

"I didn't want to put you in danger, and I truly believed you'd keep your promise to stop investigating."

Poldi bowed her head. "I'm sorry, Vito."

Montana sighed as if laboring under a heavy burden.

"I think they'd have killed Antonella in any case. They used her to lay a trap for you. At least there's one good side to all that shit—getting you arrested and so on: it shows they're scared. Maybe we're getting warmer than we know."

"Yes, I think so too. How do you plan to proceed?"

"We."

Poldi put her head on one side. "Did you just say 'we,' *tesoro*?"

"I've been suspended," Montana said coolly, "so we're a team now."

• • •

In movies this is always the moment when dramatic, heroic background music strikes up and we get to see a montage that shows how, after all their amiable but unproductive bickering in the past, two ill-matched cops start working together like a well-oiled machine. How they promptly pool their information, fit pieces of the jigsaw puzzle together, put the screws on squalid small-time crooks, go without sleep, drink coffee out of cardboard cups, pin suspects' mug shots to corkboards and link them with wool threads—in short, how they carry on the fight against crime. I like montages of that kind, in fact I wouldn't mind if my whole life consisted of them, but for one thing we aren't in a movie, and for another, not all gangsters are complete knuckleheads. *It may be the other way round,* I sometimes think. *Perhaps the rest of us are knuckleheads.*

Montana had scarcely uttered the words "So we're a team now" when Poldi pounced on him even more avidly than before. It was just a reflex triggered by the "we" from a dear and fortuitously naked lover. She was simply obeying her nature.

Immediately afterward, however, the pair of them switched to hunting mode with total professionalism. They pulled on some clothes and Poldi made coffee and smoothies. Then, outside in the courtyard, they summarized what they knew. It simply didn't add up.

"Sister Rita hadn't been a nun for long, even if she ever was one," Montana began. "In fact, she'd been working as an escort six months earlier. Her real name was Rita Lombardi."

He put a photo on the table. It showed Rita posing in front of the Colosseum for her social media channel. Torn jeans, an off-the-shoulder blouse, toothpaste smile, expensive handbag, fluffy little dog in her arms, penciled eyebrows, perfect makeup, perfect hairdo. She looked lighthearted and likable — every inch the successful but approachable beauty from next door.

"The owner of the escort agency told me that Rita was one of her most popular girls," Montana went on. "Lots of clients from industry, society, and politics."

"And the Church?" Poldi put in.

"I naturally queried that right away, but the signora wouldn't comment. Anyway, three months ago Rita disappeared into thin air."

"Family?"

"Rita came from Messina. Her mother says she had no contact with her for the last four years."

"Curious, isn't it?" said Poldi. "She enters a convent one day and attends an exorcism the next. How can that be?"

"I questioned that priest — that Padre Stefano, the one who keeps apologizing," Montana continued. "He claims never to have seen Sister Rita before the exorcism. Antonella Pandolfino is no less mysterious. As a baby, she was found in a basket outside a church in Agrigento. Her parents were never identified. She was adopted by a family soon afterward. Humble circumstances, but all very unremarkable. After school, she dropped out of a medical assistant's course when some guy promised to make her into a film star. Obvious what that meant, isn't it? She was sucked into the porn industry and later went whoring for her pimp. Drink, drugs, violence — you can imagine. In her midtwenties she developed an anxiety disorder that grew steadily more intense. She hardly ever left Librino for the last twelve years and became more and more run-down. And then, quite suddenly, she made a trip to Rome under a false name."

"What did she live on?"

"She had a job with the vehicle registration authority in Catania, but she never took up the post—never spent a day there but was paid a small salary nonetheless."

"Hush money?"

"Possibly. On the other hand, there are these cases where parents with connections and enough money for a one-time payment get their uneducated children into local government or the civil service, where they simply while away their time or never show up for work but still draw a salary and a pension. You've no idea how many illiterates work in the post office, for instance."

Poldi brushed this aside. She knew it all.

"Do you think Antonella and Rita knew each other from having been sex workers?"

"That's the most obvious connection, isn't it?"

But because Poldi knew from experience that, whether in love, buffets, or murder inquiries, one should never reach for what's nearest, she sought another connection between the two murder victims.

"It simply doesn't add up," she summarized. "A former porn actress and prostitute who had been going to seed for years in a flat in Librino suddenly underwent an exorcism in Rome under a false name and spoke in my voice. Present at this exorcism was a former call girl who had recently entered a convent and was thrown or pushed off a roof terrace, naked, a few hours later. Antonella had been stalking me for months by that time and sending me emails from the dark net — which, by the way, is more complicated than it sounds. It calls for a bit of gumption and experience or assistance, and Antonella didn't strike me as the brightest candle on the cake. She certainly wasn't a talented voice mimic either. I also wonder why she never tried to speak to me, as stalkers often do. And it all abruptly stopped. Strange, isn't it?"

"What are you getting at, Poldi?"

She didn't reply at once.

That, I guess, was because she had just gained an initial inkling of how everything fit together: the piece of the jigsaw that made sense of the whole picture. But, as always happens when everything points in one direction, when everything could become quite simple, and when our intuition is already groaning impatiently, "Haven't you caught on *yet*?," our powers of imagination still stubbornly refuse to accept the fact, simply because we don't *want* to. That, I suspect, was what was going on inside Poldi at that moment. A name had presented itself to her mind's eye, a name she would rather have suppressed, though it was also a fact that the person to whom that name belonged had long been dead. Poldi happened to be fairly sure of this, because she had, in a manner of speaking, killed that person.

"No!"

"Yes!"

"No!"

"I pass."

"You killed someone?"

"Sort of," Poldi prevaricated.

"What does that mean? Did you or didn't you?"

"All right, I did! Happy now?"

"How? Who?"

"Long story. I don't want to talk about it."

"Why doesn't anyone in the family know about it?"

"It happened in Tanzania."

"And you were never caught?"

"It's complicated. I doubt if your stunted imagination could grasp it."

"You were on a secret mission. You were an international contract killer."

"God Almighty! Yes, if it makes you happy. May I go on now?"

"*Forza*, Poldi!"

"Does any of that make sense to you, Vito?"

Montana grimly shook his head.

"And what does that tell us?"

"You tell me, Poldi!" sighed Montana.

"It tells us we must look more closely."

Poldi opened her laptop and clicked on the image of the framed group photograph. In spite of the only moderate resolution of the mobile phone photo, certain details were discernible on the screen. Poldi beckoned Montana over and looked closely at the framed photograph.

"When do you reckon that was taken?"

"Hard to say." Montana was concentrating on the picture. "The hairstyles," he muttered. "That woman's hairdo, so short at the sides and so curly on top. And the two men's long manes of hair. It must have been taken in the eighties."

Poldi nodded.

"Recognize one of them?"

Montana shook his head. "Do you?"

"Yes, I think so."

Montana took another close look at the photo. Poldi tapped one of the women, who was standing a little to one side.

"Look at that expression. She was beautiful at that age, wasn't she? And so dainty and fragile. See how she's clasping her hands together, as if she needs to hang on to herself. She still does that."

And because Poldi suddenly felt quite sure, and because she was really fed up, and because she was now beset by an awful suspicion, she squeezed into a pair of jeans with holes in the knees, pulled on her Pussy Riot T-shirt and topped it off with my Uncle Peppe's worn old biker jacket—in other words, her better-not-tangle-with-me outfit—and strode off to the bar.

Like a buxom, angry fairy with some mistakenly granted wishes to reverse, she strode along the esplanade that clammy April evening, through air as fraught with salty humidity as it was with a resentment bottled up for too long but destined to vent itself all the more violently.

The little bar in the piazza was well patronized that evening. Over half the tables were occupied and a gaggle of youths were jostling at the counter. It was as if half the town had assembled for some conspiratorial purpose.

Signora Cocuzza, seated at the cash register and wearing her usual grumpy expression, looked aghast when Poldi strode in like a fury. Poldi saw at a glance that those present included Padre Paolo, Signor Bussacca, and Signora Anzalone from next door.

"Everyone out!" she thundered like a landslide that would

bury anyone not quick enough to get out of the way. "Every-one, and be quick about it! Not you, though!" Poldi pointed to Signora Cocuzza, Signora Anzalone, Signor Bussacca, and the priest. "You stay put! The rest of you, beat it! Go on, scat!"

"Donna Poldina!" Padre Paolo said reprovingly.

"Zip it! Not a word!"

When she lets rip in her deepest voice and most peremp-tory Bavarian, my Auntie Poldi can sound quite intimidating.

All the customers quit the bar in a hurry but promptly reconvened in the piazza, eager to follow the course of events inside at a safe distance. I heard that bets were laid on whether Donna Poldina would run amok and blaze away with a gun. In fact she exploded a kind of bomb. She shooed Signora Cocuzza, her next-door neighbor, Bussacca, and the padre together to a table.

"What's the meaning of this performance?" hissed the sad signora.

Poldi slammed a print of the photo of the strange choir down on the table. She could sense how they all instantly stiffened. All save Padre Paolo.

"Donna Poldina . . ." he began angrily, but Poldi pointed to three of the figures in the photo and looked at Signora Cocuzza, Signora Anzalone, and Signor Bussacca.

"That's you, isn't it? Don't deny it, I recognized you."

"Where . . ." Signora Anzalone began in a hesitant voice, but a look from Signora Cocuzza silenced her.

"I've never seen this photo before," the sad signora said stiffly, "and I've no idea who those people are. That's not me, anyway. You're barking up the wrong tree, Donna Poldina. You should go now."

The padre squinted at the photo and then at Signora Cocuzza. "That young woman really does look like you."

"It is her," said Poldi. "And that young woman in the middle is my next-door neighbor, and the man on the edge of the picture, the one with the long hair and the mustache, is Signor Bussacca. And now I'd like you to tell me what was going on there. What *is* going on. You want to get rid of me? By all means, you're welcome. I'll quit Torre and get out of your hair, but I'm going to solve this case first."

"No one wants to get rid of you, Donna Poldina," whispered Signora Anzalone.

"I should think not," growled the padre.

"Then for God's sake tell me what's going on." Poldi gazed at her sad friend. "You're my neighbors and friends. This place is my home, and I've you to thank for that. That's why your behavior can only mean you're nursing some dark secret."

Signora Cocuzza heaved a big sigh, looking even sadder and more despairing than usual, but she didn't speak. No one did. Signora Anzalone bit her lip, Signor Bussacca folded his arms as if in need of something to cling to, and the padre simply waited.

"What was going on there?" Poldi repeated. "What was your connection with Black Madonna?"

Silence.

"Why did you kill Sister Rita and Antonella Pandolfino?"

That question hit the little group at the table like a squall ravaging a tulip bed.

"We didn't kill anyone!"

"Not directly, perhaps, but your silence permits of no other conclusion."

Signora Anzalone started to say something again, but Signora Cocuzza laid a hand on her arm and squeezed it.

That made Poldi see red. She uttered a stream of oaths in Bavarian, then reverted to Italian.

"I'll bust the lot of you! I've plenty of evidence, and nothing's going to stop me. If you want to get rid of me you'll have to kill me."

Complete bluff, of course, but it proved effective. The two women and Signor Bussacca squirmed visibly.

"You now have a choice," Poldi thundered on. "You can talk and help me, or you can go on keeping your mouths shut and watch Madonna Nera put an end to me, deport me, stick me in jail, or simply kill me."

She waited.

The padre surveyed his table companions, then ostentatiously drew his chair closer to Poldi's and waited likewise.

"And," he boomed, "don't any of you go thinking I'll ever forget any of what I've just seen and heard. Just to be clear."

"It's late," Signora Cocuzza said with a sigh, as if speaking were an immense effort. "You must go now, Donna Poldina. You too, Padre."

Poldi rose.

"I want an answer by tomorrow."

Then she left. Outside in the piazza the crowd of inquisitive spectators parted, silently making way for her. No one uttered a word. The padre caught up with her outside the church.

"Donna Poldina, wait!"

He was breathing heavily and looked glum.

"Are you all right, Donna Poldina? We haven't had a chance to speak yet. I'm so glad you've been released."

"Don't worry, Padre, I'm fine," Poldi said with a sigh. "I wouldn't mind a spot of relaxation, though."

"I don't understand what's going on here," he said, still breathing heavily. "I mean, it's utterly crazy. I've been a priest in this town for twenty years, but I suddenly feel like a stranger."

"The reasons may lie much further in the past."

"But it's unacceptable, Donna Poldina! You and I, we belong to Torre Archirafi like Signora Cocuzza, the *tabacchi,* and the mineral-water spring. I made that very clear in my last sermon. You, Donna Poldina, are the best thing that's happened to this town for decades. You may not know it, but Torre was a somber, secretive place before you came. Something has changed in the past year, though. People have become more accessible, they laugh a lot more, and they're suddenly proud to live here. You're a fresh sea breeze in the heat of summer, Donna Poldina! You're the spirit of reconciliation after a family feud, you're the good fairy's kiss, and I'm not going to let them drive you away. I'll make Signora Cocuzza's life a misery until she spills the beans at last!"

Poldi patted the padre's cheek and summoned up a smile.

"Thanks for the kind words, Padre, but Signora Cocuzza must make up her own mind."

She started to turn away, but there was something else on the priest's mind.

"I know you called me off, Donna Poldina, but I did make a few inquiries about Sister Rita."

That captured Poldi's attention at once. "Really?"

The padre kneaded his big hands together.

"Perhaps I should tell you that I haven't always been a humble local priest. I was at a seminary in Rome and was doing brilliantly at the Vatican, but I'm very quick-tempered, as you know. Well, that doesn't go down well in the Curia, as you can imagine, especially when one attacks certain abuses at the highest level—abuses everyone would rather sweep under the carpet. Anyway, in the late nineties the Holy Father appointed me an apostolic visitor. You know what that is?"

"A kind of internal investigator?"

"Exactly. In short, an apostolic visitor looks into irregularities in the bishoprics. He reports exclusively to the pope and is invested with full powers. Being inspected by an apostolic visitor is always tantamount to a declaration of mistrust on the part of the Holy See, so it's extremely unpleasant for those affected. My job was to investigate certain transgressions committed by criminal networks at the highest Curial level." Padre Paolo cleared his throat. "I'll merely cite a keyword: prostitution, pimping, money-laundering."

Which was three keywords, but to Poldi the whole story sounded familiar anyway.

"And in the process," she said, "you trod too heavily on the corns of certain powerful people who pulled strings, framed you for something, and got you shunted off to Sicily."

"Er . . . How did you know?"

Poldi gestured dismissively.

"I bleed for you, Padre, but what has all this to do with Sister Rita?"

"Well, I still have a few contacts from those days. I discovered that before she entered the convent Sister Rita had been a prostitute."

He looked at Poldi as if he had just produced a rabbit from his biretta.

"I already knew that," she said disappointedly, "but thanks for your trouble."

"Wait! Rita wasn't just any old prostitute, she was—how do you call it?—an upmarket call girl, one of her clients being a cardinal. She was also booked for certain exclusive parties regularly held on his estate near Palermo by a certain politician and former premier, who died recently. The last was four months ago. My sources say that some form of incident occurred, because the host was beside himself with rage and Rita made herself scarce."

Electrified by this, Poldi pricked up her ears. She had not only met said politician in the course of her last case but had attended one of said parties in a rococo costume. The old man had been powerful, avaricious, and cold-blooded. He had threatened to wipe out our entire family one by one, and he would certainly have been capable of doing so had he not died suddenly soon afterward. However, thought Poldi, maybe that threat still applied, even after his death.

"May I beg a favor of you, Padre?"

"You may ask almost anything of me, Donna Poldina. Only my vow of celibacy prevents me from saying 'anything whatsoever.'"

"Padre!" Poldi chided him coquettishly. Then, more seriously, "We must find out what Signora Cocuzza, Signora Anzalone, and Signor Bussacca are up to."

"Say no more, Donna Poldina."

"Not so fast, Padre. We're dealing with some very dangerous people."

He frowned at her. "I live in a state of celibacy and I take it very seriously, but do I give the impression that I've got no balls, Donna Poldina?"

In a far better mood than she had been in an hour before, Poldi returned to the Via Baronessa and presented Montana with her stop-the-presses news.

He was no less electrified, especially by the name of the dead politician.

"That could be the crucial piece of the jigsaw! We had him on our radar back then, but we never managed to prove he was connected to Madonna Nera. Besides, he was virtually fireproof. What could have happened?"

Poldi gave her beloved *commissario* a searching stare. "That was a rhetorical question, wasn't it?"

Montana nodded. "I didn't want to come out with a premature hypothesis."

"But it's obvious that Rita stole the Black Madonna during her last attendance at that orgy. It all fits, *tesoro*. Morello and the pope spoke of 'certain networks' having stolen the Black Madonna. They were definitely talking about Madonna Nera. It's obvious: anyone who heads such a powerful secret organization needs a symbol of his power. It must be inconspicuous, but it must also be the rarest and most precious symbol in existence. If it can be taken from another, hated organization, so much the better. I met that old man, Vito. That premier wanted everything, the costliest and rarest things obtainable, and he always got what he wanted. So let's assume he possessed the Black Madonna. What then?"

"Rita gets another booking for an orgy," said Montana, thinking aloud. "She has a tête-à-tête with the old man. He falls asleep, she seizes her opportunity. She knows her way around because she's been there so often. She takes the Black Madonna, which is either on display in his quarters or he showed it to her sometime, and hightails it out of there."

"But why would she be stupid enough to do such a thing?" asked Poldi. "She must have known she could never sell such an object without assistance, and she was risking her neck."

Montana nodded. "Yes, I think the same as you. She did it because she felt safe. The theft was planned, just like her disappearance into the convent."

"Exactly!" cried Poldi. "Someone must have helped her. That someone must have credibly guaranteed her protection and been in a position to sell the Black Madonna. Perhaps she was promised a bright future."

Montana frowned and continued to think aloud. "Maybe it wasn't meant to be for sale."

"What do you mean?"

"Perhaps she was meant just to bring it back."

Poldi whistled through her teeth. "Vito, you're a genius! You mean Rita was acting on behalf of the Church?"

He shrugged. "It's possible. But perhaps she was being used by a clerical third party. Someone who knew where the Black Madonna was and wanted to return it to the Church."

"Why?"

He shrugged again.

"I'll tell you, Vito: for vanity's sake. What else? To do the big thing and be a hero. It's hard to make your mark in a world of gray mice like the Vatican—I realized that just now, when I was with Padre Paolo. He's the opposite of a gray mouse. He's got a short fuse and doesn't mince words, and that doesn't get you far in the Vatican. If you want to go places in the Curia you have to employ clever tactics, keep your trap shut, be patient, eat dirt, lick boots, trim your sails to the wind, join influential circles, and advance by taking microscopically small steps. Otherwise you'll mobilize envious rivals who'll promptly put a spoke in your wheel. But bringing back the Black Madonna—that's such a feat, all your rivals can go hang. That's a tsunami you can surf to the very top."

"You've got a point there," Montana conceded. "What do we imagine this someone is like? No gray mouse is going to roll up with the Black Madonna just like that."

"Too true, Vito. This gray mouse must have a connection to Madonna Nera. How else would they have known where the Black Madonna was?" Poldi had a sudden thought. "The most believable gray mouse would be one that happens to be an investigator as well."

Montana stared at her. "Bloody hell."

"Forget it. It was just an idea."

Montana raised a hand and pondered.

"I still don't understand how Antonella Pandolfino fits into this. And why did she have to die?"

"One thing at a time, Vito. Fear is where it's at, and I'll bet he's shitting himself, our dear friend Commissario Morello."

There, it was out. And, as always happens, once an idea has been voiced it acquires a credibility of its own.

Montana just ground his teeth.

"This success would catapult Morello to the top of the Vatican police," Poldi went on. "Straight to the seat of power, where he would be most useful to Madonna Nera. He may even have higher ambitions."

Montana said nothing. He got out his mobile phone and looked for a contact.

"Who are you calling?" Poldi asked.

"DeSantis. I'll get him to run a check on Morello. I want to know all about him."

Poldi gently removed the phone from his hand and put it down on the table. "That can wait till tomorrow, *tesoro*. It's late."

So saying, she took him by the hand and towed him — yes, where to? Give you three guesses.

I picture them, sweaty, exhausted, and in a slightly more confident mood, falling asleep after another round of "it" and dreaming *sogni d'oro,* or golden dreams, as they say in Italy: Poldi, naked save for her wig, snuggled up in Montana's arms, or the pair of them simply lying side by side like a couple exempt from the fear that their partner would be gone in the morning. That's another picture I'd like to preserve somehow, frozen forever, but something intervened, as usual.

Because, in the middle of the night, the two mature turtledoves were jolted out of their *sogni d'oro* by a loud crash. Just as Poldi sat up with a start, rather bemused, she saw two figures in motorbike masks come storming into the bedroom brandishing pistols fitted with silencers.

Instinctively she pulled the sheet up over her bosom. As so often in such situations, two inappropriate thoughts flashed through her mind: first, she wondered why the intruders bothered with silencers when they'd made such a din breaking in, and second, she wanted to put something on before dying.

"Gerrup!" yelled one of them. "Gerrup, and be quick about it!"

"Yes!" yelled the other. "Chop-chop!"

"Well, I'll be buggered!" Poldi exclaimed, because despite their masks she had naturally pegged them at once by their fluorescent sneakers, which glowed like four monstrous glowworms.

The twins planted themselves at the foot of the bed, brandishing their guns at my aunt and Montana and yelling.

"Gerrup!"

"Yeah, and come with us!"

"Chop-chop!"

"Yeah, chop-chop!"

Poldi only glimpsed Montana's reaction out of the corner of her eye. He rolled sideways out of bed and reached for something beneath it, but she heard two muffled shots. Plaster spurted from the wall beside him and there was a sudden smell of gunpowder. Poldi screamed, Montana froze.

"Shurrup! Don't move or we'll waste you here and now!"

"You bet we will!"

11

Tells of death and twins. And that's it, really. Nothing much happens, except that Poldi and Montana take a brief trip and hold hands. All right, there's also some cursing, shivering, shooting, and a plausible explanation. Plus a few nice Bavarian bons mots. But that's all, honestly.

I give my imagination free rein to pass the time, but I have problems imagining death. I don't mean my Auntie Poldi's imaginary friend, but the state itself. The irrevocable fact. We always think of our nearest and dearest as immortal. Parents, family, life's companions, friends, idols. It's unimaginable that they could die, but they do. Suddenly they're not there, and nothing, but nothing, will ever bring them back. I can't imagine that. When I try to imagine it I come up against a sort of mental block, bang, *rien ne va plus*. Poldi had moved to Sicily firmly determined to drink herself to death in comfort with a sea view, but I simply can't imagine that she'll actually die. *Perhaps I can prevent it,* I sometimes think, *if only I try really hard.* Perhaps I can immunize my Auntie Poldi against death by means of splendid adjectives and fiery verbs, simply by telling people about her. By recounting her criminal investigations, her adven-

tures, her cons and contradictions, her celeb friends and escapades. By telling of her big heart, her joie de vivre and
passionate Bavarian nature. Of the glittering trail and minor miracles she has left behind her all her life. *Perhaps,* I
sometimes think, *I can sing her song.* It would probably be a
kind of love song, and to do her justice it would naturally
have to be exuberant, brazen, opulent, fantastic, mythical,
tender, mischievous, loud, and go out with a bang. As baroque as Sicily and Bavaria, in fact. But that would also
mean I mustn't shrink from exaggeration and blarney, and
must fearlessly and openly sing about "it," which isn't really
my scene. Still, if that's how I can protect my Auntie Poldi
from death—the ultimate death of oblivion—I must risk
it, even if my narrative resources are only meager and my
little ship of adjectives and naïveté will probably founder
with its sails in tatters, overwhelmed by the typhoon of reality. So be it. Although I'm very apprehensive and have absolutely no idea how. Perhaps I can do it by slightly rewriting
my screwed-up family saga. All I know is, if I *can't* summon
up a good-enough mental image of Poldi's death, perhaps
she won't die.

Sad to say, however, all the signs at that moment were that
Poldi and Montana would very soon meet their end. The
twins might be a pair of overgrown boobies, but they were
obviously in earnest. Two shots, and the whole bedroom was
filled with the acrid stench of gunpowder.

Poldi saw Montana raise his hands and breathed a sigh of
relief.

"Vito!"

"Shurrup!"

"Yeah, shurrup!"

The twin in the fluorescent green sneakers was still aiming at Montana.

"Easy, boys," Montana growled. "Just tell us what you're after."

The twin in the fluorescent red sneakers tossed Poldi a roll of duct tape and a bunch of cable ties and jerked his pistol at Montana.

"Go on, you know what to do."

"I'm naked!" Poldi protested indignantly, pulling the sheet a little higher.

"*Madonna,* then put something on!"

"Okay, but you'll have to turn your backs."

It was worth a try, and Montana was already tensing. The twins, evidently well brought up in this respect, actually half turned away, then checked in midmovement and leveled their guns at Poldi and Montana once more.

"Very funny, I don't think!"

"Yeah, very funny!"

"Go on, put something on and then go over to him. Step on it, chop-chop!"

"Yeah, chop-chop!"

Nothing to be done.

Poldi got out of bed, glaring at the twin in the red sneakers. She started to make her way over to the wardrobe, erect and dignified, but he barred her path and pointed his gun at the bunny-eared terrycloth onesie that was draped over a chair.

"That'll do!"

"What do you plan to do with us?"

"Shurrup!"

"Yeah, shurrup!"

While Poldi was reluctantly slipping into her onesie, Montana started to reach for his clothes, but Red Sneakers stopped him.

"Not you, you're staying like that!"

"Why?" barked Montana.

"Yeah, why?" asked the other twin, who was covering him.

"Because he's a cop," said Red Sneakers, "and because a naked cop is better than a cop with his clothes on, that's why."

This evidently — and eventually — made sense to his brother.

"Oh, yeah, sure!"

Poldi made a mental note about the twins' relative IQs, because it was always advisable to know the weakest link in a chain. She did, however, qualify her mental note by adding that in spite of his stupidity, Green Sneakers might be an excellent shot. Hoodlums could be total idiots, but they were still hoodlums and/or killers. So she hastened to carry out her instructions. After getting dressed she handcuffed Montana with cable ties, gave him a kiss, and then, with a heavy heart, stuck a strip of duct tape over his mouth. She didn't like to think how painful it would be later on, ripping it off together with half his beard and mustache. After that she was likewise gagged and bound.

A delivery van quite similar to the one in Rome was parked immediately outside the house with its sliding door open. The twins shoved naked Montana and Poldi in her bunny-eared onesie into the load space. Red Sneakers got in behind the wheel while Green Sneakers sat opposite Poldi and Montana in the back.

Death was already installed beside Green Sneakers. He was holding his clipboard and fiddling around with some forms with multicolored carbon copies. He gave Poldi a wave when she was pushed in. Poldi's only response was a scowl.

On the other side of the load space she made out two closed and firmly banded plastic flasks with adhesive labels on them. That was as much as she could see, because the load space had no windows and the windshield was the only source of light.

They were already swerving through the darkness at top speed. The masked twin was leaning against the flasks, casually covering Poldi and Montana with his pistol.

Death looked at Poldi and shrugged.

In spite of her efforts to memorize their route, Poldi soon lost her bearings. All she registered was that they rounded a large number of bends and were obviously going uphill. She inferred from this that they were heading in the direction of Etna. Not a really reassuring thought. Nor were the plastic flasks, because the streetlights they passed enabled her to see that the labels bore chemical designations and warning symbols for corrosive fluids. This made her feel really apprehensive. Exchanging a glance with Montana, she could tell that the same thing was going through his head. They couldn't speak, of course.

But my Auntie Poldi possesses an extra gear, and "Where there's a will . . ." is one of her favorite mottos.

She stretched out her cuffed hands and grasped those of Montana, who promptly returned her pressure. This entailed something of a contortion, which their guard naturally noticed.

"Let go!"

Poldi vigorously shook her head.

Green Sneakers brandished his pistol, but Poldi shook her head again.

He shrugged. "If you try anything, I'll kill you both."

He said it so dispassionately they had to take him at his word.

Poldi felt the pressure of Montana's fingers. Without looking at him, she felt for the soft skin of his palm and started tapping.

Tiptaptip ... Quickly but firmly she sent Montana her first message in Morse by tapping his palm with her fingertips for varying lengths of time.

I. L.O.B.E. Y.O.O.

"Cool!" I said, sounding deliberately casual, when she described this episode this over lunch in the Via Baronessa. My notebook was half full by now. "It happens in every other B movie, but hey, who am I to cast doubt on the truth of your tall stories?"

"You mean you don't believe me?" Poldi said with a sigh, and she demonstrated on the tabletop.

Tiptap, taptaptaptip.

She really could do it quite fast, and it really did sound like Morse code.

"It wasn't completely faultless, I admit. I was a bit rusty, and I could only hope that Vito knew his Morse code."

"Where on earth did you learn it?"

"Well . . ." she said, lingering over the word, and whenever she employs that intro, I know what's coming. "It was

248

back in the day in Hollywood, midnineties, and I'd been making the costumes for a B feature. I got to know this guy Steve at the Chateau Marmont, the way you do. He was in a bad way because they'd kicked him out of his own computer firm and he wasn't happy in the new one. He looked really miserable, so I started by giving him a couple of black turtlenecks from the set of this B feature to smarten him up. Then I told him, 'Learn something new, Steve! Something, anything, to freshen up your ideas.' And so, in a festive mood, I suggested that we both do a Morse course. He was an expert on codes, was Steve, but he balked at first. 'Morse is totally obsolete,' he grumbled. 'Why should I learn it?' So I told him, 'Just because, Stevie! Just because! One more thing, Stevie: think different! Think different!' He understood that, Steve did, because sometimes you have to inject something new into your noddle—something difficult and useless, that's the main thing. It'll teach you to think laterally and come up with new ideas. Bear that in mind for your novel."

Poldi waited for Montana to respond. She could feel him move a finger—hesitantly at first, but then—*tiptaptip*—came the reply.

I. P.O.B.E. Y.O.O. T.U.O.

Poldi's heart leapt. Resolutely, she Morsed on.

W.H.O.T. U.I.L. T.H.A.Y. D.U.?

K.N.I.L. U.S.

To which Poldi replied:

P.L.A.N.?

Montana's reply came at once. He had clearly thought of something, but it took him quite a while to Morse it through. In a nutshell, he proposed to hurl himself at Green Sneakers at the earliest opportunity. Although logic prescribed that he would be shot, Poldi would at least have a chance to grab the pistol.

Poldi's reply:

Y.D.I.O.T.

Abruptly she snatched her hand away. She already had a plan, namely, the precise opposite of his. Poldi knew her definite date of death, after all, so she could afford to take a risk. She proposed to disarm the more boneheaded of the twins at the earliest opportunity, thereby giving her beloved *commissario* a chance. She had just decided it was a good plan when Montana firmly grasped her hand and began to Morse again.

W.I.L. U. M.R.R.Y. M.I.?

Poldi gave a violent start. It was not lost on Green Sneakers. "Hey, hey, hey! Keep still, you!"
Poldi stared at Montana, who unblinkingly held her gaze. She started tapping.

I.

Montana interrupted her by squeezing her hand and shaking his head vigorously. He wanted an unequivocal answer.

Poldi heaved a sigh, remembering "Latin Lover," her conversation with Gianna Nannini, and her unequivocal negative, for which—as Poldi herself knew—there were more than enough reasons. And because she knew all this, she shook her head and tapped:

Y.E.S.

O.V. C.O.R.S.E.
I.D.E.O.T.

Plus, in case of a fault in transmission:

Y.E.S. Y.E.S. Y.E.S.

Montana blinked and growled something. Poldi bent over and kissed him. That's to say, she pressed her duct tape to his.

"Hey!" Green Sneakers cried angrily, brandishing his pistol again. "Cut that out!"

Sighing, Poldi leaned back against the side of the van, simultaneously happy and unhappy. She really did want to marry Vito, in defiance of all reason, but the present state of affairs suggested that either it wouldn't happen or their marriage would be a very brief one. She glowered at Death, who merely gave an apologetic shrug and shuffled his papers in a sheepish way.

They rounded one bend after another. Poldi lost her sense of time, but they pulled up at last and the engine fell silent.

She felt Montana tense beside her and hoped he wasn't planning to do something stupid now that they were virtually engaged.

The door slid open and the twin in red sneakers gestured with his pistol.

"Out, the pair of you! Chop-chop!"

Poldi found it hard to get up. Her legs were numb and the cable ties were biting painfully into her wrists. It was also unpleasantly cold at this altitude. Emerging from the van with a groan, she saw that it was just getting light.

Although the sun had not quite cleared the horizon, it was light enough to see that they had pulled up beside a road in the midst of a wide expanse of lava resembling a frozen black sea. Looming up in front of Poldi was the peak of Etna, gilded by the morning sun. If she turned her head a little she could see a patch of woodland. The spot seemed familiar to her somehow. Her surroundings were absolutely silent. Not even a bird could be heard, just the wind blowing hard in the direction of the summit as if trying to cleanse the whole mountain of some impurity.

Montana gave himself some vigorous slaps to restore the circulation in his legs and warm his naked body and was also looking around.

Their surroundings offered scant grounds for optimism. Just the road and a rugged expanse of lava wherever one looked, and in the distance the small clump of greenery. A good field of fire, in other words, especially as it would be impossible to escape across such rough ground barefoot or wearing a bunny-eared onesie.

Rrrippp! Before she knew what was happening, Red

Sneakers had wrenched the duct tape first off her mouth and then — *rrripppp!* — off Montana's.

"Ouch! Bugger me!"

"Yell all you like, no one'll hear you up here," said Red Sneakers.

Montana was cursing and grimacing with pain. His handsome beard had acquired a little bald patch, but it was a nice feeling, being able to breathe freely and also speak.

Poldi held out her cable-tied wrists.

"They're staying like that."

"You bet they are!"

"So what happens now?" Montana demanded.

The twins pointed along the road in the direction of the wood.

"Get moving," said Red Sneakers. "Nice and slow, though, or it'll be *kaboom!*"

"Yeah, *kaboom,*" Green Sneakers chimed in. "*Kaboom* — that's good."

"Why don't you simply kaboom us here and dissolve us in that acid?"

Momentary bewilderment.

"Because . . . well, because!" Red Sneakers replied. "Boss's orders. Now move!"

Poldi exchanged a glance with Montana and saw that the same thought had crossed his mind.

This entailed a postponement. A postponement meant hope, and hope might mean escape.

Red Sneakers prodded Poldi with his gun. "Get moving."

"Haven't you at least got a blanket for me?" growled Montana. "It's bloody cold, or hadn't you noticed?"

"No blanket," said Red Sneakers.

They slowly got under way, Poldi in her terry-towel onesie and slippers, Montana in his birthday suit with Death alongside.

Montana was miserably cold, but he walked along the road with his head erect. In spite of his no-longer-youthful physique, his little tummy and his rolls of fat, his wrinkles and incipient liver spots, he looked muscular and full of life and *sicilianità*. Poldi realized at that moment that she had never met a more handsome, splendid, dignified man, and she felt proud of her lover. That's to say, her fiancé.

"All right, *tesoro*?"

Montana nodded.

"So what's the plan now?"

"Well, you stick a ring on my finger, I stick one on yours, and we both say yes. Or are you getting cold feet already?" He grinned at her. "For someone who never wanted to get married, you said yes pretty damn quick. Be honest, you're looking for a provider, that's all."

"You can put your own socks away, and don't go thinking you can slack off after the wedding. Four times a week is compulsory, I want that in writing or I'll look for someone else."

"Three times," groaned Montana. "Please! Neither of us is getting any younger."

Poldi looked at him tenderly. She would so much have liked to take his hand at that moment. His strong, shapely, hairy hand.

"Oh Vito, if only you knew!"

Voices from behind them:

"Pipe down!"

"Yeah, pipe down!"

"Well?" Montana whispered.

"Why ask *me?*"

"You're the boss. Tell me what the plan is. I'm in."

Poldi thought for a moment.

"I assume we're going to meet the big man before they rub us out. That may give us some leeway. Besides, I don't think it's just pure chance or bloody-mindedness that you're naked and I'm having to traipse around in this onesie."

"So?"

"Someone wants to humiliate us."

"Oh, who?"

"It's only a guess, *tesoro,* but if I'm right you must leave the talking to me, okay?"

"You're the boss, Donna Poldina."

"No, we're a team, and don't forget it. Do you trust me?"

"How senile do you think I am?"

Poldi ignored this.

"When I say, 'Run!' you run, understand? I don't know how much time I can gain, so you must run like the devil, promise me that."

"What about you?"

Poldi glanced over at Death.

"Promise me, *tesoro.*"

"Beh!" Montana said with a sigh. "All right, but woe betide you if you get yourself killed. I might change my mind about the wedding."

The road led straight across Etna's lunar landscape above the tree line. At least the wind was dropping. The twins then directed Montana and Poldi along a dusty little track leading off the road and into the lava fields. That was when Poldi guessed where they were going.

The track was uncomfortable for Montana in his bare feet, but he kept up.

When they set foot in the enchanted green clearing, Poldi could not help thinking of Signor Mezzapelle activating the Earth Snake with his drum. A healing activity, but as things stood now, Poldi and Montana were to be zapped right here, in her favorite spot. Poldi found this rather sad and hoped that nice Signor Mezzapelle would never hear of it.

The twins instructed Poldi and Montana to sit down on the flat, shiny boulder in the middle of the clearing and keep quiet. While Green Sneakers kept them covered, Red Sneakers stepped aside and made a phone call. They were both looking nervous—always an ominous sign in killers.

"What are we waiting for, boys?" Poldi asked in a studiously casual tone, just to keep talking. "Not that we're in any great rush to die. Just asking."

"Shurrup!"

"Yeah, shurrup!"

"I don't suppose you thought of ordering us some coffee?"

That was going too far, because without warning Green Sneakers angrily put his gun to her head.

"Shurrup!" he said. "Hold your stupid tongue or I'll blow your head off, *kaboom!* I'm sick of your billing and cooing. My brother said we're to wait, so we'll wait. *Basta!*"

Poldi emitted a startled squeak. Montana took her hand and squeezed it.

They didn't have long to wait, because the twins had only just calmed down when a figure approached from the other side of the clearing. A woman. Wearing the same patterned tracksuit as Rosaria in the video of the exorcism and carrying a jute bag, she uttered a string of oaths as she strode over to Poldi and Montana.

Poldi groaned softly.

"Porca Madonna!" Montana exclaimed when he recognized the woman.

"No!"

"Starting that again?"

"No! No, absolutely not!"

I slammed my notebook down on the table, jumped to my feet, and paced up and down the courtyard.

"No! No resurrections, please!"

"God Almighty!" Poldi cried angrily. "Then go on denying reality and living in your dream world of petty bourgeois bliss!"

"Which of us is living in a dream world? You try to sell me one tall story after another, and for what? Because you think I'm naive, that's why! You're shameless! I've been really patient—exorcisms, people who speak with your voice, secret societies, Death, your celeb buddies, et cetera. I do have a bit of imagination myself, but there are limits. If you bring Rosaria/Antonella back to life, I'm out. That's it."

"May I, just this once, go on telling you about this in peace?"

"No."

She looked at me with a smile.

"What if I promise you there's an entirely plausible, logical, watertight explanation?"

I stared at her suspiciously.

"You're only pulling another fast one on me."

She shook her head and raised one hand. "I swear," she said innocently.

"You don't think I'm naive?"

"Perish the very thought."

I calmed down a little, fetched myself a beer, and resumed my seat.

"Okay, last chance, but I promise you, one more tall story like that and I'm out for good."

"Effing bloody volcano," the woman in the tracksuit could be heard swearing as she came. "First this effing wood with its effing roots and twigs and branches everywhere. You either get tripped up or get poked in the eye. And it smells of effing mushrooms. I hate mushrooms."

She strode across the mossy ground with the air of someone having to wade through a disgusting morass.

"And then this effing lava! You're likely to break an ankle every step you take!"

"Tell me it isn't true, Poldi!" Montana said in a low voice.

"Keep calm, *tesoro*," Poldi whispered back. "Leave the talking to me and stick to the plan."

"Morning, boss," Red Sneakers said nervously when the woman in the tracksuit had reached the boulder and was, with a look of relief, catching her breath.

She was panting like someone at the end of a long trek, but her face was also excessively and rather unflatteringly made up.

"Morning, boss" came Green Sneaker's echo. "Shall we—"

The woman cut him short with a "Ssh!" and a curt gesture. Then she planted herself in front of Poldi. Poldi got up and looked her in the eye.

"Well, what do you say now, Poldi?"

Poldi said nothing.

"Dumbstruck, are you?"

"*Porca Madonna!*" breathed Montana.

No wonder, because despite the woman's heavy makeup and although she wasn't wearing a wig—her short haircut was less a haircut than the result of wind, weather, and erosion—the resemblance was really uncanny.

Poldi heaved a loud sigh and said in German, "Hello, Maria, nice to see you again." She turned to Montana. "Vito, may I introduce Maria? She's my twin sister."

"Yes, the one you tried to kill!" Maria screeched, suddenly beside herself with rage. She grabbed Poldi by the throat and squeezed it like a madwoman. "But I've got you at last, you miserable wretch! You won't escape me this time, you dirty bitch! I'm going to finish you, you pig's arsehole, you streak of shit, you filthy slut, you . . . you whore!"

The Bavarian language has any number of colorful epithets applicable to women.

12

*Tells of survival, of family and love, envy and death.
Poldi runs out of time, Montana turns blue, and
everything goes according to plan for Maria. Or
nearly so, because, as always, something intervenes.
In this instance, a little bird. The result is that Montana has to reveal a personal secret, a bug is found
under Poldi's sofa, and her nephew gets maximum
points.*

My Auntie Poldi looked at me as if she was waiting for
my usual reaction, but I think I merely stared at her.
She waved a hand to and fro in front of my eyes to see if
there was any reaction.

"Feeling better?"

I considered this. I felt I'd completely overcooked a bend
and was trying somehow to get back on track. A thousand
questions were swirling around in my head. One in particular.

"Why didn't you ever say you had a twin sister?"

"Who says I didn't?"

"Hello? This is the first I've heard of it."

"Speak for yourself."

"Er . . . So who else knows all about Maria?"

"Well, Peppe knew, of course. And your other aunts and Uncle Martino, they know."

"So why the devil did no one ever mention it?"

Poldi sighed.

"Can't you think? Because I didn't want them to, that's why. Shall I go on or not?"

I nodded.

She emitted another long sigh.

"I've spent my entire life running away from things. School, parents, getting too close to people, men I loved, big opportunities, responsibility. Myself too."

I started to contest this, but she cut me short with a curt gesture.

"Most of all I've run away from Maria all my life. But as usually happens, no matter what you run away from, it catches up with you sooner or later, and it's bigger and worse than before. That's what it's like with Maria; she always catches me up."

She sipped at her drink and then went on without looking at me. Her eyes were focused on something far, far beyond me.

"So Maria is my twin sister, but although we're as outwardly indistinguishable as two peas from the same pod, she's quite different from me. I was a happy child. I was funny and had a lot of friends, as you may imagine, but there was always something dark about Maria. Something that strikes fear into you even though you don't know at first what it is. That's why she never had many friends and the few she did have soon sheered off. She never had an easy time of it, Maria didn't, and although she wasn't stupid—far from it—she always found reading and writing a problem. I could kick myself for not having caught on at once when those emails came from Antonella, but I thought Maria was dead."

She took another drink.

"She was always envious of people. It was like she'd been born with a sort of skin she couldn't slough off. Some people are like that, you know. They're firmly convinced that life has shortchanged them and that everyone wants to deprive them of something. That's why they soon start taking things away from other people, simply because they feel entitled to. They've no sense of shame or remorse. Maria was envious and jealous of everyone, but mainly of me. I don't know why. I loved her because she was my sister, but Maria always thought everything dropped into my lap and she got nothing. She was always trying to break my possessions or steal them. First of all my dolls, but later on she did her best to alienate my women friends and my earliest lovers. Once, while I was on location in Australia, she even sneaked into our bed and waited for Peppe to come home, can you imagine? Peppe kicked her out at once, of course. So you may be able to understand why I soon steered clear of her and have never felt safe from her. Only in the last couple of years, because I thought she must be dead."

I said nothing.

Poldi took another sip.

"We must have been about six when our parents noticed she was setting traps around the house. She caught little creatures in them and watched them die. They were really ingenious, those traps, so it was obvious Maria wasn't stupid—that she actually had a high IQ when it came to stealing and torturing. None of the therapists my parents dragged her to managed to drive that out of her. She merely became more ingenious than ever. At twelve she burned down our old house in the middle of the night. It was an inferno—my parents and I only just managed to get out in time. Maria was standing in the garden, calmly watching. A detective inspector's daughter! My father didn't utter a word for weeks. There was only one solution: Maria was consigned to an 'institution,' as they're known. Locked up, in other words. Of course, that was far from the end of it. On her release she continued to dog my footsteps and try to make my life a misery, take my place and ultimately get rid of me. Because I was the shadow that darkened her life, whether I liked it or not. I always felt guilty about this and tried to right a few of the wrongs she'd committed, but I'll tell you about all that another time. All you need to know right now is, the last time we saw each other was in Tanzania. Maria was working for Kigumbe, and there was—let's say—an accident. Which I couldn't—let's say—have prevented. With a car. Maria was in it, and it caught fire, and I wasn't able to save her. Or maybe I didn't want to save her, I don't know. Although I knew who and what she was, it broke my heart, because I thought she was dead. But she wasn't. She turned up again, and she had a plan."

I picture the two of them, my Auntie Poldi and her sister Maria, trying to throttle each other in that clearing like a brace of Furies, Poldi in her bunny-eared onesie, Maria in her patterned tracksuit. Their resemblance was striking, especially in that incandescent state, but the more I picture this scene, the more differences I discern. Poldi's rage was ultra-Bavarian and sprang from the same source as her effervescent love and generosity. She bestowed her rage, like her love, from the bottom of her heart, without hatred and in the firm belief that she could improve the world with passion and, if need be, with a few knuckle sandwiches. Maria's rage, by contrast, sprang from a dark place, for where Poldi keeps her heart, all Maria possessed was a dirty glacier of hatred and envy. Or so I imagine. Envy and an incapacity for love had made her age far more unfavorably than Poldi. Booze, tobacco, and love affairs notwithstanding, Poldi still has fine, pearly skin adorned with wrinkles resembling a slightly wind-ruffled sea that's a pleasure to behold. Maria's face looked furrowed and bloated, its burst capillaries inadequately disguised with makeup. Then there were her eyes —the eyes that had ultimately betrayed her on the exorcism video. Maria's eyes had originally been as brown as Poldi's ever-sparkling boot-button eyes, but they had lost all their color, becoming pale and empty.

While the sisters were trying to throttle each other, the twins merely watched in amusement, naked Montana in disbelief. And still standing on the edge of the clearing, fiddling with the papers on his clipboard like an uninvolved expert, was Death.

Midway between heaven and earth, the clearing was a really good place where something ancient and pure seemed to be sleeping. It was a place in which to find peace and have a little chat with the universe.

Yet it was there, of all fine places, that Maria and Poldi now went for one another, growling and snarling, cursing and gasping. Although she looked older, Maria was in better shape than Poldi, so the fight quickly ceased to be an amusing scuffle between two sisters and became a life-or-death struggle.

Still handcuffed but taking no notice of Maria's two thugs, Montana eventually stepped in.

"*Basta!*" he yelled. "That's enough! Stop this at once!"

He tried to separate the sisters but was promptly punched by Maria. Montana is a gentleman of the old school. As a street urchin in Giarre, on the other hand, he had learned to stand up for himself at an early age, in keeping with the old, gender-neutral rule: one punch gets two in return. Before Maria knew what was happening, his cuffed hands had mutated into fists and dealt her a haymaker.

With a yell, she let go of Poldi and measured her length on the mossy ground. Red and Green Sneakers were momentarily taken aback; then they leveled their guns at Montana.

"That's enough!" he bellowed. "Lower your weapons! We're all going to cool it, is that clear? Easy now!"

"You hit the boss!" Red Sneakers said indignantly.

"Yeah, you did!" said Green Sneakers.

Maria got to her feet and sat down on the boulder, and Poldi, breathing hard, did likewise. Tempers cooled a little. Maria spat.

"Ah, the Signor Commissario!" she said to Poldi in German, one eye on Montana. "You and your thing for policemen. Still, he looks very virile. That appeals to me. Maybe I'll let him live a little longer if he gives me a demonstration of his *sicilianità*, what do you think?"

"What do you want, Maria?"

Maria made a show of having to consider the question. Then, innocence personified: "Revenge? Compensation for all you've done to me?"

"I've never done anything to you, Maria."

"You tried to kill me!" snarled Maria, flying off the handle again. "You left me to die in that car, cool as a cucumber!"

Poldi shook her head and strove to remain calm.

"That's not true, Maria, and you know it. It was simply impossible. There was fire everywhere, and you know what fire does to me—you best of all."

"Oh, you poor thing!"

"How did you get out of the car in the end?"

Maria grinned. "I wasn't in it."

Poldi shook her head. "That's not possible. I saw you."

"How stupid can you get! You only saw me get in, and the next thing you saw was an explosion and smoke and then fire. By that time I'd switched to a car of Kigumbe's. It was all prearranged, of course. Or did you really think I'd let myself get arrested so easily?"

"So you weren't in the car at all?"

"No."

"And for over two years I've been reproaching myself for not having managed to save you, Maria!"

"Serves you right."

"But I'd have lost my own life if I'd tried."

"Well, at least it would have sweetened my memories of you."

Poldi heaved a despairing sigh and glanced over at Montana. He looked ready to pounce, but the suspicious twins were holding him in check. Briefly reminded of a long-ago night out at the Oktoberfest with Maria, Teresa, Caterina, and Luisa, Poldi could find no residue of sisterly affection in her heart. Instead she decided it was time to settle certain accounts, draw a line under the past, and deliver her sister into the hands of the authorities for good. First, though, she wanted some answers.

"Why did you kill Sister Rita and Antonella, Maria?"

Maria looked surprised.

"What? I didn't kill either of them. All right, I admit that was the original plan, at least where that slut Rita was concerned. But something always intervenes in this shitty country. I've never understood what you like about Italy, but you've never had a clue about anything."

"So who was it?" Poldi demanded, unimpressed.

Maria chuckled. "Wouldn't you like to know? Sadly, you're going to have to bite the dust with that question unanswered. No, delete the 'sadly.' Everything worked out perfectly in the end, didn't it? You fell into my traps, you swallowed every false lead of mine. The emails from Antonella, the exorcism, Russo's cartons, and now the statue of the lost Madonna . . . You're such a fool! For a whole year now, you've failed to grasp that I've had a finger in every one of your cases. That surprises you, doesn't it? And now we're here for the grand finale."

"Why here particularly, Maria?"

"Good God, how stupid can you get! Think, Poldi."

"Because it's a favorite place of mine?"

"Spot on! Because I know all about you. Such a nice place, isn't it? So pure and unspoiled, it's enough to make you sick. You won't be here long, though, you'll see."

Maria got up with a groan. She reached into her jute bag and produced an automatic.

Montana braced himself.

Poldi, who saw that Death was spreading out his forms on the mossy ground, got up too.

"So this is it?" said Montana. "All this effort, just to gun us down and dissolve us in acid?"

Maria stared at him in surprise.

"Ah yes, the flasks of acid," she said in Italian, as though she had only just remembered them. "No, they weren't meant for you."

"Really?" Montana sounded puzzled. "Who, then?"

Maria sighed resignedly, like a teacher deploring the incorrigible stupidity of a pupil at the back of the class, pointed her automatic at Red Sneakers, and—*plop!*—shot him. He fell to the ground with a final groan of surprise.

Before his brother could utter a word, still less point his gun at her, Maria calmly turned and—*plop!*—shot him too. Just like that.

"Stupidity deserves to be punished, don't you agree?" said Maria.

Montana prepared to hurl himself at her, but she spun round and leveled her gun at Poldi, shaking her head reprovingly. Montana subsided, grinding his teeth. Poldi stationed herself beside him.

"Do you have the Black Madonna? The original?"

"Of course," Maria said irritably. "And I'll be rewarded for it by Madonna Nera. What did you think? That little slut Sister Rita got there before me? I always get what I want in the end, don't I? And now I got you too. The Black Madonna was the perfect honeypot to get you here."

Poldi briefly debated how she could extricate her Vito from this mess unscathed. There were two dead bodies lying there already, and she wanted at all costs to prevent Montana from joining them. The trouble was, she was bereft of ideas and Maria still had her gun. All she could do now was gain time.

"But if you've been wanting to kill me all this time, why trouble to get me suspected of murder, spray threats on my house, try to deport me, et cetera?"

Maria rolled her eyes.

"Christ Almighty! Because it was fun, of course! The gentlemen from Madonna Nera want their statue back at all costs, and my little game raised the stakes, so to speak. Get it?"

Poldi nodded.

"Listen, Maria, that time in Tanzania—"

"Shush!" Maria broke in. "I know you're only trying to stall, but fuck that. We're finishing this here and now. I still have to take care of your nephew. It's touching, the way the poor fool worships you and tries to be like you. Really idiotic."

"Leave him out of it, Maria! He has nothing to do with all this."

"All right, I'll think about it as long as you kneel down and say sorry." Maria pointed her pistol at the ground. "Convincingly, mind!"

Poldi knew that kneeling on her bad knee would leave her ill-equipped for an ultimate showdown, but she also knew Maria. It was high time to call on her repertoire of dirty tricks.

Instead of kneeling, she took a step toward Maria and started, very softly, to sing:

Were I a little bird
and had two little wings,

I would fly to you.
But since that cannot be,
but since that cannot be,
I shall stay here.

Although Montana didn't understand a word, he recognized the tune of the old German folk song. To his surprise, he saw that Maria was trembling, seemingly in the throes of some profound emotion.

"Shut up!" she hissed at Poldi. "Stop that!"

But Poldi sang softly on.

Although I'm far from you,
I'm with you while asleep
and speak with you.
On awakening, though,
on awakening, though,
I find myself alone.

"Stop that, I tell you!" Maria screamed.

But she was trembling more and more convulsively. Despite herself, the tender words and simple melody of that old, innocent lullaby seemed to be resonating somewhere deep within her. There where her heart had once been, perhaps they were mingling with buried memories of something childishly good, building up into a choir and calling to her. Trembling, sweating, and breathing heavily, Maria was visibly striving to resist the song and her memories and everything associated with them. With a groan, she tried to raise her gun, but the gentle song was robbing her of all her strength. Poldi saw her eyes grow moist. By the time the third verse came, Maria finally gave way and joined in as if she simply couldn't help it. She sang in a choking voice, like someone suddenly finding comfort and redemption.

> *Not an hour of the night goes by*
> *that my heart fails to awaken*
> *and remember that you*
> *many a thousand times,*
> *many a thousand times,*
> *have given me your heart.*

Spellbound, Montana listened to Poldi and her grotesque replica singing a German folk song in an enchanted place with two dead bodies lying at their feet, as if that gentle old melody could heal and revive them. He also saw a weeping Maria lower her gun like she could scarcely retain her grip on it. A moment later he saw Poldi kick Maria on the shin with all her might.

Maria screamed and doubled up. Quick as a flash, Poldi wrenched the gun away from her sister and leveled it at her.

"Run!" she shouted to Montana.

But Montana—who'd have thought it?—didn't budge.

"You dirty bitch!" screeched Maria, hopping on the spot and clutching her leg.

"I'm sorry, Maria, but you left me no choice." Poldi stepped back out of Maria's reach, continuing to hold the gun in her outstretched, still cable-tied hands. "Facedown on the ground! And you, Vito, get going!"

"Forget it," he growled. "Give me the gun."

But Poldi continued to aim at her sister.

"You've no heart!" Maria wailed. "How could you do this to me?"

"You were going to kill me, Maria, or had you forgotten?"

"I will, too, take it from me!"

"Give me that gun, Poldi!" ordered Montana.

"Shut up and do as I say, both of you!" Poldi tightened her grip on the pistol. "The game's up, Maria. Lie facedown with your hands behind your back."

"What are you going to do now, shoot me?"

"No, hand you over to the police. Vito, would you be good enough to fish a cable tie out of that guy's pocket and cuff my sister? Careful, though, she's dangerous."

Montana promptly inserted his hand in Red Sneakers's pocket, but Maria didn't lie down. She straightened up and stretched.

"You're so naive, Poldi. You seriously think I'd turn myself in?"

"Don't make me do it, Maria."

Maria coolly shrugged her shoulders.

"Nonsense. You don't have the guts."

She turned and started to hobble back the way she'd come.

"Maria! Stop!" Poldi cried desperately. "Stop or I'll fire!"

Maria turned and gave her a wave. "Bang, bang!"

Poldi gripped the pistol even more tightly and aimed it at her.

Montana came up beside her. "Give me the gun, Poldi. I can stop her without having to kill her."

Poldi shook her head. "Stop, Maria! Please!"

Maria was walking faster now. Montana took the weapon from Poldi's hand. She was too weak to resist. He at once took aim at Maria's receding figure and yelled, "Stop!"

But Maria had no intention of stopping. Montana fired a warning shot in the air, but the gun still had a silencer fitted and just went *plop*. Maria continued on her way, undeterred and slightly faster than before. He aimed at her legs, then lowered the gun.

"I can't do it," he groaned. "She looks so like you. It'd be like shooting you."

"It's okay, *tesoro*," Poldi said quietly. "It's okay."

They had to look on impotently as Maria disappeared from view. Pursuit was out of the question, thanks to Montana's bare feet.

He at least found a clasp knife in one of the dead twins' pockets and was able to cut their cable ties at last. Groaning as she massaged her chafed wrists, Poldi saw that Montana was punching a number into Red Sneakers's mobile phone. He was shivering all over with cold.

"Who are you calling?"

"Headquarters. They must launch a manhunt and send a unit up here."

"No, don't." Poldi took the phone out of his hand. "You can't call the police."

"Look, Poldi, I know she's your sister and all, but she's just killed two men and I'm a cop."

"No, at this moment you *aren't* a cop," Poldi insisted. "You're suspended, and your lot are busy trying to pin things on you so you never become one again. Besides, our story sounds pretty crazy, doesn't it? A phantom—one that's allegedly the spitting image of me—tried to kill us but first shot the twins who abducted us, me in a bunny-eared onesie and you stark naked. And, funnily enough, the only fingerprints on the weapon are mine and yours."

"There'll be plenty of pointers to Maria."

Poldi shook her head.

"You don't know her. She's never left any traces behind. You can bet her fingers and palms are silicon-protected. No one will believe our story. They'll book us and put the screws on us, the way they've been wanting to the whole time. No, we must get out of here as fast as possible."

"*Porca Madonna!*" Montana exclaimed as the extent of their predicament sank in.

"I'll call Uncle Martino—he knows the spot."

Montana shook his head. "In view of the situation, better keep your family out of this." He sighed. "Okay, there's another alternative."

With a frown that suggested he was going to find it hard, he stepped aside and made a brief phone call.

Poldi was worried about his ability to withstand the cold for so long without a stitch of clothing. Turning, she saw that Death was standing over the twins and completing his forms without taking any notice of her. She found that faintly reassuring.

"Who did you call?" she asked when Montana returned.

"You'll soon see," he told her. "In three quarters of an hour's time we'll be picked up on the road up there. I'll just have to grin and bear it till then. Let's go, I must keep moving. Maybe we'll find something in the van."

Poldi had her doubts.

"I told you," she said with a sigh. "Maria has never yet left any traces behind. That's why I'm afraid we—"

That was as far as she got, because a distant explosion rent the early morning air and enveloped them in its reverberations.

Montana stared at her.

"I told you," she repeated. "No traces, not ever."

"So much for giving Madonna Nera a kick up the backside."

Poldi put her arms around him and rubbed his back to warm him. He was as cold as the morning breeze.

"All right, *tesoro*?"

He nodded.

"That was a lovely song," he mumbled into her terrycloth.

"Do you still want to marry me?" she whispered. "I mean, I'd understand it if you aren't as keen any longer, now you've met my sister. She'll never leave us in peace. I'd be an imposition."

"You're the sexiest imposition I've ever met," Montana assured her, teeth chattering. "Of course we're going to get married. And if your sister shows up again, it'll be the biggest mistake she's ever made in her life."

At this point Poldi heaved a long, ruminative sigh, and Totti, from under the table, let out a long, ruminative fart. Afternoon in Torre Archirafi was taking its course. Children's voices could be heard coming from the Via Baronessa. I looked at her admiringly and played an imaginary violin.

"Yes, well, Vito is an incurable romantic," said Poldi. "Sicilian, detective inspector, sexual force of nature, lover, rejuvenator, comforter, soulmate, and romantic. I've never missed an opportunity in life, you know. That's because I always thought Maria would be the end of me. But if life asks you what you really want, what do you say?"

"Er . . . 'No thanks'?"

"No, you dumb cluck! You say, 'One of everything, please. *Con tutto*. To go, what's more.'"

My Auntie Poldi knew a thing or two about life, love, and *con tutto*.

"But I've met such a soulmate," she went on, "just as my time runs out. I suppose that's called the irony of fate."

"You don't seriously think you're going to die on your birthday?"

"Of course. Death is very finicky about these things. My birthday's my deadline, and that's that."

I couldn't help being upset by this.

"I won't let it happen," I said. "I mean, I don't believe it! It's utter nonsense, Poldi. Death isn't a person, understand? No ninja, no clipboard! We'll celebrate your birthday, and afterward you'll get married and go on investigating, loving, drinking, and enjoying 'it.' Enough already! *Basta*!"

I pushed my chair back a little and shouted at the evening sky. "Can you hear me, life? You've never asked, but I'm happy to put this on record: I'll have one of everything, please! *Con tutto e con Poldi!* To go, what's more!" I turned back to Poldi. "Don't look like that! It makes me mad, that attitude. I don't want to hear any more of that shit, okay?"

Poldi rolled her eyes.

"So who came and picked you up?"

"Why, Russo."

"No!"

"Yes!"

"No!"

She rolled her eyes again.

• • •

"Well, I'll be buggered!"

Poldi recognized the beefy Mercedes SUV with the tinted windows from a long way off. It had taken only half an hour, so it must have raced through the towns on Etna and negotiated the mountain's umpteen switchbacks at breakneck speed. Now it was approaching the spot where Poldi and Montana were waiting.

The volcanic landscape was littered with shattered, smoking fragments of the twins' van. The remains of its tires were still burning, and the road surface was scorched. Poldi and Montana were standing at the roadside. They hadn't moved from the spot, and Poldi had spent the whole time cuddling and warming her beloved, shivering *commissario*.

Without a word of greeting, Russo emerged from the car holding a blanket, which he threw over Montana. Hans and Franz hurled themselves at Poldi and jumped up at her, barking frenziedly.

Just imagine: the man whom Poldi believed to be a *mafioso* in chief, a crime boss whom she thought the worst of and had been trying to nail for a year, whom she had flirted with and even kissed—it was Italo Russo, of all people, whom Montana had called, and who had, without hesitation, driven up Etna to collect them.

"Are you okay?" he asked.

Montana nodded.

"And you, Poldi?"

It took until then for Poldi to recover the power of speech.

"What the devil's going on here?" she demanded.

"I was going to tell you," Montana began. "I mean, you'd have found out sooner or later."

"Tell me what, Vito?"

278

"We're cousins," said Russo.

Which, it should be noted, doesn't mean much in Italy, and Sicily in particular. "Permit me to introduce my cousin Fabrizia" tells you nothing about the speaker's exact relationship to Fabrizia. For example, I get the impression that I'm related to half my generation in Catania. When I'm out with my (first!) cousin Ciro and he bumps into someone, he'll tell me later it was a cousin of ours. One is always indirectly related or connected to someone or other, and since nobody knows exactly, "cousin" is a universal remedy. All envy and mistrust notwithstanding, it creates a special, almost conspiratorial bond between all Sicilians. As it turned out, however, Montana and Russo really were first cousins.

"No!" cried Poldi.

"Yes," Montana said almost apologetically.

"No!"

"We shouldn't stand around here," said Russo.

Even with the heating turned up full, Montana couldn't stop shivering in the back. His cheeks were pale, his lips blue. Poldi, who was very concerned about him, caught a worried glance from Russo in the rearview mirror.

"We spent the whole of our childhood together," he told her. "Vito is like a brother to me. I was a rather sickly child. Vito always defended me against the other boys, and he made me realize I could achieve anything if I tried. He also saved me from drowning on one occasion."

Poldi asked no more questions. She merely gave Russo a brief account of what had happened, and he listened without interrupting her. Even when she told him about Maria, he remained as imperturbable as a barista when dehydrated backpackers come stumbling into his café on an August afternoon.

Russo drove Montana and Poldi to his property near Femminamorta. While Montana was warming up under the shower, he sent for some clothes from the Via Baronessa and made some phone calls. He looked focused and determined and as intrepid as usual. *Like a general on the eve of battle,* thought Poldi.

"Do you still want to marry me?" Montana called from under the shower.

"Why ask?"

"Don't let's kid ourselves. You and I both know that Italo is far more than just a successful nurseryman. As a policeman, I oughtn't to have any contact with him."

"But?"

"Italo isn't a bad person," Montana replied after a moment's hesitation. "He isn't a killer, nor has he ever taken out a contract on anyone. And he really is like a brother to me. He's family, and to keep things that way we came to an agreement many years ago: I would never personally investigate him or inform on him. In return, Italo occasionally passes on information I would never obtain otherwise."

Poldi was dumbfounded. "He's a snitch of yours?"

"If you want to put it that way. Well, what do you say now?"

"You're my man, Vito. I live in a greenhouse myself — who would I be to throw stones? Mind you, I can't promise that *I* won't go on investigating him."

Montana turned off the water and got out of the shower. He was looking much better now, pink-skinned after all that hot water.

"I think Italo might even enjoy that. I almost get the impression he fancies you."

Poldi deemed it wiser not to comment.

But what really robbed her of speech was when she walked into Russo's office a little later and saw Ravi sitting on the sofa.

He gave her a broad smile and said in perfect Italian, "How nice to see you again, Donna Poldina."

"Well, go on, say it," my Auntie Poldi said with a sigh, when I failed to react in the usual way.

I shook my head. "No, no problem. So Ravi was sitting there."

"Don't you find that a bit unbelievable?"

"Your twin sister a contract killer, Mafia boss a police informant . . . Why should I be surprised by a snooping sitar player?" I really couldn't summon up more than a weary smile. "Hey, come on, Poldi!"

"You'll get another clip round the ear if you aren't careful. Want one?"

I leaned forward a little.

"I always thought there was something a bit unkosher about Ravi. Okay, what do I get if I guess why he was sitting there?"

"If you want to make it a game, why don't you set the terms?"

"If I guess right, you must stop all this talk about dying on your birthday." I put out my hand. "Okay?"

She glared at me angrily. "Know what you can do? You can go to hell."

"No thanks."

I continued to hold my hand out, grinning.

Poldi capitulated. "But only on one condition."

"I'm listening."

"You have to put me in at least one chapter of your novel. It doesn't have to be a long one, a short one'll do. Make a character out of me if you like. It's got to be juicy, mind. *Con tutto*. Earthy, brash, nerve-racking, dramatic. But unpretentious too, and full of heart, and above all funny. The way I am myself. Or was, whichever."

"Hey, Poldi, it doesn't work like that," I grumbled. "Honestly, I doubt if I'm up to it at all, this writing business. And being funny certainly isn't my bag. Comedy's the hardest thing of the lot to pull off, everyone says so."

"What should you say if you'd like to try something you've never done before but which you do think you're capable of, and some fool says, 'Yes, but that's the hardest thing of all'?"

"Er . . ."

"Then you say—listen carefully—'I'm well aware of that because'"—short pause—"'I'm very good at it.'"

"But that would be a barefaced lie."

"Nonsense! Moderation is a sign of weakness. Say it!"

"I'm well aware of that because, er . . . I'm very good at it."

"No, say it like this: 'I'm well aware of that'"—short pause—"'because I'm very good at it.' Again."

I had to recite the sentence three times before Poldi was reasonably satisfied.

"Well?" Poldi demanded, her eyes sparkling because she had turned the tables on me yet again. "Deal?"

"Okay, deal." I sighed, and she slapped my palm.

"You'll never guess what Ravi was doing there, not with your limited imagination, but let's hear you try."

"Well, the way I see it," I said, sitting back in my chair, "Russo planted Ravi on you to look after you and do a little snooping when he saw there was something wrong with you. Ravi probably works for him in any case. And because Ravi happens to play the sitar as well—something that would appeal to an ex-hippie like you—he made the ideal Trojan horse. You were bound to give him a job."

Poldi stared at me the way Verrocchio probably stared at young Leonardo when he saw how well the lad from Vinci could paint drapery. I felt pretty good.

"*Cento punti,* my boy! Ravi is a mathematical genius— he manages Russo's finances. And he's so modest too. His job wasn't to spy on me though, just to take care of me."

Ravi had brought something with him: a ziplock bag full of electronic components and wires. Poldi could guess what it was.

"I located them in your house using a special device, Donna Poldina. In the telephone, beneath the table lamp, behind the television—your house was thoroughly bugged. The bedroom too, and your nephew's attic room."

He beamed at Poldi as if he had found buried treasure. Montana groaned. Russo gave Ravi a nod.

"Maria," Poldi whispered in dismay. "She knew everything the whole time."

"I'm afraid there's another party involved," Ravi went on. "One of the bugs is very different from the others—not as efficient. It was stuck to the underside of the sofa."

"I see . . ." Poldi considered this.

"I think it'd be best if you lie low for a while," said Russo.

"Out of the question," she said.

"He's right, Poldi," said Montana.

"What part of 'out of the question' didn't you understand?"

Montana looked at his cousin and shook his head in despair.

Poldi turned back to Ravi. "Which side of the sofa?"

13

Tells of church pews and lies, friends and frustra-
tion, love and intimacy, home and naïveté. Poldi now
has a plan, but first she has to swallow a bitter pill.
Information is compiled in the Via Baronessa, the
ball starts rolling, and a wedding is planned. Padre
Paolo touches on a dark chapter in Italian history,
and soon afterward Poldi sneaks out of the house.

At this point in the tale, Poldi was interrupted by someone ringing the doorbell.

"Ah," she said, getting up to answer it, "that'll be Vito."

Outside, evening had already overtaken afternoon, bringing with it the scent of grilled fish and wild fennel, and I was
gradually recovering my appetite. The church clock struck
seven. A television quiz show was blaring somewhere in the
neighborhood. I heard voices at the door, then Poldi came
back into the courtyard with Montana, who was looking
cool in bleached jeans and a T-shirt. He greeted me warmly,
then turned to Poldi.

"It's all set. Does he know?"

"We're nearly ready," Poldi told him. "Then we can go."

I smelled a rat.

"Hey, what's going on, folks?"

"It's almost time," Poldi said in German. "We must go as soon as it's dark."

"Er . . . Where to?"

"To extract a confession from a murderer, smash Madonna Nera, and, with a bit of luck, catch Maria. Why did you think I was telling you all this?"

"You're shitting me."

"Not at all. Or, to use your own words, no."

Montana looked at his watch. "Is there a problem?"

"No," said Poldi.

"Yes!" I cried, aghast. "Have you lost your mind, Poldi? You can't just tell me, out of the blue, that we're setting off on a lethal suicide mission!"

"Don't start that again!" Poldi rolled her eyes. "Don't be so niminy-piminy. Are we a team or aren't we?"

"But we aren't Batman and Robin, we're just Don Quixote and Sancho Panza, and they got a thrashing every time."

"Don't wet your knickers. We've planned everything down to the last detail—tonight is the moment of truth. I'll make us a smoothie."

She disappeared into the kitchen. Montana was smoking serenely.

What was I to do?

I took one of his cigarettes.

"Has she told you?" he whispered to me when Poldi was out of earshot. "I mean, about us?"

"Yes. Congratulations."

He leaned forward a little. "You know her. Think she'll get cold feet?"

I shook my head.

Montana grinned at me.

"Ever been a best man?"

"You're crazy," I said. "You're all crazy."

Poldi, coming back with the smoothies, saw the look on my face.

"Look, my boy, it's not easy. We can either sit here and wait for Maria or Madonna Nera to kill us all, or we can take charge of our own destiny. Well, which is it to be?"

I was feeling sick.

"Why can't I be the brilliant computer genius who controls the whole operation from his keyboard and hacks through all the security systems so the heroes have a free hand?"

Poldi patted my hand. "Because your IQ only equips you to be a hero."

Then she told me about the last part of her investigations leading up to my return from France.

"I'm sorry," Padre Stefano said as usual when Poldi sat down on the pew beside him, and he instinctively recoiled a little.

The young priest was incessantly kneading his hairy hands together on his lap. His gawky frame seemed to have caved in. What with his pallor, his five o'clock shadow, and the film of perspiration on his forehead, he looked much older than his age and as nervous as a confirmed bachelor before his first blind date.

"How nice to see you again, Donna Poldina."

Poldi had chosen the little church of San Sebastiano in Acireale as a meeting place because they could talk there without fear of eavesdroppers. At this hour, shortly after noon, no one was there but a few elderly widows, but she kept an eye on them all just in case.

"It's really terrible, what they've imputed to you," the priest continued in a whisper, without looking at her.

"Weeds never die, as they say here."

"Thanks, I'll remember that. How can I help you?"

"How well do you know Commissario Morello?"

The priest turned to her in surprise.

"I'm sorry?"

"You heard me."

"Commissario Morello is undoubtedly an estimable servant of the Holy See and a devout Christian."

Poldi said nothing.

Padre Stefano sighed and kneaded his hands together. "You place me in an awkward position, Donna Poldina."

"Then please excuse my effrontery." Poldi rose to her feet.

"Wait!" whispered the priest. She sat down again.

"I may personally have had a few doubts about his integrity, but I haven't hitherto ventured to confide in anyone for lack of evidence."

Poldi looked at him keenly.

"What sort of doubts?"

"Commissario Morello has occasionally expressed sympathy for certain groups on the extreme right wing of the political spectrum. That, mind you, is not a crime in itself. Freedom of speech holds good in the Vatican as well. But once, when I discreetly suggested focusing on a certain criminal network named Madonna Nera in connection with the theft of the Black Madonna, he became extremely angry. He told me to mind my own business and leave him to do his job."

"And that was it?"

Padre Stefano squirmed. "It comes under the seal of the

confessional. I once heard Sister Rita's confession, and she"
—he cleared his throat and lowered his voice still further—
"she implicated Commissario Morello. With the best will in
the world, I can tell you no more."

At that moment, I imagine, Poldi's POLDI must have
clicked on again. While the priest was speaking, Poldi registered his facial expressions and various involuntary eye
movements. That must also have been the moment when her
subconscious put the name Death had whispered to her—
and which had appeared on her mind map—in the out-box.

She stared at Padre Stefano as if she were seeing him for
the first time.

"Bugger me, how could I have been so stupid!"

"I'm sorry?"

Poldi forced herself to remain coolly professional.

"Know something, Padre? The evening the two of you
were at my house, there was a certain amount of toing and
froing on the sofa while I was in the kitchen. I couldn't at
first recall which of you was sitting where, but now I think
I've remembered."

"What do you mean, Donna Poldina?"

Poldi just looked at him.

Suddenly: *Brrrooom! Brrrooom!*

"So sorry!"

Feverishly the priest felt in his trouser pocket.

The sinister sound filled the little church like the buzzing
of some hellish insect. Several of the widows turned their
heads indignantly.

Poldi produced her mobile phone from her handbag and
held it up. Padre Stefano's name was on the display. She had
secretly called him.

"A bit satanic for a priest's ringtone, don't you think?"

Padre Stefano had found his phone by now and turned it off. The ringtone fell silent, but to Poldi it seemed to hang in the still church air like a sulfurous haze.

"Touché," Padre Stefano said in a glacial voice, silently clapping his hands. "I congratulate you. Is your *commissario* waiting impatiently outside?"

"Yes."

"And listening in as well, I'm sure."

"Precisely."

Padre Stefano leaned forward. "Hello there, Commissario Montana. Nice try, but disappointingly ineffectual, I'm afraid." Turning to Poldi, he said, "A ringtone. I ask you!"

"Did my sister put you up to it?"

He merely gave an apologetic shrug.

"No, she didn't have to," Poldi surmised. "All she had to do was set things up—that's her forte. You did the rest when Sister Rita flew into a panic and everything threatened to come out."

"You have a vivid imagination, Donna Poldina."

"You may belong to Madonna Nera, Padre, but you're already on Maria's hit list. Then she'll sell off the Black Madonna to the highest bidder. She's like that, so you'd be wise to come with me and make a clean breast of everything."

"Perhaps you're also on that list, Donna Poldina. You, Commissario Montana, your nephew, and many other people dear to you, who knows? Maybe we'll simply bide our time. What do you think?"

"Why?" whispered Poldi.

"Perhaps I've got designs on the papacy." He laughed. "That would be a joke." He got to his feet. "If we trust in

God's mercy in silence and humility, perhaps He will, in His goodness, grant us and our dear ones a long life. Perhaps. That's the most we can hope for, isn't it?"

"You're disgusting," Poldi hissed. "The word 'God' should never pass your lips."

But all she could do was watch impotently as Padre Stefano made his way down the gloomy nave and out into the open. She could see Montana silhouetted in the doorway. Padre Stefano simply strode past him without a word, unimpeded.

"No!" I exclaimed again — relatively predictably.

"Yes!" This time it was Montana who said it. "It's enough to make one sick. We can't prove anything against him. I called Morello at once and was told he'd been temporarily suspended on suspicion of having molested a female Spanish pilgrim. It looks like they plan to neutralize him too. Morello wants to help us as much as he can, but things are getting tricky."

"Another tentacle of the Madonna Nera octopus," Poldi said grimly.

I well know what it feels like to be brought up short when you're going full speed ahead or just after the start. It's the story of my life, so to speak. Usually the obstacle is me, so I give up right away and start on something new. Or give up altogether. Not so my Auntie Poldi, even if she says different, like she's always run away from everything and so on. She's not to be believed, because Poldi, in her heart of hearts, is a terrier who'll fight till she drops if she believes in something. Setbacks only activate her reserves of energy. Sure, in her depressive phases she'll hit the bottle and want everything to end, but she's a phoenix, my Auntie Poldi. She always bounces back.

Poldi never wants to be a burden to anyone, but unlike me she has no inhibitions about asking for help if need be. And in contrast to me she has masses of friends—the coolest and most wonderful friends imaginable.

On sober reflection, though, the situation really did look bleak: no solid evidence against Padre Stefano, a murderous sister breathing down her neck, and a powerful criminal organization after her and the town where she lived.

Run-of-the-mills like me would quietly strike camp, pack up, move out, disappear, knuckle under. Not so my Auntie Poldi. Whoever was behind Madonna Nera, they now had to deal with a ferocious and determined adversary. I saw it as a contest between David and Goliath, except that the David in this case was not in the first flush of youth and wore a wig.

"I want to know all about that godless priest," Poldi told Montana grimly when they returned, frustrated, to Torre Archirafi that afternoon. "Family background, favorite dish, what circles he moves in, where he damn well is now—simply everything. Can you manage that, Vito?"

Montana nodded. "Officially my hands are tied, but Italo can take care of that sort of thing. I can consult DeSantis in Rome, and back at headquarters I can rely on Zanotta. I'll also have a word with Morello, but the whole thing won't be easy."

The two of them spent the time until evening making a series of phone calls, some of which might set the odd ball rolling, but some not. For the moment, that was the most they could do.

Although Poldi did not believe that Maria would show up again so soon, Russo insisted on sending an inconspicuous team to patrol the Via Baronessa at regular intervals. He also put a tail on Padre Stefano, because Poldi surmised that he and Maria would soon meet for a handover of the Black Madonna.

During the several days that went by like this, spring hurriedly packed its bags and made way for summer, the true ruler of Sicily. The aunts, Uncle Martino, and Totti blew into the Via Baronessa like a fresh breeze laden with good humor and deliberate optimism, bringing pasta bakes, pickled vegetables, and *gelati* with them. In spite of everything, Poldi began to feel a bit more at home again. The aunts insisted on knowing how she proposed to celebrate (a) her birthday, and (b)—most importantly, of course—her nuptials. In Sicily a wedding beats everything, even the final of the World Cup. Understandably, given their current situation, Montana and Poldi were not in the mood for a party, so the aunts delightedly undertook to organize one. *Con tutto*. Don't get me wrong. Teresa, Caterina, and Luisa aren't blind to reality, far from it. They do, however, possess one wonderful attribute: unshakable optimism. They cherish a firm belief that all will end well, that there's always some way out of every mess, that justice exists, and that death can sometimes be thwarted by pigheaded self-assurance.

Apropos of Death, he looked in from time to time and made timid attempts to speak to Poldi in private. He evidently had something on his mind, but Poldi ignored him.

She had decided not to waste any of her last few weeks on earth thinking about Death.

Another visitor was Assistente Zanotta, who regularly dropped in to kiss Poldi's hand and, with a conspiratorial air, to provide his suspended boss with copies he had made —not entirely legally—of certain documents. These included some that had reached him by a discreetly roundabout route from Rome, together with friendly messages from Montana's former colleagues there. Zanotta reported that the dead twins had been identified as two brothers from Cefalù who had spent a good proportion of their short lives behind bars.

Poldi surmised from this that Maria had been—or was still—living in the Cefalù area. At any rate, she had disappeared.

Padre Stefano made no move. He spent most of the time at his mother's house in Linguaglossa and only occasionally went to Mass there.

Everyone seemed to be waiting for something.

Ravi played the sitar in the courtyard and compiled all the items of information that came in on a laptop. Thanks to all the comings and goings that occurred at this period, it could be said that Poldi's home resembled a dovecote.

I picture it as a little commune that discreetly dispersed toward evening to allow the engaged couple to enjoy some relaxation and "it." Poldi told me later that those nights were different from usual. No less passionate, of course, because their lovemaking was still a collision between two forces of nature, but somehow quieter and more intimate —heartfelt to the point of self-dissolution. They scarcely moved. Poldi devised a term for it: holding still. Closely entwined and conjoined, my Auntie Poldi and Vito Montana "held still," perhaps as a way of halting the passage of time. Or simply because they loved each other so deeply.

On the evening of the third day something happened. Padre Paolo called at No. 29 Via Baronessa looking pale and tired, but in his face Poldi at once detected the familiar glow of an investigator hot on the trail.

"Her name wasn't always Cocuzza!" he blurted out after the first coffee. "Young Alessio D'Anunzio, who works in the Comune di Riposto, owed me a favor because some years ago I helped to get him off a charge of shoplifting. That's how I obtained a look at her entry in the residential register."

In a place like Sicily, where many aspects of daily life can be really complicated thanks to bureaucracy, corruption, fatalism, and disorganization, it's always helpful to know someone who owes you a little favor. It usually works quite well, and without anyone having to keep accounts. Recipients of little favors always know they will one day have to repay them. That, for instance, is why the dozen bottles of Nero d'Avola and the splendid *panettone* we give our janitor for Christmas aren't an act of bribery, because he can't just graciously accept the wine and the cake and leave it at that. No, wine and *panettone* are a little favor that places the janitor ever so slightly in our debt—a debt he will naturally have to repay in due course. For example, the next time there's a leak and we urgently need a plumber. And that, in turn, will be a little favor which *we* will have to repay someday. The janitor knows this, we know it, the plumber knows it, Alessio knows it, everyone knows it. Little favors keep the machinery of Italian society running and are often a more stable currency than the euro.

So Padre Paolo had found out that Signora Cocuzza was a widow twice over. Her second husband, the confectioner Salvatore Cocuzza, with whom she had opened the café bar in Torre Archirafi, had died in the tenth year of their marriage. Cause of death: blood poisoning after a routine operation performed by a slipshod surgeon in Acireale. That in itself would have accounted for Signora Cocuzza's melancholy frame of mind.

"But many years earlier," Padre Paolo went on excitedly, "when she was a very young woman, she was married to a Daniele Grasso from Caltagirone. The couple moved to Torre Archirafi, but Daniele died in the second year of their marriage. The cause of death is described on his death certificate as 'accidental.'"

The name Daniele Grasso rang a bell with Montana. He hurriedly leafed through the document copies brought him by Zanossa and, after a brief search, struck oil.

"Someone named Daniele Grasso lost his life in the devastating bomb attack on Bologna's main-line station in 1980," he reported, "one of the worst terrorist atrocities in Italian history. Eighty-five dead, over two hundred injured. There was total chaos — I still recall how traumatic it was. The authorities originally assumed that the extreme left-wing Red Brigades were responsible, but inquiries soon indicated that the attack had been carried out by a neofascist network. I took part in those investigations from the mideighties onward, but our work was obstructed and delayed at every level. Although there were a few convictions, the true background to the atrocity has never been fully elucidated. One year previously, Daniele Grasso had been recruited as an informant by the Polizia di Prevenzione because of his links to Madonna Nera, but then he disappeared. I mean, we're talking about a time without computers, central databanks, and so on. Grasso simply disappeared off the radar and did not reappear until that bomb went off in Bologna."

"And you think he's the same Daniele Grasso as Signora Cocuzza's late husband?"

Montana shrugged. "It needs checking, but these things take time."

"But you must at least have known if he was married."

He shook his head. "Files disappeared, official inquiries petered out, sources dried up, witnesses were intimidated. A successful investigation was almost impossible."

Poldi thought for a moment.

"With the best will in the world, I can't see Signora Cocuzza as a terrorist."

Her initial impulse was to confront the sad signora with that assumption, but she was afraid her friend would be even more unapproachable than before.

She looked again at the phone picture she'd taken of the old group photo showing her friends and neighbors in their youth. They looked so young and serious. *Like a choir,* she thought, *but too serious for a choir.* The resolution of the phone picture was not very good, but she zoomed into it a bit for a better look at the faces. Although they seemed to float in a sea of pixels, Poldi suddenly made out something different. Something she had hitherto mistaken for a shadow.

"Well, I'll be buggered!"

Beyond the heads of the group, on the building the young people were standing in front of were some pixelated but relatively legible fragments of lettering in angular, well-spaced block capitals.

QUADI

Poldi recognized the letters and knew at once what that faded inscription meant in full. She passed it every day.

It was time for a little local on-site inspection.

I picture my Auntie Poldi in black stretch trousers, black T-shirt, and her biker jacket, her face and hands blackened, flashlight in one hand, crowbar in the other. As a grande dame of the international secret agents association, in other words. I picture her stealing out of the house in the middle of the night, because she has naturally refrained, yet again, from telling Montana anything about her intentions. Poldi is funny that way; whenever she ventures into a lion's den, she has to do so on her own. It occurs to me that this may be because of Maria. She may simply be reluctant to embroil anyone else in some mess involving her sister. And perhaps that is what has made Poldi so lonely and brought her so much *han*, because in spite of her many lovers, her celeb friends, and all the dear ones who crowd around her like scouts around a campfire, my Auntie Poldi is a lonely soul. Sounds incredible, but it's true. On the other hand, who isn't a lonely soul? Ultimately we're all on our own.

I picture Poldi flitting noiselessly down the Via Baronessa like the shadow of a shadow of a ninja, then along the esplanade and past the church of Santa Maria del Rosario, then across the piazza, past the closed and deserted bar, to the pier. All Torre Archirafi is wrapped in slumber, though the flicker of a television can sometimes be glimpsed through the shutters. There's no one about. Poldi is all alone, the sound of her footsteps mingling with the whisper of wavelets breaking sluggishly on the rocky shore. Or so I imagine.

The object of her nocturnal excursion was situated beside Torre Archirafi's small marina at the far end of the esplanade. Poldi had hitherto paid little attention to the building with the forbiddingly bricked-up windows, but she had seen from the photo that they were still open when it was taken. The building must once have been painted a luminous solar yellow, the color of a Sicilian afternoon, but decades of abandonment and neglect had left the paintwork badly weatherworn.

Poldi crouched down behind a fig tree and watched the building until she felt sure there was no one in the vicinity. In the light of a solitary streetlamp she made out the old lettering, which had once been coral-red.

ACQUADITORRE

Torre Archirafi's mineral-water spring had reputedly been known back in the Middle Ages. The water that comes bubbling to the surface there from deep in the volcanic rock is rich in sulfur and magnesium and does, alas, taste that way. For one thing, Sicilians in earlier times were less choosy and happy to have a source of fresh water close at hand; and second, in the early years of the last century Torre's water enjoyed great popularity in upper-class circles because of its purgative effect. The boom didn't last, though, and Acqua di Torre sadly had to close its bottling plant in the 1970s. The spring continues to effervesce, however, and brass taps on one side of the building enable anyone to draw water free of charge.

Poldi had hitherto assumed that the bottling plant had simply been left to deteriorate since its closure, but the longer she looked at the building, the more she doubted this. The big roller shutter on the side appeared to be in good order, and the steel door over the staff entrance facing the street was secured with a shiny new padlock.

Poldi emerged from behind her tree and stole over to the steel door. A brief professional check, then she quickly inserted the crowbar and—*clunk*—the door was open.

She slipped into the interior of the building. Her flashlight revealed the remains of the former bottling and labeling equipment. Most of it had been dismantled and sold off after the concern went bankrupt. Only the least movable items remained. Still stacked against one wall were some pallets laden with dusty bottles. The floor was littered with fragments of glass that crunched at every step Poldi took, and the dust she stirred up hung in the motionless air. She couldn't help sneezing. Without exactly knowing what she was looking for, she roamed through the derelict building until she came to a storage room that had clearly been used after the bankruptcy for quite different purposes.

In the middle was a large circular wooden table with at least twenty chairs surrounding it. There was plenty of dust here too, but standing on the table were two big cast-iron candelabra encrusted with wax and still holding the stub ends of candles.

Shining the flashlight in all directions, Poldi uttered a little squeak of alarm when she saw that the walls of the storage room were covered to head height with paintings. The paint was faded and the plaster flaking off in places, but she made out a host of grotesque figures: monsters, angels, demons, mythical beasts. The paintings were no masterpieces. The images and motifs looked naive and devoid of perspective, but they weren't all that bad either. They reminded Poldi of medieval representations of the War in Heaven or the temptation of Saint Anthony. Some of them were even reminiscent of Hieronymus Bosch, particularly where groups of naked figures were depicted standing dreamily around in a kind of Garden of Eden inhabited by fabulous winged beasts and dwarfish trolls. On one wall were some very strange representations of naked adults floating like embryos in amniotic sacs connected by a maze of tubes. The series of images was interspersed with symbols and unfamiliar characters that looked as if they had been carelessly scrawled on the plaster. Finally, enthroned on an outside wall beneath the bricked-up windows was a huge portrayal of the Black Madonna—or rather, of a kind of Black Madonna. It depicted her, almost naked, sitting cross-legged and surrounded by rainbow-colored rings. The woman was wearing a sort of crown but nothing else apart from beads and flowers all over her body, and her eight arms were spread out like a peacock's tail. This picture was not particularly well painted either. Poldi surmised that it was meant to portray or at least be reminiscent of the Indian goddess Kali. Inscribed in Italian beneath it were the words DO AS THOU WILT!

Rather uneasily, Poldi continued her tour of inspection. Beside the storage room she discovered a big kitchen complete with old saucepans and dishes, a wet room containing six showers, and two rooms containing bunk beds with mildewed mattresses. Here too the walls were covered with paintings.

All in all, the whole complex suggested that a group of about twenty persons had lived together there for a while and then, from one day to the next, abandoned the place. They might have sung together on occasion, but they certainly hadn't been a choir, thought Poldi, who knew a thing or two about communes and hippie sects. Wondering what it all had to do with her case, she decided to go home and consult Montana.

But something intervened yet again. As she came back into the hall, she was dazzled by three flashlights. Instinctively she tightened her grip on the crowbar.

"I was afraid you'd find out someday," said a familiar voice in the darkness. "But you'd have done better to forget it."

Poldi started to say something, but Signora Cocuzza cut her short.

"Come with us."

The other two flashlight carriers were Signor Bussacca and Poldi's next-door neighbor, Signora Anzalone. She debated whether to simply make a run for it, but she was too intrigued, so she let the trio shepherd her to the big round table.

The sad signora lit the stubby candles, probably for the first time in decades.

By their light, Poldi saw her three friends sit down facing her across the table. They were looking disconsolate.

"You realize we can't just let you go, don't you?" the sad signora said with a sigh.

Poldi put the crowbar on the table.

"So what do you propose to do now?"

They looked at one another, thoroughly at a loss.

"Kill me like Sister Rita and Antonella Pandolfino?"

"We didn't kill them!" said Signora Anzalone.

"I know," said Poldi. "But why give me all this grief? We're friends, neighbors."

Signora Anzalone and Signor Bussacca didn't move. Their gaze was fixed on Signora Cocuzza.

She suddenly covered her face with her hands and bent over as though in pain.

"I can't do this anymore. I'm so sick of the whole damned business!"

Poldi saw her shoulders heave. Signora Anzalone put a hand on her shoulder. Poldi would have done likewise, but she was too far away. All she could do was pass a handkerchief across the table.

"Thanks," sniffed Signora Cocuzza, and she blew her nose.

"What was this place?" Poldi asked quietly.

"Our home," said the sad signora. "Our home and our future. At least, that's what we believed in our naïveté. We were a Thelemic commune."

14

Tells of charlatans and flower children, mothers and Black Madonnas, youthful dreams, guilt, and pain. Poldi devises a crazy scheme, sewing machines run hot in Rome, Totti earns praise, and the nephew undergoes another crisis. First to collapse after a nocturnal conversation is a mommy's boy, then Montana and an entire building. And Poldi is forced to recognize that people can't save themselves from themselves.

When I just can't make any progress with my family saga, I sometimes wish I were a charlatan—someone with a load of tricks up his sleeve and any amount of devilish charisma. A trifle squalid and ill-shaven, perhaps, but irresistible. A self-confident Pied Piper and frequenter of wild parties—here today, gone tomorrow—who captures hearts and passes dud checks wherever he goes. Sadly, I'm not a great one for wild parties and possess absolutely no devilish charisma. I probably lack all the soft skills essential to charlatanry.

But there have always been others endowed with plenty of such attributes. The British occultist Aleister Crowley, for example, who was compelled by debts and a lot of bad luck to decamp from England in the twenties of the last century. Seriously addicted to heroin, he founded an occult commune near Cefalù, the Abbey of Thelema. The little farmhouse still exists. Dilapidated, overgrown, and hard to find, it continues to attract a handful of cranks and amateur photographers.

Crowley and a few adherents spent three years in Cefalù, where they indulged in some rather unappetizing sexual practices and excessive drug-taking that ultimately led to the death of two people and Crowley's expulsion from Italy. This did not, however, spell his own end or that of the Thelemic movement. Because of his crude theories about a new world order, the right of the stronger, and the movement's motto, "Do what thou wilt," Crowley was hyped by nationalists of all colors and regarded himself as the Nazis' occult ideologist in chief. The Thelemic movement lived on in small cells after World War I and Crowley's death, still traveling in the slipstream of neofascist movements like — you've guessed it — Madonna Nera.

And that was the origin of the sad signora's unhappiness. She had simply been a flower child who enjoyed the odd spliff and dreamed of love and freedom. This, it must be borne in mind, was a time when girls in certain Sicilian villages were forbidden to wear trousers. In order to escape her oppressive little world in the hinterland of Sciacca, the not yet sad young woman had joined a hippie commune which, in accordance with the alluring motto "Do what thou wilt," lived in an old mineral-water bottling plant in a sleepy little town named Torre Archirafi. She took absolutely no interest in politics but a great deal of interest in handsome Daniele Grasso. By the time she finally realized what a mess she was in and handsome Daniele had been blown to pieces by a bomb in Bologna station because he was a police informant, it was too late.

"We didn't know all this, you must believe me, Donna Poldina," sobbed the sad signora. "When Daniele was killed and everything became clear to me, I died too. The commune broke up soon after the bomb attack. People came and threatened to kill us and our families if we didn't keep our mouths shut, so we remained silent and tried to start a new life. I don't know if you can imagine how ashamed of this I am, Donna Poldina."

They were sitting together in Poldi's courtyard drinking grappa: Signora Cocuzza, Signora Anzalone, Signor Bussacca, Vito Montana, and my Auntie Poldi.

Poldi laid a hand on her friend's arm.

"Who else in the town knew?"

"Not everyone, but the rest must have guessed. Some of them moved away, others just wanted to forget. And then Madonna Nera came. Everyone is so incredibly sorry."

"Who sprayed those graffiti on my wall?" Poldi demanded in a stern voice.

"I did," Signor Bussacca said sheepishly. "But I never meant them."

"We thought," Signora Anzalone amplified, "that if only we could drive you away, at least you'd be safe."

"Ssh!" Poldi made a curt gesture and Signora Anzalone fell silent, looking dismayed.

No one spoke.

Poldi deliberated.

Then, with a sigh as big as Italy's national debt, she said,

"You're a queer bunch, but, *Madonna,* you're my friends."
She looked at them all in turn. "Let's forget it. Everything's
going to be okay."

"No!" Signora Cocuzza exclaimed in an agonized voice.
"These people will never give up!"

"Do you remember any names from back then?" Montana put in.

Signora Cocuzza nodded. The other two former flower
children nodded likewise.

"Would you be willing to testify?"

An exchange of glances, more silent nods.

"Who was Antonella Pandolfino?" asked Poldi.

"We think she was the daughter of Rosaria," said Signora Anzalone, tapping a young woman in the group
photo. "Rosaria was pregnant by Alessandro, who headed
the commune and was a Madonna Nera contact man, as
we realized later. The baby was born the day after the
bomb attack. For fear that it might be harmed, Rosaria
drove it to Agrigento by night, shortly after the birth, and
left it outside a church. She was fatally injured in a road
accident the following year. That finally made it clear to
us that we must never talk."

"But why did Rosaria put the photo of you all in the basket with the baby?"

Signora Cocuzza shrugged.

"Perhaps she simply wanted to leave the baby with something of herself. Early this year Antonella appeared in the
bar, showed me the photo, and asked if I recognized anyone
in it. I said no and sent her away. She never came back, but
soon afterward we all received threats again—after years."

"So poor Antonella went in search of her birth mother

and attracted the attention of Madonna Nera. Was Padre Stefano ever here?"

They shook their heads.

"I don't know how we can ever make it up to you," sobbed the sad signora.

"But I do," said Poldi.

For by then, or so I imagine, she had already devised this absolutely crazy, hopeless, suicidal, crackbrained plan.

"That's the craziest, most hopeless, suicidal, crackbrained plan I've ever heard," I said. I tried to catch Montana's eye. "And you're joining in this stupid malarkey?"

"I like you," Montana growled, "but call one of your aunt's plans stupid again and I'll have your guts for garters."

"He's an author," Poldi said apologetically. "Dramatizing and exaggerating are part of the job." And turning to me, in a schoolmarmish tone, "What do you say if someone tries to explain that what you have in mind is a near impossibility?"

"Leave me out of it!" I cried defiantly.

Poldi sighed.

Montana glanced at his watch. "T minus sixty."

"Er, what?"

"Good God, another hour of this!" Poldi exclaimed indignantly. "Haven't you ever watched an action film?"

"But this isn't Hollywood!" I yelled. "We'll all die!"

"True," said Poldi. "But not tonight."

"So to recap," I said, striving to sound reasonable, "you plan to pose as your twin sister in order to extract a confession from a twofold murderer and member of a powerful terrorist network while pretending to hand over the Black Madonna. Where can you go wrong!"

I think I may have giggled hysterically at that point.

By contrast, Poldi and Montana remained entirely serious.

"Spot on, my boy. You've now got the rough idea."

Parallel universe, I thought again. *This isn't happening, you're simply stuck in some matrix or other.*

"But folks—*ding-dong*—the guy will immediately spot it's only a cheap copy."

"Copy be damned! I've got the original."

Before I could say "Er . . . ," she got up and disappeared into the house. I heard her moving around in the living room, then the sound of a cupboard door closing. Poldi came back into the courtyard carrying something bulky swathed in cloth. Depositing it carefully on the table, she proceeded to unwrap it.

My unoriginal response to seeing the Black Madonna for the first time was "Wow!"

The same shivers run down my spine whenever I look back on that moment. I'm no expert, but even I could tell at once that the figure was a masterpiece of the woodcarver's art, its finely worked facial features and long limbs having miraculously survived the centuries in every detail. Carved out of ebony, the figure was almost entirely black. The color of the Virgin's robe had largely faded, but it was still clearly evident from specks of pigment and gilding that the figure with the child in its arms had been brightly painted and adorned with gold leaf. But it was the look on the Madonna's face that captivated me most of all: an expression so forlorn and sad, so utterly not of this world, that it rent my heart. That ancient ebony figure, presumably created in homage to a maternal deity from biblical times, seemed to shoulder all the *han* in the world as a way of bestowing a little redemption on us.

"Isn't it just?" Poldi said softly when she saw how overcome I was.

"Where . . ." I said. "I mean, how . . ."

"Totti," Poldi said in explanation, and as though on cue Totti let out a fart beneath the table. Only a very subdued one, though, as if he didn't want to upset the Black Madonna.

"In that clearing up on Etna, that's where," Poldi went on. "Unlike me, my sister had a penchant for drama. Maria always wanted to break things. If something was good, she wanted to ruin it. Like that clearing, which is now steeped in blood. But it didn't occur to me that she'd wanted to ruin something else until I was reminded of Signor Mezzapelle with his drum and his Earth Snake. He'd said that something good and old was sleeping there. He meant the Earth Snake, but then I thought he might have sensed something else too. I know a thing or two about vibes, so Vito, Martino, Teresa, and I went back up there and let Totti sniff around a bit on the off chance. And — ta-daaa! — as you see, he's not only a good truffle hound but an excellent Madonna hound as well. It was buried just beneath the spot where Maria stood in front of me with her gun. The way I see it — don't laugh! — is that the Black Madonna saved our lives, mine and Vito's."

"Does Maria know you have it?"

"That's a rather naive question, my lad — you can see that yourself, can't you? If Maria hadn't caught on, she would scarcely have lured you back from France and tried to total us in the car yesterday, would she? That's why the plan needs putting into effect—fast. Well, how about it? Are you coming with us or not?"

I found it hard to tear my eyes away from the Black Madonna. She seemed to be entreating me to do something—something that would slightly mitigate her pain and her *han*. I looked at my Auntie Poldi and nodded.

During the two weeks before my return from France the plan took shape in the truest sense of the word. The preparations were incredibly complex and called for some extremely elaborate logistics. Above all, though, they entailed the strictest secrecy and most watertight security measures, because Poldi was afraid Maria might turn up at any moment. But she didn't. Maria remained below the radar, and round-the-clock surveillance of Padre Stefano produced no indication of any contact between the two. That emboldened Poldi to take a very risky step that might have derailed the whole plan, but one without which it could not succeed.

At the same time, Gammarelli's sewing machines were whirring away in Rome after the clerical outfitters had received a rather unusual order from Poldi via an anonymous middleman. Her plan this time meant gambling on her accumulated experience from an earlier life. Its motto: "Always overdress!"

Even so, the whole scheme just barely succeeded. Because of me, to be precise. By the time I made my swift and unexpected return from France, Poldi realized that Maria had become active again.

Consequently, although preparations had still to be completed, Poldi decided to put her plan into effect as soon as possible. While she was coolly telling me everything over ayurvedic smoothies, Montana had unobtrusively made the final arrangements.

The night I resumed work on my novel, Poldi had finally contacted Padre Stefano and, in an imperious tone, dictated the conditions under which the handover to her sister was to take place.

The question was, would he bite?

There were plenty of other questions as well, but by the time Ravi appeared in the Via Baronessa a little later and good-humoredly opened his laptop to coordinate the whole operation like a sort of mission control, I was past asking them. I simply didn't care. I wasn't really myself. I was somewhere else, on autopilot, in a trance, whatever. Or possibly in hunting mode.

Soon after midnight an SUV with tinted windows drove into the town. Aimlessly, or so it seemed, it cruised through the deserted streets, then turned off onto the esplanade and drove along it to the mineral-water bottling plant, where it pulled up and extinguished its headlights. No one got out. The car just stood there as if trying to dissolve into the darkness. Nothing happened for a while.

Half an hour later a second SUV appeared. With its headlights off, it headed straight for the old bottling plant and parked outside it. A man dressed in black got out, looked around briefly like an animal taking scent, and then went inside. The steel door was already open. In a movie this would have been an ideal moment for some *Brrrooom!*

From my hiding place I had a good view of Padre Stefano entering the storage room, because Poldi had placed lighted candles all around the walls. Also burning on the big round table were the two candelabra, and in the middle stood the Black Madonna. There were now only two chairs at the table. Seated on one of them was Poldi, wearing a cheap, patterned tracksuit. The chair facing hers was unoccupied. The whole scene was reminiscent of a birthday surprise for a good friend. The priest paused in the entrance at first, taking it in.

"Well, come on in!" Poldi called to him. "Let's get it over. I don't have all night."

"What is all this?" he asked suspiciously.

"I dolled the place up a bit. I thought you'd like it." Poldi gave a throaty, mirthless laugh.

I held my breath.

The priest came over to the table and stiffly sat down just beneath the eight-armed Kali-Madonna. Like an idea made tellingly visible, the words DO WHAT THOU WILT hovered in the air above his head.

"In the interests of further fruitful cooperation, our mutual friends would welcome it if this transaction could be completed without any"—he cleared his throat—"collateral damage."

Poldi emitted another harsh, hostile laugh.

"Stop wasting time. Do you have it?"

Padre Stefano took a small cotton bag from his pocket and slid it across the table. Poldi opened the drawstring to enable some of the diamonds to spill out and examined one of the stones in the candlelight. The priest bent forward a little and scrutinized the Black Madonna, then sat back looking more relaxed.

"You've used me, Maria," he said, "but there's always another time. One day I shall be pope."

Poldi put the diamond back on the table and looked at him.

"Oh no, I don't think so," she said in her normal voice.

"I'm sorry?" The words just slipped out.

"Namaste!" Poldi said loudly.

That was our cue.

Emerging from the room's two entrances came figures clad in pale cotton robes and wearing pointed hoods like those familiar from Easter processions in Spain. The origins of this special type of hood are Roman Catholic and have a centuries-old penitential tradition behind them. The hooded figures included Aunts Teresa, Caterina, and Luisa plus Uncle Martino. Vito Montana was somewhere among them, as were Signora Cocuzza, Signora Anzalone, Signor Bussacca, Padre Paolo, and yours truly. But they included many more —half Torre Archirafi, in fact. Silently and with measured tread, some three hundred people crowded into the room, because they had finally had enough and wanted to atone. It was in response to a request from a supreme authority that Gammarelli's workshops had at the last minute managed to produce so many costumes based on my Auntie Poldi's design. Each figure bore a candle and a large portrait photograph.

Poldi had planned it all down to the last detail.

"What is this?" gasped Padre Stefano, looking startled.

Quick as lightning, he grabbed the little bag of diamonds and jumped to his feet.

"Siddown!" Poldi hissed at him. "And come clean at last!"

He shrank back.

"You're crazy, Donna Poldina. You're a crazy murderess and thief and a danger to the public." He sat down again.

"This performance will do you no good at all!" he shouted, crossing his arms defiantly.

But that failed to impress anyone. The hooded figures paraded past the murderous priest one after another, displaying each photo portrait in turn, then formed a circle around the table. The photographs were of young people, old people, men, women, children, office workers, smiling holiday-makers, and children in front of Christmas trees. All had met their deaths in the bomb attack in Bologna and other atrocities staged by Madonna Nera. As each portrait went by, Poldi called out the subject's name.

"Antonella Ceci . . . Silvana Serravalli . . . Roberto De Marchi . . . Vittorio Vaccaro . . . Viviana Bugamelli . . . Angelo Priore . . . Carla Gozzi . . . Fausto Venturi . . ."

And so many more.

When I myself passed the priest, I could tell that Poldi's mise-en-scène was having an effect. Stefano was looking dismayed. On the other hand, it only seemed to be reinforcing his stubborn defiance. He was breathing heavily and struggling to maintain his composure, but he remained silent.

One of the last hooded figures bore a photo of Sister Rita laughing coquettishly in her nun's habit. On reaching Padre Stefano the figure removed its hood. It was Commissario Morello.

"You'll regret this, *Commissario*!" the priest snarled.

"Simply confess," Morello told him, unimpressed. "The evidence is overwhelming. It's only a matter of time before we find some DNA that confirms it. The Holy Father has already decreed your excommunication."

"This is a conspiracy!" gasped Padre Stefano. "I'm innocent!"

Without another word, Morello stepped aside and lined up with the rest.

A last figure approached Padre Stefano. Small and hesitant, it was carrying a photograph of Antonella Pandolfino. On reaching the priest it removed its hood. From my place in the crowd I could clearly see him give a violent start.

"Mamma!"

The elderly lady was very refined in appearance and affected the short, practical hairdo so popular with Sicilian women of her generation. She was trembling.

Silence reigned in the hall. All that could be heard was the priest's heavy breathing.

"No, Mamma, no!" he cried in an agonized voice. "*Madonna*, what are you doing here? None of this is true! For the love of God, I—"

Padre Stefano's mother brusquely interrupted him. "Signora Poldi and the two *commissari* came to see me," she said, quietly but distinctly. "I have even spoken on the phone with the Holy Father. I couldn't believe it of you, Stefano, not you! Not my son, whose life was dedicated to God and who always made me so proud, but it seems you deserted God long ago. I'm ashamed of you."

"Mamma, no!" He was whimpering now.

The old lady was clearly struggling to remain calm.

"I want you to confess what you've done," she said firmly, "and I want you to say all you know about this terrible organization. If you fail to do so, you will no longer be my son."

If ever the lifelong dependence on their mothers of Italian *mammoni* and *bamboccioni* proved beneficial, it was now. Slumped in his chair, the priest burst into tears.

"I'm sorry!" he sobbed. "Sorry, Mamma, sorry! I was simply besotted with Rita! I was infatuated, utterly obsessed. But after the exorcism she flew into a panic. She snapped. I tried to calm her down, but she wouldn't listen. She wanted to go to the police. And then I simply lost my head . . ." He gave vent to another paroxysm of sobbing.

"Yes, well," Poldi put in, "but Antonella Pandolfino's murder was carefully planned."

"Your accursed sister manipulated me!" Stefano yelled. "I was a victim of Satan! Mamma, you have to believe me!"

Taking his mother gently by the arm, Poldi shepherded her over to the aunts, who took her under their wing.

"That's enough," said Montana, who had also removed his hood, and he and Morello led Stefano away.

The others, throwing back their hoods as well, stared after the priest and his mother in embarrassed silence.

"I'd like to thank you all!" cried Poldi, and there was no triumphalism in her voice. "I love you and I'm proud to be one of you." She clasped her hands together and bowed in all directions. "Namaste!"

On that note the meeting broke up. Rather irresolutely at first, as though the participants didn't really know where to go. Then, slowly, they began to move. One after another, they shuffled out into the darkness. After a few minutes the room with the grotesque murals was deserted once more.

I went over to Poldi, who was still standing beside the table, clearly struggling with her emotions.

"I'm proud of you, Poldi."

She wiped her eyes.

"Crybaby," I said softly, and she laughed.

"You'll get another clip round the ear if you're not careful!"

She grinned at me and reached for the Black Madonna, intending to wrap it up again.

And then all hell broke loose.

I had only just glimpsed the figure in the doorway leading to the former dormitory when a giant fist knocked me off my feet and sent me hurtling across the floor. There followed an ear-splitting bang. When I next drew breath I saw smoke and flames everywhere.

The side wall of the bottling plant was missing; the explosion had completely demolished it.

Deafened and dazed, I struggled to my feet and saw Poldi not far away, gray with dust and coughing. She appeared to be looking for something.

And then I saw Maria emerge from the doorway leading to the former living quarters and come out into the room. She was holding a *caffettiera* by the handle. It looked as if her sole intention was to offer us some coffee, but at that moment nothing would have surprised me.

Meanwhile, Poldi had retrieved the Black Madonna and seemed to guess what the coffeepot portended. When Maria drew back her arm, she held the wooden figure protectively above her head.

Instead of throwing the coffeepot at us, Maria flung it with all her might at the ceiling. There was a flash and a bang and liquid fire rained down on us from above. It was the first and only Molotov *caffettiera* I'd ever seen. But, to repeat, nothing would have surprised me. All I saw then was that the old wooden ceiling had caught fire, and I took cover.

"Got you, you bitch!" screamed Maria. She drew an automatic.

I saw Poldi, with the Black Madonna in her arms, dive behind the massive oak table, which had overturned. *Good idea,* I thought, and followed suit. We had only just made it when Maria opened fire.

By this time the whole room was filled with flames, smoke, and dust. Splinters were flying about our ears. It was only a question of time before the table disintegrated under Maria's fusillade.

Poldi thrust the Black Madonna into my hands.

"As soon as she has to reload, make a run for it! Don't hesitate, run as fast as you can!"

"What about you?"

"This is a family matter, sonny."

I was going to make some objection, but at that moment I saw Montana dash through the flames in the doorway and stand there in the smoke like a phantom, gun at the ready, trying to get his bearings. Then he sighted Maria and took aim.

But Maria was quicker. She fired twice, and Montana fell to the floor as though poleaxed.

"*VITO!*" screamed Poldi.

The firing suddenly ceased. Maria was having to reload.

"Run!" Poldi shouted to me.

And I ran, but not with the Black Madonna, which I put down beside her. I don't remember what, if anything, went through my mind, but I simply ran over to Montana. He lay doubled up on the floor, coughing and groaning. No idea how I did it, but I somehow managed to drag him out of the burning building. All I remember is that I laid him out in the open air, so much smoke and dust in my own lungs that I could hardly draw breath.

People were standing around me at a safe distance from the heat. They shouted something, and I turned to see that the whole building was ablaze, the roof timbers going up in flames. Shots could be heard inside. No idea where he'd come from, but Totti suddenly appeared beside me. He barked at me excitedly, something he very seldom does, and three things occurred to me. First, my Auntie Poldi was inside there; second, as long as shots were being fired she was still alive; and third, I'd promised to look after her.

I don't think I had any clear idea of what I was doing, and courage didn't come into it. I simply dashed back into the building through the smoke and flames.

The firing ceased as I blundered into the hall. Stumbling through the smoke, I saw Poldi and Maria grappling with each other, fighting for possession of the Black Madonna like two maddened hellcats. Maria, whose hair had caught fire, resembled a human torch. I didn't know what to do until the Black Madonna escaped the sisters' clutches and fell to the floor.

It still breaks my heart to remember what happened then. I shall feel guilty all my life, and I hope my karmic punishment will not be too severe.

"Aunt Maria!" I yelled. "Look!"

I snatched up the heavy wooden figure and hurled it as far from me as I could. It crashed to the floor near the flames.

Maria stared at me as if I were a ghost.

"You stupid fool!" she screamed. She thrust me aside, meaning to run and retrieve the figure, but Poldi caught hold of her leg.

"No, Maria!" she gasped. "You'll never make it! We must get out of here. Come on, please. We'll settle matters outside any way you want, but please come!"

Maria kicked herself free and dashed toward the spot where the Black Madonna had landed. I saw her take the statue and hold it up like a trophy. Or perhaps like some lost child.

"It's mine!" she shouted out triumphantly. "It has always been—this is proof of my genius and my invincibility. I'm the most amazing criminal in the world!"

I didn't know what she meant. Most likely the smoke was confusing her mind already. Visibility was almost nonexistent by now, and Maria was starting to disappear into the fog like the Flying Dutchman. Just then a sinister, ominous groaning sound came from overhead. The joists were giving way.

Poldi made to follow her sister, but I held her back.

"No! The roof's collapsing, we must get out of here!"

"I can't leave without Maria! I have to look after her, I promised Mutti."

She struggled to free herself, and I had no choice but to slap her face forehand and backhand. Sorry, I know it was bad form, doing that to my aunt. Just add it to my karmic tab, it doesn't matter anymore.

For all that, the two slaps proved effective. Poldi stared at me in amazement. She might have been seeing me for the first time.

"Hey, where did you spring from?"

"We've got to get out of here, Poldi. Please come on, Mutti's waiting."

Yes, I know, that was bad form too, but I had no choice. I

took her hand and looked around for the exit. I could hardly breathe, the smoke was so thick. I'd completely lost my bearings and didn't know which way to go.

Then something tugged at my leg. Totti! He barked at me, gave my jeans another tug, and went on ahead. As in my dream. Firmly gripping my aunt's hand, I followed him outside. Poldi had stopped resisting.

People came rushing over to us with blankets. There were firefighters everywhere. Totti bounded around us, barking.

Poldi turned to face the building once more.

"I'm going to have a little drink, then I'll go and get Maria," she said. Just then, with the most frightful crash I had ever heard, the bottling plant's roof collapsed.

Flames shot up into the sky. A smoky red bubble expanded into the darkness. It hung in the air for a while as though irresolute, then silently imploded.

15

*Tells of friendship, death, and happiness. There is
mourning, laughter, music-making, flirtation, dancing, and thanksgiving. Names are named, stages
built, and backs patted. Poldi uses the time she has
left as best she can, her nephew hides himself away,
and Montana sends a text message. And then Poldi
ducks out of her own party because of the final
score.*

I'm wrong: perhaps we aren't all alone in the end. I don't
have a great talent for friendship, and I can only try to
combat death and oblivion with limited resources, but I realize I'm wrong when I look at my Auntie Poldi. Although it
doesn't always help me to combat depression and loneliness,
or the fact that we're our own worst enemies, it's a comfort.
As long as we can join the family for Sunday lunch and argue
about the best way to cook *parmigiana di melanzane,* and as
long as we can sit silently in the piazza with a sad friend, and
as long as someone invites us to a barbecue or says "Glad
you're back"—as long as we're welcome somewhere, all our
whims and frailties notwithstanding—there's still hope.

That's why I'm all the more appalled by the fate of Antonella Pandolfino, because it makes me wonder how badly

screwed up a life must become before a person feels lonely enough to put their faith in someone like Maria, who appears out of the blue one day. Because from everything Montana and Morello found out in the ensuing weeks, that must have been the way of it. Maria must have kept Poldi under close observation for a year and waited for the right moment. Having somehow discovered that Antonella had turned up in the bar with the photo, she must then have spent weeks gaining her trust—at least, Antonella's neighbors in Librino told of regular visits to her by a woman matching Maria's description. And all the time Maria had been using poor Antonella for her treacherous plan. No one could turn the clock back—no one could give Antonella a hug or invite her to a barbecue; they could only try not to forget her. Halfway along the esplanade was a small, nameless *piazzetta* with a nice view of the sea and Etna. Padre Paolo's proposal that it should be named after her met with widespread public approval.

Torre Archirafi's former mineral-water bottling plant burned down to its foundations. The acrid stench of smoke hung over the site for days like the dying echo of a final threat.

But when Signora Cocuzza left a bunch of roses outside the ruins next morning, she smiled as she did so. I saw that myself.

My knowledge of everything else is only secondhand, because for the next few weeks I took refuge in my attic room in the Via Baronessa, being unable to cope with all the congratulations, back-patting, and invitations to barbecues I received because of my alleged heroism.

I think Vito Montana knew how I was feeling. The morning after the fire I received a text message from him: "THANKS." Just that, nor did he ever make another reference to that fateful night, but whenever we see one another I detect a benevolent gleam in his eye that honors me more than any pat on the back or request for a selfie.

Maria had wounded him badly in the shoulder. He may never be able to stretch out his arm to its fullest extent and was suffering, like the rest of us, from smoke inhalation, but after three days he discharged himself from the hospital and moved into No. 29 Via Baronessa. For one thing, he was engaged to Poldi; for another, she was in a pretty bad way.

She didn't leave the house for days, could hardly breathe, coughed up black phlegm, and regularly needed oxygen. I was worried. Far worse than her physical symptoms, however, were her grief and despair at the death of Maria, whom she had once more been unable to save. Poldi was a picture of misery.

But when she shuffled into the courtyard for breakfast on the morning of the third day, she said, "I've never thanked you, my boy."

"Yes you have."

"No I haven't. I'm not completely gaga and senile yet. It's important to say thanks and apologize if you make a mess of things. If you can't say thanks or sorry you've got no heart, and a belated thank-you is a poor thank-you—bear that in mind. So thank you, my boy, for saving my life." She folded her hands and bowed to me. "*Namaste.*"

To cover my embarrassment, I said, "Honestly, Poldi, that's all balls and bang-me-arse."

She gave me a friendly clip on the back of the head and poured herself some coffee.

"Now ask me for something."

"Forget it, Poldi, there's no need."

"Hell's bells, can't you leave that to me to decide? Well, go on, ask me for something. I want to give you something as a thank-you."

I didn't have to think for long.

"Tell me about her," I said. "About the old days. About the folk song you sang together."

"It'll make me blub like a baby, though."

"So be it."

My Aunts Teresa, Caterina, and Luisa clearly found the subject distasteful. They displayed unexpected obduracy when I raised the subject of Maria with them at lunch the next Sunday. Where she was concerned, they seemed to have imposed a sort of *omertà* upon themselves.

"The past should be left in peace," said Caterina.

"Have another slice of this delicious peppered sheep's cheese," said Teresa.

"One shouldn't speak ill of the dead," said Luisa.

"For God's sake, then say something nice about her!" I cried, feeling like Poldi.

The aunts looked at each other.

"We'd like to," said Caterina, "but alas, there's nothing nice to be said."

"That's impossible. Poldi spoke very affectionately of her."

Silence.

"Maria could be very charming when she wanted to be," Caterina went on eventually. "But she always used her charm to get the worst out of people, and believe me, she was talented at that. Think of all of Poldi's wonderful attributes and pervert them into their diametrical opposite — that's Maria for you. After various unpleasant incidents had occurred in Munich, we decided never to speak of her again. What Poldi tells you is her business, but we" — Caterina glanced around at the others — "will continue not to speak of her. Don't think we're being disrespectful of the dead, but for us Maria died a long time ago."

That concluded the matter as far as they were concerned, and anyone who knows my aunts knows they're unbeatable at two things: kindness and obstinacy.

I, on the other hand, was thoroughly galvanized — breathless with excitement, as may perhaps be imagined. A dark family secret! *Namaste,* universe! It would lend my hitherto rather naive and plodding family saga the requisite drama, spice, and bestsellerism. I would naturally have to change names and only hint at certain details, but those were the only concessions I could afford to make. Determined to ruthlessly exploit this dark family secret, I proposed to carry out some thorough and unsparing research as soon as I returned to Germany, combing through archives and police records and tracing contemporary witnesses. But, as may also be imagined, Sicily is complicated and something naturally intervened, as it always does.

So life gradually resumed its accustomed course. Sicily is like that, and that is how Tomasi di Lampedusa puts it in *The Leopard:* "Everything must change so it stays the same."

Montana's suspension was swiftly lifted, but — the old story — he could forget about receiving an apology from the powers that be.

In Rome, Padre Stefano made a full confession. Admittedly, he incriminated Maria, claiming that she had incited him to commit the two murders, but this ultimately did him little good. In order to reduce the severity of his sentence, avert his excommunication, and above all retain the love of his mamma, he came out with names, addresses, bank account details, passwords, and who did what with whom and when—simply everything he knew.

This sufficed to warrant a series of house searches and arrests in the Vatican as well as elsewhere, and will even, with a little luck, result in some successful prosecutions in the next few years. It will not, of course, suffice to smash Madonna Nera completely, because it is in the nature of such organizations that they can regenerate severed limbs like an axolotl. However, Madonna Nera at least presented no threat for the time being, and the former flower children Cocuzza, Anzalone, and Bussacca had no immediate need to fear its vengeance. That was why they declined to be taken into the witness protection program.

Everything is complicated and things keep intervening, but life goes on. And because this is so, and because Poldi is a phoenix, it wasn't long—only a few days—before she was once more sitting outside the café bar in the piazza with her friends Signora Cocuzza and Padre Paolo, licking a *gelato pistacchio e cioccolato*.

"This pistachio ice could be a trifle saltier," the priest complained.

"You smoke too much," Signora Cocuzza retorted. "It's ruined your palate."

Poldi heaved a sigh. "It's my birthday in four weeks," she said abruptly.

"No!"

"Yes!"

"No!"

"I'm thinking of throwing a little *serata*. Just a handful of people. What do you think?"

The others stared at her as if she'd just said something very silly, then sat back.

"Great, but you can forget about the handful," said Signora Cocuzza. She raised her fist and Padre Paolo gave it a nonchalant bump with his own.

It must also have been during those first few weeks after the fire that Poldi received a phone call from her new acquaintance.

"How are you, Donna Poldina?" the pope inquired.

"I've felt better." She coughed. "I'm getting there, though. Many thanks for your help."

"No, it's for me to thank you. Your courage and self-sacrifice have been exemplary."

"Fiddle-faddle. I couldn't even save the Black Madonna from the fire."

"That's an irreplaceable loss, of course, but it wasn't your fault, Donna Poldina. You've done the Church and the Italian state great service. Tell me what I can do for you."

"Your assistance with Gammarelli and Padre Stefano's mother was help enough. If you wish, you can say a Mass for Antonella Pandolfino."

"Gladly, but don't you have a personal wish?"

Poldi thought for a moment.

"If you permit, I'd like to ask you a personal question."

"By all means."

"Are you afraid of death?"

It turned into a longish conversation. By the end Poldi felt a little bit less depressed. She resolved to face her forthcoming birthday bravely and screw Montana as often as possible in the time that remained.

The next few weeks were relatively uneventful. I received some short text messages from Valérie asking how I was and whether we could meet, but I asked her to give me a bit more time. Not because I was playing games; I simply wasn't up to it yet.

Anyway, it was suddenly there like a surprise visitor from overseas—one whose arrival had almost been forgotten: Poldi's birthday.

She was becoming a little nervous, as may well be imagined. Just before midnight she had sent Montana off to bed, telling him that she wanted to sit on the terrace for a while, seeing in her birthday by herself with a glass of Prosecco. She felt convinced that Death would be awaiting her there, but he wasn't. He wasn't waiting in the courtyard or beside the kitchen sink, and he didn't show his face the next morning. He didn't show his face all that day, so things took their long-planned course. And that meant the party!

For days now the area outside the bar in the piazza had been a scene of great activity. A small timber platform had been erected, tables and benches imported, colored lights and loudspeakers installed. A transformer had burned out, several of the persons involved had sworn at each other and made it up, and hovering over Torre Archirafi was a barbecue haze and the most delicious culinary aromas imaginable. I had been requested to keep Poldi in the house until I was notified by text. The call came at nine that evening, and Death had failed to put in an appearance even then.

Instead, gifts had arrived. They transformed No. 29 Via Baronessa into an Aladdin's cave of glitter, ribbons, and rustling gold foil. Poldi's living room was piled high with wrapped gifts of every size and color — with one exception: there were no bottles. Many of the parcels smelled alluringly of vanilla and marzipan, others of fragrant soaps or unguents. Neighbors kept popping in throughout the day, laden with flowers, parcels, and baskets of fruit, with the result that Poldi scarcely found time to think about Death.

Until that evening.

This time, being the self-effacing person she is, Poldi wore something rather restrained: a backless gold silk gown with two dragons curling around her generous décolleté, together with a pair of pointed gold slippers, also embroidered with little dragons, that would have suited any fairy queen. Her cheeks were dusted with glitter powder and little rhinestones glittered in her wig. No idea how she'd attached them.

"What do you think?"

She rotated on the spot in front of me and struck a couple of coquettish poses.

"Fantastic!" I said. "Enough to give anyone a heart attack. A regular sugar rush!"

"That'll do," she broke in, rolling her eyes. "Your compliments still need some work."

I offered her my arm. It had been a hot July day, and the evening was still so warm that I'd dispensed with a jacket. I was wearing black trousers and a black shirt with the sleeves rolled up.

"Hey, what's this?" Poldi exclaimed in surprise when she spotted the octopus declaration of love on my right arm.

"Er . . ."

"Well, I declare, an octopus. When did you get that done?"

"Last week."

She took my arm and continued her examination of my new tattoo. The octopus was black and wound its way around my forearm as though palpating it. It was pretty detailed and wore an amiable expression—I'd insisted on that. If I twisted my arm a bit or clenched my fist it looked as if it were stretching this way and that.

"That's brilliant work," said Poldi. "Did Marco do it?"

"No, I went to a professional in Messina. Like it?"

She looked at me. "It's really great. But how are things between you?"

I shook my head.

"We're just friends now."

What else can I say about that evening? We had a real blast. Half Torre Archirafi turned out to celebrate my Auntie Poldi's sixty-first birthday, and everyone had contributed something to the gigantic buffet supper. My three Sicilian aunts and uncle were there, my cousins, and of course Totti, Signora Cocuzza, Signora Anzalone, Signor Bussacca, Padre Paolo, Commissario Morello, and Italo Russo. Someone had even dug out Signor Mezzapelle. Assistente Zanotta was there, as were Ravi, Mago Rampulla from Santa Venerina, and—very briefly—Dottore Bonacorsi. I spotted Valérie and numerous well-known society and showbiz faces among the guests, because several of my aunt's celeb friends had accepted invitations with alacrity. For reasons of discretion, though, I'm afraid I can't name any names.

My appearance in the piazza with Poldi on my arm was the signal for applause to ring out and a local cover band to strike up "Eye of the Tiger." When Montana went over to Poldi to ask her for the first dance, there was a minor pyrotechnic explosion at the edge of the stage. Then Gianna Nannini leapt onto it and sang "Happy Birthday" for Poldi, followed—word of honor—by "Latin Lover."

I really wanted to make my way over to Valérie, but I had to undergo some more back-slapping and couldn't extricate myself.

"Handsome couple, aren't they?" someone beside me suddenly said in German with a slight Italian accent. A woman of my own age in a strapless red dress, she had the same green eyes as her father and the same little furrow between her eyebrows. A combination of warmth and anger.

I think I just stared at her.

"I'm Marta," she said with a smile, extending her hand. "Vito Montana's daughter."

"Er . . . I know."

"Nice tattoo." She took my arm and ran her fingers over it.

"Thanks," I muttered.

"They're an incredibly smart couple, did you know that?"

"Yes, I was hoping a bit of it might rub off on me."

She regarded me with a curious expression I couldn't interpret.

We watched in silence as Poldi and Montana continued to dance. Marta swayed in time to the music, from time to time nudging me—probably by chance—with her shoulder. I saw Montana signal to me from the dance floor with two fingers, indicating that he was keeping a close eye on me.

"See you later," said Marta, and she disappeared in the direction of the buffet.

I wondered for a moment if this was an invitation, but before I could come to any conclusion Valérie was standing beside me.

"Who was that?"

"Er, Marta. Montana's daughter."

"Do you know each other well? It looked like it."

"Where's David?" I asked.

"Gone. Cameroon."

"Ah."

She took hold of my arm and looked at the octopus. "*Mon Dieu,* you actually did it."

"Mm."

"Shall we dance? If you say 'er' or 'mm' again, I swear this is the last you'll see of me."

Shortly before midnight I saw Poldi wave to someone. I turned around but couldn't see who it was. Then I saw her pick up a bottle of *spumante* and two glasses and unobtrusively slip away in the direction of the quay. She clambered over the rocks forming the sea wall, still holding the bottle, and disappeared into the darkness. Behind me, someone started whistling the tune of "Were I a Little Bird," but when I turned to look there was no one there and the whistling ceased. Feeling uneasy, I perched on the low wall enclosing the esplanade and waited for Poldi.

Seated with his clipboard at the far end of the pier was Death, nervously puffing at a cigarette.

"Smoking is lethal," said Poldi, sitting down beside him.

Death coughed.

"I only do it because it looks cool."

Poldi uncorked her bottle.

"You can drink a toast with me."

"Because it's you, Poldi. But only a drop."

"So you're on duty," she said bravely. "In that case, let's get this over and done with. I've had the best party of my life, and I'm not—"

"Poldi!" Death broke in angrily. "Could you once, just once, put aside your hurtful mistrust of me and shut your trap?"

Poldi fell silent.

"I've, er . . . something to show you."

He reached for something beside him and suddenly held up his scorecard. Ten out of ten.

"What does that mean?"

"Well . . ." He hesitated. "Your birthday and the deadline, they don't, er . . ." He cleared his throat. "They aren't a perfect match."

"Meaning what?"

"They don't coincide."

"Are you saying I don't have to die today?"

"I was joking, trying it on. I know I said one out of ten, but I was irritated by your vacillation, your eternal shilly-shallying. 'I want to die. No, I don't. Yes, I do.' Honestly! So I wanted to test you a bit."

"Test me?" Poldi said in a low, menacing voice.

"Sorry, it won't happen again. I mean, I realize I can't change people, you least of all—who am I to even try?—but I thought it might make you aware of your priorities."

"So I still have a bit more time here?"

"You know that's something I'm not allowed to say. Let me put it this way: you've probably got enough time for a wedding."

Poldi filled the glasses and handed him one.

"What shall we drink to?" he asked.

"To friendship."

After a while I saw her coming back from the pier and went to meet her, feeling relieved and anxious in equal measure.

"Everything okay?"

Poldi looked at me, and I think her eyes were a trifle moist.

"Everything's okay, my boy. I needed a bit of time on my own, that's all. Are you having fun, you and your eight-armed new friend?"

"Are you really okay? You know what I mean."

She laid a hand on my chest.

"Yes, really," she said. "And now let's whoop it up with a vengeance! We'll go on investigating together—we're a team, after all—and in a couple of months' time there'll be a wedding to celebrate, and then we'll whoop it up again. And again and again, because that's life, and life is wonderful. How does that sound?"

I drew in a lungful of velvety Sicilian night air. The sea was saying something in a sleepy whisper.

"Sounds like a plan."

Acknowledgments

This book again could not have been written without the outstanding support and magic from so many lovely people. So thanks to my friends Guido, Ute, and Yeo-Rhim for their valuable feedback and questions on the first draft. Big thanks go out to my German editor, Daniela, from Bastei Lübbe, and to Helen Atsma, Jenny Xu, and Taryn Roeder and the whole wonderful team from HMH for their enthusiasm, dedication, accuracy, and courage. I'd like to thank my agents, Sibylle and Felix, for all of their efforts and support, and then all of my friends for their understanding and love when I become as unsocial as a Sicilian barista in August during writing phases. Much love goes out to all my dear readers, bloggers, booksellers, and Poldi's former friends and colleagues, whose touching emails and letters sometimes reach me right in the most difficult moments of writing. *Namaste!*